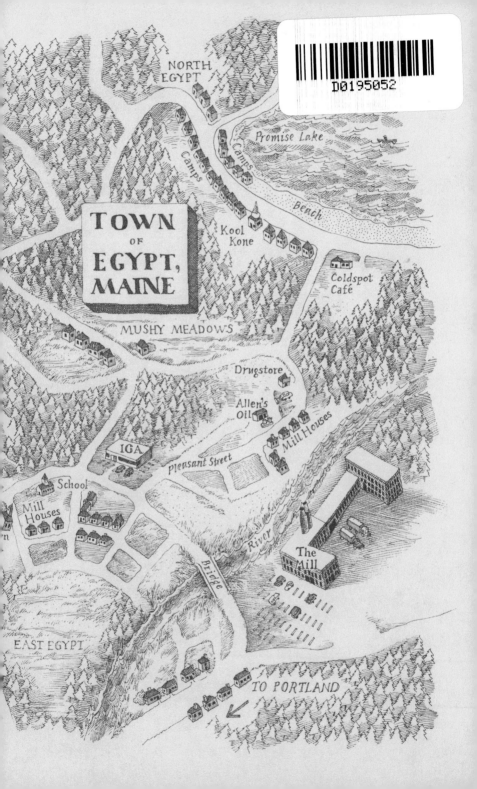

Letourneau's
Used Auto Parts

Letourneau's Used Auto Parts

Carolyn Chute

TICKNOR & FIELDS

New York

1988

Thank you, Jaquie Giasson Fuller.

Copyright © 1988 by Carolyn Chute.
All Rights Reserved.

For information about permission to reproduce selections
from this book, write to Permissions, Ticknor & Fields,
52 Vanderbilt Avenue, New York, New York 10017

Library of Congress Cataloging-in-Publication Data

Chute, Carolyn.
Letourneau's Used Auto Parts.
I. Title.
PS3553.H87L48   1988   813'.54   88-2210
ISBN 0-89919-500-8

Printed in the United States of America

P 10 9 8 7 6 5 4 3 2 1

Portions of this book have appeared, in slightly different
form, in *Agni Review, Northeast,* and *Shenandoah.*

Endpaper map by Leslie Evans.

For all the Bleeding Hearts and Hearts of Gold.

Any bird, bug, or animal including the human animal can be self-serving, cool, and steely-hearted. It is only the superhuman who can rise to Compassion.

Contents

Letourneau's
Used Auto Parts

Big Lucien Letourneau

Flavie	Memère Poulin	Armand
HIS OLDEST SISTER	HIS MOTHER	HIS YOUNGER BROTHER
		Severin
		ARMAND'S SON

Some of His Children

By Maxine
Norman
Little Lucien
Missy
Michel
Ryan

By Lillian Greenlaw
June Marie

By Marilyn
Dinah

By Keezhia
May

E. Blackstone Babbidge

Lillian Greenlaw   Ernie Train
HIS SECOND WIFE   HIS HALF-BROTHER

His Children by His First Wife

Luke
Eugenia
Mark
Anastasia
Jennifer Ann

Stacy
Michelle
Benjamin
Christopher
Jason Robert

ONE

Crowe Bovey's Burning Cold

1

THE SCOUT CROW, lean in winter, makes a sweep over the outer ring of wrecks and junks. Everything in the salvage yard is sealed in new snow. The scout crow opens his toes and swings down to perch on the boom of the yard wrecker. He checks for signs of life.

2

The room over the drugstore is hot and the bedcovers are in a ball on the floor. The only thing Crowe Bovey is wearing is his metal-rimmed glasses. He pokes at Jill Luce. She's not really sleeping, just pretending . . . holding back a giggle. Jill's body breathes and un-braids, the stomach muscles careening porpoiselike. When Jill Luce is wearing clothes, they are the kind with high tight waists. Crowe Bovey pokes her again and the waterbed rolls. Jill pretends to have a dream. She whimpers.

Up on his elbows, Crowe Bovey listens to Jill's FM radio, hard rock. He has a long broad body, but short legs . . . hands darker than his body . . . tattooed by auto grease. His eyes slide contemp-tuously over the posters on the wall. On the closet door is the Van Halen lead in leather pants and heavy chains. The chained man's face shows no alarm . . . In fact, he's almost dozing. Crowe picks the label off the instant coffee jar on the nightstand and shreds it . . . shreds it some more. He opens his hand and the shreds flutter on Jill like colored snow. She opens her eyes. He locks himself to her for another round. They have not left this hot place for three days.

3

Volunteers shout over the grind of pumps while water rumbles down the timbers that have caved into the cellar. You can't tell a child's wristbone from a pencil in the black debris and mud.

A neighbor just arriving sighs, "Lost them all, didn't they?" Another neighbor nods.

"I seen a couple of them yesterday in the window there . . . lookin' out . . . the redhead one and that other light one."

A whisper: "They just found the mother . . . at least they *think* it's the mother."

More neighbors arrive, parking beyond the fire hoses. "I don't see Crowe's truck. Where's his truck?" a neighbor in bedroom slippers asks as she rocks from foot to foot, hugging herself.

"Good question," says another.

Another one shrugs.

The hoses kick. Water sprays on some of the neighbors. They shriek and step back. One says through his fingers, "They found Crowe yet?"

"Don't look as though he was home," says another.

"Nobody's seen his truck in the yard for three days," says another. "THREE DAYS!!"

"S'pose they weren't getting along?"

A news van has arrived. A cameraman in sweater and jeans moves among the neighbors. "TeeVeeeeee!!!" squeals a child.

Between the dozens of cars and trucks and three rescue units parked along the road, glides the new pickup truck of Crowe Bovey. The slush whispers.

"Jesus! There he is."

As he steers with one hand, he pulls at his cheek with the other, his habit. You can't see his eyes for the gray day, and gray tree limbs scutter over his metal-rimmed glasses. His green workshirt which reads LETOURNEAU'S USED AUTO PARTS on the back is buttoned to the throat.

Rescuers move over the ice with his wife's mother between them. She has just arrived in her station wagon. Neighbors have become silent. The mother-in-law makes gagging cries and wrenches at the rescuers' orange jackets. The rescuers slide away from her on the ice . . . then toward her . . . like comic skaters.

Crowe Bovey shuts off his engine and gets out. His dark hair is streaked gold from working bare-headed. He stands with the neighbors among the fire hoses and watches the volunteers flood the timbers, the timbers steaming and hissing like a dying dragon. He watches his mother-in-law go onto her knees, her red screaming face in folds like a dewy rose. Then he looks into some of the neighbors' faces. They avert their eyes.

After a minute, he gets back into his rig, turns around on the slushy crown, then drives back up Seavey Road like he's just another curious neighbor going back home.

4

Crowe Bovey parks his new pickup at the locked salvage yard gate. He sits with the windows rolled up, his hand on the wheel. He watches a single crow circling over the wrecks and junks. The crow dips almost playfully as it passes over the salvage office. Now Crowe Bovey sees others on the woodline, a tree of crows waiting, noisy, jubilant, more than he can count.

5

Big Lucien Letourneau's current wife hangs shirts in the kitchen of the big house behind the salvage yard. Big Lucien's old sister, Tante Flavie, is upstairs making beds tight and white as tables. The shirts the wife is hanging are green and say LETOURNEAU'S USED AUTO PARTS on the backs in yellow-gold. On the pockets they say BIG LUCIEN. The kids walk the kitchen counters like cats.

6

It is the next day, about 8 A.M. Big Lucien's wife's name is Karen. She sleeps alone in a tangle of blankets. She *loves* to sleep. When she hears the first shot, she pulls a pillow over her head. The second shot . . . she sits up blinking, giving the safety pin at the neck of her gown a frantic feel. She drops from the high bed, runs barefoot downstairs through the big house to the piazza. The old sister is in the bathroom . . . probably scrubbing the tub. The kids have been up early, walking the kitchen counters, messing with the cupboards. They run to the piazza with Karen and stare out into the brightness with round hazel eyes. A splatter of black feathers lies a few yards away. Crowe Bovey stands coatless in the opening between gnarled lilac bushes, a shotgun against one thigh.

"What are you DOING!!" Karen screams.

Crowe Bovey smiles.

Karen leans down and makes a loose snowball from snow on the step. She pitches it at his face, but he ducks, trotting away . . . laughing.

7

He sits square-shouldered . . . always square-shouldered . . . in his only clothes, his workshirt buttoned to the throat. The shirt says LETOURNEAU'S USED AUTO PARTS on the back. . . . CROWE on the pocket. Among the reds and whites and golds of flowers along the wall, members of the family embrace. The funeral parlor is vaporous with their sobs, a little bit stinky from velvet curtains, Chinese rugs, and years and years of dark light.

Now and then one or two of the sisters-in-law look over at the dark row of chairs where Crowe Bovey sits so square-shouldered, and they search his face for signs of grief.

When Karen Letourneau comes to the doorway of the kitchen that afternoon, she sees her husband's old sister, Flavie, headed out through the shed with a bag of trash, slamming doors as she works her way toward the barn . . . Then, almost in the same moment, Flavie's sewing machine begins its hearty thrum upstairs. The old woman is EVERYWHERE.

Crowe Bovey sits square-shouldered at the table, pulling at his cheek and three days' whiskers.

Karen rubs her eyes with her palms. "Gawd. It's you," she says.

Snow whirls outside the windows, and the lilac bushes only a few yards away are lost in the brilliance.

Still in their pajamas, Karen's children scurry over the kitchen counters. "Get off them counters!!!" she screams, and the kids plop off all at once with a box of Lucky Charms.

The kitchen floor churns with cats . . . cats of all colors, but mostly white cats. When Karen sees the shotgun, she raises one eyebrow.

Crowe Bovey says, "Your husband *said* I could stay here a few days till I get situated. I been sleeping in my Ford." He wipes his shotgun with a soft cloth, his fingers pressing along the thickness of the barrel in hard, elongated strokes.

The cats bash themselves against Karen's bare legs.

Karen wonders if this means Crowe has finally left his wife . . . or has she kicked him out . . . after all that carrying on with that college kid Jill Luce . . . Twenty-year-old Jill Luce with the high, hard-on-the-ears giggle and all those high, noisy clogs, different colors to match different clothes. Everybody in town knows about Jill Luce and Crowe Bovey. But also everybody has heard about the fire. Everybody except Karen Letourneau, who sleeps. She yawns. Her lavender eyes water. Big beautiful lavender eyes. All Big Lucien's wives have had beautiful eyes.

"Well, well, well." She sighs. "Lucien don't tell me nothing. You never know who's gonna turn up here. Every morning's a new surprise! Dogs in the barn, drunks on the floor . . . pregnant cats in the tub . . . half-wits watching my TV. I come downstairs in my nightclothes and bingo! . . . A new face!"

The kids arrange plastic bowls on the floor and the cats scramble over and look in the bowls. The kids shake cereal in the bowls, then pour on milk. They eat without spoons like cats. And the cats push in around them.

Crowe Bovey watches his boss's wife with a haughty half-smile.

"Why you got that gun in here around my kids?" she hisses.

"Ain't loaded."

She sniffs. "Yep . . . Big Lucien has what you call a HEART OF GOLD! He'd take in a poison snake if it begged him."

He watches her hard. Her bleached hair lies on her neck like a deflated yellow balloon. Her big freckles seem to churn.

The kids leave their bowls with the milk and soggy cereal, but the cats keep on. The kids get out their police cars, fire trucks, school buses, bulldozers, and wee sporty cars. One child tips a bowl and the milk runs down the steeply slanted floor with colored cereal spinning on top.

"Quit foolin' around!!" Karen screams. She fidgets with the safety pin on her gown. Crowe Bovey watches the fingers on the safety pin. His half-smile is eerie, for his eyes are expressionless, fixed.

Karen exclaims, "KIDS!! This is the man Papa sent up here to be with us for today! Maybe longer! He ain't as bad as the last one. You guys ain't forgot HARRY, have ya? Harry, that one with the yukky eye."

They all shake their heads and scrinch up their noses.

The dark spotty light of the Letourneau kitchen crawls over Crowe's glasses.

"This one's just a crow killer," says Karen.

One kid runs its tongue out at Crowe Bovey.

Crowe's eyes slide onto the children. He cracks his knuckles. With red wet smiles, the kids all watch him do this. They copy him.

Karen pads barefoot to an open drawer and takes out a spoon. The cats are ramming her legs again, more frantic than before, flexing bodies, flexing tails.

Crowe fondles his gun, the heavy, almost-black stock, but his eyes are on Karen's broad back.

None of the kids can get sound to come out of their knuckles. They pull on their fingers in various ways.

The man leans back on two legs of the chair. "You . . . Karen," he says. "You pretty sentimental 'bout crows, huh? You like birdies?"

Karen frowns.

The kids pull each other's fingers. At last a sharp CRACK! A scream. "Aw-waaaaaaahh!!!"

Karen crosses the slanted floor to inspect the finger. "For crissakes! Would you guys find something to do! Ain't *Sesame* on?"

They rush for their toy cars. Some of the cats run under the table in among Big Lucien's magazines and Crowe Bovey's feet.

Karen starts coffee.

On the buffet is a stack of greasy recipe books . . . showing the old sister's large handwriting . . . all in French. Karen has never laid eyes on the books before. She almost touches one. The storm shakes the house, screeches across the openness of the salvage yard. Karen jerks her hand back. She just stands there with her hands at her sides, watching the coffee beating up inside the glass knob. She listens for the sewing machine's thrum, or the old woman's hard shoes, but it's quiet up there.

The kids roll their cars and trucks down the steeply slanted floor. They shriek to imitate sirens. The trucks smash into the wall. "Not so rough!!!" Karen screams.

They do it again and again and again.

Karen watches the coffee beating darker, darker, darker.

Crowe Bovey pulls his cheek and the kids standing along the wall pull their cheeks.

Karen says, "You guys go see if *Sesame's* on."

They stretch their cheeks grotesquely. One cheek makes a snapping noise as it lets go.

Karen keeps her back to them all, listening to the storm rattle the house. She hears Crowe Bovey's wet boots shift under the table, but the kids get strangely quiet.

The man's eyes on Karen's back are like the eyes of a soldier at attention.

Karen wishes she were back in bed. It's a high old metal bed painted gray. She pours two mugs of coffee. When she turns, she sees all three kids are up on the table while the man lets them feel the gun.

"GET DOWN!" she screams. They plop down like cats. As she runs at the table some of the hot coffee sloshes over her hands. The kids vanish.

Crowe rocks slowly on the back legs of his chair. Standing near him, Karen can smell his dirty shirt and dungarees, the blackened hands. He smells like the inside of a motor running hot. Karen holds her burned hand hard against her gown.

He pulls one of the coffees toward him.

"Don't you want milk?" she asks.

He shakes his head.

She pulls out the chair across the table from him. It has a cat in it. She dumps the cat off, then straddles the chair.

"He's paying me a dollar a crow, you know," he says, smiling. "Maybe you don't know that. He wants them cleaned up."

"He?"

He almost giggles. "HIM! Your *husband!*"

Karen looks grief-stricken. "That's ridiculous. Lucien ain't like that. He LOVES animals . . . birds, bugs . . . GERMS if he could see 'em. So tell me another story."

"You have a crow problem around here . . . Overpopulation. You'll be sorry if you don't eliminate a few."

"They just fly around," she says.

He chuckles. "They do more than fly around. They are BAD NEWS!"

She says, "I don't believe Big Lucien would let you shoot at ANY-THING on this property."

"A buck a crow." He smiles, eyes steady.

Karen leans forward, her eyes fluttering. "Well, let me tell you something, Mister Man. Big Lucien's off on a drunk. AIN'T HERE. You shoot any more crows and I'll call the deputy. Try me."

He wipes his mouth on his sleeve. "You're dumb," he says softly. He swallows deeply of the coffee. Steam charges up around his glasses. "DUMB. Crows ain't good for nothing. They got no pur-pose."

"I *like* 'em," she says icily. She adds canned milk to her coffee . . . stirs it . . . the spoon clinks.

"I've been huntin' crow since I was five years old. I musta blasted two thousand of them cocksuckas so far. POW!!" He aims a pretend gun. The invisible gun kicks his shoulder.

Karen glares at him.

He leans back on the chair legs, rocks to and fro. "I ain't got a dot a mercy for them bastardly things. Coons either," he says.

"You're a weird man," she says.

"Ain't nuthin' wrong with killin'. You like *meat*, dontcha?"

She fiddles with her safety pin. He watches her pulling hard on it. "Maybe," she says.

"Maybe, maybe," he jeers. His lip curls.

"I think you looked pretty silly the other day picking on them birds with your stupid ol' . . . crow gun."

Crowe laughs . . . a high ominous shriek. "Ain't any crow guns. Boy! You know a lot!"

"Whatever."

"There's no gun called a crow gun, Karen."

"Don't matter."

He drops his head, kisses the gun. "This dandy is a Marlin pump action twelve-gauge. It's a shotgun . . . see . . . a SHOTGUN."

"Big deal."

"Well, if you wanna learn something instead of being dim."

9

Karen Letourneau's kids dress themselves. They go out and watch the yard men strip cars for the crusher. The kids run over the hoods of cars like cats. They find Crowe Bovey pulling a transmission behind the office. He works his wrench fast so that short wizened breaths fly frozen from his face. His hands are wrecked with sores. In time the kids find the crows in the bed of Crowe's truck. The uncounted pile of crows. They stand on the back bumper and look at each other with awe quivering in their round hazel eyes. "Yukk!" they say. They pat the dead crows.

His glasses are next to the lamp. He sleeps on the divan without taking off his wet boots. In all other available space, there is curled-up cats. The parlor has taken on the scent of his dirty shirt and dungarees. He lies on his face.

Karen's children cross the old fern-print linoleum . . . munching. Their hands go in and out of cereal boxes. They stand at the edge of the divan and look down on Crowe Bovey, at the back of his shirt which says LETOURNEAU'S USED AUTO PARTS. They look at each other solemnly. One of them drops a handful of Apple Jacks on the shirt. They wait. The shirt rises and falls, uninterrupted. They look at each other. Another hand opens over the sun-streaked hair.

11

She wears a coat over her gown. She seldom dresses. As she steps off the piazza, huge pieces of frozen breath are torn from her face by the subzero wind. She sees Crowe Bovey has made a path in the snow with his comings and going. His new pickup is parked at a crazy angle by the lilacs that obscure the old house. The openness of the salvage yard is noisy with wind. She follows the man's path, swinging her arms. As she passes his truck, she hears him. "Twenty-eight, twenty-nine, thirty, thirty-one . . ."

"What are you doing!" she rasps.

"Countin'," he says.

She pulls herself up to the tailgate with both hands.

"A buck a crow," he says, grinning, his dark eyes steady on her freckled face . . . only a small part of it showing inside her hood.

"You lie," she says. "Big Lucien is NUTS over animals!" Her eyes move over the crows . . . crow heads, wide-open crow beaks, crow feet, pieces of crows, whole crows, and on this heap the man squats, one hand on one knee . . . large grinning mouth.

"Shows you how much you know him," he snorts.

Slowly she lowers herself back to the ground.

There is another storm. Karen emerges in her faded gown. Cats surge from counters, cupboards, and chairs and make a yowling stampede toward her. The walls thrum with old Flavie's sewing machine.

Crowe Bovey is at the big table playing with a book of matches. Snow plops off his boots, drizzles away down the slanted floor. He doesn't look up. His smell is more enormous. There is a bloodiness on the table under his hands. And next to his hands is the two-week-old *Evening Express* with the headline SIX KILLED IN MORNING BLAZE. There are fingerprints in blood and grease around the edges.

Karen takes egg salad from the refrigerator and cats stand on their hind legs. She says, "If you want some clean clothes, you are welcome to use some of Lucien's . . . And we have some Willie left here last spring."

He cracks his knuckles. This time the kids don't copy. They just hang close to Karen . . . like the cats. When Karen turns, she sees the man has shredded the matchbook cover and popped off all the match heads.

There's a buzz in the distance.

"Is that Lucien coming to plow us out?" Karen asks.

Crowe leans toward the window. He nods.

"Oh, boy," says Karen. She puts the egg salad and a loaf of cheap bread on the table. The round hazel eyes of her children watch her hands make the sandwiches.

The buzz comes through the storm, closer, closer.

The kids watch Crowe Bovey shred the light-bill envelope.

Karen says, "You kids ain't gonna eat this dinnah . . . You're probably all full up on cereal."

Crowe makes shreds of the shreds, smaller and smaller shreds.

Karen passes out the sandwiches.

The plow clatters into the dooryard. The kids clutch their sandwiches and run to the window. Karen sighs. "Well, kids . . . here's your papa in his plow, home at last from his wine, women, and song!! Bet he's hung over 'n' hurtin'. Probably have one of his seizures on the kitchen floor tonight . . . Give us all a show . . . scare us out of our wits." She gives a pretend giggle. "Gosh . . . don't that man love to plow. Oooooooeeeeh! Plow! Plow! Plow! Let's see what he wrecks this time, kids. Last time he smooshed your swing set . . . remember?"

The kids nod. Their mouths tear at the sandwiches.

Crowe breaks his sandwich into four equal pieces with his black gashed fingers . . . arranges them to cover the headline of the paper.

Big Lucien is plowing so close to the house now that the glasses and plates in the cupboards clink together. Karen says cheerfully, "Don't that man love to plow! He's a real artist with a jeep, ain't he, kids?"

The kids chew slowly, staring wide-eyed into the crazy soaring lights. One child's cheeks are flushed violet. It stands off to one side, opening its sandwich and studying the egg salad.

Big Lucien backs up, rams the snow toward the house, higher, higher, higher.

The flushed child rolls its shoulder against its mother's thigh, against the faded gown. "Poor sick baby," Karen sighs. She stoops to wipe its nose with the hem of her gown. The man's eyes widen on the bare freckled leg.

"Baby's got the bug," says Karen.

The child's bleak round hazel eyes are like night eyes. Its hair is flat with sweat. Crowe Bovey moves his eyes up and down the child. The child throws its sandwich on the floor.

"STOP THAT!!!!" Karen screams.

The spinning light on the jeep fills the kitchen, drizzles over Crowe Bovey's glasses. Karen pulls out a chair, straddles it, and the child climbs into her lap.

"What the hell's that under my foot!" She looks under the table. It's an egg salad sandwich.

The other kids get tired of watching the plow job. They vanish.

Suddenly the TV in the parlor is louder than the plow. The channels switch crazily. Karen screams, "SHUT IT OFF!!"

But they don't.

Meanwhile, the old rowboat by the barn splinters to a million pieces. Big Lucien backs up and rams it again.

The TV goes louder.

When the plow rams the house, a bit of plaster lets go from above and slaps into Crowe Bovey's lap. "Jesus!!" he gasps.

Along the edge of the house Big Lucien Letourneau makes the snow hang in vertical bluish walls nearly as high as the house. The monstrous snow. The amber light on the cab churns through the kitchen, gleams on Crowe Bovey's glasses. He flexes his fingers.

Big Lucien rams snow to the east and west, his rear wheels spinning . . . wailing. The snow heaves up, covers one kitchen window. The plow thumps around the yard, eats up a rubbish barrel. Snow explodes against the piazza. The headlights and plow lights flood the kitchen . . . a hard, broad, steady light.

Crowe goes white.

Karen's lavender eyes tear up with laughter. "He's just plowing his heart out!" she shrieks. "Don't look so shook. You look shook! You oughta SEE yourself!!" She wipes her eyes dry on her sleeve.

Crowe stands up with his hands out away from his body while the yellow cab light sweeps across his belt buckle, making it glimmer. "It ain't *that* funny." His voice is coarse.

The lights of Big Lucien's jeep pull away, then burst in at a different side of the ell. Karen's laugh is almost a SCREAM.

Crowe steps over cereal bowls, trucks, and tricycles. His shirt is partly tucked in, partly yanked out.

Karen snickers, "You're getting funnier by the minute! You oughta SEE yourself!"

He pushes his hands into his pockets. The sick child's eyes follow him, its cheeks now red like a clown's. "Ahhh, sweetie . . . Poor sick sweetie sweetcums," Karen murmurs.

Crowe wheels around and around, the smell of his dirtiness toiling toward Karen as he passes.

The plow strikes the house. The walls groan. Crowe cries, "What's he trying to do, anyways! Bust his way in!!! He mad at you or something? This the way you guys settle a fight???"

"He always does this," Karen says softly. "It's how he plows." But she is starting to look a little uncertain. Crowe's pacing has an actual rhythm to it now.

Crowe laughs, rubs his hair, paces.

Karen rocks from side to side with the child. She blows across the red cheek, traces the small damp head with a thumb. Crowe watches the child and the child watches him, eyes locked, both sets of eyes silvery in the eerie shifting light. As Crowe circles the room, the child has to turn its head to keep him in view.

Karen speaks. "My father used to have a crow . . . a PET crow, her name was Phyllis . . . before I was born."

"Well, I *figured* there was something behind all this syrupy, poor-cute-little-crows shit!" the man says softly, almost to himself.

"My father says crows are smarter than people."

"That's garbage." His voice gets low . . . a dangerous-sounding low.

Karen leans down, spits on her hem. "That makes them smarter than anything," she simpers.

"Crows ain't smarter than humans," he says . . . very low.

"At least as smart as," says Karen.

"That is pretty silly. Crows can't invent stuff!"

"My father says Phyllis was good company. She said TWENTY words." She smiles. She draws the hem of her gown up, spits on it again, wipes the child's crusty nose with it. The man glares at her long freckled legs and the child pushing its face up into the wetness of the gown.

Big Lucien's jeep retreats, becomes a far-off buzz. Then the sighing of the storm, the drumming of the sewing machine upstairs, the purring of the cats, the croaky TV in the next room, and the sick child breathing noisily through its open mouth all seem like a kind of peace.

"Maybe it was thirty words." Karen sighs. "I'm not sure exactly."

Crowe laughs. "Thirty words ain't much."

She cocks her head and looks at him past her hang-down hair. She says, "Lucien has said THREE words to me in the past three weeks."

The storm gives the house a furious shake. Crowe puts one blackened hand out to her. "I give up. You win, Karen. Can't win a friggin' argument with a woman . . . I learned that long ago!!" His voice has gone high now, a dangerous high.

The child closes its hand around Crowe's right thumb.

Crowe makes a sound in his chest.

The two kids who have been in the next room reappear with mangled-looking mouths. Karen knows it's only grape jelly, or maybe

Jell-O powder . . . one of their raids. Crowe's eyes zero in on those mouths. He jerks his thumb free of the sick child's grip. He makes a quick silly little hop over one of the wee sporty cars . . . over a cat . . . over a spoon. He pulls at the back door as if to tear it off. But there is no outdoors.

There is only the hard-packed bluish wall of snow Big Lucien has playfully plowed up there flush with the door. Crowe just stands there looking surprised.

Karen shouts. "Well, look at that, aye!!! Look at what Papa's gone and done to us! Blocked our door up. How are we going to ever get out?"

The children stare with awe at the wall of snow.

Crowe says, "Pretty gawwwddam fuckin' funny." Then come the hard gobbly sobs of grief.

TWO

Leaving Freddie

1

LILLIAN GREENLAW, the mother, is sitting on the tub in her black velour robe with white lace collar. She is one of Big Lucien's many ex-girlfriends. The water isn't out of the tub yet so everything is in a big hot fog. Junie, the daughter, stands in front of the sink. This is always the way it goes when Lillian is about to tell secrets about MEN. Junie knows everything about Lillian's present boyfriend, Freddie. Lillian often marvels, "Freddie would have a bird to know all the stuff you know about him, Junie!!!"

At this very moment, Freddie is having another one of his toothaches. Sometimes his teeth are so torturing, he just lies on the living room rug with both hands over his face. But mostly he takes to bed. No matter how torturing his toothaches go, he never makes a peep. "A silent sufferer," Lillian calls him.

Lillian whispers through the fog, "Our troubles are over." Lillian's gray uneasy eyes move all over Junie as she speaks. "It is *finally* over."

Junie says, "Oh, yuh?"

Lillian and Junie both fix their hair the modern way . . . root perms, they are called, the shaggy raggedy look . . . and both use gold clips or old bandannas to tie up their shaggy raggedy hair into frenzied ponytails. The bandannas are often red to match their look-alike red sweaters with white lambs across the chest. When they are dressed exactly alike, Freddie calls them "the Greenlaw twins" even though Lillian is blond and Junie is dark, dark . . . the dark, dark blood of Big Lucien Letourneau, a man of the past. Big Lucien comes up occasionally in Lillian and Junie's secret talks about MEN.

Now Lillian is whispering, "How would you like some brothers and sisters . . . some instant ones . . . big as you?"

Junie sucks in her left cheek which makes her thick bottom lip thicker . . . the lip Lillian always calls "the Letourneau lip." It makes Junie look like she's been backhanded there.

"June Marie! Heavens to Betsy! Don't do that with your mouth!!"

Junie says, "Are we ever going to see Freddie again?"

Lillian gasps, "OF COURSE! He's not going to be dead! He'll be around."

Junie narrows her eyes, penny-color eyes . . . the blend of Big Lucien Letourneau's dark, dark and Lillian's uneasy gray. "Has where we are going got anything to do with that guy with the DOGS?" Junie asks.

Lillian stands up, tightens her sash. "Sweetie! You are too clever!" She throws her arms around Junie's narrow shoulders, gives her a big squeeze . . . then pulls the door open. They leave the bathroom, one by one in a secret, secret way.

2

E. Blackstone Babbidge's children don't move a muscle in church. They are square-shouldered, thick-necked, almost military. In fact, nothing is moving in this church . . . just Pastor Paul's right hand turning the pages of his white leather Bible. Pastor Paul's eyes are closed.

June Marie Greenlaw's eyes are fixed upon the back of her mother's long cream-color dress. She sees that her mother is taller than Blackstone.

Pastor Paul opens his eyes and speaks to Blackstone and Lillian in a high pale young voice. He makes them hold hands. Pastor Paul has whitish eyebrows and lashes and chapped lips and beautiful bluish hands, one held quavering in the frozen sunlight that whirls down from the tall windows above.

Blackstone's children's eyes are blue with black lashes . . . ICY EYES.

Lillian giggles at something that Pastor Paul murmurs and her ponytail, brushed to a yeasty thickness, catches the sun, turns it snow-white. She looks into E. Blackstone Babbidge's icy eyes.

Junie sucks in her left cheek.

The big gas heater at the back of the church clicks on.

Junie studies Blackstone's lushly thick black mustache . . . the kind that plunges . . . an out-of-control mustache.

When Pastor Paul says, "Eugene, do you take this woman to be your lawful wedded wife?" Blackstone says, "Yessss," in a deep unfriendly voice and a little tornado of frozen breath issues from his face.

3

They are wearing their matching sheep sweaters and matching red bandannas knotted around their shaggy raggedy ponytails.

"I'm going to start a business," says Junie. "Birch logs. I know where I can get some. I'm going to make a million." Her penny-color eyes study her mother's face.

"There goes my little businesswoman . . . at it again!" says Lillian cheerfully.

On the Horne Hill Road, the Malibu engine works hot and hard while the yellow woods blur past.

At the top of the mile-long hill there's a one-lane iron bridge and then the Babbidge house which sets close to the road. The house looks like a train of many cars: blue shingles, then brown shingles, then board-and-batten, then the last section is a pretty gold. The dooryard is full of bony, chained-up dogs, a van, a truck, and a tree. Off to the west is the howling windy sky, miles and miles of sky over the tops of trees. The Babbidge house sets high.

Junie says, "I'll charge two bucks each. Freddie always says outer staters will give *anything* for a pretty birch log."

Lillian eases the Malibu up into the yard close to the house. She is looking hard at Blackstone, who is working on his truck. All that shows of him is the back of his LETOURNEAU'S USED AUTO PARTS shirt and the stained wrecked rear of his jeans. Lillian touches her heart with her fingertips. "My Gawd . . . I can hardly BREATHE when I lay eyes on that man!"

Junie looks the other way, over the tops of the trees to the purplish piles of bigger mountains beyond Egypt. "Do you think the wind is worse up here than it was in East Egypt? Mark says it's worse," says Junie.

Blackstone's youngest kids and grandkids appear around the Malibu with aluminum foil twisted around their necks and wrists . . . and aluminum foil twisted into the shapes of guns. They slide their icy eyes over Junie and Lillian.

"There's the little sweeties now," says Lillian. She opens the car door. The kids vanish.

The trees scream with wind and the eaves of the house whistle. Yellow leaves stick leechlike to Junie's and Lillian's bare legs. Lillian pulls some bags from the car. The bags pulse and snap like fire. Lillian giggles loudly like she's listening to herself giggle.

Out of thin air, Mark Babbidge appears, Blackstone's next-oldest son.

"Big Columbus Day sale!" Lillian chirps.

Mark holds the storm door wide.

"Thanks, Good-Lookin'!" exclaims Lillian, looking directly into his icy eyes.

He doesn't smile. He has a fat neck and thick wrists but a hard mean skinny look around the eyes. "Bags, bags, bags, bags," he says and lets the door slam.

4

In the Babbidge bathroom, Lillian sits on the toilet lid, which has a red fake-fur toilet lid cover, while she and Junie secretly open bags.

Lillian gives a little plaid dress a sniff. "Like new!" She giggles.

Junie pulls a pair of tiny sneakers from a bag. "Freddie always said you was a yard sale whiz, Mama."

Lillian giggles. "Yes, he always said that, didn't he? That's 'cause of all the nice shirts I found him that day we went with Stephanie." She whispers, "He looked wonderful in that suede jacket, didn't he, Junie?"

"Yep," says Junie. She makes a line in front of the door with the small bags, then squats down and pulls things from them . . . mostly things to fit Blackstone's youngest children and grandchildren.

"You think they'll start to warm up to us when they see these?" Lillian asks, giving a fuzzy red-footed sleeper a delicate shake.

"I don't think they'll *ever* warm up, Mama," Junie sighs. "They are chilly people." She holds a blue dress up to her boylike chest and studies herself.

Lillian says huskily, "June . . . put that on right now. RIGHT NOW. You will look scrumptious in it!!! Wait till they see you at Daddy Blackstone's church in that one. My Gawd! Put it on!" Lillian jumps from the toilet lid, tosses down the footed sleeper. She gives the blue dress a little feel. "Try it on, June! Wear it out to the yard. Let Daddy Blackstone look at you in it. He'll be proud. Gosh, he'll be PROUD! PROUD! PROUD! Blue is definitely YOUR COLOR."

Junie narrows her penny-color eyes on the pipes under the sink.

Lillian gasps, "Hurry, sweetie! Put the dress on! Let him look at you in it!"

"I don't want him to look at me," Junie says.

5

Before supper, E. Blackstone Babbidge stands with his granddaughter, baby Crystal, on his shoulders, swaying, staring into the kettle of boiling potatoes. He is wearing his denim workcap with the bill bent straight up in a way that would look goofy on anybody else. The baby hugs his head.

Junie stares at the words on the back of his shirt: LETOUR-NEAU'S USED AUTO PARTS. The words are in yellow-gold.

"It's ready!!" squalls Eugenia, Blackstone's oldest girl. There is something pregnant about her though she hasn't got a big belly yet. But there's *something*. Probably the flat slap of her gray Nikes on the linoleum and the stately way she carries the kettle of potatoes.

The table fills up fast.

Some of the smaller children already have their hands folded, waiting for the blessing.

Anastasia, younger than Eugenia, sits at Blackstone's right. She is a short, thick-waisted girl . . . her arms softly darkly haired, her shoulders almost manly. Her complexion is a white, white pallor against her tufty black hair . . . a sick-looking pallor . . . a hospital pallor . . . a grave pallor. And yet she is unnervingly beautiful . . . the kind of beauty that seems FREAKY in the company of ordinary people.

Blackstone fixes his workcap on his knee and amazingly it clings there. Blackstone and his oldest son, Luke, look just alike at times . . . with their thick necks and half-shaves and sweaty mangled-looking hair . . . except that Blackstone has some spears of gray along the jaws. Even though it is really Luke's house, Blackstone always sits at the head of the table.

"Time for the blessing," says Eugenia.

Junie glances around the table at all the folded hands.

Blackstone just grips the table like he's about to shove it through the wall and whispers hoarsely, "PRAISE GOD FOR THIS FAMILY."

Junie doesn't close her eyes all the way. She takes the opportunity to get a good close look at Blackstone's tattoo. It is a moon in what Lillian has explained to her is "the last quarter." It is bright yellow and black. The moon's lips are stretched out like it's in the middle of a big kiss and its single eye is wide open . . . staring right into Junie's eyes. It is a tattoo of "unusual detail," Lillian has said . . . "A work of art." But Blackstone's forearms are hairy so the moon at all times looks lost in a storm.

There is a silence after "PRAISE GOD FOR THIS FAMILY," like everybody sort of expects there to be more. But there is no more.

Eugenia whispers, "Amen."

Beautiful, pallid Anastasia pushes the margarine tub, the bread dish, and the salt closer to Blackstone's plate.

Mark loads his plate with nothing but hot dogs. He squirts mustard all over them, then slashes them with his knife and fork. Lillian watches him hard. "Thank you for being so helpful today, Mark," she says.

Mark looks at her. The gap in his front teeth shows, but it isn't actually a smile. He says gravely, "Any time, Miss Lily-Ann."

Lillian takes a forkful of potato and chews it up fast, her gray eyes looking especially merry as she glances around.

Nobody makes many eating noises. They are all cautious eaters.

Lillian says with a giggle, "You know, Mark . . . once I heard that in Greece in the old days they believed a space between the front teeth meant you were highly sexed."

Blackstone spits something into his napkin and gives his thick mustache about eight wipes.

Junie looks to see who he is looking at. But he's not looking at anybody. He just looks dumbstruck.

6

Blackstone looks from face to face, the Easter movie tape in his hand. "Ready?" he asks, his voice soft.

"Yes Daddy!" "Yes Daddy!" "Yes Grampuh!" they say.

Lillian sits cross-legged on the rug. With the end table lamp behind her, her flaring raggedy topknot looks white-hot at the edges. Blackstone's eyes fix on her a moment. She lowers her eyes to her hands folded in her lap.

Junie speaks up. "Why we seeing an Easter movie? This is Columbus Day. Didn't they have any Columbus movies?" She giggles, flaps her left foot nervously.

Christopher, Benjamin, and Jason Robert, sprawled out on the rug in front of Junie, look into each other's eyes and titter, "COLUMBUS MOVIES!!"

Lillian leans toward Junie. "Daddy Blackstone says we can *learn* from this movie." Lillian's voice is not her normal voice, but the one she uses when she is listening to herself.

Eugenia comes from the kitchen and squats on a vinyl hassock in the kitchen doorway, rubbing her eyes that have a tired violet look around them. "I seen this movie *five* times. It's good." She smiles at Junie.

There's something about the air in the room that says this is not going to be an Easter movie with rabbits.

Junie's eyes drift over to Anastasia, the wrinkled yellow nightie, the black knee socks, the little worms of her just-washed hair, the BEAUTIFUL FACE. The BEAUTIFUL FACE has been crying.

Blackstone drops into the old spring rocker and folds his arms across his chest, knees wide apart. He shoves his denim workcap to the back of his head. He never makes the chair rock. He is not the rocking type.

Children on the rug inch closer to him. The littlest of the three Jennifers settles between his feet and knees, hugging his legs, her pale eyes dreamy. Kids are all over the rug and along the wall. And there's no room on the divan. Not with Luke's wife there, sleeping off the mill. Her left hand hangs out from a mint-color blanket.

The movie has clashing thrumming big music, big skies, long gloomy hallways with people sneaking around.

Junie stretches her legs, wiggles her feet with the big red sneakers . . . stares at her sneakers. She is thinking about the birch log business.

Blackstone looks around the room studying the faces. The two younger Jennifers have dozed off, one with her head propped on a soft-bodied plastic-faced monkey.

As Blackstone's icy eyes sweep around, they hold hard to beautiful Anastasia, who has suddenly hidden her face in her arms.

"This is the awful part," Eugenia whispers from her hassock. "This really gets awful, Miss June, Miss Lily-Ann." She smiles sadly. "You know what happens."

"We know what happens!" says Lillian with a giggle.

Blackstone narrows his eyes on the screen. There's the cross being dragged by Jesus through screeching taunters. It thumps along down over stone stairs.

Blackstone's voice makes everybody jump. "What's the matter with you, Anastasia!"

Now Anastasia has both arms wrapped around her head.

The oldest Jennifer sighs, "She don't like this movie, Daddy."

Blackstone says hoarsely, "You ain't *supposed* to like this movie." He snaps off a piece of the jade plant on the window sill and pitches it at Anastasia's broad back.

What sounds at first like a toy whistle is Anastasia . . . then one of her hard sobs.

"Don't make me get out of this chair," says Blackstone.

"It's just actors, Anastasia," says Eugenia . . . still smiling sadly.

There's a THWONK! THWONK! THWONK! from the TV. They are driving the nails now.

Blackstone pushes away the child from between his knees and stands.

"They're just ACTORS!" little Michelle gasps. "Don't cry, Anastasia!" She pats her big sister's arm.

Blackstone draws his hand over his mustache, then looks back at the screen. There's a wide shot showing the three crosses, the three slumped, pale, battered, speared, and spit-on men, the navy-blue distances of earth and sky blackening, sizzling.

Blackstone steps over the sleepy kids, grabs Anastasia.

"Ain't real blood!" shrieks Michelle, covering her own face now, eyes glittering between spread fingers.

Anastasia hangs dead weight from Blackstone's forearms, making him grunt as he steers her close to the TV screen.

Jason Robert, Benjamin, and Christopher try to see around their father's legs.

"Is he dead yet?" one of them asks.

"No," says another. "I seen one small breath."

7

Junie lies on her little aluminum-frame fold-up bed staring at the jars of pickles and vegetables that look a ghosty blue in the moonlight along the wall. Her room is the shed where Blackstone's ex-wife liked to keep her canning. Junie listens to Blackstone getting up onto his knees on the creaky bed beyond the wall, hears the sheet slide off his back. She can hear his tongue move in his mouth. She can hear Lillian's arms go around him. Junie's eyes glide among the ice augers, broom handles, creepers and rope, then to the door. Her eyes stop on the doorknob.

8

The next night during supper, they hear Luke's truck in the dooryard. He gets home later and later each night, then leaves again before dessert.

It's like this every year at the harvest, according to Eugenia . . . Eugenia, who is starting to warm up a little bit.

"There's Daddy!" squeals Jennifer, not the Jennifer by Luke's wife but the Jennifer by the Ballard girl Luke went with in high school.

Jennifer is everybody's favorite name, Lillian likes to say when there's a mix-up on Jennifers. "There can't be too many Jennifers!" she always says. All three Jennifers, including Blackstone's Jennifer, have grown to their soft, soft name.

"There's Daddy!" squeals Jennifer again as they hear the truck door slam.

"Eat your supper," says Blackstone.

Anastasia watches every move Blackstone makes. She sees he needs oleo. She pushes the oleo tub toward him.

Tonight Lillian is wearing a white knit top which Junie has never seen before . . . the kind of top Lillian used to say she'd never be caught dead in.

Luke takes a long time coming in. They can hear him talking to the dogs, leaning what sounds like a rake against the house.

The baby, Crystal, drops a piece of fried baloney off her highchair tray and it rolls like a little tire across the linoleum, hits the mopboard, and falls.

Christopher, Benjamin, and Jason Robert titter into their glasses of milk.

"Little kids think the dumbest things are funny," says Mark gravely, squirting mustard in crisscrosses over about ten pieces of baloney stacked pancake style on his plate.

With his cheek full of biscuit, Blackstone says deeply, "Somebody get that meat."

Eugenia gets up.

Luke comes in wearing no jacket even though it's cold. He shuts the door by backing up to it. He sniffs. "Smells like hot dogs!"

"Wronnnnnnnng!" says Jason Robert.

Luke goes straight to the sink and lets the water run and run while he gets a tumbler. The water pump under the floor starts clacking.

Eugenia holds the runaway baloney up to the light, picks off something, and flips it back over into the baby's highchair tray.

Luke stands behind his father and drinks the whole tumbler full of water without taking a breath.

A Jennifer says, "Daddy! Do an imitation of Kenny Rogers for Miss Lily-Ann. She don't believe you can do it!!!"

Lillian eats in a dainty way that Junie knows is not Lillian's true way of eating. Lillian wipes her mouth with a napkin and says softly, "Well, I didn't say he couldn't do it at all, Jennifer Denise."

Eugenia says, "As it turns out, Kenny Rogers is Miss Lily-Ann's favorite singer, Luke . . . so it would mean a lot to her you could do it."

Luke gives his mustache a couple of thoughtful pulls, looking Lillian up and down. He bursts out singing, his face scrunched up, a make-believe microphone in his hand. He does several lines of "Daytime Friends, Nighttime Lovers."

"Do a chicken!" Jason Robert says excitedly.

Luke does a chicken. He sounds just like one. Then he does other birds . . . pretty singing birds. Then he does Daffy Duck.

Blackstone puts a little salt on his string beans. He sets the salt shaker back real easy. His icy eyes stay on his plate.

Now Luke does a horse.

All the little kids giggle. Anastasia laughs with a mouthful of milk. It kind of sprays.

Luke does a dog . . . a dog whimpering softly. He shivers as he does it. "That's one of Dad's dogs," he says.

9

After school the next day, Junie heaves her books onto her bed and looks hard at the glass doorknob to Blackstone and Lillian's room, the last room in the long house, the most private room other than Luke and Diane's which is upstairs in the finished part of the house.

She turns the knob.

The big bed is made up with a comforter of large gold and blue flowers. There are two doorless closets heaped with cardboard boxes. The lamp and clock are on the floor.

She sits on the bed.

The room is icy although it has been a warm afternoon.

Junie gives a little bounce and the bed ernks.

She stretches out. On the ceiling the foil of the insulation reads ASSURED THERMAL PERFORMANCE. The walls do, too. Everywhere she looks it says ASSURED THERMAL PERFORM-ANCE. She pulls the comforter back. She lays her head on Lillian's pillow. She rocks her head from side to side. She stops moving, listening hard to the kids in the dooryard playing Outer Space and to the now-and-then whimper of one of Blackstone's chained-up, bony dogs.

She sniffs Lillian's pillow. Then she sniffs Blackstone's pillow.

10

The black night brings rain, a cold stinging hard rain . . . a ghoulish rain. The dogs on their short chains study the house silently with squinted eyes and drooping tails. A small black terrier perches trembling on the tipped-over snowmobile, his teeth showing like a tiny smile. On into the night the bleary dark rain beats every square inch of every dog, but they keep standing . . . facing the house with the same squinty expressions.

11

After supper the next night, Luke comes in. He looks like he's lost ten pounds during the day. His red chamois shirt is unbuttoned and hangs over his belt. He sits on a chair by the door pulling off his boots.

Lillian and Blackstone are at one end of the big leaf table with just a little paper-shade lamp on, a warm yellow island of light on Blackstone's big forearms and on Lillian's hands turning the pages of the Bible. She is reading: ". . . walk in love, as Christ also hath loved us, and hath given himself for us an offering and a . . ."

"Ain't this romantic," says Luke.

Junie is at the dark end of the table counting quarters from a Hi-C can. She has a red bandanna tied around her shaggy hair. She watches Luke pawing through a pile of stiff gloves and wool socks behind the door. He smiles at her. She smiles.

He takes a pair of socks back to the chair. Blackstone's icy eyes and Luke's icy eyes meet.

Lillian keeps reading: "For this ye know, that no whoremonger, nor unclean person, nor covetous man, who is an idolater, hath any inheritance in the kingdom of Christ and of God . . ."

Luke laces his boots up fast.

Lillian stops reading suddenly. She strokes the open Bible. "Feels like flower petals!" she says. "Like irises! Or roses! I wonder how they do that!" She pushes the Bible across the yellow circle of light to Blackstone's battered hands. He says, "I'll take your word for it, Miss Lily-Ann. You know I can't feel nuthin' right."

Luke stands up, crosses to the wall switch, strikes the switch with the back of his hand. The kitchen fills with glare. Everybody squints.

He lifts his plastic cap off by the bill, puts it back on his sweaty hair more securely, like he's trying to screw it on. The cap has no advertisement on it, just a small crisp American flag.

He says, "June . . . you want to go with me to check on the crews?"

Junie looks at Lillian. Lillian is turning in her chair to glimpse at Luke, who is unbuckling his belt to tuck in his shirt.

"How nice!" she says cheerily. "How special to get to know your new brother!"

Blackstone leans forward on his forearms, head bowed as if in prayer, but his eyes are WIDE.

12

Luke is a big boss man . . . manager, they call it, of T. M. KEELY FARMS. "Executives own it," he says.

Junie likes it that somebody might see her riding along with Luke through Egypt village. When Luke stops for gas, she looks around to see who is seeing her up on the high seat of the farm truck. There's nobody around . . . just Luke bent over with the gas nozzle. She looks through the back of the cab into the face of one of Blackstone's dogs. Rambo, King, and Melissa . . . Luke takes them places a lot . . . He doesn't ask his father if it's okay. He just does it.

"How's school?" he asks Junie on the long stretch through the Freetchie woods.

She says, "Stinks."

After that, neither of them talks. Luke gulps from his Thermos and steers with one hand. It looks to Junie like he's got big things on his mind.

They hit the darkening potato field on Emmons Road going too fast. Junie hangs on. The headlights bounce.

A harvester and loaded truck move in tandem against the sunset which is cold and white and windy. Luke drives like he intends to ram the rear of the harvester, then jams the brakes, making the big dogs thud around in back.

Luke jumps from the truck.

The harvester and truck of potatoes lurch to a stop.

Junie hears Luke screaming out there, his voice high and squeaky and squealy like some other voice . . . like one of his imitations. "Do any of you know what a ROCK looks like?!!!" he squeals.

The dogs prance and circulate, making Luke's truck shimmy. Luke and a bald man in a parka hustle around to the back and Luke shows him some rocks heaped against the tailgate. The dogs kiss Luke. "THESE," Luke screams, "showed up in your last load!"

"You're kidding," says a low voice.

"NOOO! . . . I'm not kidding! Lookit! That one there's bigger than your head!"

Junie gets down from the cab, feeling for vines with the toes of her new dress-up sandals. She wants them all to see her with Luke. Junie's eyes graze over the silhouettes of the women on the bridge of the harvester . . . kerchiefs, big hats . . . one of them cranking on a cigarette lighter but having no luck in the wind.

Luke and the bald man go back to the harvester.

Tufts of witchgrass wag in the wind.

Everywhere are the roars of engines. Everywhere is Luke's voice like there are ten Lukes.

Junie steps closer to the harvester, feeling the eyes of the women on her . . . their kerchiefs flapping in her peripheral vision.

Luke keeps screaming and the word "ROCKS" is repeated about a dozen times. Then his screams stop.

Junie rushes back to the truck, pulls herself up onto the high seat. Luke's Thermos is there, uncovered, steaming, looking like it's about to tip over.

He's back at the door before she realizes. She jumps almost out of her skin.

13

The sign says PRETTY BIRCH LOGS . . . $5 EACH.

Promise Lake is violet-color, dreamy. A warm soft sunless October day. Not many customers.

Gussie Crocker says, "You can go to jail for a long time for skipping school. Ain't that right, Anastasia?"

Anastasia watches a car pass on the black tar highway, her dark-lashed pale eyes wide. "I don't know. I've never done it before. What if the teachers go out looking for you? What if one drives by?"

"They got big nets," says Gussie. "Makes you feel foolish when they got you in one."

Junie sneers, "Quit talking dumb. I'm counting. Please." Junie flattens out five-dollar bills on her knee, getting out the wrinkles.

On the beach an oldish couple strolls past with their oldish dachshund. Anastasia watches them uneasily.

Gussie Crocker says, "Let's take some of that money and go over and get a banana boat."

Junie says, "You guys got a bottomless pit."

Gussie snarls, "You're a crummy boss. We haven't had no dinnah, no breaks!" Gussie has sunglasses so you can't see her eyes.

Junie says, "What do we need a break from? We're just sitting here doing nuthin' . . . just rakin' in the dough." She mashes a wob of money into a pocket of her baggy camouflage shorts which used to be Freddie's. She adds, "When I give you your salaries, you can do what you want with your money. You can waste it on crap if you want. But what I'm doing with *mine* is *saving*. I'm going to get a Two-Eighty Z. Red. With red interior. All red."

Gussie turns her head toward the crowded Kool Kone parking lot across the road. "You can have a banana boat made with butterscotch if you ask 'em. You just got to give up the chocolate sauce. Or the strawberry. Or the pineapple. I *hate* pineapple. Too chunky." She swipes off her black corduroy beret and twirls it on the end of one finger. You can't read her eyes behind those glasses. She has such a smooth style.

A green LTD pulls off the road into the Kool Kone parking lot. It has Massachusetts plates. Junie studies this. "They certainly look like the birch-log type. Maybe after they fill their faces, they'll ease on over and spend some money here." She sniffs. "I hate to brag but I'm really *into* business now. Really into it. I can tell about those people. I have a feel for the customer."

Anastasia sighs. "Kool Kone has all kinds of customers. We've only had two the whole day."

Gussie Crocker snorts. "That's because people *got* to eat. They don't need a silly piece of white wood."

A loaded ramp truck rumbles through the dark tunnel of trees. The truck comes slow and easy. The driver's left arm is stretched along the open window, the face a gray shape in the private gloom of the cab. Anastasia makes an ugly little cry.

Gussie's head turns as the truck creaks past the beach. She says, "Don't sweat it, Anastasia. It ain't your dad. It's probably whatchacallit . . . Big Lucien Letourneau . . . the one with the metal head and other metal stuff . . . HAND, I think. He's got a big metal hand."

"Gross!" gasps Anastasia.

Gussie says deeply, "He's about as gross as they come."

Junie frowns, pretends to be hardly interested. The truck door says LETOURNEAU'S USED AUTO PARTS, EGYPT, MAINE in yellow-gold. The driver has the fingers of his left hand hooked around the big side mirror . . . normal-looking fingers. Dark green shirt.

"Watch!" says Gussie. "You want to see him CLOSE UP??? You want to see his metal hand . . . metal head . . . whatever it is?

WATCH!!!" A rock appears in her freckly hand. When it hits the ramp truck door, it sounds like a firecracker.

The truck whines to a stop, its load, a long silver Eldorado, gives a little sensual bounce.

"I'm getting out of here!" Anastasia gasps.

The gears seem to rip up the insides of the old truck. It is backing up.

The girls see the face.

"Ain't nobody," says Gussie. "Just fat Ricky from Miracle City." She snatches up another rock and wings it. Another hit. CRACK!

"Hey! Cut the shit!" screams the face.

14

When Blackstone gets home from the salvage, he doesn't look at anybody's face. He hangs his denim cap on a nail behind the door and pulls off his jacket.

Lillian and the beautiful Anastasia are cleaning mackerels out of a white plastic pail.

Lillian calls out, "Junie!!! Come check the cookies! My hands are all gooshy."

Junie comes from the living room . . . sees Blackstone at the table, his hands and one forearm a satiny black. She drops her eyes, moves cautiously like she's crossing a stream on stones.

"Look at me," says Blackstone.

Lillian, Junie, and Anastasia all look up quick. Anastasia's mouth looks tight.

Lillian's hands keep working. She wraps a fish head in wax paper. She does a neat job of it like the heads are little birthday presents.

"Miss Lily-Ann," says Blackstone. "Did you know these girls have been playing hooky from school for three days?"

"Yes," says Lillian, almost too softly to hear.

"What?" says Blackstone. "Speak up."

"Yesssss," says Lillian.

Junie says, "They need a few more minutes, Mama." She closes the oven door easy.

Blackstone says, "Where you want your lickin', Anastasia? Somewhere private? Or right here in the kitchen in front of everybody?"

Anastasia closes her eyes.

Lillian says, "Oh, Blackstone . . . My God. That's awful. Please don't."

Blackstone breaks out into one of his big scary grins. All his little teeth show. It opens up his whole face. He says, "I've been using the belt on them kids for twenty-seven years and . . ." He stands up slow and achingly. "Let's get one thing straight, Miss Lily-Ann. These kids are MINE . . ." He jerks his thumb toward Junie. ". . . that one is YOURS."

Anastasia runs out of the room, the quirky toy-whistle sound of her cry moving down the long long shape of the house.

Lillian looks like she's about to sling a handful of fish guts at the back of Blackstone's head as he turns away, the fish stomachs and fish livers quivering there between her fingers, yellow, purple, and umber. She hisses, "June Marie . . . get Eugenia to watch the cookies . . . You and I are going for a little walk."

15

The dogs growl low in their throats as Junie and Lillian stride through the darkness in their matching black suede jackets, their raggedy topknot ponytails swinging in a frisky way. Lillian never zips her jacket, just squeezes it across her narrow chest like she does with her bathrobe.

When they get up onto the narrow bridge, Lillian stops to hug one of the cold iron trusses. She's out of breath but she's sort of laughing, too. The river moving under the bridge sounds like a huge swallowing mouth.

As Junie comes close to her, Lillian runs to the next truss.

Junie snarls, "This a game or what?"

Lillian giggles, then turns to gaze out over the treetops to the lights of Egypt village below . . . more far off than stars.

Lillian is quiet.

Junie takes a step toward her. Lillian bolts, disappears into the dark.

Junie cries. "Stop it, Mama! Let's not do this!!"

Junie feels her way to the dark end of the bridge, far from the Babbidge porch light. She asks, "What are you thinking, Mama?"

"Nothing," Lillian replies.

Junie squats down in the middle of the bridge and holds her knees. She says, "Nobody can think *nothing* unless they are dead."

Lillian giggles. "I wish I were."

One of Blackstone's dogs breaks the rules, howls . . . a sweet note held long, prayerlike.

Lillian says, "I hate him, Junie. I really hate him. My love for him is subsiding."

Junie says, "Well, I hate him, too."

16

Luke's company truck is brand new. Black. But at all times it is dusty and splattered. Under the crescent of scarlet letters that read T. M. KEELY FARMS, NORTH EGYPT, MAINE is the potato that Junie hates. A bright pink potato. It looks for all the world like flesh and blood. It could pass for a human baby born without arms or legs or head.

Being with Luke has become a regular thing. He even shows up at school. Through the windows in last-period English class Junie can see the truck with the potato on it, pulling up behind the ring of yellow buses . . . waiting for the last bell. She writes *luke babbidge* on one of the last pages of her English text in tiny tiny secret print.

When she comes outside with her books, Luke says, "Hey, Junie! Little buddy! What's up?" His icy eyes graze over the long low windows of the school's old section.

He has told her EVERYTHING there is to know about the potato business. Sometimes she stands around the office while he makes calls, and while he talks he makes funny faces to her. He tells her juicy gossip about the packers, the weighers, the stackers, and the young boys who pick out chefs after school. Sometimes she just sits in the truck while he messes with the belt on one of the harvesters. She keeps the heater on for her legs and feet. He lets her wear his digital light-up watch. When they ride along the back roads after dark, the red numbers flicker excitedly.

They are working two fields tonight . . . Bond Road and the big one near Ace Pond. The harvester they are using in the biggest field Luke says is worth a MILLION DOLLARS. Luke likes to tell Junie astonishing stuff, then he makes a funny face to imitate her look of surprise. He likes to imitate her voice, too. *"Really!"* he swoons in a lilty girlish voice.

The black truck hits the big field going way too fast. As it comes bounding and bouncing toward the million-dollar harvester, Luke stomps the brake and the dogs crash against the cab. Luke is screaming even before he has his door open. "What the fuck! What the fuck! What the FUCK!!"

The harvester and half-loaded potato truck are stopped. There are lighted cigarettes glowing everywhere in the darkness.

"So what do we have here? The royal fuck-off!!!?" Luke screams.

The dogs bound off the back and cruise around, lifting their legs on the million-dollar harvester.

Junie gets down from the seat, still in her school sandals and pantyhose and pretty gray outfit, feeling for vines with her toe.

From the harvester a woman's voice, low as a man's, moans, "Hey, boss man . . . time to quit. We can't see for diddly-shit."

The stars are coming out now with foamy spaces between them which are quadriptillions more stars.

The dogs zoom through the cockeyed headlights of the big potato truck.

There's a woman on her knees vomiting, her big hands spread on the thighs of her jeans. Right away Junie knows her. It's Gussie Crocker's mother. Junie steps closer.

Luke's pale jeans and boots appear in the headlights. "Well, what do you say, dear!" he screams over the engines.

The woman wipes her mouth on her sleeve.

Luke shouts, "You are plopped down here in front of the last order of the day. GET UP!!!"

The woman strains forward, vomits a huge steamy pool between her knees.

Luke points at the drivers and both engines die. He says hoarsely, "Mrs. Crocker, do you *hear* me?"

There is only the sound of somebody's lips on a cigarette.

Luke's legs are cocked like he has the power to hop a mile. The deep-as-a-man's voice speaks from the harvester, "She can't take motion, Mr. Babbidge. We all got our days. Maybe she needs a few days on the grader. That's what I would do if I was you . . . put her on the grader."

Another voice: "Last fall it happened to Dee Dee, only she just got a lot of water come to her mouth, you know."

"Yeh, but last year we was *all* gaggin' over mushy potatoes . . . Even Luke hisself looked a little green."

Everybody chuckles.

Another voice, "It was gettin' so we . . ."

Luke bellers, "What are you all blabberin' about!!!!" He moves deeper into the headlights of the big truck. The dogs rush with him, black and bony, their hollow flanks rippling like banners. "We can't stand around here listening to you women's life stories. You can do it on your own time, but you're not going to do it on KEELY time."

A cigarette shoots like a little star from the harvester. One dog runs at it, gives it a sniff. Somebody laughs.

Another dog smells the sick woman's palamino-color ponytail spread on her back. Another smells the pool of vomit.

"GET!!" Luke waves his arms and the dogs lunge out of the circle of light.

Luke points at the harvester. "Everybody get ready to roll . . . PLEEEEZE! We've got russets to dig. You all think it's too dark to work, aye? Well . . . you know what a russet FEELS like. And you know what a vine feels like. And you know a vine from a rock and your head from your ass . . . I hope! This isn't *Days of Our Lives*, ladies! This is the REEEEL world. We're not going home for supper till we finish this order. The longer we fart around, the later it gets. It's close to six-thirty now! TRACTOR MAN! Move that tractor PLEEEEZE! Mister TRUCK MAN! EVERYBODY, back up! Start on the other side of Mrs. Crocker."

The engines roar to life. The harvester lurches, clangs, jangles. Luke whistles for the dogs, a two-fingered whistle. The truck lights slide away. The sick woman is dissolved in darkness.

Luke's voice is suddenly close to Junie's face, his hand pushing at the middle of her back. He is saying softly, almost reverently, "What are you doing out of that truck? You shouldn't have got out of that truck. You wanna go and get your new sandals spoiled?"

17

Junie slams her bike down, bursts into the kitchen . . . her hair untied . . . her penny-color eyes bleary from the cold and smeared with something black.

Beautiful Anastasia is alone at the big table with a sketch pad and pencil. The pencil is not a regular pencil. This one whispers. She says, "Where you been all day? You quitting school for good?"

Junie empties her pockets on the table . . . pennies and dimes, a St. Christopher's medal, a plastic cowboy with bowed legs, a gummy sailing-ship earring, and a cast-iron paw. Her hands are as smeared as her face and rosy with cold. "I been going through cars down at the salvage. You wouldn't believe the neat stuff. Mostly money. I'm gonna get rich at this."

Anastasia keeps drawing. "Daddy says if he ever catches anybody at the salvage, they get strapped . . . And he WILL," she says.

"That's stupid. Why not?" Junie snarls, pulls from her pockets three more pennies.

"He don't say why. But it's something creepy probably. And the same goes for Miracle City. You hang out there, you get the strap. Ask Mark about that. Daddy caught *him* in Miracle City twice."

Junie wipes her hands on her jacket, studies the wall of coats and jackets behind the door a long moment. Then she leans on the table opposite Anastasia. "What's that?"

Anastasia smiles. "What does it look like?"

Junie screws up her face. "Upside down, it looks like a potato."

"That's it!" says Anastasia with a small smile. She puts the pencil down, picks up another. Some of the pencils are colors. Junie leans closer. Anastasia whispers to herself like she's giving gentle orders to her hand.

In other parts of the long, long house doors slam, the TV talks low.

Anastasia's potato is tasty-looking. It has dimples and dents. A cold-looking potato. Juicy. Full of rain. Full of the long summer.

Junie thinks of the hideous pulsating pink potato on the doors of the Keely Farms truck fleet.

Junie whispers, "You draw pretty good potatoes."

"Thank you," says Anastasia. "I'll give you this one to hang in your room."

18

While the Babbidge family sleeps, a hoarse wind comes up. Frost forms on the old windows of the unfinished part of the house. The dogs sigh. They curl themselves up hard and small. They look like a lot of furry funny basketballs left around the dooryard.

But the little black terrier tied to the tipped-over snowmobile doesn't rest. He perches on top of the machine, his teeth bared in a little smile. His trembling is out of control . . . almost mothlike.

When the little terrier wails, Blackstone doesn't raise his head from his pillow or speak, but his eyes are wide in the dark.

Then the terrier is silent a while, but the wind clashes objects around in the yard, and the trees crackle like fire.

Lillian whispers, "Poor animals. They must be freezing to death."

"Won't hurt 'em," says Blackstone. "They are made for it."

"I don't know," sighs Lillian. "They don't seem very happy."

Blackstone is silent.

Lillian thrashes the heavy blankets around a bit. She says almost cheerfully, "I don't understand why you don't fix them up some little houses . . . to keep them out of the weather, you know. It wouldn't take much."

"It would take *plenty*," Blackstone snorts. "Lumber costs *plenty*. I don't spend good money on a buncha damned dogs. I have a *family*."

"They must be so cold," Lillian insists.

Blackstone grunts. He reaches for her head and hair, the nape of her neck, spreading his fingers there . . . though he can't feel her . . . His battered hands can't ever feel softness. He says, "Outdoor dogs ain't supposed to be made of. It'll ruin 'em. You want lap dogs you do one thing, you want watchdogs you do another. Those are *watchdogs* out there, Miss Lily-Ann. It may not please you, but it's

38

got to be. Life isn't an easy road. You better face that now and get it over with. Life ain't no Walt Disney pi'ture."

The small black terrier begins yipping.

Blackstone doesn't raise his head off the pillow or shift the great hulking thickness of blankets. He just bellers. "SHUT UP AND LAY DOWN!"

There is only the roar of the wind for the rest of the night.

19

Coming back from bringing his wife to work, Luke and Junie ride the roads slow. It is after midnight. Sometimes it seems the truck almost comes to a stop. But then Luke gives it the gas on a good straightaway. Baby Crystal is asleep, her head in Junie's lap.

As they pass the school bus–stop shed at Mushy Meadows, Luke says, "You been missing a lot of school, Junie."

Junie looks out at the black space and stars.

He says, "Don't want to talk about it, huh, brat?"

"Why *you* want to talk about it?" she asks.

He feels the keys that dangle from the switch. "I . . . I'm curious. That's all. Curious about you."

Junie looks at him, the bill of his American flag cap low, just little sparkles where his pale eyes are. She thinks he smiles. She's not sure. The mustache squirms around some.

He says, "Is Mr. Dunlop still there . . . that puts kids in the trashcan?"

Junie says, "Nobody named Mr. Dunlop."

"You ain't heard of no Dunlop?"

"No."

He feels the keys in the switch again. "You ever get in trouble in school? Get detention?"

"Just for stuff I didn't really do," she says.

He chuckles. "Girl after my own heart."

Junie squeezes her knees.

He says, "Is Mrs. Mountain still there?"

"She's a creep," Junie says.

Luke leans toward Junie. "NAME. DATE. AND DIVISION.

IN UPPER LEFT HAND CORNER OF YOUR PAPERS . . .
FIFTH PERIOD IN THE RIGHT. NUMBER FROM ONE TO
TWENTY. PENZZZZZZZZZZZZZZZ ONLY!!!!!" He does Mrs.
Mountain's voice perfectly.

Junie snickers.

Baby Crystal is steamy against Junie's lap.

Junie says, "Mrs. Mountain is a creeping creep."

At the foot of Horne Hill, the nose of the farm truck lifts up in front of them . . . up, up, and up. The motor works hard and hot. Luke shifts, but doesn't give the truck much gas. He looks over at Junie, the eyes sparkling under the bill of his cap. He says softly, "Mr. Dunlop put me in the trashcan once. Right in front of all the kids. He says, 'This is what we do with those who don't PAY AT-TENTION!' And you know . . . right in front of all those kids I . . . I . . . you know . . . cried."

Junie looks at him, her mouth ajar.

He rams the gas, makes the engine holler. Then rams the brake. The truck swerves a little. He punches the horn with his fist and stomps the dimmer switch about six times with his boot. The trees and stone walls on both sides of the road flutter like an old-time movie.

Like Daffy Duck, he says, "Disthpicable!"

Then he twists the knob which makes blue stuff squirt out.

20

Lillian and Junie sit on the bed of big blue and gold flowers with the door shut. The house is quiet. Outdoors is quiet. There's just Lillian's voice in the whisper she uses for secrets. She says, "We haven't had a nice talk like this in so long."

"Busy, I guess," says Junie, waving her legs around over the edge of the high bed. Her jeans fit loose, some Eugenia gave her.

Lillian studies Junie's mouth like there might be something on the lips, a cookie crumb or some mustard. But there's nothing on the lips, just the bottom lip thickening like all Letourneaus' when they are doubtful.

Junie swings her legs faster. "This room gets pretty chilly, huh, Mama?"

Lillian says, "Yeah . . . frosty. And it's not even winter yet." She sighs deeply. She says, "June Marie . . . I have something I want to ask you." She sighs again. "Do you have any secrets to tell me?"

Junie frowns. "Secrets?"

Lillian giggles but her gray eyes are full of fright. "You know . . . secrets about MEN."

Junie's feet stop swinging. She narrows her eyes on the little window that is a sea of yellow beech leaves and sun.

Lillian hisses, "Nobody likes Luke . . . he's not *like*able."

"I like him," says Junie.

Lillian's eyes fill fast with tears. "My GOD, Junie! You're not even fifteen!! You get pregnant and your life will be over!"

One of Junie's knees jerks. "MAMA!" she cries out, grinning madly.

Lillian flings herself off the bed, wailing, hiding her face in her hands. "That bastard! That bastard!!!"

Junie stops grinning. "Luke is nice. He's *very* nice. NICE. NICE!!! Stop bawling. I hate it! It makes you look numb."

Lillian scooches down beside the bed, pulls out a fat orange box. She stands with the box, waves it a little. "Does he use these? I can give you some of these if he don't."

Junie stares at the box.

21

Junie slumps in her desk. She watches the back of Little Lucien Letourneau's black T-shirt. "Frenchmen love to wear black T-shirts," Lillian always says.

The back of Mrs. Mountain's wide navy dress has chalk marks from leaning against the board while she talks. Yellow chalk. She is talking about PARTICIPLES.

Junie would like to have a word with Little Lucien Letourneau, but she and Little Lucien have never had much to say. And besides, he's cocky.

Junie's maroon corduroy drawstring satchel lies in a thick way on top of her books by her foot.

22

When she gets home Junie doesn't waste any time getting out of her school clothes. She just leaves them in a pile on the bathroom floor. Lately it seems business ideas are popping up right and left in Junie's head. She shoves cereal boxes and folded washrags down to Blackstone's end of the table, then gets a bunch of Sunday papers from the shed.

She stops to bust up hot dogs for the baby, who loves them cold. "Gogs!!" Crystal cheers.

Junie sits Indian style on the stool against the window, the late-day sun at her back, weak and autumnal and orange.

Anastasia comes from the back rooms of the house, still in her school outfit. One side of her face is red from napping. And there on her calves, looking less purple than this morning, the marks of Blackstone's belt . . . this time over what he called "sassing."

"Whatcha making?" she asks.

Junie replies, "You'll see in a minute."

Junie's big sneakered feet wag with excitement as she dumps a package of KRAZY GLUE from a bag.

"I love art, you know," Anastasia breathes.

"Ain't art. Art is for babies. This is business," Junie tells her. She leans over the highchair tray and breaks up another hot dog, then wipes her hands on her jeans.

They hear a grunt and look through the doorway at Luke's wife's hand that hangs from the mint-color blanket on the living room divan. The hand jerks a time or two, then goes limp.

Anastasia says, "Can't I help you with this you're making?"

Junie says, "Last time you was my employee, you did nothing but complain."

Anastasia says, "Well, I'm near food and water now. I'm not so weak."

Crystal shrieks, "Gogs! Gogs! Aaaaaaaaaaaaaah-waaaaaaaah!"

Junie breaks up another hot dog in the tray.

Anastasia looks intently at the newspapers and purple cardboard and glue.

Out in the living room there's a show on TV with doctors shouting. Handsome doctors. No funny-looking doctors. On top of the TV are all Blackstone's birthday cards, mostly from his people in Aroostook, where he's from. And mixed in are two gold-framed graduation photos of Luke and Eugenia.

Anastasia giggles. "Mark told me you was selling condoms in school today. You find *them* in a junk car?"

"Maybe," Junie says, then adds, "Anybody you know that's interested, tell them I ain't got but three left."

"Okay," says Anastasia, then giggles again.

Junie cuts a star shape from a newspaper.

Anastasia flops to a chair, close to Junie.

Baby Crystal is a powerful thin-haired big-faced baby, her striped shirt tight across her back. She picks up a hunk of hot dog in her left hand and squishes it . . . then squishes one in her right hand. She has great power on both sides.

Anastasia reaches for the scissors and makes about ten perfect stars. Junie glares at Anastasia's stars. Dozens of stars flutter from those scissors, stars that look made by a machine.

Crystal throws a piece of squashed hot dog straight up. It arcs. Drops straight down into the sink.

Junie holds the glue close to her face. "Bonds to almost ANYTHING," she reads aloud, her voice deep and grave. "Bonds SKIN INSTANTLY . . . Gaaaawd." She sucks in her left cheek. She reads on. "Surfaces must MATE CLOSELY. What do you suppose that means?" Her eyes slide onto Anastasia's freakishly perfect face, the lovely wide mouth whispering to itself as her hands work the scissors.

Crystal spits hot dog. Hot dog and goo shoot in all directions.

Anastasia gives the baby's hand a hard slap.

Junie looks for a long moment at the baby's big square wailing mouth. Then she rips open the glue package and an eensie tube rattles to the table. "This is wicked stuff," she breathes.

Anastasia hoists the baby out of the highchair.

Junie glances another long moment at the baby's crying mouth. She squirts a couple of drops of glue onto the purple cardboard. She says, "This is such powerful stuff that if I wanted to, I could glue you to your desk at school . . . and glue Mrs. Mountain on top of you." She aims the tube at Anastasia like a loaded gun, squinting one eye.

Anastasia says, "Very funny."

Junie shapes the cardboard into a big cone, vises it with clothespins. Then she glues on a few stars, a couple of paper moons.

Anastasia makes huge fart noises into the baby's neck. The baby laughs deep, thick-necked laughs.

Junie hisses, "That ain't your baby."

Anastasia says, "Is, too. I'm her auntie. That's pretty close."

Junie glues on more stars, not looking up, her skinny shoulders hunched in her work.

Anastasia says, "You are mean."

Junie says, "You are retarded."

Anastasia says, "You ain't nuthin' here. I ain't your sister. This ain't your niece. And LUKE ain't your BROTHER. You act like Luke is your brother. But he's not!!!"

"So?" says Junie.

Anastasia jounces the baby on her hip. "Nobody is your brother or sister. You ain't got none."

"Yessuh!" howls Junie. "Little Lucien Letourneau is my real brother and Missy Letourneau is my real real sister. Ask my mother!"

At this Anastasia giggles hysterically. She dances with the baby around the kitchen. The baby laughs, too . . . till she loses her breath and gags.

Junie glues on more stars.

Anastasia comes back to the table, breathing hard, her eyes runny with wild humor.

Junie says, "Tonight when you are asleep, I'm going to sneak right in your room and glue your eyes shut. Then I'm going to glue you to the bed. No . . . first I'm going to glue your big fat mouth so you can't holler and get somebody to give you a rescue."

Anastasia flutters her eyes. "You talk like a baby. What a baby. Baby! Baby! Baby!"

At supper, during Blackstone's deep-voice blessing, Junie watches Anastasia and catches her looking back. She can tell Anastasia is worried. She probably thinks Junie might really glue her tonight.

She will huddle there tonight in the big bed she shares with Stacy and Michelle, worried sick about falling off to sleep.

23

Junie lies on her little aluminum-frame fold-up bed, her feet sticking out at the end, her eyes wide.

The jiggling of the doorknob to Blackstone and Lillian's room has awakened her. She figures it is one of them feeling their way out to the bathroom.

Then something clobbers the door and she hears her mother shriek.

Junie grips the sides of her tiny bed.

"PLEEEEEEEZ!" Lillian bawls.

The wall goes thwonk! thwonk!

"I can't take it!" Lillian gasps. "I can't take it!! I'm tellin' ya." She gags. "Oh . . . pleeeeeez stop! Pleeeeeeez. God. Stop!" She gags again. "You think I'm foolin' about the nightmares! Why don't I tickle you! Then you can see what it's like, you bastard!" Then she giggles crazily and the wall thwonks once. "If I get a dream tonight, it'll be your fault," she says faintly like there's something covering her face.

Junie can't imagine Blackstone tickling Lillian . . . or tickling anybody. He's not the tickling type. She sucks in her left cheek . . . then once on the right.

"You'll pay!" Lillian sort of sobs.

Then there is running. There's no space in their room for running. But it sounds like a big race. Then the bed boings. Then something smashes the wall, an elbow or a shoulder, maybe a head. There's a deep grunt.

Lillian giggles. "Seeeeeee, Mister Smarty . . . Now you know how it feels!"

45

24

Junie stands on the dark side of the big leaf table, her mother in the sun. They are face to face.

Lillian's hands smooth out Blackstone's jeans. Three pair. Riddled with battery acid. The knees and flies are snow-white.

Then she folds three dark-green shirts with LETOURNEAU'S USED AUTO PARTS across the backs . . . GENE over the pockets. Yellow-gold.

Junie makes towers out of folded washrags and sucks her right cheek in. Outside the kids are playing Outer Space . . . giving each other commands . . . voices too deep, too soft, too deadly serious to be children.

She looks across to Lillian's face. "I could use more of them things," she says in a whisper.

Lillian smiles. "What things?"

"The Trojan things," says Junie.

Lillian's face whitens. She doesn't say anything, just pulls a yellow fuzzy-footed sleeper from the basket.

Junie says, "Can I have some *more*, Mama?"

Lillian keeps her eyes down. She folds three sleepers. She looks dumbstruck. She folds another sleeper. A pair of socks. "June, I gave you a DOZEN."

Junie starts a new pile of washrags. She doesn't have to watch her hands fold. Her hands snatch this way and that all by themselves . . . like little trick dogs. "Well . . . if you give me a bunch more, I'll go easy on 'em this time."

Lillian stops folding. She looks into her daughter's penny-color penny-round eyes. "Sweetie, did you and him really do it all that many times? It's only been THREE DAYS."

Junie reddens. "I guess." She looks down at her hands.

Lillian's voice gets husky. "He must be a regular rooster, huh?"

Junie sighs. "Yes. It's pretty bad."

Lillian's eyes blur with tears. "Don't you let him . . . Well, don't do anything you don't want to do, will you? By Gawd, you're just a kid. He's twenty-SEVEN. He's different, you know. Big and pushy. Don't do anything you don't want . . . You hear me, June? Only if you feel good about it. I don't know . . . but I'm starting to get kinda *scared."*

Junie sucks one cheek in and her bottom lip thickens.

Lillian looks off into the darkmost corner of the kitchen and whispers, "Men are monsters. I'll be glad when I'm in my grave all by myself."

25

Saturday the beach is busy. It's one of those hot yellowy October days when a haze hides the mountains. Around the Kool Kone parking lot and along the road, the tall-grass bugs sing like mad.

Junie's Hi-C can is full of dollar bills. She sits squarely on a rock with her knees apart, wearing a tall purple cone-shaped cap with stars and moons. Even between customers she wears a dazed and mystical expression. The sign taped to her TV tray says FUTURES . . . $1.00.

Up on the road a three-quarter-ton pickup with a pink flesh-and-blood-looking potato on each door rolls to a stop under a pine. Junie's eyes widen on the truck. Then she pretends not to notice. A boy smelling like barbecue potato chips and having what looks like pollen on the fine hairs around his mouth asks Junie, "Can I know about Christmas . . . What I'm gettin'?"

Junie narrows her eyes. "For one dollar, I can tell you about all Christmases for the rest of your life."

Luke appears beside the boy. He looks thinner, more haggard. The visor of his American flag cap makes a black shade across his white-blue eyes. His messy T-shirt is stuck to him. His arms drip. He smells like gasoline. He says, "How's the little businesswoman?" and he chuckles.

She retains her dazed and mystical expression. "Fine."

He looks at the low neck of her crisp gauzy gypsy blouse, blue-white against her dark skin. She is fully decked out today . . . huge flowery floppy skirt, a necklace of outrageous large cream-color shells, Eugenia's silver bracelets . . . *eight* of them.

47

He spreads his hand on the hot metal TV tray. "Come on up to the farm for dinnah. I'll get you an Italian and chips."

"What for?" says Junie, keeping her mystical expression and mystical voice.

"What do you mean, 'what for?' " he asks.

"Why you want me to come up there and eat with you?"

The boy beside Luke says, "I was first, you know."

Luke pushes his cap back on his head, turns, and gives the boy an icy study. The boy shrugs and moves away.

Luke pulls the cardboard sign off the tray. "How can we write OUT TO LUNCH on the back of this? You got a pen?" He paws his pockets.

Junie says, "I'm not hungry today."

Luke says, "Well, you can come along anyway. We can shoot the shit."

"What do you want to talk about?" she asks, narrowing her eyes on his tensed Adam's apple.

"Same things we always talk about!" His voice is getting the squeak to it that means he's working up to a scream . . . although he has never before screamed at Junie.

She says, "Maybe I ought to stay here today." She squints into the blinding yellow haze of the long beach. "Business is pretty good."

Gently he tapes the sign back on the tray. He chuckles. But even the chuckle has a squeak. "You're not *mad* at me, are you, Junie?"

Junie shrugs.

"What in hell's brought all this on??!" It's an almost-scream.

Junie shrugs again.

"Have I said something wrong?"

Junie says, "Well, sometimes you're bossy . . . wicked bossy. And pushy . . . *big* and pushy. It gets on my nerves, you know. I'm not your real sister, you know. If I was your real sister, I might let you boss me . . . a little . . . but . . . I ain't. Or if I was your GIRL-FRIEND, you might be able to boss me, but I ain't that either!" She looks out at the lake.

He chuckles. "I can't remember a time I ever bossed you! I don't know what the hell you're talking about. We get along real good . . . We get along *perfect*! We've covered every goddam subject . . . school, parents, politics, ice fishing, business, TV, TROPICAL

FISH, pilgrims, sports, cars . . . SNOW! I've been very nice to you. You are, it looks to me, trying to put a little drama into your life. I ain't never seen the beat of it! It's because nobody ever puts you straight! You got free rein far as I can see . . . Just your mommy's little spoiled brat!!" He chuckles, but it's not a real chuckle. "Well . . . I can't stand around here all day . . . Goddam orders are piling up. Toodle-oo!" He turns and trudges through the deep yellow sand back to the truck. Junie watches him with a chilly, mystical expression.

26

This is the very first time the Jennifers and Christopher have come into her "room." They sit on her narrow aluminum-frame bed swinging their legs and looking around. They are warming up, Junie thinks.

Junie says, "Everybody close your eyes and cover them."

She closes the door nice and easy and pushes a box of empty canning jars against it with her foot. Her hands are black and the front of her sweatshirt is streaked and spotty. She goes down on her knees by her bed and pulls out the paper bag with the pickled puppy in it. She opens the bag and holds the quart-sized blue Ball jar to the light. "Okay!" she says. "You can look."

Their pale eyes fix on the jar in her upraised hand.

"What izzzzzit?" one of them whispers.

"A dead dog," says Junie. "I got it at the salvage."

Christopher's eyes slide down her arm onto her face. "Uh-oh! You ain't supposed to go there. Daddy says."

"They got all kinds of stuff in the cars . . . money and jewels even. I seen TREASURE. You guys are pansies." She lowers her voice. "HE don't scare me."

The late-day sun wraps around Junie's wrist like a yellow bracelet and the blue jar shimmers. The puppy slowly turns, its yellowed umbilical cord trailing like a sash . . . A little ballerina, its face dreamy, forever in repose.

"This puppy is a girl," says Junie.

"Is it DEAD?" one of the Jennifers asks. She zips her jacket up, then zips it down, then up, then down. Fast.

Junie gives the jar a shake. The puppy turns faster through its yellowy raggedy sediment. "Maybe not," she breathes.

"Open it up!" says Christopher.

Junie starts to work the wires. All four kids rear back, eyes aflutter.

"Just kidding," says Junie. "I can't open this up. I don't want to wreck it. It's worth a LOT OF MONEY."

She thrusts the jar back into the bag . . . then back under the bed. The kids drop off the bed, head for the door. "HEY!" Junie cries. "Don't go! Maybe I got something else you can see."

"Like what?" asks the oldest Jennifer.

Junie almost trips over the box of canning jars, flattens her back to the closed door.

"You got stuff from SPACE here?" Christopher asks.

"Outer space, you mean?" Junie asks.

"Yuh," says Christopher.

"Maybe," says Junie.

They all look at her blackened empty hands.

27

It's a cold smoky-smelling blue and gold afternoon on the Ginn Road Lookout, where you can see for miles and miles. A silver Dodge Charger with black pinstripes and loud, thrumming music rumbles up to the very edge of the drop-off. Anastasia Babbidge screams.

Everybody laughs.

"Pluto to Earth! Pluto to Earth! This is the captain speaking!" Scott Reed speaks into his hand. He flicks the key and the big engine dies.

"What if your brakes didn't work, Scottie?" Anastasia gasps.

He says, "We'd all be hist'ry, I guess."

Everybody laughs.

Keith Crocker rolls a joint on the knee of his jeans.

Nobody looks at the view.

Now and then a window cranks down to let a cigarette fly out into the weeds. Out with each cigarette come the clangs and wails and rivets of music and Anastasia's nervous giggle.

Rick Ballard says, "June . . . what's this I heard you got fifteen bucks for that canned dog?"

Scott Reed howls, "NO SHIT!!"

Keith Crocker puts the joint into Junie's outstretched fingers.

"A CANNED DOG? Who needs it?" sneers Scott Reed.

"Colby needed it," Rick Ballard chuckles.

"Figures," says Scott Reed. "Probably to go with that stagecoach wheel and nurse's shoe."

"He's into trivial," says Rick Ballard.

Scott turns to look back at Junie. "Hey, Rich Woman, you want to go in on some really tough weed from Reynolds on Friday?"

Junie passes the joint up front to Anastasia and speaks while holding back her smoke. "Nah. I'm saving up. I'm going to get a Z."

Scott Reed snickers.

Keith Crocker says softly, "You know how much one of them babies goes for? It's going to take you till you're forty to have that kind of money saved up."

"You'll probably have to go for a loan," says Rick.

Scott snickers. "Junie? Get a loan? I can just see it. You're not even old enough for your license yet, are you?"

Junie lays her head back against the seat, still holding her smoke, her eyes closed.

"Come on, Junie," urges Scott. "Put in on the weed. Chance of a lifetime."

"Naw . . . not this time."

"What an old maid. Jesus, Junie . . . sometimes I don't know about you." Scott shakes his head, takes the joint from Anastasia. "Maybe, June, you ought to get yourself a good rocking chair."

They all titter.

Junie lets out her smoke. "Well, if you mean I ain't getting married, you are right. Men are jerks."

Scott, Rick, and Keith all groan at this.

Junie continues. "I'm going to be a working woman . . . sales probably . . . make piles of money."

"Marry me, O Rich Woman!" Keith Crocker beseeches.

Junie says, "I'm not marrying anybody. But Scottie, you are

51

wrong, wrong, wrong . . . I won't ever be no OLD MAID!" She keeps her eyes shut tight and wears a pleasant little smile. "All old maids do is dust their house . . . stuff like that. But me . . . I'm going to cruise around in my Z and have a nice life."

28

Another bad black night. Black rain. Black wind. Deep black eddies are around the doorstep and around the stakes and small trees and concrete blocks where E. Blackstone Babbidge's dogs are tied, where they run their tight forever-circles that eat away the earth. The wind makes the dogs' ears flutter and twist. The rain pounds their faces.

The sound of a truck creaking up onto the iron bridge is hardly a sound at all, lost in the howl of the black weather. But the dogs hear it. Their ears open out like cups. Rambo, Crackers, Princess, Big Boy, and Sam lean hard into their collars, stand straight up like men.

The truck has no headlights, no visible driver. It just idles there, a kind of ghost of a truck, a faint illumination in the shape of a windshield, a floating windshield, and the low unearthly thrum of its motor.

The tiny black terrier snarls and spins and gags, jumps on and off the old snowmobile, his teeth snapping.

"It's probably nothing," Lillian tells Blackstone.

The windshield-shaped illumination now floats backwards and vanishes into the storm. But the dogs have lost their minds.

The porch light comes on . . . a puny light through the black rags of rain. The storm door whooshes open and Blackstone appears in a white T-shirt and jeans and boots with trailing laces. His icy eyes zero in on each dog face. They have nearly lost their voices, some of them gone onto their knees and croaking . . . some foamy on the chin.

29

The three girls pedal along down the main aisle of the salvage yard, Junie in the lead, her skinny legs working in a pinkish blur, her gypsy skirt in a flutter of gaudy purples and reds. Everywhere are the twinkles of cracked mirrors and busted glass struck by the warm autumn sun. Everywhere the tall-grass bugs sing.

"Hang a left!" Junie commands. They shortcut their bikes between two battered vans.

In the distance is the saggy-roofed paintless house and barn of Big Lucien Letourneau . . . Not the house you'd expect the MAN OF GOLD to live in, rich rich rich Big Lucien Letourneau. The trees in the forest around it are low-limbed and sinister-looking.

At the end of the aisle is a shirtless thick-waisted man working on a pile of tires.

"Hey ho!" Junie calls and comes to a smooth stop. "Are you Big Lucien Letourneau?" Like she has magic to her voice, a cloud swallows up the sun and the air seems suddenly freezing.

The man reaches for another tire. The muscles of his back and arms thicken and furl. The tattoo on his upper arm and shoulder is a dragon: black, bright green, and red. He mutters, "Lit-tle Lucien iss *big* while Big Lucien . . . he iss *lit-tle*." He is breathing so hard and his accent is so thick that Junie squints to make him out.

"What?" she says.

The man doesn't answer, just slings more tires like they are Frisbees. The yellow salvage yard dust droops around his humped-over back.

Anastasia and Gussie Crocker stop their bikes alongside Junie. Gussie's eyes can't be seen behind her white plastic-frame sunglasses, but Anastasia's eyes are round with fright, scanning the rows of cars, scanning the woods. Gussie slams her bike down and locates a rimmed tire to scooch on.

Junie says to the man, "Big sale on futures today. Only one dollar. Want to know what's in your future, mister?" The sun returns bigger than ever, something like the headlight of an oncoming freight train. She unties the purple cone hat from her bike and fixes it on her head.

The man jerks a tire off the changer and heaves it onto a pile. He grunts. "Not now."

"One dollar isn't much for something as wonderful as *your* future," Junie says in a solemn way. The sun flashes crazily.

The man gasps. "I got better to do wit my money dan pay you to hang around."

Junie presses on. "One dollar is a wicked deal. At the fairs you give three bucks. If you want to know your future for cheap, here's your big opportunity."

He pulls a red bandanna from his pocket, wipes his face. His chest heaves like he's working up to his last breath.

Junie says, "It's got to be either travel, love, or business." The sun shimmers on each of the topics as she names them. "Or if you are curious about what you are going to get for Christmas . . . I been good at that."

He almost smiles.

Anastasia steps over heater hoses and busted glass to join Gussie on the tire. She sits with a soft, worried sigh.

The man pounces off the tire pile and picks his shirt off the door handle of a red and white Chevy truck. Across the back of the shirt it reads LETOURNEAU'S USED AUTO PARTS. And over the pocket it says ARMAND. He gets cigarettes from the pocket, picks at his belt buckle with a match, leans against the truck which looks hot enough to fry his back. He lights up. He narrows his eyes on Junie. "You look familiar," he says. "You live around here?"

"No," Junie replies quickly. "I'm an exchange student from South America."

The two girls on the tire giggle like mad.

Junie gives them a scorching look. "In about five minutes you are both going to be fired . . . FOREVER!" she hisses.

"How come you act so suspicious?" he asks. He smokes ravenously. His dark eyes study her shell necklace, silver bracelets and floppy skirt, and cool gauzy blouse.

"I ain't," she says softly.

He crosses his arms over his chest, breathing noisily even now. He points with his cigarette toward the paintless house. "Go bug de women. All dey got to do iss sit around."

Junie squints at the paintless house. She sucks in her left cheek, then her right. A few aisles away, a yard wrecker roars. Chains clang. "Okay, for crissakes. Go ahead. Look into your silver ball." He chuckles.

Junie pats down a place in the weeds, sits cross-legged with her floppy bright skirt spread out in a pretty way. She looks up . . . straight at the dripping chest and arms . . . the red flames, red eyes of the dragon. She closes her eyes.

She still sees a red eye. She says, "Wow. I see hundreds of women."

The man gives his cigarette a vicious suck.

Junie snarls, "Mister! You've got to be quiet! I'm in an altered state. There's no fooling around."

Again, he looks like he might smile . . . but he just blows smoke.

Junie says in a mystical voice, "I see them coming from everywheres, even California. Good ones. Like they look on TV. They are rich. Got tans. Pretty clothes. Two-Eighty Z's. Trans Ams. They stop at North Windham to ask directions. They say, 'Hurry up and tell us where's Egypt? Where's that guy with the huge muscles and green monster on his shoulder and a name begins with A?' . . . Armand, I guess it is . . . I only saw it real quick. There gets to be wicked traffic. Buyin' up all the maps. Runnin' out of gas on the road. Leaving their Two-Eighty Z's and Trans Ams and Rolls-Royces behind. All they got on their minds is BIG MUSCLES and the dragon with the huge fiery breath. No women left in California or Florida or Boston or the places of communists. Those escape. They come in boats and things. On camels. They all come here just to give you a BIG KISS."

Anastasia and Gussie gasp and gag with laughter. Gussie makes a huge hollow kissing noise with her cheeks.

Junie keeps her eyes shut tight.

The man pitches his cigarette into the dirt. It's hard to tell if he thinks it's a good future or a bad one. He drives his hand into the pocket of his smeared dungarees and pulls out a flat-looking wallet.

Junie opens her eyes when she hears the rustle of paper money. But what she sees first is the man's upper body twinkling like busted glass, busted mirrors, tiny suns.

30

The sound of Blackstone's belt on Anastasia in the kitchen is like firecrackers. Junie lies on her little fold-up bed, her eyes on Blackstone's ex-wife's jars of pickles.

Lillian is out there in the kitchen, too. "Stop it! Stop it!" she wails. Junie covers her ears a while.

When her bed starts to tremble, she knows it's Lillian running through the long, long house, giving each and every door a slam. When she reaches Junie's room, Junie makes like she's deep in sleep. When the last door slams, Junie opens her eyes. She listens to Lillian sobbing in the room with the bright flowery bed. "I HATE HIM! I HATE HIM!" Lillian screeches.

31

The next night Blackstone sits at the long dark leaf table with only the light from the paper-shade lamp. Lillian says, "Come to bed," but he just stares at the outside door.

Everyone else goes to bed, clicking off the lights in the long train of narrow rooms.

In the morning he is still there at the table, asleep with his face in his arms, his denim cap, which Luke calls "the commie cap," is by his foot on the floor.

Lillian says, "How about some eggs?"

Without lifting his face he says, "No thank you."

The kids gobble cereal, their eyes wide on each other.

Eugenia comes to stand behind her father. She says, "Did you call up over to Mama's? . . . She's probably there at Mama's. Anastasia and Mama've always been close."

Blackstone raises his head. "Your mama ain't seen her."

Eugenia starts to place her hands on his shoulders, but something makes her change her mind. "If I make you a little toast, Daddy, will you eat it?"

"Not now," he says.

"Maybe we should call the deputy!" exclaims the oldest Jennifer.

"Yeah," says Stacy gravely. "Somebody crazy mighta got her, huh?"

When the wall phone starts up ringing, Blackstone is out of his chair to snatch it off the hook before the first long ring has finished. "Hello," he says deeply.

He turns toward the wall. "Where are you?" He glances up at the rooster clock over the refrigerator. "Where ARE you? I'll come get you." He listens. The room is silent with his listening.

"No, I won't," he says. "I promise. Tell me where you are."

He listens. He lays his forehead against the wall. He says, "I can't understand you . . . Get yourself together!" He rubs the back of his neck.

Lillian brings him a chair from the table. He sits easy. Rubs his hair. "If I promise I won't, I WON'T!"

He listens.

"You have to come back. You ain't but a baby!!"

He listens. He rubs his hair hard. "Okay . . . say it right out. SAY IT!!!"

He listens. Then it is a long, long time that he's not saying anything, just gripping the phone with his shoulder.

Eugenia murmurs, "Dad . . . she hung up, didn't she?"

Lillian says, "She'll be back home soon. Kids do that sort of thing all the time."

He stands up fast, the phone receiver hitting the wall, swinging like a hung man. He is vomiting even before he reaches the sink.

Nobody talks. The retching in the sink is noisy, half-strangling, half-sobs. All eyes watch this uneasy thing happen.

32

When Junie gets home from school that day, her mother's Malibu is gone, but the truck with potatoes on the doors is in the yard. It makes a tinking noise like it hasn't been home for more than a minute.

"Hi Toto!" She greets the wee black terrier perched on the snowmobile. But he won't look her in the eye. He stares off into the

57

distances, the great gray piles of hills, the high-up cottage-cheese clouds, birds, planes. He is trembling mightily.

Some of the larger dogs yearn toward her, their tails swaying, but they don't bark or yelp any hellos.

In the kitchen there are muddy prints the size of Luke's feet. "What pigs men are!" Junie says softly. She hangs her black suede jacket on the wall of coats.

The toilet lid clatters in the bathroom. But otherwise the long house is silent.

Junie gets a stick of oleo, peels off the paper. She measures out some sugar. She hunts up a spoon. She can tell Luke's having trouble with the toilet because of the big GURGLE GURGLE in the drain of the kitchen sink.

Junie chuckles.

Luke ambles out of the bathroom and stands by a window looking out. The sun looks dusty across his arms. He glances over at the divan with his wife's hand hanging from the mint-color blanket.

Junie busts a couple of eggs into a bowl.

The pipes running new water into the toilet shut off.

Luke says, "Wake up. I want to talk to you."

"Add vanilla," Junie whispers. She hunts up the vanilla. Somebody has used it all and put the empty bottle back on the shelf.

Luke moves toward the divan. "DIANE!!" he screams.

Her hand just hangs there.

He kicks the divan.

Junie gets a butter knife to scrape out what's left of the peanut butter. She feels the shape of it. It is real silver, very old, has roses on the handle. She loves how sometimes hard things feel soft. It starts to take on the heat of her hand.

She turns the peanut butter pail on its side and starts scraping.

Luke paws around under the mint-color blanket and gets a good grip on Diane . . . looks to Junie like maybe her neck. "Diane," he says. "You hear me?"

Diane groans.

Luke sits on the divan.

Diane sighs. "You guys go play."

"Diane!" he wails. "It's ME!" He lies down alongside her. He looks like he's all by himself, spread out on a mint-green blanket.

Minutes go by, time for Junie to cut out cookies and crisscross them with a fork. But Luke hasn't moved a muscle yet. He's still just lying there face down. Junie thinks he is sleeping. But maybe he's just lying there thinking or something.

33

Outside it's Indian summer . . . yellowy and hot. Inside the Cold-spot Café the air is black and icy. Anastasia has the chills. Out-of-control chills and a bad, bad purplish sunburn.

Bruce Springsteen is Vikki Karnes's favorite singer. Vikki mashes enough quarters in the slot to make that voice go on forever and ever.

The waitress brings two Cokes with ice. She is Armand Letourneau's wife, Patty . . . full-blood Passamaquoddy who everybody thinks is Japanese. Perhaps because she has such dainty ways. She says, "We're out of straws, dear." This makes Anastasia giggle a wild heinous drunken giggle. "So silly," says the waitress . . . and disappears . . . or so it seems. Anastasia lays her face on the cool table.

There is a cold whirring sound between Bruce Springsteen songs.

Vikki Karnes leans onto the lighted console of the jukebox, singing with the music, wiggling her rear, tossing her hazy yellow hair. Her bikini is pink. In the dark Coldspot light, she looks entirely BARE.

Anastasia wears a bikini, too . . . one of Vikki's spares. It's a print of yellow sunfishes. It has a bright-yellow terry cover-up top. But it's still not warm enough . . . nothing like the broad warm beach across the road where they have spent the morning. Anastasia's teeth chatter. She pushes the cold Cokes away. One tips over, spills on the floor. She looks around for the waitress . . . but sees only the quiet bar . . . No one there.

Vikki appears at the table. "You are shit-faced!" She heaps some paper napkins onto the pool of Coke.

"Yep," says Anastasia softly.

"I told you you wouldn't feel it at first, to go easy . . . but no no no. Now all we got for tonight's 'bout a third of a fifth . . . We might as well stay home tonight if we haven't got anything to take. I'm not

59

showing up at Lori's with nothing to put in . . . I don't know about you, but it's not CLASSY."

Anastasia giggles. "Oh-kaaay."

Vikki leans toward Anastasia, her face nearly hidden by the yellow scribbles of her root perm. "Let's get out of here. That waitress is up to something. She was just on the phone. Don't think for a minute she doesn't know your folks are looking for you . . . SHE KNOWS . . . I can tell."

The waitress scurries past with huge pizzas for three men at a table by the door.

Vikki says, "Let's go back to the house and watch some soaps."

Anastasia says, "Nawww."

"I'll fix you a baking soda bath for your burn . . . It works."

Anastasia groans. "Nawww."

Vikki hisses, "If you don't sleep off that V.O., you aren't going to be worth much tonight . . . COME ON . . . before something happens here. I'm tellin' ya, that waitress is acting VERY suspicious."

"I'm sick of hiding," says Anastasia. "Sick of it . . . sick . . . sick . . . sick of soaps, sick of your living room . . . sick of your little brother." Her teeth clatter. She lays her face on the cool table again. "I ain't going nowhere. It's nice here. Nice and great."

Bruce Springsteen's voice goes on forever. Anastasia keeps her head on the table, her face to the paneled wall. She thinks maybe Vikki has gone to play pool with the gang out back in the game room . . . But Vikki *might* still be sitting right there across the table for all Anastasia knows.

Endless Bruce Springsteen . . . and the cool feel of people walking by her booth . . . making a breeze. She keeps her eyes wide on the wall.

"Anastasia," she hears her father say.

She turns her face to the left. She sees a belt buckle and a pair of blackened hands . . . another belt buckle and more hands. She can't count the hands.

"Please, Jesus," she says softly.

Blackstone yanks her to her feet, every inch of her skin set on fire. "Arrr!" she howls. "My burn!!"

"Where have you been?" he murmurs . . . the ugly murmur he uses just before he tells one of his kids to bend over.

60

She sobs. "My burn . . . my burn. Please, Daddy . . . It's SORE."

He loosens his grip a little, looks to his left into the face of Crowe Bovey. The whole place has gotten quiet, even Bruce Springsteen. Blackstone speaks into Crowe Bovey's haughty dark eyes, "What do I do with these friggin' kids?"

Crowe is pulling off his shirt . . . the green workshirt with LE-TOURNEAU'S USED AUTO PARTS on back, CROWE over the pocket . . . fixes it on Anastasia's shoulders. He grins crookedly at Blackstone. He shrugs. He doesn't seem to have the answer either.

34

It is November. The black bitter evening booms with a rain that thunders from the ell into the calf-deep water by the steps. Blackstone and most of the children have gone to Wednesday night prayer meeting. Eugenia and Lillian are at the table telling baby stories with Sanka gone cold in their cups. Lillian wears a pair of aqua-green pants made of a spongy material she used to say she'd never be caught dead in. Eugenia's new maternity top is a plaid of bright, almost gory oranges, reds, and purples. She gives her thick thighs a couple of squeezes. She says, "I've got to stop eating cookies."

Junie and Luke play Monopoly under the paper-shade lamp. They have been on a real Monopoly streak lately . . . now that the harvest is done. Luke keeps giving his mustache a sinister twist and saying, "Things are looking mighty grim for poor sweet June."

"I don't know what you're talking about," Junie says. "I'm the one that owns everything."

"Not for long! Not for long, poor sweet June," he says, giving his mustache another twist.

Headlights flutter on the wall. Junie leans back to look out. It is a truck with LETOURNEAU'S USED AUTO PARTS, EGYPT, MAINE on the doors. It pulls up under the beech tree close to the house. Its windshield wipers slash. The dogs silently go round and round on their short chains and ropes. Some stand on their hind legs.

The truck doors open . . .

"Who is it, Junie?" Eugenia asks.

Junie replies, "I don't know."

There are two men moving through the ragged darkness, one with a rifle. The dogs lunge at them but the short ropes and chains jerk them back . . . They are barking now. The man with the rifle hollers out, "STAY INSIDE, WILL YOU!"

"Somebody is hollering to us," says Lillian.

Luke stands up . . . but before he gets to the window, there are two shots.

Lillian screams, jumps from her chair.

Luke looks out and sees two dogs floating on the broad water. He says, "Everybody sit down."

Lillian sinks into her chair. "My God. What izzz it? What's happening?"

The dogs bark in unison . . . one BIG bark. The man with the rifle is standing just out of reach of Rambo's snapping teeth. He aims the rifle at the teeth.

Luke goes back to the table and sits.

Junie covers her ears, watching Luke, trying to read him.

There are more shots . . . spaced . . . filled with a kaiyaiying, with barking and the boiling dark rain. Once there's a CLANNNNNGGGG!, what sounds like a shot hitting the swing set by mistake.

One by one the dogs' voices disappear.

"Why don't you DOOO something, Luke!" Lillian cries.

"I'm calling the deputy," says Eugenia, pushing to get up.

"Sit down!" Luke snarls. Then he says softly, "It's what we always wanted, isn't it?"

"Toto," says Junie softly.

"It's what we always wanted," Luke says, glaring at them all. "I'm sorry . . . but I'm not sad."

The headlights slide down the wall and away.

Luke stands up . . . goes to the window. "It was just a mattera time . . . I coulda told ya . . . how far-reaching the golden hand of Big Lucien Letourneau is. I mean, goddammit, that's impressive."

The rain thickens.

.

62

THREE

Springtime in Miracle City

1

THERE ARE more trailers and camps in Miracle City than there were a month ago.

Things have gotten out of hand in Miracle City, the selectmen all say.

"Big Lucien Letourneau always lets his heart of gold get the better of him," one of them says.

"Heart of gold isn't what I'd call it," another one sneers. "It's just plain ignorance!"

"But where will it stop?" says the next one. "He hasn't got much land left that's buildable anyway. Nothing but rocks and ridge."

"But he always finds a way to squeeze in one more."

"He'll be doing high rises next." Chuckle.

"You know, he lets them stay there for nothing. Every one of them!"

"I heard something to that effect."

"That's just plain bad business. The man will go under before long anyway."

"He's not someone you can reason with either. When Barry gets off the phone with him, he just shakes his head."

Another one sighs. "Trailers between trailers."

"And those shacks, too!" the first one says with a wrinkling of the nose.

"And there are places where you can see that mess from the road. It's a disgrace to our town. People will think Egypt is the *slums!!*"

"Only one or two of them actually has a toilet, you know."

Gasp!

Gasp!

"If we can get those new codes to pass, we can stop him."

2

It's a warm mint-color evening in Miracle City. The deputy, Erroll Anderson, rides with his bare forearm out the window of his jeep, his eyes narrow. There's at least three new particle board camps thrown together since the last time he was down in here.

He is looking for Little Lucien Letourneau . . . fifteen years old . . . who they say is bigger than Big Lucien . . . no doubt way bigger than the last time he drove down in here to track him down. They say Little Lucien lifts weights, has become a regular Mr. Maine.

The deputy blows his horn at a cat. He says "Nice night" to a woman in her doorway working a washcloth in her ear as he passes. But there's no sign of the boy who is built like Mr. Maine . . . even at the gray and porchless camp where he lives, there's no answer when the deputy knocks.

3

Norman Letourneau, Little Lucien's older brother, never plays cards. He must not like cards. He doesn't actually say. But when Uncle Armand or Crowe Bovey asks, "Hey, Norm . . . poker tonight?" he just says "Naw."

He likes to sit in Big Lucien's chair with the paws and grin his weird grin that shows all his tongue. And he drinks a little beer.

They play in Big Lucien's kitchen, glaring with lights, cats surging. But Big Lucien himself is rarely around . . . off making a deal somewhere, no doubt.

Little Lucien comes over with Norman. He is always with Norman . . . forever close . . . except when he's over to Blanchards doing bench presses and squats. Little Lucien Letourneau . . . so broad across the chest that OXFORD PLAINS SPEEDWAY on his T-shirt looks like a *command*. He has a deep, tired, bluish look of triumph around his eyes these days . . . working in the woods with Norman . . . *making money.* He leans way back on two legs of his chair, his cards face down on his crotch, a beer on one knee. He says deeply, as low as his boy's voice will go, "Your draw, Mon Oncle."

Armand Letourneau says, "Okey-dokey!" Armand wears a dark-green LETOURNEAU'S USED AUTO PARTS shirt tonight so none of the dragon is visible. And yet everyone in the room knows the dragon is there . . . Even if they didn't know, they'd know. They'd know it by his posture, by his voice, by his numerous showy ways.

The screen door screels open. A couple of cats and an old old collie dog charge in . . . and then a short thick hippie woman. None of the men at the table seems astonished to see the hippie although this is the first time any of them has seen her in ten years. She is just one of Big Lucien's many ex-wives. It happens sooner or later. They come back.

She looks nothing like she did when she left for California . . . The stabbing happened in California. And she is a much thicker woman, all hips, all thighs . . . She even looks *shorter.* With her aluminum cane she prods her way along the steeply slanted floor. There are cats in all the cushiony chairs, men in all the hard ones . . . No sign of the old sister, Flavie . . . Nobody gets up for the hippie . . . Nobody says hello. Over by the cold woodstove, the hippie dumps a cat out of a straight-back chair.

The cat skids across the slanted floor and appears in Norman's lap. Norman busts into one of his big grins. Norman looks wet tonight . . . long stringy wet-looking beard. He is often wet-looking, wet with his work, wet with bad weather. His wet-looking outgrown crewcut has got flattened out on one side.

The hippie says, "Well, well, well, you sure have grown, Little Lucien. You aren't what I expected . . . but I know it's you . . . same face . . ." Her voice is damaged . . . hoarse, broken, terrible . . . the kind of thing that would break Big Lucien's heart. The voice continues. "I thought I'd come over and see if you were here . . . let you know the law is hot on your trail . . . truancy, he tells me . . . maybe give you a chance to jump out the back window and head for the hills." She chuckles. A broken hissy chuckle.

65

Little Lucien upends his beer, then looks into the hole at the top of the can. He says as deeply as he can, "Anderson don't sweat me none."

Sargent flattens three bright jacks and two tens onto the table one at a time.

Crowe Bovey looks hard at the middle of Sargent's throat.

"Shit," groans Armand.

Mark Babbidge chuckles. "Ain't talent. Just luck."

There is a purring of many cats . . . and the purring of Armand Letourneau's emphysema and the fathomless creaking of the woods in back of the old house.

The hippie wears a beautiful skirt . . . something perfectly hippieish . . . a purplish print of lusty-looking minotaurs. In her vast lap a cat appears . . . a wide-awake-looking black cat with white-yellow eyes. All over the hippie's forearms are scars that look like lips. She wears a denim workshirt open at the throat and the scars there on the throat look like lips, too . . . bright lips . . . like the lips of little boys and girls. Her real lips are set in a hard white line, a worried smile. She looks over at Norman, who is patting the cat in his lap. She says, "How have you been, Pitoo? In ten years, you haven't changed a bit."

Norman grins at her . . . a sheepish grin.

"He doan answer you any to Pitoo anymore," says Armand. "He doan recognize it."

The hippie's eyes slide onto Armand's thick right upper arm. It's easy to see that she knows the dragon is there. She then looks into Armand's face and smiles at him gravely.

Sargent makes little towers of the silver he has won.

"What's that you say? P-2?" Mark Babbidge asks with a snicker. "That some kinda outer space name? P-2 D-2?" In one corner of his mouth is a sewing needle. It glimmers. Chewing on sewing needles has been a continual habit of Mark's since he started working in the woods for Sargent. Sometimes the needle will disappear all of a sudden. Then it reappears on the other side of his mouth.

The hippie's broken voice says, "He'll always be Pitoo to me! Hard to break old habits."

"Well, you better break *dat* one," sneers Armand . . . Then he laughs, looking not at her but at the faces of the other men.

Norman is still grinning at the hippie, hands in the pockets of his workpants, the sleeves of his brown reindeer sweater drooped over his bony wrists. It sounds like he's purring. But it's the cat on his lap curled up tight like a large yellow snail.

4

Maxine Letourneau, an ex-wife of Big Lucien's, mother of Norman and Little Lucien, snaps a no-nonsense stainless steel lighter under a fresh Tiparillo and studies the dipstick of her truck with a no-nonsense expression. The truck is yellow . . . a wee Chevy Luv . . . too wee and too yellow a truck for such a rugged-built woman . . . but good on gas.

The tailgate has been painted with a bold unshaky hand: GOD BLESS AMERICA . . . GOD BLESS PRESIDENT REAGAN . . . slightly mud-splattered, slightly dusty, but still very readable.

Maxine's two younger boys, Ryan and Michel, have Big Lucien's dark dark blood, dark looks, thick bottom lip. One is whipping the roots of a tree with a stick. Both boys have no-nonsense spring haircuts . . . pretty close to bald.

Across the narrow rutted road the hippie is out on her doorstep with a book. Her camp has been thrown together in a big hurry by the salvage yard guys . . . Big Lucien's orders . . . Waferboard that still smells strong, blond, and sweet. The hippie is so thick-hipped, thick-thighed, she seems to fit too tight in her tiny doorway. Her graying dark hair bursts from its pins . . .

When the hippie catches Maxine's eye, she lowers her book and waves. Maxine is not the waving type. She just nods.

"Mama," whispers one of the boys. "Let's go over and sit with the new lady a minute."

Maxine says thickly, "You let me catch you over anywheres near that hippie and you're going to be DEAD MEAT."

Both boys look at the hippie across the rutty road, their dark dark Letourneau eyes gleaming. One boy sucks in his left cheek.

5

It is noontime in the New Hampshire woods . . . the saws and skidders silenced. All around the men's mouths and in the curves of their ears are the squashed blackflies . . . also silenced.

Sargent chuckles. "And she says to him, 'You'll always be Pitoo to me! . . . Hard to break old habits.' "

"PEEEEE TOOO!" screams Sonny Ballard, who always screams even when he's close to your ear.

Norman spits a mouthful of blackflies next to Sargent's foot, not breaking the rhythm of his file. Norman Letourneau has a way with a file . . . a filing genius, they say. "Genius" is not a word you could use on Norman for much, they say . . . But when Norman takes a file to a chainsaw, something unexplainably lucky happens between his yellowy bony hands and his dark lusty weird eyes. Sitting next to him on the tailgate is Little Lucien, his brother, forever close.

Sonny Ballard screams, "That's French for 'my sweeetie'!"

The men howl with laughter. Norman keeps his head bent over the saw, his long scraggled beard drooping through the circle of his arms. The blackflies look like dark weather around his neck and ears.

Mark Babbidge says, "P-2 ain't French. It's special hippie code. Right, Norm? You got a little hippie in ya, dontcha? . . . You like to toke up a few now 'n' then, dontcha?"

"God-DAM!" screams Sonny Ballard. "Hippie code! Prob'ly means one pecker doing the job of two . . . P-2 . . . GET IT!!!!"

Some of the men howl over this.

"Hippies ain't got no limits," snickers Mark Babbidge.

Old Man Taber says almost to himself, "I thought hippies was in the past. There ain't no such thing as hippies anymore."

Mark says, "*This* was a hippie. An old an' gray hippie . . . but absolutely GENUINE hippie . . . Ain't she, Norm? An' using that special hippie code on you."

Little Lucien speaks up, his voice as deep as possible. "All the old ladies call him that . . . Pitoo . . . it doesn't mean *anything*."

Silence.

Little Lucien's eyes widen on his older brother's scrawny shoulders. He says, "Norm . . . you don't have anything to do with Papa's old ugly hippie woman, do ya?"

Norman says thickly, almost inaudibly, "Nawww. I only fuck with trees all day." There is always a thickness with Norman's voice, like something hung up in his throat . . . something half-swallowed . . . what his mother, Maxine, calls "born damaged."

Little Lucien gets up off the tailgate, says quickly, "I'm starved. I'm not going to use up my dinnertime smackin' flies." He grins a little. A no-nonsense grin. He is not the grinning type.

Old Man Taber and Jeff Bean start to move away . . . ambling toward the landing where the other trucks are parked. But Sonny Ballard is looking hard at Norman. "What's that you say, Norm? You say you fuck trees?"

Little Lucien says, "He didn't say nuthin'. He's just bullshittin' ya."

Sonny Ballard says huskily, "I think he *meant* it."

Mark Babbidge says, "Sure he means it. Norm don't bullshit nobody . . . Do ya, Norm?"

Norman keeps his head down, feeling a couple of the rakers with his thumb.

Sonny Ballard says, "What's this ol' world coming to . . . man! Everywheres you look nowadays, we got mother-fuckers, daughter-fuckers, pony-fuckers, CHICKEN-fuckers . . . Why not TREE-fuckers . . . aye, Norm?" He gives Norman's shoulder a slap. Nobody can see Norman's face, just the shudders down his narrow back which means he is laughing one of his weird soundless laughs that show his tongue.

Mark Babbidge says deeply, "Tree-fuckers ain't nothing modern . . . They go way back."

"BEFORE CHRIST!" screams Sonny Ballard.

"You're all nuts," snarls Sargent, moving away.

"Show us how it's done, Norm," Mark Babbidge says. "I can't quite figure the blueprint on that one. I mean . . . TREES don't have . . . you know . . . a place to put it!"

"Yeah . . . P-2, show us how you fuck a tree!" Sonny Ballard almost loses his voice.

Little Lucien says, "Aren't you guys starved? We got ten minutes left to eat."

Mark says, "Ten minutes is *plenty* of time for Norm. He strikes me as the fast type. Right, Letourneau? You'd only need a coupla *seconds* to do a small tree, aye?"

Norman raises his face . . . grinning like mad. He stands up, says very very softly, "Allll right."

Mark Babbidge says, "Mmmmmm . . . trees." He sidles up to a beech sapling and gets a grip on it. "Take this one, Norm. I'll hold her steady for ya . . . She's trying like hell to get away."

"Young stuff!" screams Sonny Ballard.

Norman steps up to the sapling, locks his left leg around it.

Mark whispers, his eyes wide on Norman's face, "You REALLY gonna do it, ain't ya . . . you weird bastard!"

"B'en, alle a des grosses branches, eh? Quiens, j'vais embracer sa bedaine," Norman says, chuckling to himself . . . gives the trunk one small kiss. Then he lets out a long weird lusty yowl and feels for his fly.

Little Lucien's face goes gray.

6

On the long ride home from New Hampshire, Little Lucien sleeps, his head rocking against the truck door, his hair flickering.

Norman watches the land, the details of stone walls, gapways, and overgrown family graveyards. As he downshifts onto the Bond Road, the last stretch home, he hears Lucien's head hit the door. Lucien rubs his head, murmurs, "Jesus. Jesus. Jesus."

Norman watches the woods.

Little Lucien sits up, yawns . . . paws his pocket for a cigarette. He says, "Nobody makes money in school. School is for fairies."

Norman's strange dark eyes turn on him. He laughs . . . nothing but his tongue showing.

7

The night is thick and there's a wide pink moon over the mountain. Big Lucien has a new golden bug bulb for the piazza . . .

70

makes all the ladies, babies, and kids have handsome bronze-color faces.

Out from the darkness of parked cars and trucks, Norman Letourneau's thick voice calls, "Papa home?"

"He and Crowe have gone after a car!" calls Big Lucien's old sister, Flavie. She stands on the edge of the piazza . . . tall, tall mean-looking old woman with bulging apron pockets that clang when she walks. "Hey!! Come up here a minute!" she bellers. "You especially, Little Lucien. Your mot'er iss here."

The two brothers appear in the yellowy light . . . Little Lucien fresh from lifting weights at Blanchards . . . more thick-necked, small-waisted than even a few hours ago . . . his face charged red as fire.

"I want your ass on that school bus tomorrow morning, Lucien," snarls his mother Maxine's voice from the dark end of the piazza. He stares into the darkness, trying to see. At last he makes her out, sitting there on an inverted pail, swinging her foot in a circle. Next to her his big girl cousins are beautying up Memère Poulin's hair, putting it into bows and barrettes. They are looking at him . . . on the verge of laughter, it seems.

He says, "School's for fairies." He tries to make his voice deep. But in his big neck, his voice is still a boy's voice.

There is a smell of hot cake from the kitchen. Old Tante Flavie turns and strides into that smell which is as thick and yellow as the light.

Norman grins one of his biggest, most foolish-looking grins. He moves away from Little Lucien, but Little Lucien keeps him in his peripheral vision.

Maxine's foot swings harder. She is wearing her best cowboy boots, dark, glossy. She says, "I don't wanna hear shit."

The girl cousins look at each other, on the verge of great rippling waves of giggles.

"Deputy been around again, Mama?" Little Lucien asks.

Maxine gets a Tiparillo started with her no-nonsense stainless steel lighter, snaps it shut, returns it to the chest pocket of her shirt. "Yesss," she says and big smoke comes out on her yesss.

"Depitty Dawwwg," says Norman from the distant darkness . . . then the soft gagging sounds of his weird laugh.

71

The tantes and other ladies all in their rockers give Norman scorching looks. One says, "Won't ever amount to anyt'ing wit'out a good education."

"Won't amount to a pile a shit!" snarls Maxine.

Tante Flavie reappears with cake. Up and down the long piazza the plates of yellow cake go. As the old tante passes Norman in the darkness, he pats her upper arm. He is not afraid of the black and bitter meanness of her eyes.

Little Lucien watches this.

Next Norman moves toward a chair with a new old woman in it. Lately, Big Lucien, whose heart is gold, has been taking in old ladies right and left. This old lady has her hands folded in her lap, a tight new perm, blue plastic-frame glasses, and a look in her eyes like a wild horse.

"Dearie! Dearie!" Norman says huskily, grabs a hold of her button-up sweater, kisses her cheek.

"Leave her alone, Peeee-too!" Tante Flavie commands. "She's not right."

Norman grins, pulls a frilled footstool up in front of this new old woman, straddles it, stares into her wild eyes.

"They are going to cut off my head," says the new old woman, looking down at her hands.

Little Lucien has settled into an empty rocker and two cats have filled his lap. The old collie dog's head is on his knee. He looks ready for a smoke. But he never smokes in front of Maxine.

Norman leans toward the new old woman to kiss her again and his long rag of a beard rakes against her leg. "Debbie's dead," she says into his eyes.

Norman rubs his outgrown crewcut violently, then reaches for her two child-sized hands . . .

Maxine says, with her Tiparillo wagging on her lip, "What you're going to learn, Lucien, from your big brother is how to make a fool of yourself all the time . . . That your idea of an education?"

The girl cousins titter at last.

Little Lucien keeps his face down, patting the cats, patting the dog.

Norman asks the new old woman, "What's your name, dear?"

The new old woman just looks at him. She is smiling a little.

"Her name iss Grace," says Tante Marie Louise. "She iss not right. Doan keep pawing her."

Norman says softly, "Grace."

8

Today is Norman's thirtieth birthday . . . "The big THREE ZERO," Maxine calls it. His sister Missy will have made a nice cake . . . candles . . . everything for tonight. But there is nothing different about the day. Cutting popple, cutting beech. Hot like summer. The hot exhaust, the hot noise, the hot sun . . . with blackflies in all the cool spaces. Blackflies in the ears, in the mouth, in the nose.

On the ride home, both Norman and Little Lucien slouch, each with one arm out in the thick evening air. Coming into Egypt, there is a green, cool, almost prehistoric haze along the roads. When the first FOR SALE sign appears, Little Lucien's eyes slide over onto his brother to see how he is taking it. It is the look of their father, the one raised eyebrow . . . the thickening bottom lip.

Little Lucien feels for his Luckies.

Then there is another FOR SALE sign. Then another. A rhythm of signs.

"Well, well, well," says Little Lucien, folding his arms across his huge chest, making his muscles under his black T-shirt writhe in a showy way. "Land's goin' ta hell."

"Yep," says Norman in a voice that makes it seem like he hasn't a brain in his head.

9

The night is checkered with the lights of Miracle City and chuckling with the sound of many TV's.

Norman Letourneau studies the hippie's wide-open door, the black, black look of it. The door is always wide, day and night . . . no screen . . . just bugs going in and going out on their own accord. The hippie likes air, they all say. He knows this is true. He remembers her well . . . remembers her ways. He knows she is in there sewing in the dark, sewing Santas . . . one Santa after another . . . and Mrs. Santas . . . what his papa used to call *mass production*. Sewing in the dark, her hands as good as eyes. He knows her dark eyes are watching him. Small dark eyes. Beady, Maxine has described them.

Maxine says she is sick and tired of being WATCHED.

Norman walks toward the dark wide-open door. He takes a step onto the pale new porch. He takes three steps inside. He smells her weird hippie food, her weird hippie ways.

The croaky broken whisper speaks into the dark, "Aren't you EVER alone, Pitoo!" She is trying to sound friendly, perhaps.

No, he is never alone. He strikes a match. His young brothers, Ryan and Michel, hang near him, staring hard at the hippie's scarred throat and arms.

"Wow . . . it's little in here," says Ryan. His left cheek is swollen, looks like it hurts. But it's only gum.

The hippie is right by the door in a frazzled old cloth chair. The Mrs. Santa in her vast lap has no face yet.

The match burns down to Norman's finger. He strikes another to light the lamp that the hippie keeps by the sink. The hippie uses the sweet kind of kerosene that comes in colors. Norman grins.

The hippie stands up, uses the chair arm and then the table to help her go along. She goes to work making tea on the blue propane flame.

Ryan doesn't move his gum around in his mouth, just stands there with his one vast cheek, eyes gaping at the hippie.

The hippie touches Norman's arm. She says how glad she is that he has come over. Ryan and Michel study the hand on the arm.

The hippie asks them if they saw the six o'clock news on their TV. She says her little radio doesn't pick up much in these hills. She doesn't wait for answers . . . she just talks. She says the only thing her radio picks up is "ta-da ch ch ch p-ch p-ch!!! This is hard rock, if you don't understand my imitation," she tells them. She shakes her big hips.

Not much for news, not really, they tell her.

She talks and talks. Even with her broken raspy voice, her accent is plain as day, out-of-state, BIG CITY. She gets Norman and the two boys to sit at the little table which is piled high with half-finished Santas and Mrs. Santas. She says, "Doesn't it look like rain?"

The finished Santas stare down from various shelves, eyes flickering in the lamplight like live eyes. What substance does she use for the eyes? anyone would wonder from this distance. They are not your usual chubby rosy Santas.

The hippie says, "Pitoo, where is Little Lucien, your most devoted follower?"

"Over to Blanchards workin' out," says Ryan around his big gum.

"Working out?" wonders the hippie.

"WEIGHTS," says Ryan.

"Oh," says the hippie. She chuckles. "Maybe he'll be like the Hulk someday." She moves around the table, bearing onto her good leg. She places a jar of black lurid-looking honey near Norman's hands. She gives some Santas a shove with her forearm to make space. Then she pours the tea. It is hard to tell what smells like mice, the tea or the hippie. She says, "Pitoo, happy birthday."

He is startled.

"I remember birthdays," she croaks. "I keep mental lists. I'm a real birthday kind of gal."

"You eavesdrop," Norman says, watching her shove the big upholstered chair up to the table. "You can hear us across the road. Heard them singing 'Happy Birthday, Dear Norman,' didn't you?"

She says, "My dear person . . . in Miracle City, it isn't called EAVESDROP. I would have to wear earplugs not to hear your toilet flush."

"Yooo can hear our toilet flush???!" Ryan gasps.

The hippie smiles. "I can hear your thoughts."

Norman says, "Don't get scared, you guys. The old hippie woman loves to pull people's legs."

The hippie gobs honey into her tea. The smell of mice gets warmer, larger. She says, with a tight, worried smile, "It's only been ten years, Pitoo, since your papa and I were together. I remember *all* of your birthdays. You can test me if you want."

He looks at her hard scarred throat.

The boys' eyes slide over to Norman. Norman's bottom lip is thickening. Beneath the scraggly whiskers, they can see him sucking in his left cheek . . . the look of Letourneaus whenever one of them is in doubt.

It is almost noontime in the woods.

Sonny Ballard and Jeff Bean and Little Lucien Letourneau are all working fast, the deep murderous groan of Sargent's skidder close behind them. Up on the ridge descending trees crackle like fire. It's Norman up there, working alone.

Norman never eats, just a little tea . . . beer on the weekends. Noon means nothing to Norman. He'd just go on and on forever, cutting up along the ridge, if you didn't stop him.

Little Lucien appears on the tangled skidder path, following the scream of his brother's Stihl. When he sees through the gloom of pines the white of Norman's old ratty thermal shirt, he shouts, "Dinner!" But his voice is drowned out. He leans up under a beech that has the orange X. The blackflies boil thickly around his face. He lights up a Lucky. Don't blackflies hate Lucky Strikes!

Norman kicks out the notch, moves around to the other side of the tree, squats, sort of facing Lucien . . . but he still doesn't see him. Lucien grunts . . . Norman is pretty weird with trees. Something like a *human* relationship. Sometimes you see him, when he doesn't know you are there, he'll spread his hand open on the bark as if he feels heat and heartbeat.

Now he hikes the saw up, gives it the gas.

Lucien feels hungrier by the second. He thinks of the little watch Mrs. Callahan wears on her wrist. During quizzes she strides between the plastic desks, tunking the watch's face with her thumb. Sometimes Lucien would forget himself and start staring at the big clock on the wall. She would materialize at his side and thrust her little watch to his face. "About done?" she would ask in a loud voice.

He thinks how right this minute in room 11, it is twelve o'clock.

He hears the CRACK! then the crackle-crackle-crackle of the popple letting go . . . dropping to his left. He sees his brother move his eyes toward him . . . the raised eyebrow. He can tell, Norman is happy to see him.

11

The trailer the Johnsons have been living in is dark-green enamel with a thickness of hemlocks around the door . . . a nice porch and flagstones. Each of the bedroom windows has a decal of a fireman rescuing a child from flames.

Maxine Letourneau sits at her picnic table with a *National Enquirer* spread out before her and a can of Coke as the Johnsons strap down their last load of furniture and wave goodbye. The husband, Dave, lays on the horn all the way out of Miracle City so that a full minute later it is still a tiny wail in the distance.

Old Mr. Staples calls from his doorway, "The Johnsons were nice people, weren't they?"

Maxine lets a ring of smoke drift from her lips toward the empty trailer. "The Johnsons were assholes!" she snarls. "Thought they was King and Queen Shit. Good to see 'em go!"

12

The hippie has no idea how long she's been asleep in her old upholstered chair, no idea of the time. But it seems like around three. What has awakened her is the cold hard boil of rain outside her door. She feels a legless, armless Santa Claus face-up in her vast lap.

Then she hears somebody move. "Who's here?" she rasps.

She cocks her head. She has her shoes off, her big socks piled around her ankles like ropes. She says, "Where are you?"

"Right here," he says. He is very close, close enough to grab her by the throat if he were that kind of man.

"What time is it?" she croaks.

"Three," he says.

She says quickly, "Let's light the lamp."

"Naw," he says. "Let's not." His voice is in a new place. She thinks he might be sitting on her little bed behind the table. The bed is heaped most of the time with half-done Santas, faceless Santas, footless Santas. But there'd be room perhaps for scrawny Pitoo.

"Where *are* you!" she insists.

"Right here," he says. You can hear the thick idiot sound of his voice all the better in darkness.

"Who's with you?"

"Nobody."

She stands up, feels along the counter for matches, strikes one in a hurry, holds it up.

He is not on the bed now, but right beside her. He always has had a way of doing that . . . disappearing . . . reappearing . . . like a rat. She sees his oversized messy thermal shirt hanging on his body so loose it is like a white flag, a signal. The match goes out.

She strikes another, holds it up to his face as if to set his beard on fire. He isn't smiling. He looks nervous and dead set on something. She studies the swimmy dark center of each eye till the match gets too short. She strikes another one. He is gone. He is at the table, also with a match. He lights the lamp.

She says, "Where is your crew? Your followers?" She tosses her match into a pan of water.

"In bed," he says. He keeps his hand on the lamp. He keeps playing with the wick, raising it, lowering it, his eyes on the flame. "I couldn't get to sleep. The no-see-ums were coming through the screen." He doesn't look at her. She realizes he's being *sheepish*. "I can't believe you don't have the little cocksuckers in here . . . with your door wide open like that." He chuckles.

She is amazed. This sheepishness. Amazing.

"And then I saw your door open . . . and thought I'd come on over." His hand is still on the lamp. How vastly quiet.

"Would you like tea? . . . Maybe a little mint tea would help."

"Naww," he says, eyes on the lamp.

"You are upset about the Freetchie land," she croaks.

He looks at her. "You've been eavesdropping."

"No I haven't, sir. Don't you men know there's no secrets among women!! And everybody talks about you . . . old women . . . young women. Even your old girlfriends come around. Everybody talks about Pitoo. You are a great mystery."

He sidles back over to the bed, sits there on the Santas with his face in his hands.

Her guts tremble.

He says into his fingers, "Land's going to hell. Everywhere you look."

She pivots on her good leg closer to the bed. It is hard to tell what he is up to. It could be *anything*.

He says into his fingers, "All I want is a regular life. I'm not the fast-money type . . . Can't keep up with them yuppies these days."

His messy shirt, buried in front by his beard, seems whitest of whites, a little bit electric.

The hippie croaks, "Listen here, Pitoo . . . I don't want you sitting on my bed if you are loaded with woodticks."

He drops his hands from his face. He has a look ten times more sheepish than a minute ago. The rain thickens, drums on the roof . . . cold, cold endless rain.

She puts her hands on her hips. "Okay, Pitoo. Let's get one thing straight. I don't believe in big families. So you better have condoms on you. I'm fresh out."

He raises one eyebrow like his papa does when he's on the kitchen phone making a deal. He says softly, "Shit."

He stands up quick, pulls up his shirt.

She grunts. "Thought so."

He is spotted with ticks. TICK CITY, as Maxine would say. There are actual constellations of ticks on his yellowy ribs . . . one settled-looking one, big as a grape.

They spend the rest of the night pulling them off and squashing them in the sink. No sex. There is no further mention of it.

13

There is screaming and dying on Maxine Letourneau's big color TV. Ryan is stretched out on the rug on his belly, sucking the water out of a squirt gun. Around him the rug is wet.

Through the archway he can see Maxine in the kitchen, leaning over the sink. She whips her short graying hair back with a wet comb, first one side, then the other. When she's done, she stabs the comb into the pocket of her shirt. She packs her Adidas bag with sandwiches . . . checks her watch . . . 2:15 P.M. . . . running late.

79

She steps between Ryan and the TV and says, "I'm leaving. Missy and Lori should be along. Stay where you are. If I find out you been over at that sleazy hippie's again, you're dead meat."

The child looks out into the dapply afternoon light on the doorway, then back at the TV.

Maxine says, "You think it's funny but if that hippie gets you on drugs, your life won't be worth living."

He looks out through the screen door again and says, "What if she forces her way in here with a gun or something?"

Maxine fixes a fresh Tiparillo on her bottom lip, snaps her lighter under it. The smoke rides up the right side of her face so she narrows that eye. "Hippies don't believe in guns. They just use drugs and sex."

Ryan seizes her by the right ankle.

"Not now, Ryan!" she snarls. "I'm late for work!"

He lets go. "Kiss me goodbye," he says.

She squats down, takes his face into her hands. His mouth smells like the plastic squirt gun. She kisses his mouth.

He grabs her around the neck and gives her a screechy kiss in her left ear.

"Goddamya little turd-face!" she bellers. She stands up, rubs her ear.

She jerks her comb from the pocket of her cowboy shirt, gives her hair a quickie repair. The cowboy shirt, made for a broad-shouldered man, is a soft baby blue. The boy's dark eyes show two pale reflections as he studies her. "If you don't like being smooched, Mama, then don't fix up so nice," he says sullenly.

14

He is waiting for her out in the yard, not in *her* yard but *his* yard, which he has tried to start a little grass growing on. The new neighbor, Bobby Drummond. He has the sleeves of his plaid shirt rolled up so there's no missing his hairy arms.

He says "Mrs. Letourneau" deeply . . . a murmur.

He is a red-haired, red-faced, white-teeth type. Small cars . . . two of them . . . one for him, one for his wife. You never hear him or his wife talking . . . not even when they are in their little yard planting the grass. You know they *must* have conversation. But not even a syllable floats over into the other yards. Maxine has been wondering since they moved in almost two weeks ago what it is about them that Big Lucien Letourneau has found to pity.

Maxine slings her Adidas bag into the back of her little yellow truck, narrows her eyes on Bobby Drummond, her Tiparillo in one corner of her mouth putting off a humungous smoke. "What's up?" she says.

He murmurs, "Please come over here. I want to talk to you."

She keeps her hand on her truck, doesn't budge.

Bobby Drummond's eyes move over her. He murmurs, "You and your kids and your company are not to park vehicles in my dooryard anymore . . . or use my driveway to turn around in. You have your own yard. If you put some thought into it, I'm sure you can arrange them all over there just fine."

Maxine's thick neck quivers. "What do you care where people park . . . This ain't Connecticut. This is the WOODS!" She is starting to tell him about how she has no control over what her company does, about how one of them might whip right into his dooryard to turn around before she could stop them . . . but he is walking away from her.

After his trailer door closes, the quietest door-closing Maxine has ever heard, she heads for her door. She has to step high because of no porch. Inside, she crosses the kitchen to the sink, stands there looking into the drain.

"What happened, Mama?" Ryan asks. He comes up behind her, gives her pretty blue cowboy shirt a little pull.

"The usual," says Maxine, mashing her Tiparillo in the sink. "The usual half-brained idiotic mother-fuckin' crap represented by eighty-nine percent of the human being population . . . Damn them all to hell. I've HAD it."

"What are you going to do?" he asks, looking around at the bright open door to the yard.

"I don't know," she snarls. "We're outnumbered, for crissake."

15

That evening the hippie woman sits on her sweet blond porch in the dark, sewing a Santa.

She spies the white thermal shirt right up under the closest hemlock, the flag, the signal. "How wily you are!" she croaks. Her guts tremble.

He walks toward her now, his special gait . . . ratlike. He smells like one of his sister Missy's big suppers . . . a big gummy roast and lots of potatoes. He sits on the bottom step at her feet.

There is laughter on the TV in the Reed trailer next door. Norman glances that way and grins one of his weird grins. You'd never know the man had teeth. Just tongue.

"So you are alone tonight?" She sighs. "Did you bring condoms or what?"

He hugs his knees. "Naw," he says thickly.

She makes tighter and tighter stitches on Santa's left wrist.

"I missed you," she says. "Thought you might be mad."

"Naw . . . just busy."

"Well . . . you left here unfulfilled. Figured you went someplace else."

"Naw." He looks at her, one eyebrow raised. In the dark, his face is Big Lucien's face . . . Gross Monsieur Pluto . . . man of gold. She says, "Do you remember Stan? The man I went to California with?"

He rubs his outgrown crewcut hard . . . on the side that always looks flat. "I remember him."

She says, "You know, in California I died. They kept this ol' body going . . . torn to hell . . . but I died on that kitchen floor."

He hugs his knees hard, rocks a little. "Naww," he says. "You love to pull a leg, dontcha?"

She sighs. "Know what I was thinking when Stan went after me with that knife?" Because of the angle at which the hippie is looking at him and Maxine's gray porch light across the road, the hippie's steel-rimmed glasses look empty of eyes.

He says, "Naw, what?"

"This is what I was thinking, dear Pitoo . . . dear good person . . . I was thinking, 'I'm *shit*.' "

He rocks just a little harder, like listening to a lullaby.

She says, "Even afterward when everybody said what a bastard Stan was . . . I'm thinking to myself, 'I'm SHIT.' "

He rocks a little harder, his head turned away.

Her broken voice above his shoulder says, "I wish I could go back to just *one* of those moments when I was married to your papa. I don't mean I want to be married to him again. I just mean I want to see him looking at me from across that big table. I just want to be the me I was then . . . to see me through *his* eyes . . . because in Lucien's eyes everything is dear . . . C'est plus qu'on voit . . . Everything is a miracle. You know what I mean about your papa?"

He says, "Yep."

16

It looks like Norman has a black eye but really it's just something that's bit him. In the springtime you are just a piece of meat to so many. In the truck cab, Little Lucien with his sandwich and Norman with his Thermos of tea look out at the blackflies in their dark boiling strata, trying to beat their way in through the windshield.

Norman says, "Tonight I'll just drop you off at the house, but no supper for me . . . I've got to go to Tamworth."

Little Lucien looks at him. Little Lucien's cheeks get bright color when he eats . . . a rose to each cheek. And then there's the dark, dark eyes. And his forever-cocky expression. He kind of snickers. He always looks his cockiest when he's scared. He keeps looking at Norman . . . but not too steady . . . just in a smooth and cocky way.

Off in the sunny distances of glittering mosquitoes and blackflies, beyond Sargent's skidder parked in a twisted agonized-looking angle on a heap of logs, are the screams of Sonny Ballard . . . probably screaming one of his gorilla jokes too close to Old Man Taber's ear.

Lucien says, "So what's in Tamworth?"

"Barn . . . doing a metal roof for a barn . . . Cooper's friends, the ones at Pal's party."

Lucien snickers. "What do you know about barns?"

"Same as anything, you roof 'em."

Lucien looks away, chewing fast. "Won't it be dark?"

"They got these big lights, Cooper says. We plan to go till midnight. I say what the hell."

"Big lights," Lucien snickers.

"What's so funny about big lights?" You'd swear it was Norman who has the tunafish sandwich in his mouth, so thick his voice is.

"Nothing. It's just all such a joke."

Norman pokes into his mouth with his thumb and some of his teeth show . . . the teeth that his big grins never reveal . . . large, tea-stained teeth . . . rather large, dangerous-looking teeth for so short and scrawny a man. He picks around a minute like he has food caught in there . . . although his wee bowl of Cheerios was hours and hours ago. He says, "Friggin' blackflies. You know, if you don't inhale or exhale, they won't bother you. It's breathing that attracts them."

"No shit," says Little Lucien as deep as he can.

17

Junebugs growl like bulldozers in the corners of Big Lucien Letourneau's slanty old piazza and the old twisty tree-sized lilac bushes put off a smell. Big Lucien is nowhere around tonight. Norman is not around. Little Lucien is squatted with his back against the clapboards, his eyes closed, listening to the tantes whisper in French just inside the screen door . . . something about the gas stove, he surmises . . . His face looks grief-stricken.

Maxine snarls, "Don't them lilacs stink. Big Lucien ought to take the old chainsaw to them goddam things. Ain't good for nuthin'."

Little Lucien opens his eyes and sees his Oncle Armand standing there under the gold bug light with his fiddle. Tante Lucienne leans close to the new old woman's ear. "Grace! Grace!" she hollers. "Diss iss Armand, Big Lucien's brot'er, come to play the fiddle for us!!! Look! Look up!"

The new old woman raises her wild eyes to the middle of Armand's gauzy old T-shirt, snowy white.

"She doan know what's going on!" says old Flavie from the screen door, her hands on her hips. Flavie looks in charge . . . the head old woman . . . the last word.

"Is that Armand out there?" a voice calls from the front room.

"Yes," says Tante Flavie. "Get out here now!"

Some of the newer old women gawk at Armand's upper arm. They are the only people who don't already know about Armand's most showy self. In warm weather Armand is his most showy self without even opening his mouth. There's the green dragon tail roiling out from the T-shirt sleeve, stout and well proportioned, the Mr. Maine of dragons . . . although Armand himself has a beer gut and, plain as day, you can see his belly button, deep as a woodchuck hole, through the gauzy T-shirt.

Little Lucien sighs.

Armand settles himself on the ruffled footstool with his fiddle across his knee. His breathing is worse tonight. He closes his eyes a good minute.

A couple of cats push against Little Lucien, against his hands that just hang there between his knees. This is the way they hint for pats, Beatrice and Sally, two of his papa's most favorite cats.

Armand raises the fiddle. He has such a queer manner with the old paint-splattered family fiddle. He acts kind of humble, kind of shy. This is not your true Armand.

When he begins, the cats flatten out their ears. One goes skidding off the piazza into the night. The collie dog hunkers up close to old Flavie's leg. But the noise coming from that fiddle, for humans, has a power. Big Lucien's brand-new wife, Keezhia, stands in the kitchen door in her scruffy quilted robe, too pregnant for clothes . . . tapping her foot. Everybody is in kind of a daze. As Armand slashes away, he never looks up, his face red like somebody ashamed. He rips from one screely seesawing tune right into another . . . on and on and on . . . the women as red as he is, as though with shame. Now and then he howls. But nothing like the howls he used to produce before his emphysema. But they are great howls. It makes the women go another, deeper shade of red. The howls are like pictures. Worth more than words.

When he is done everyone claps . . . those who have their minds . . . Not Memère Poulin with her GI Joe doll in her lap and not the newest old woman with the wild eyes and pretty sweater.

Now Armand is hunkered forward, gasping, his forearms on his knees . . . his eyes wide on Little Lucien. He sucks for air for nearly a minute while everybody pretends he's not.

Finally he looks into his old sister's eyes, old old Flavie, and says, "What's de matter wit Lit-tle Lucien?"

Maxine grunts from the dark end of the porch.

"Nothing's the matter," says Little Lucien as deep and cocky as he can.

"Hiss brot'er iss moonlighting a few weeks," says Flavie. Her hands move around in her pockets so the stuff she carries starts to clank and clang like a drawer full of forks and knives. "Roofing."

"So what iss de problem! What iss de problem!!" Armand howls.

Nobody has the answer.

Armand says, "Somebody didn' know Norman, didn' know Little Lucien, might say, dere goes a couple off dem fags. Dey say, dere goes a couple off fags or what?"

Tante Marie Louise cries out, "ARMAND! Go say you a good Contrition for dat. Nobody lissen to hiss words!"

Armand grins. "Well, he juss look so luff-sick!"

Little Lucien's cheeks are flamed.

Tante Flavie has taken a couple of long-legged strides to her brother, gives his tattooed arm a poke. "Play, you! Play an old nice song for dese ladies and close your mouth."

Armand says deeply, "I apologize to de ladies. I wass juss give Little Lucien a hard time. Not serious. Juss fun." He doesn't look at Little Lucien at all, but nuzzles the fiddle up under his chin.

The new old woman named Grace says, "Phil is at work."

Down at the low dark end of the piazza, Maxine is deathly silent.

18

There's only two women out on Big Lucien's sagging piazza tonight, his current wife and the hippie, who has come for a little visit. They sit in the dark with the gold bug light switched off.

The hippie says in her croaky broken voice, her out-of-state, BIG CITY accent, "So where is everyone tonight?"

The wife shrugs. "Tupperware party." The wife, too pregnant for clothes, seems more pregnant by the minute . . . pregnant legs, pregnant arms, pregnant hands. At times it seems to the hippie that Big Lucien is like The Thing in the movies which took over bodies . . . took them over from the inside out. At first the person looked normal . . . then suddenly the whole body would rip open and The Thing would come pouring out lashing, slashing, howling, bubbling, gummy and gooey.

The hippie says, "How are you feeling tonight?"

"Okay," says the wife. She slaps a mosquito, then another.

The hippie sits with her knees apart, rocking gently, her deep lap filled with her sewing. In the near distance, beyond the black thickness of the woods, there is shouting and arguing . . . the usual neighbor troubles of Miracle City.

The hippie's glasses, just two circles of ghosty gray light, turn upon the wife. "There isn't too much to a Tupperware party anyway," she says. "No wine, no music, no good-looking men."

The wife giggles. "I know." She looks at the hippie. The wall phone near the back door rings out through the slanty empty house, one jangling ring, then another. The wife groans, pushes herself up to answer it.

"He's not here," the hippie hears the wife say into the phone.

When the wife comes back over the creaky floor, her slippers slisking, the hippie gives her a hard long stare. The wife is young. Barely twenty. Her teeth are terrible but she has such a classy way of tossing her thick hair. In the dark, she is striking.

Beyond the trees, there is more arguing, then the blare of a car horn . . . a door slamming . . . then more arguing.

"Gosh," says the wife.

The hippie says, "Springtime in Miracle City. It's always the same, they say." What the hippie is working on tonight is the white helpless head of a Santa, no body. She says, "I'm sorry, but nobody told me your name."

"Keezhia," says the wife.

The hippie is quiet a long minute.

The arguing has quieted in Miracle City. There is just the purring of Big Lucien's grateful cats and the two chairs creaking.

The hippie says almost prayerfully, "*Keezhia*. That's the most beautiful name I ever heard."

The wife sighs. "It ain't very common."

19

The hippie has her shoes off, bare feet, bare legs, and a soft old summery skirt . . . a hippie-looking skirt. She says, "Where's Pitoo tonight?"

Ryan says, "He's gone to Tamworth."

The evening is warm. Almost watery. There's the smell of all those Miracle City suppers still on the air . . . onions, meat . . .

Little Lucien smokes. Looks around. His eyes are slitted when he draws smoke. This goes with his cocky ways.

Ryan says, "Mrs. Hippie, are there drugs in this tea?"

There's no lamp lit yet . . . just the greenish-looking twilight coming in patches through the hemlocks. And then there's the red-hot end of Little Lucien's Lucky Strike.

The hippie chuckles. "Worse than drugs. It's some part of a goat. It'll make you smell in school."

The two younger brothers look at each other. "Hippies are always joking," says Ryan.

Michel nods.

Little Lucien has nothing to say. Now and then he spits something through his lips . . . a bit of tobacco. He wears a small superior-looking smile.

From the shelves over the sink and stove and bed, the finished Santas and Mrs. Santas look on. The women say she gets fifty bucks apiece for them at the malls at Christmastime. They say these Santas are not to play with. The eyes might come off and a baby could choke. And even with the eyes on securely, there's something about the faces of these Santas that scares the daylights out of kids. The whiteness, perhaps, the long noses, thin mouths . . .

The hippie is having one of her talk-talk-talk spells. It is easy to see she is glad they have come over. As she talks about what the President and the First Lady spent on a place setting of china, Little Lucien stubs his Lucky out in his tea saucer and lights another . . .

His eyes steady on the hippie . . . especially the bare feet that are strong-looking feet and very very flat against the new sweet blond floor. The hippie says the country is doomed.

Little Lucien blows smoke hard through his nose.

The hippie cracks a joke. She tells them she sometimes puts bats in her tea.

Ryan titters, gives her big left knee a poke. "Be serious!!" he scolds.

The hippie bites her thread, knots it . . . talks awhile about the Civil War and the Revolutionary War . . . and what we should have learned from history. She gets into the Industrial Revolution. She covers *years*. She says, "We are just animals. Not even good as whales. Now, whales . . . There you have altruism!!"

Because of the wide-open door there is a horrid whiny commotion of mosquitoes about their heads. But the hippie insists that if you don't have your lights on, you won't draw mosquitoes.

Then the hippie tells what she knows about mercury lights, what makes them work.

Suddenly Little Lucien says right into her eyes, "So what makes you know so much? You aren't a friggin' schoolteacher, are you?"

"No," croaks the hippie. "But I almost was . . . before I changed my major . . ."

Ryan says, "LUCIEN! Cut out being a jerk to her. She's nice."

The hippie stops talking for two or three long minutes. Two cars pass on the narrow dirt road, turning in down at the Farringtons' trailer. Coons crash around in the trashcans next door. But without the hippie telling all she knows, there's not much conversation. Little Lucien stubs his cigarette out, lights another. Now and then he makes his big neck muscles jerk around, then his shoulder muscles. He has good control over his muscles.

The hippie's horrible voice is now a throaty whisper. "Lucien . . . you were only about four or five when I was married to your father. You don't really remember me, do you?"

He says, "I remember you."

Maxine wakes him by giving his bed a little kick with her cowboy boot.

He doesn't turn over and look. He just says "What, Ma?" in a deep and cocky way.

She doesn't say anything. The hiss of her Tiparillo smoke through her teeth is worth a thousand words.

He flips to his side, sees her silhouette against the kitchen light. "Now what?" he says.

"So you been over to that sleazy woman's gettin' laid, huh?"

"Christ." He sighs. He covers his face with his hands.

She rakes her fingers through her short short graying hair, says, "Well?? Were you??"

"No way. Which one of your spies can I thank?"

"The whole friggin' neighborhood! And I want it known, Lucien, here and NOW, that if you drag your two innocent brothers along again, you can sleep out in a tree from now on."

"Ma . . . I didn't see no drugs over there. She's just an old hen like you."

"What you need is a good slap in the face!" She grabs him by the face, squeezes his cheeks. He wrenches his face away.

"Come on, Ma . . . not *now*. This is the middle of the night!! The rest of the world isn't on backwards time, you know."

"If you went to school instead of busting your ass in the woods, you'd be a normal boy again. You'd *fight* to stay up late. And you'd have normal sweet high school girls to go rutting after . . . not pothead, sleazy commie hippie types!"

"Don't talk so loud."

"I WILL TALK LOUD IF I WISH!! OKAY!!"

He sits up, the covers dropping to his waist. Across the vast chest, the words BORN AGAIN PAGAN on his scarlet T-shirt look like a *command*.

Maxine smokes no-handed, raking her hair with her hands over and over.

Lucien says, "Ma, you want me to get up awhile? Is that what you want?"

"Maybe a few minutes. You know what happens when I gotta talk."

"Yep," he says.

Maxine is alone eating eggs. She has her favorite tape on low, the voice of Waylon Jennings just humming. She swings one cowboy boot in hard happy circles. "Mmmmmmmmmm," she hums along.

"Mrs. Letourneau, please come here," a voice says softly, a sort of Waylon Jennings murmur. Maxine narrows her eyes, pulls the curtains apart.

"Please come here. I want to talk to you," Bobby Drummond says from the edge of her dooryard.

Maxine runs her tongue around the inside walls of her mouth. The Waylon Jennings tape shuts off. Then there's silence.

She heaves herself up, strides to the door. He is wearing his sporty-looking shirt with the number 8 on it . . . tucked in . . . Even though he's short, he looks enormous . . . a regular Mr. Maine.

"What's the matter now?" she snarls.

"Please come here," he says.

She jumps off the sill to the broken soft boards which were once her little porch. She says, "What? What? What? What?" as she ambles toward him.

He says, "Mrs. Letourneau. You listen to me. I want no more turning in my driveway or parking on this side of that tree. See where the grass begins? That's my yard. Okay?"

"When's this . . . all this parking and turning?" Maxine asks with a curled upper lip.

"A good lot of the time. When my wife and I are at work, my yard becomes Grand Central Station, they say."

"THEY? Who's they?" She glares up and down the road. "Tell me which one of these goddam shithead neighbors hasn't got better things to do than watch where my kids and friends turn their vehicles around? . . . when they might spend their time better by keeping the eagle eye sharp on a sneaking little creep like you and figuring out what all your tiptoeing sneakiness amounts to!!"

He smiles a slow wide smile.

Maxine smiles, too. "How quickly we forget this is Big Lucien Letourneau's land, that we live here for FREE . . . you and me BOTH. WE don't have PROPERTY, honey. WE don't have YARDS. So you can stick that MY YARD bullshit up your ass!"

She steps sideways, plants one cowboy boot in *his* yard, gives one of his low-hanging hemlock limbs a little friendly pat.

He says, "Keep it up and I call the deputy. He already knows where you live." He steps away from her, ducking the great drooping hemlock limbs.

Maxine snorts with laughter. "Deputy peputy creputy . . . that goofball. I mean, I'm really scared. Try the National Guard."

He murmurs, "Oh, and while we're at it . . . maybe the *Health Department*. My wife has seen some of your older kids standing right there in your doorway, dumping grease from the pan . . . probably garbage, too."

Maxine pats the pocket of her cowboy shirt, not ready to light up one of her Tiparillos, but she likes to know they are there. She says, "Look here . . . this is crazy. Let's figure this thing out. I mean . . . let's try to be sensible. WE aren't being very NEIGHBORLY, are we?" She reaches to touch his shoulder.

He jerks away.

Maxine's face goes on fire. She balls up her fist. "Want this, you asshole cunthead!!!" She gives his collarbone a thonk with her palm.

He just stands there, his eyes fixed on her face.

"Why don't you fight back, you pussy-faced little twerp!" she almost sobs.

Neighbors come to their doors.

Maxine pokes his chest.

He murmurs very softly, "Quit it."

She pokes him again. She snarls, "What's the matter? Why don't you fight back? 'Fraid I might lay you right out flat and you'll feel like a fool? Hee, hee, hee. Maybe you just like to mash up that little squeaky insect of a woman you got yourself over there so you can be *sure* you'll win. Bet anybody wants to if they cared to . . . put an ear up to your door at night, they might hear *plenty* of weird squeaky things going on in there. Right? I'm right, ain't I?"

He just keeps studying the center of her face.

She shoves him. He grabs for a hemlock limb to keep his balance. She shoves him again.

He murmurs, "I don't believe in hitting women . . ." He pauses. His eyes slide over her cowboy shirt. ". . . even if it's one that *looks* like a man."

Maxine smacks him in the mouth.

He throws up one fist between Maxine and his face . . . but he doesn't strike back. His bottom lip is swollen, orchid-color. Maxine veers away. She makes the high porchless doorway of her camp with one leap . . . gracefully . . . from practice.

22

When Maxine gets home from the mill at midnight, Little Lucien is standing against the kitchen sink, a lighted Lucky in his fingers. It's the first time he has ever smoked in front of his mother. She throws her Adidas bag on the table and snarls, "What are you doing up this late? You're not going to be worth shit come four-thirty, a point you've been trying to prove to me for quite some time around here."

"Too many mosquitoes in my room."

"Kids been leaving open the screen. What they need is a good kick in the ass." She finds a can of Coke in the refrigerator.

He watches her hard as she gulps from the can.

He says, "What was there, a shoot-out here or something today?"

She smoothes her straight, straight graying hair with a little spit. "Why?"

"Missy says the deputy was here . . . Something about you and whatchacallits next door."

"That's right!" she snarls.

He puts his cigarette to his lips, his eyes steady on her.

She burps. "Well, I say frig 'em all." She crosses the room to where he's standing. She studies the pan of cold spaghetti in the

sink. She finishes the Coke, then whales the can into the trash . . .
burps again. He looks at his feet. He hears the click of her lighter,
then the long easy smoky sigh. "Yep, I say frig 'em all!" she says.
She leans against the sink like he's doing. She grunts. "You know
something, Lucien, there's one thing you're going to learn real quick
out there in the world . . . now that you're out there circulatin' . . .
and that thing is that short men always got to act like they've got a
brick stuck up the ass."

He draws on his Lucky Strike, feels the smoke thickening in him
. . . even in his arms. It feels good.

23

Little Lucien sleeps in Michel's bed tonight. He sleeps in different
beds different nights . . . different brothers . . . nobody complains.
He is easy to sleep with. He doesn't toss. Even when he's wide awake
for hours. He just smokes. The darkness is jarring and black, except
for the lighted end of his Lucky.

"I remember you," he says aloud.

It was in the days before Miracle City . . . just the old house and
barn, just the woods and a pretty field . . . just the salvage yard. It
was in the days when somebody started to call his papa Man of Gold
and Gross Monsieur Pluto. "Dere iss money in de used car parts
bissness!" his Oncle Armand always exclaimed. And it was true. Big
Lucien's pockets were always thick with change. He'd jangle it when
he was on the kitchen phone making a deal . . . or out in the dooryard standing around with the hippies.

For it was in the days when the hippies were there, loads of hippies, men hippies, women hippies, baby hippies . . . hippie dogs.
The hippies had tents behind the barn . . . The pretty field was noisy
with hippies' lives. Hippies liked outdoors. They were real out-
doorsy people.

And it was in the days when he was about four years old . . .
thereabouts.

The hippies liked him. Said he was big for his age . . . said he
was smart.

His mother, freshly divorced from Big Lucien, would bring Little

Lucien for his visits . . . and she'd say, "Stay away from those hippie tents!"

But the hippies were everywhere . . . in the big kitchen using the phone, out by the bulkhead filling their water jugs with the hose. Hippies were always smiling, carrying things . . . boxes and baskets . . . babies. Some hippies sang . . . sang right out as they walked along. But the hippie he remembers best was the one with THE HAIR. Black hair pinned up in back, but bursting from its pins. Frisky hair. There was nothing special about that actually. All hippies had great hair. And all hippies had that way of talking . . . BIG CITY, Maxine called it. But . . .

Some days Maxine took Little Lucien with her up on the ledge to *watch*.

The hippies probably knew they were being watched by the two eensie figures hunkered on the mossy ledge above . . . but . . . the hippies didn't mind being watched, Maxine said. Hippies *like* being watched. Hippies are showy people.

Little Lucien hardly watched the hippies. He lay on his back and pushed his sneakers into his mother's hip. Or he hunted for special rocks.

He remembers it was that hippie with the black and frisky hair who was down there among the tents getting playful with his papa. She had no clothes. A sock or something . . . but otherwise PURE PINK. Right there with other hippies walking by with their water jugs . . . and a couple of hippie beagle-type dogs watching from the closest tent door. Maxine didn't look surprised. She just watched hard. It wasn't the first time she or Little Lucien had seen a full-grown hippie without clothes . . . OUTDOORS. That was the hippie way.

But Big Lucien wore clothes . . . his green workshirt and something for pants. Actually Big Lucien and the hippie woman were so far away down there, you'd hardly know them . . . if you didn't know them.

Big Lucien nuzzled his face around in the back of the hippie's hair . . . the hippie gripping the picnic table. Big Lucien worked that hair with his teeth till it exploded from the pins and dragged all over the dirty plates. A dog, a setter type, barked at them, thinking this was a fight.

Then Big Lucien was like a man riding a pony . . .

It was nothing new to see Big Lucien doing this to hippies. On his visits, Little Lucien had seen his father with other hippies this way . . . in the sumac, in cars . . . in the old house. It was nothing. And Maxine had come upon Big Lucien doing this to hippies before . . . lots of times before . . . but today was a kind of LAST STRAW.

Big, hard, meanish Maxine. He remembers turning to look at her because she was so *quiet*. And there was her mouth a big wide square. She was bawling. Silently. But big.

But it was only that once that his father was down there while both of them watched together from the mossy ledge. The rest of the time it was just hippies busy with their chores . . . their big garden . . . their bee boxes . . . their kids and their dogs. His father usually wasn't around. Gone up to the salvage office. Or gone off.

Maxine was pretty weird about hippies. But then she was weird about a lot of things . . . especially Big Lucien. When he came over to the Graves Falls Road place to visit her where she stayed with her sister, she let him make Missy and Michel and Ryan. She let Big Lucien do ANYTHING he wanted . . . just to have him look at her from across the room . . . to see herself through his eyes.

Then Little Lucien was with his father in the old Ford ramp truck they had in those days . . . no words on the doors. The hippie drove. His father had been having his seizures right and left in those days . . . had to do with the metal plates in his head. The hippie drove pretty good. She had strong-looking arms. They took a shortcut coming home . . . with a Volkswagen winched up high on back and sumac and other bushes slapping in at the open window on his father's side.

The hippie talked constantly.

It was a bad thing . . . up ahead . . . Even before he saw it, he knew, because the sound his father made was a warning sound. Then he said, "Stop de truck, Eve."

Then Big Lucien was gone . . . just the truck door hanging open, crackling and hissing against the sumac fronds because the truck was still rolling.

Little Lucien saw it. A head on a post. Then he didn't look anymore.

His father called back to the truck in such thick French-English that the hippie said, "WHAT?"

But then his father didn't repeat it.

His father went to the back for tools. He seemed to be having a bad time getting the head off the post. There were the whacks of a hammer or wrecking bar . . . Little Lucien didn't look. He just kept his face hard-flat against the hippie's sweater. The hippie said, "It's okay, baby," and fooled with his hair. "It's somebody's witty idea for a pig cookout invitation . . . I guess," she told him. "Whoever lives up that driveway." Her voice was not broken and raspy then. It was a plain voice. But a voice that was hard with BIG CITY.

His father was OUT THERE. The whacks went on forever.

Finally there was a THUMP in back. Must be the head, Little Lucien was sure. He kept his face fixed upon the hippie, breathing a wet place on her sweater . . . even when his father was back up on the high seat . . . panting and smelling afraid.

"What do we do now?" the hippie asked.

"We get de hell out off here before dose bastards come down dat driveway looking for dere pig." His father spoke softly. The more bad a thing was, the more disgusted Big Lucien was with people, the more soft his voice would go.

"What are you going to do with it?" the hippie asked.

"*Bury it,*" Big Lucien whispered.

The hippie was having a time working the gears around Little Lucien. But she was very nice about it, he remembers.

His father was very quiet as the loaded ramp truck creaked along, headed home . . . not even jangling his pockets of thick change. Except for the weight of him on the seat, it was like nobody was there. It made Little Lucien want to look to be sure he hadn't leapt out into the bushes again. But he didn't look. He didn't want to look at his father's face when there was somebody disgusting and wrong in those eyes.

Then the hippie's BIG CITY voice wondered, "Do you see anybody coming, Lucien?"

Little Lucien froze. He wasn't sure which Lucien she meant . . . They were BOTH Lucien.

24

There's too many at Big Lucien's table for Sunday dinner . . . although Big Lucien himself is not around.

The new old woman says, "They are going to kill every one of us. Better not wait around."

The table is made for many, one of Big Lucien's quickie creations . . . A piece of CDX plywood on a two-by-four frame and at one end of it the deer-foot lamp he found in the trunk of a Ford Escort.

It's one of Tante Flavie's dark lustrous soups again. You never know what's in it.

Ryan has gone under the table to check out Big Lucien's magazines and other treasures . . . Rubik's Cube . . . a raccoon puppet . . . chess pieces . . .

"Get up here in your seat!" Maxine snarls. "Unless you want your ass smashed!"

The teenage girl cousins are on the verge of giggles. But Mary Warren giggles right out. Mary Warren, Big Lucien's grown daughter from Unity.

"Maxine iss too rough on dem," says one of the tantes.

"She should say a good Contrition for her meanness," says another.

Maxine grunts.

The hippie and Big Lucien's current wife, Keezhia, sit against the wall. They have been spending time together these days. Maxine calls it GETTING THICK. The hippie has sewed some pretty things for the baby. And she is always brushing the wife's hair with her hippie boar bristle brush . . . which according to the hippie makes healthy hair. And she and the wife talk about babies . . . babies, babies, babies. And the hippie reads to the wife out of hippie magazines about trimesters and natural childbirth and breast feeding.

Keezhia right now is wearing her scruffy light-blue bathrobe, her belly ready-looking . . . like a bomb.

Norman looks like a bomb . . . tired and touchy. He is almost never around anymore. And when he is, he just keeps his hands in his pockets and yawns big watery-eyed yawns.

Armand hollers over his shoulder to his wife, "Patty, dere are people here wit'out spoons. Isn' dere enough spoons?"

Patty gets more spoons.

Armand, Crowe Bovey, and Bobby Ward all wear their green salvage shirts. Crowe Bovey's eyes seem like they are on the wallpaper above the hippie's head but that is Crowe Bovey's way of studying a person.

Tante Flavie ladles some of the dark soup into Armand's bowl first. Everybody studies Armand's bowl . . . which is kind of the bowl-of-honor. Tante Flavie moves on to the next bowl and as she works the ladle her cross, which is dark with tarnish and housefly-sized, swings out from the crisp check of her apron toward the bowl she is filling and hovers quivering there.

Armand says, "Isn' dat turkey remain from Christmas?!" He gives his soup a frisky stirring. He winks at the other men.

Little Lucien is watching the hippie. Eve. He looks at her necklace of tiny shellacked shells, her hair. THE HAIR. Pinned up. You could never know how much hair . . . unless you knew.

He is leaning back on two legs of his chair, his arms folded over his chest . . . his neck muscles flexing. When Tante Flavie gives his shoulder a nudge, it jumps him. She loads his bowl to the brim with dark soup. He says "Merci." He says it deeply, deeply, deeply . . .

The hippie turns to the wife, Keezhia, and whispers in her damaged voice how you have to be careful with turkey meat, no leaving it out long on the platter like people have always done . . . and you have to scald all the utensils.

Armand bellers, "Dat iss de worse buncha crap I ever heard!" He looks at all the men's faces with his secret secret look of dismay. "Memère raise six kids wit leaving all dat turkey meat out and every last person iss still alive dat not die off somet'ing else!"

Norman's head drops back against the window frame . . . it actually makes a THWONK . . . and everybody is looking . . . sees it's only one of his weird laughs. He is almost strangling with laughter. He seems cut off from his air.

Crowe Bovey sneers, "If you believe everything you read in those ladies' magazines, you'd not be able to eat *anything.*"

Norman is out of his mind with laughter, wagging his head back and forth.

The hippie croaks, "I don't read *ladies'* magazines. This was public radio."

"Commie radio," snarls Armand.

Norman thrashes around in the paw-foot chair, thwonks his head against the window frame hard . . . thwonk, thwonk, thwonk!

Patty Letourneau fixes the new old woman a biscuit and murmurs, "You have on your pretty pearls today, Grace!"

The new old woman smiles . . . a small smile.

Maxine is very very very quiet.

Crowe Bovey says, "Goddam health freaks get more bullshit stirred up. Just trying to scare the public. And they're doing a damn good job of it, too!! I'd like to see just one of 'em outlive my grandfather who lived to be ninety-one on nothing but pork and beans."

"Jezuss!" howls Armand. "Betcha couldn' light a match at hiss house!!"

Old Flavie loads Bobby Ward's bowl . . . chubby Bobby Ward, shy to the point of agony. "Thank you, ma'am," he says in a soft, soft way.

Armand cries, "Arrgh! I got a little turkey meat on my hand! You t'ink I'll make it!!!"

The men howl.

Tante Flavie starts work on the women's bowls.

Norman forks out bread 'n' butters into a saucer . . . his head cocked sideways, his body bent . . . as though sore from his laughter.

Some of the old tantes cross themselves before eating.

"Debbie's dead," says the new old woman, her biscuit plopping into her lap, saucer and all.

. Armand presses one hand between his thighs. "My God! I need de ambulance. Diss turkey iss burning to de bone!!"

Crowe gasps, "Jesus! I think I swallowed some." He bugs his eyes out.

Norman is now forking bread 'n' butters into his mouth straight from the jar . . . one after another . . . green seeds on his beard . . . his eyes merry.

As Tante Flavie fills the hippie's bowl, Norman looks into the hippie's eyes.

The hippie's black, black eyes stare back at him . . . fixed on his mouth slisking away on the pickles. His grin gets bigger and bigger and finally he says *very very* sweet and sheepishly into those hippie eyes, "What about pickles? Suppose they cause sterility in men?"

The hippie flings her bowl of scorching soup upended on his right hand.

He cries out, "AAAARRR!" then aims for her right hand with his fork . . . but misses . . . stabs the table instead.

"Phil's at work," says the new old woman into the sudden silence.

Norman flings the fork across the room . . . which about eight cats dash over to smell.

The hippie lowers her eyes, drops her hands to her lap. "Shit," she says softly.

25

He lies there in the night, his hair plastered to his forehead. He is a sticky naked muscular weight on his side of the bed. He is smoking. Thinking. He is thinking how his brother Michel smells like pennies when it is hot like this.

He thinks of the day. The long day. Most days are the same . . . groans, shouts, clangs, blue with exhaust, burning with bugs. And Sonny Ballard's sick gorilla jokes.

They say it hit 80 today. In the woods it was a thousand. He likes to think of that at night . . . the misery of his work . . . to think of it from a distance.

He thinks about the hippies . . . about that summer when his father had seizures galore . . . and headaches. He was afraid of his father then. Awed.

That summer Maxine said he was probably old enough to hear about his father and not be scared . . . this thing about his father . . . which until now might have been too scary for him. "But now you are very big and brave," she said. He'd nodded. "Yep," he had said as deeply as a four-year-old can go. "*Big* and brave."

She explained that inside Papa, in his right arm and right hip and right thigh and inside his head, is made of metal . . . and this was because of an accident he and some others were in at the mill where he worked when he was about nineteen years old. She told him all this with a matter-of-fact voice and said, "See, there's nothing scary about it. He's just a regular papa . . . a little bit like the bionic man on TV only he can't jump high." She said this is why your papa falls on the floors sometimes and twists around . . . also the headaches . . . also the times when he gets quiet in a chair and won't answer you. She said, "You understand all that, don't you, Lucien?"

"Uh-huh," he said.

She was sitting on his bed and smoking while she told him this . . . then started on to other things . . . her work, her friends, her ENEMIES, and Grandma and Grampa's trip to Florida. But he wanted her to keep talking about his papa's metal head and other metal parts. He wanted to hear about it and hear about it and hear about it . . . but he was too scared to ask her to go back to it . . . for he could hardly say the word "Papa." It was, for the moment, too tremendous a word to pronounce . . . kind of thick.

Then there was one of the headaches . . . a warm lemon-color evening at the end of the summer. Nobody talked about the headache. They acted like it was just your average evening. They were all in the front room with the TV, even a couple of hippies.

Little Lucien studied the old paintless house with narrowed eyes, keeping his loaded machine gun under his arm. In the growing darkness, broken toys . . . a lawn chair . . . old Flavie's lawnmower all looked like dangerous shapes. But he wanted to save on his "ammunition," not wanting to go back into the lighted house to fill up again and get trapped by the tantes. He worked his way around a La Salle fender and gave the faded maple leaf flag nailed to the barn door one small blast of his ammunition, growling, "COMMIE FLAG!"

Now he burst through the open space of the dooryard with his weapon held chest high, then skidded to the blackness of the low-hanging hemlock boughs. From here he could see the dormer over the piazza. Up there the room was dark. He held his breath a little, shaking the water around in his weapon, studying the dormer, hearing the hippies and the tantes having their "average evening," hearing the hippies in the field, hearing the tall-grass bugs . . . waiting. He knew a scream would come. All day there had been just one scream after another. He watched that dark dormer window with all his might.

The scream came. It made his supper thicken inside him. He was used to women crying . . . it happened now and then. Their high cries. Their letting go. But this was none of that.

He could imagine his father's dark shape on the bed, writhing. He could imagine the eyes . . . terrible eyes . . . metal eyes.

But then soon there was the evening which smelled of wet streets, wet brakes . . . riding in the ramp truck, going after a car in Portland. Oncle Armand drove.

Little Lucien lay in his father's arms with the top of his head against the door, his hair fluttering in the breeze. His father and Armand talked French softly, thinking he was asleep . . . though now and then Armand would forget himself and hoot.

Little Lucien didn't understand any of it. The lights of the city flickered outside his closed eyes and the great old truck whined to a stop again and again in the laboring traffic.

It seemed that his uncle and his father weren't talking words, but round contented sounds like the burbles of doves.

And he found that if he moaned a little, his papa, who thought he was sleeping, would tighten his arms around him.

He moans now . . . gives the smoke a fierce blast out through his teeth.

26

They are trying out the new bug zapper tonight . . . one of Big Lucien's fabulous finds. It came in just today in the trunk of a smashed 1980 Aspen. When the bugs fly into it, they sparkle like stars . . . and the women say, "There goes one!"

The hippie has been brushing Keezhia's hair.

It is not quite dark, but a deep color everywhere like beets. Keezhia steps off the piazza to go pull down a few sheets from the line. The sheets are white-blue and as electric as Big Lucien's killer light. All the Letourneau sheets are this kind of white . . . the work of Tante Flavie and Tante Josephine, who are big on bleach.

Keezhia struts like a little queen these days. The bigger her belly gets, the more light her step. The hippie watches Keezhia. All but Keezhia's light-moving feet disappear between the two lines of sheets.

Two men appear wearing bug netting on their heads . . . a tape measure rippling between them . . . crunching along in the leaves from behind the house, along the stone wall, along the border of Big Lucien's land. And then a woman. The woman carries a clipboard. Her bug netting is stuffed into the rear pocket of her beige corduroy slacks . . . Looks like a little gauzy green tail to Keezhia.

Keezhia gasps, "Ooh! You scared the daylights outa me! Thought you were coy dogs!" She giggles. She looks into the eyes of the woman, but the woman turns her eyes to the woods and says to the men, "About thirty more feet to the metal stake, then it makes a fifty-degree angle toward the other stone wall."

The tape measure is sucked up into the hand of one man and the two men move away. The woman studies her clipboard.

"Somebody selling that land?" Keezhia asks the woman.

The woman's eyes leap to Keezhia's face, then quickly return to her clipboard. "That's right," she says, then steps away.

Keezhia stands between the bleach-smelling sheets a long while after she no longer hears the crashes of the woman and men in the trees.

Inside the house the phone rings. Somebody with a deal for Big Lucien or somebody hoping to borrow a few bucks.

She stands there a little bit paralyzed by the good bleach smell. And by the feel of her own glands thickening, like clockwork. Until two minutes ago she believed she was the most beautiful woman in the world.

The bug zapper crackles.

"Who wants cake?" Tante Lucienne's voice wonders.

"What kind?" A child's voice.

"Plain."

"Yukk."

27

Maxine prances around the rug to the beat of her latest Dolly Parton tape as another carload of her mill friends show up, all of them carrying six-packs of beer. "HEY MAXINE!!" they holler.

Maxine wiggles her Tiparillo, wags her eyebrows.

Little Lucien fills the La-Z-Boy, his feet higher than his head, so he has to look between his sneakers at the TV which has no sound. He is pulsing and flushed from lifting weights at Blanchards. He is barechested. What looks like a large gray flat parasite fixed to one rib is actually his St. Anthony's medal . . . so delicate the chain.

The women put their beer on the table, shake the rain out of their hair. One wipes her face and arms on a dish towel.

Maxine turns the music up. "Shake 'em up tonight, girls!!!" she howls.

Little Lucien tries to imagine what sounds the TV would be making if he had the volume on. Canned laughter, he is sure.

One of the women holds a Waylon Jennings tape above her head . . . "Maxy! What will you give me to hold this close to your heart?"

"Where'd you get THAT! I thought they hadn't released it yet!" Maxine snarls.

The woman dances around with the tape like it's the actual Waylon Jennings . . . then ducks between the other women to escape Maxine.

Little Lucien scratches his elbow, slides his eyes over to the unopened beers on the table.

Maxine gets her clutches on the tape, gives it a kiss. "Mmmmmm, baby!" she moans. "Waylon, Baby!!!" She kisses it five times.

Little Lucien thinks the sound coming from the TV if it were turned up would be whimpers because the woman on the screen has her face in her hands.

"Don't look so pissed off, big sweetie," says a close-by voice.

He looks up.

It's his mother's friend, the one who bombs around in a red Nova. He knows them by their cars. She puts a beer, kind of warm, into his hand. He curls his fingers around it.

"Thanks," he says as deeply as he can.

Now she's pressing a beer into the hand of one of the other women, the one who drives the brand-new blue-gray Grand Am.

The rain thickens. He thinks maybe Norm will be along . . .

rained out of Tamworth. He likes to picture Norman sidling in with that weird grin, his dungarees torn to pieces and his outgrown crew-cut flattened out on one side . . . and the ratty beard . . . coming home early to give Maxine's friends a hard time . . . chase them around, making exaggerated kissing noises in their ears . . . then whispering in French. And Norman always goes just a little too far.

His mother snaps Dolly Parton off mid-croon . . . puts on Waylon Jennings. But she is also watching Little Lucien out of the corner of her eye . . . sees him popping the can of Schlitz open. She stares into his face. He holds her stare.

She wiggles her Tiparillo, wags her eyebrows.

He makes the first gulp a good one.

28

It is not the first time Norman has come up behind her at the IGA and made a scene, but it's the first time since the FORK.

She is in BAKING NEEDS, leaning onto her aluminum cane, pondering Durkee's dried chives. It is always the same. His suddenness. Like a rat. Out of nowhere there are his arms squeezing, his voice against her hair, "Bonjour, ma belle." She loses her balance, a can of Crisco hits the floor, goes speeding down the long aisle toward Little Lucien, who has a six-pack of Molson's in each hand.

"Quit it, Pitoo!" she croaks.

Little Lucien stops the rolling Crisco can with his foot. The cap he is wearing today says STEEGO and his T-shirt, which was red once, is faded to a soft, soft rose. He doesn't look anything like a boy these days, and yet there's something not quite ripe about him . . . not broken or scarred enough.

The hippie pivots on her cane to face Norman's big grin with her small black narrowed unfriendly eyes. But he's not grinning. He's just standing there in an old frayed green salvage shirt that says BIG LUCIEN over the pocket in yellow-gold, one of his father's castoffs . . . nothing anybody but Norman would wear. He watches her read the name.

Little Lucien calls hoarsely from the distance, "Come on, Norm . . . let's get going. Christ."

The hippie looks over toward Little Lucien, but past him . . . all the way to the far end of the aisle. She croaks, "Don't look now but that person in the suit jacket coming our way is Gaston, the one who scoffed up Freetchie's land and the Cook land last fall . . . and now that land next door."

Norman and Lucien watch Gaston squeeze around the hippie's grocery cart. He carries a pint of half-and-half in each hand.

The hippie goes on tiptoe on her one good leg and whispers into Norman's ear, "He got that land next door for five thousand . . . selling it for thirty. Everybody can kiss that land goodbye."

"How do you know so much?" Norman says.

She sees his fingers on her grocery cart, two of them gummy with blood, the nails crushed . . . the usual.

"You think I made it up?!" she croaks.

"Naw," he says. "You're a good girl." He moves away from her. "I gotta go . . . We left the truck running . . . Starter's going to hell."

She reaches out and grips his wrist . . . a hungry, deadly kind of grip . . . but then she makes a joke of it. "We should meet in the IGA like this more often, Pitoo!"

He pulls at his mustache and says sheepishly, "You hippies ain't got no limits."

29

The "yard boys" are starting to get frisky, yowling, hooting, throwing things at each other. It's not late yet, but they've been there for hours. The bartender keeps watching Little Lucien. There is definitely *something* about him that doesn't look twenty-one. He doesn't order anything . . . just looks out through the big window and smokes.

"How's the parts business, Mon Oncle?" he asks.

"Got-dam piss-poor," says Armand breathlessly. "We doan part dem. We juss crush dem to pay fast bills. It doan look good."

Little Lucien glances at the thickening crowd. Big Lucien was supposed to meet them here after the auto auction but every time the door opens, it's not his face.

Little Lucien sees that the bartender is watching Bobby Ward, too

. . . Shy, chubby Bobby Ward . . . almost thirty . . . looks like twelve.

Maxine told Little Lucien that if he went off with that BUNCH tonight, he would have to sleep in a tree when he got home. She always says this about the tree lately . . . instead of her old threats of smashing his ass or making him into DEAD MEAT.

Wayne Hutchins wears his denim vest with its Sherpa lining over his salvage shirt although it is hot here, the kind of hot a crowd makes. He has a hopping kind of walk, like a jay, coming back from the bar with another Narragansett and a bag of cheese curls. He flings the bag of cheese curls onto the table against Little Lucien's thick, folded forearms.

Little Lucien says, "Thanks."

A young woman appears at the table, squinting at the faces of the yard boys and Lucien and she says, "Which one of you is Big Lucien?"

They all look her over, the designer jeans, the gauzy pink summer top, the necklace of teensy moons and stars, the white-blond Dutch-girl haircut . . . the way she needs to squeeze the back of Crowe Bovey's chair to stand straight.

Armand chuckles. "Well . . . de answer iss simple. De Big Lucien iss lit-tle while de lit-tle Lucien . . . he iss VERY BIG."

All the yard boys hoot and howl over this. Little Lucien smiles, a big rose coming to each of his cheeks.

The young woman laughs along, her grip on the back of Crowe Bovey's chair getting more of a white-knuckled look.

"You want him for an emergency?" Donnie Lowd asks . . . grinning . . . he has not much for teeth . . . a couple.

Everybody is grinning. They watch the hands on the back of Crowe's chair. They watch the gauzy pink blouse.

"Well," she sighs. "My friend, Adele . . . she met him here last week. Said he was very nice. She's an art person you know . . . she teaches art . . . high school level . . . drawing, painting, you know." She giggles into her hand. "Me . . ." She giggles. "I am HISTORY and ENGLISH . . . same school. Boston." She giggles. "Adele wanted to draw him but she didn't have the materials with her at the time . . . So he agreed that if she came here tonight again with her materials this time, he would pose. We had to come all the way from Boston. It's something she wanted to do, you know. If you knew my friend, you'd know what I mean." She giggles. "She is a determined little thing." She giggles, then adds, "She said he had great EYES."

Armand makes a deep sound in his chest, a sort of signal to the others to snicker and groan.

Armand says, "We all have nice eyes at de yard."

The young teacher's necklace glitters in the barroom gloom as she shifts from foot to foot. Her eyes settle solidly on the exposed tail of Armand's dragon.

Little Lucien thinks about getting a tattoo, tears open his bag of cheese curls.

"So you think he might be around?" she asks.

Armand grunts. "He iss a hard man to catch up wit . . . a regular streak off light!" He looks into the eyes of the boys so they will snicker.

"Well," the teacher sighs, swaying. "Maybe she would settle for one of you guys. I don't know. She was really set on this Lucien guy." She scrutinizes each face. "Any of you want your portrait done?"

Wayne Hutchins blinks his eyes. "Isn't it kind of dark in here to draw pictures?"

"Where iss diss artist female person?" Armand wonders, turning in his seat to study the crowd . . . gasping for breath as he turns.

"She *was* just in the ladies' room," says the teacher. "I'll go check on her." They watch her move away, bearing onto the backs of other people's chairs as she crosses the crowded bar.

When she reappears, she spreads drawing pencils on the table, makes room for the fancy paper . . . wiping up spots of beer with napkins . . . pulls up an empty chair from one of the other tables.

"There's something weird here," says Donnie Lowd.

"Yeah, where is that artist?" says Wayne Hutchins.

She replies, using a clear teacherly voice, "Still in the ladies' room. Now you must be patient!" Then she giggles like mad . . . leans hard on the table . . . beer bottles clink together.

"Whoa!" says Armand.

She says, "I have to warn you . . . Adele is nervous. She has been talking about this Lucien fellow steady . . . as an art subject, you know. He must have a wonderful face. I hope he shows up soon." She says this a little sadly.

Little Lucien watches Crowe Bovey making shreds of beer bottle labels . . . then his eyes slide over to chubby Bobby Ward. Bobby Ward catches him looking at him. Lucien averts his eyes quick.

"I guess I better go check on her," the teacher says, then disappears.

Crowe leans back in his seat, pushes his steel-rimmed glasses higher on his nose, and says with curling lip, "I don't trust them. It's a trick. They are probably really Jehovah Witnesses."

The boys thrash the table with their laughter . . . A bottle goes over. The surging wetness misses the drawing paper but heads for Donnie Lowd's lap. Donnie leaps up in time.

The artist arrives, the blond teacher holding her straight. The artist wears a dress . . . a very teacherly dress . . . and Little Lucien feels something icy move between his shoulder blades. He drives himself back onto two legs of his chair, smoking no-handed, just the short cigarette on the bottom lip and the squinted-up right eye.

The Dutch-haircut teacher lets go of the other one right over the empty chair. The artist hits the chair hard, throws her head back, and bleats, "Baaaaaaaaaaaaa!"

All the yard boys get quiet. They watch the woman's throat jerking with that weird sound, shaking her hair . . . teacherly hair, short, brown, and curly.

Wayne Hutchins murmurs, "Sounds like a sheep."

The Dutch-haircut teacher says, "Who wants to have Adele do a beautiful portrait of them? . . . She's a very talented gal, let me warn you." The Dutch-haircut teacher's eyes are grayed and sleepy with her drunkenness.

Wayne points at the artist. "I would give anything to see this sheep-woman do pictures!"

A crumpled package of Pall Malls hits him in the ear.

"Good shot, Donnie!" says Armand, laughing . . . but his laugh turns into one of his long strangling coughs, which ends with him spitting in a paper ashtray.

"Do you want a profile or a full face?" The Dutch-haircut teacher giggles. "I think Adele needs a little boost right now . . . Which is it? . . . Profile, maybe?"

Wayne jumps up, almost knocks his chair over. He says deeply, "I want ALL of me!" He pulls off his denim vest, flings it to the floor.

The boys scream over this. People at other tables keep turning to see what's so funny. Wayne takes a bow. His hair shifts, flips sideways off his hidden bald spot.

Armand bellers, "Wayne! Want us to go out to de ramp, get you somet'ing to hold? Do you want a picture off yourself holting a nice big ratchet?"

Donnie Lowd loses a mouthful of beer on his sudden guffaw.

The artist gives her chair a couple of jounces like it's a rocking horse, then her face drops onto the table.

"This should be a great picture," Crowe murmurs, his eyes on the advertisement napkin he is tearing into two equal pieces.

The Dutch-haircut teacher borrows a couple of citronella candles from the other tables, arranges them on the window sill, drags another chair over. She points at Wayne. "Sit here," she orders in a teacherly way.

Wayne does a little dance, opening and closing his half-unbuttoned salvage shirt. "I want her to do ALL of me, don't forget," he says huskily.

"Which ain't a hell of a lot," murmurs Crowe.

Donnie Lowd loses more beer over this. It SPRAYS.

More people arrive, packing into the next table. There aren't enough chairs. They look over at the extra chair next to the candles, but they don't speak up.

The artist stands up. The chair under her tips over. She falls to the floor. "Baaaaaaaaaa-ha-ha-ha-ha-haaaaa!" She thrashes around among the men's feet and the table legs, her teacherly dress twisted around her.

The other teacher stoops for her arm. "Adele! Get up! How are you going to draw if you can't even sit right?!" She stoops a little more, almost stumbles onto the floor, too . . . giggles. People at many other tables are craning their necks, looking on.

Little Lucien glances at the bar . . . the bartender busy with a new huge bunch of people.

The artist has lost one of her dressy buckle shoes. The other teacher is looking for it. She says, "He looks easy to draw, Adele."

She points up at Wayne, who is standing over them with his arms folded across his chest. He wiggles his eyebrows at the artist. The artist covers her face with her fingers. "Ba-haaaa!"

Wayne says, "Never mind the picture, dear. Get her to do a sheep." He doesn't take his eyes off the curly-haired woman on the floor. She is drawing what looks like an X with her finger on his left workboot. He nudges his boot closer to her, closer and closer till it's against her leg.

"A sheep?" The blond one giggles. "How do you mean?"

The yard boys watch gravely.

"You mean *pretend* to be a sheep?" the blond teacher says, her eyes seeming to sober up in an instant . . . clear and fixed on Wayne's face.

"Yes," says Wayne.

"Baaaa-hahahah!" the woman on the floor cries out.

Wayne sneers. "Okay, WALK like one!"

What sounds like somebody busting up small sticks for a campfire is Crowe Bovey giving his knuckles a few stiff cracks.

The blond teacher says, "Come on, Adele . . . this isn't working out. These guys are jerks. Let's go back to our table." She turns toward the next table. "Will somebody over there help me get my friend on her feet . . . PLEASE?"

Three strangers stand.

The curly-haired teacher pushes herself up onto all fours, takes a couple of shaky sheeplike steps.

Wayne sort of laughs, sort of sobs. The men from the other table can't get around Wayne.

"Be a sheep, you goddam cunt! Be a sheep!" He pushes her face to the floor with his left boot.

"Quit the shit!" Crowe Bovey is out of his seat, seizes Wayne by his shirt.

The blond teacher grabs Wayne by the hair.

The men from the next table are yanking on Wayne.

Armand gets to his feet gasping.

Bobby Ward and Little Lucien get to their feet. Shy, shy Bobby Ward nudges Little Lucien, says softly, "Ain't you always wanted to get yourself a teacher down like that?"

Little Lucien can't see anything anymore with all the strangers

pushing around him . . . just one quickie flash of his Oncle's back
. . . the gold lettering . . . He says in his most cocky way, "Yep, I
have."

30

Her name is May. None of her dark hair shows because of the little
hooded outfit she wears, embroidered richly with leaves and rose-
buds and bees . . . one of the hippie woman's many creations.

Keezhia rocks slowly, the baby in the crook of one knee. She
whispers to the hippie, "She scares me."

The hippie nods, her lap piled with her sewing.

At the other end of the piazza the killer light crackles while all
the tantes underneath it are murmuring in French.

Keezhia leans toward the hippie and whispers, "Boy babies are
like . . . like teddies . . . cuddly teddies. Know what I mean?"

The hippie nods, not breaking the rhythm of her stitches.

Keezhia frowns at baby May's blank wide-open eyes. "Girl babies
are different. They are like . . . like women . . . like small women."

"More human," says the hippie.

Keezhia looks at the hippie. "Gawsh . . . That's it . . . But don't
it sound awful?"

The hippie nods. "Truth is hard sometimes."

31

There are no real stars tonight. The sky is pure black. But the killer
light sparkles and the trees all around the dooryard blink and twinkle
like mad with fireflies. There is yellow cake going around. Old bald
Mrs. Bean, the newest new old woman, has the baby in her big
spotted hands.

From the kitchen Wendy Ballard's voice: "Gross Monsieur Pluto
doesn't ALLOW people to keep bugs in jars! Go let 'em out . . .
NOW!"

"But Mama . . . he LIKES it in there!"

"No, he don't. Let him out."

At the dark end of the piazza the hippie is brushing Keezhia's hair . . . running the brush deep. Such deep hair . . . like harrowing up earth. Whenever the hippie is brushing the wife's hair, the wife gets speechless and quite still . . . almost paralyzed. And the hippie, who would usually talk your ear off, has nothing to say either.

"Come have a look at your new sister, you two!" Mrs. Bean says when Norman and Little Lucien arrive.

Little Lucien acts like he's a little hard of hearing . . . as if the voices of women are not anything he recognizes. He leans against the closest lathed column and pulls off his advertisement cap to inspect it for woodchips.

Norman sidles over to Keezhia, his dark eyes unreadable in the poor light. His mangled gray T-shirt says BOWDOIN across the chest . . . something his papa found under the seat of a wreck, no doubt. As always the T-shirt, the jeans, are dappled with bar and chain oil, the pinkest, smelliest kind. The hippie's eyes are also unreadable in the dark, but for certain, her eyes are on him.

Norman drops to his knees in front of his father's wife, steadies himself against one of her knees as he pulls his thick wallet from his pants. He empties it into her lap . . . bright stiff bills . . . tens and twenties. The hippie stops brushing.

"What are you doing!!" Keezhia squeals.

"For you to get yourself pretty blouses!" He spreads one hand on her stomach . . . which gives her a start. She draws her rocker back as far as it goes. "The salvage biz ain't worth a shit!" he snarls. He kisses her hands . . . the palms, the wrists, each and every finger . . . ticklish whiskery kisses. "Ain't nothing to come from goddam salvage no matter how many rigs the old man crushes. No such thing as FAST money. Just fast weeks, fast months, fast years flying by. And you just gave the old man what he loves best!"

She glances over at the baby, blue-looking under the bug killer and wide awake against the new old woman's monstrous flower-print bosom.

Little Lucien, leaning against the lathed column, studies the kitchen through the screen door . . . the visor of his STEEGO cap low over his eyes. He is watching one of his father's favorite cats eating yellow cake up on the counter. Little Lucien's whole body seems

114

to flicker with contempt and weariness . . . No one need read his eyes.

Norman's knees crack as he rises from the floor. He goes for a look at the baby. He gets one of his big moronic grins, his long beard lashing against old bald Mrs. Bean's knee. "Sweet . . . sweeeeeet!" says Norman in a squeaky voice. He seizes the baby so roughly it seems she will fuss.

Keezhia bristles.

"Use her careful," says Mrs. Bean.

He dances around, making huge horrible kissing noises on the baby. "B'en, garde ça, la petit' . . . ma belle," he says huskily. Then he sidles ratlike off into the darkness, baby and all.

Keezhia gets off the rocker, leans against the piazza rail. "He makes me nervous," she says.

"Iss no woman he spares," says Tante Marie Louise.

Little Lucien finds an empty rocker and sprawls there, strikes a match on the clapboards.

Wendy Ballard's oldest comes ramming out of the kitchen through the screen door, holds a jar out to Little Lucien. The jar glimmers . . . a single firefly.

"You think he likes it in there? I gave him grass."

Little Lucien leans back, says deeply, "He needs friends . . . other bugs. You better let him go."

32

Norman points to the distant twinkling trees. "SPRINGTIME. Can you say it? SPRINNNNGTIME."

He gives the baby's cheeks little squeezes forcing her mouth into an O. She just lies there . . . on his knees, eyes wide and blank.

"BLUE BAPTIST BUS. Can you say that? BLUE BAPTIST BUS." He squeezes the baby's cheeks. She just lies there . . . on his knees.

He is sitting on the step of the ravaged bus in the middle aisle of the salvage yard . . . the heart of the salvage yard. He stares into the black spots that are the baby's eyes . . . the dim gray of her face.

"Sweet," he says.

There are fireflies inside the bus. The windows twinkle like mad . . . Everywhere is the writhing, unbraiding light.

The baby makes weird wet noises with the walls of her mouth.

He jiggles his legs. "You are getting ready to cry, aren't you?" He smoothes her face with his thumbs.

She stiffens a little.

"Sweeeeeee-eet!" he says in his squeaky for-babies voice.

She stiffens again.

"If you start up that crying shit, I'll have to take you back," he warns. "I can tell you aren't going to be much fun for a long time." He stands up slow. His knees crack.

33

Maxine Letourneau sits at her picnic table in the dark, thwomping mosquitoes with a rolled-up *Natural History* magazine . . . and smoking. She has just gotten home from the mill . . . after midnight . . . and here are new neighbors moving in, the ones to replace "shithead Bobby Drummond." In a way, these people are as quiet as the last. Quiet is a bad sign.

There is no way to get much of a look in the darkness. She hates these sneaky types who move in after dark.

A pickup truck backs up to the old green trailer door, snapping and crackling the hemlock limbs . . . another loaded truck waiting in the road . . . the pink wash of the brake lights . . . the white T-shirt of the man waving his arms. "Whoa," he says. Softly. It's the deep deep chilling murmur of E. Blackstone Babbidge . . . one of Big Lucien's yard men. He's on the short side. Another bad sign. There's the slamming of truck doors, more murmurs, tailgate chains jangling . . .

Maxine lowers her Tiparillo, her hand steady as she does it. She is very quiet. There's not even the sound of her smoke coming out. This is the way it goes when she is crying . . . the big square wide-open mouth, the tears streaming . . . but no noise.

34

He is standing with his back to Tante Flavie when she sees him . . .
looking out the window. He hears her of course, but he doesn't turn
around . . . How queer, Pitoo . . . He could be up to ANYTHING.

Flavie is on fire with making beds. She makes three at once, shaking sheets, crisscrossing the worn linoleum on her hard, hard shoes.
Her apron pockets clash. The whole time he doesn't turn around
. . . doesn't try to kiss her hair or bite her neck. He is wearing one
of his papa's old castoff salvage shirts . . . the big yellow-gold lettering on the back badly fuzzed.

She heaves a few trucks into the closet . . . and a bunch of those
ugly robot things with skull faces that kids have to have these days
. . . Everything they see they want.

She stoops to mash the dirty sheets into the basket, looks at Pitoo
from the corner of her eye. She asks in French if he is okay.

He answers that he is.

The beds along the wall have come out white and tight as dinner
tables. She tries to see what he is looking at. It's the mountain . . .
the great pointed one . . . its rock face and pointed firs, the lavender
look of its new snow . . . the blond gouges of construction going on
up there . . . new homes . . . big and filled with strangers . . . nobody Pitoo will ever know . . . the old Freetchie land . . . GONE.

She can't see his face . . . but . . . she knows what's there on it.

35

Outside the IGA the hippie pulls off her mittens, slaps them into
the child seat of her grocery cart . . . stoops to spread her hand on
a nice-shaped pumpkin . . . certainly the biggest in the pile. A
mother with a cart full of kids pauses too, saying sharply, "They'll
be there *next* week, Heather," and one of the kids begins its wail of
grief. The mother wheels the cart away toward the automatic doors.

Another cart wheels past the hippie.

Then another. And people carrying loaded bags in and out of the
cold orange of October sun.

The hippie glances over at the Indian corn . . . blue hubbards . . . apples . . . and jugs of cider . . . gourds. And three man-sized smiling paper scarecrows looking on. She leans her cane against the high glass window . . . tries to get a grip on the pumpkin.

The push of his knee into the back of her skirt makes her shriek. The shriek . . . just what he wants.

She hoists the pumpkin into the cart, her bad leg trembling like the high-strung hind leg of a poodle, she thinks . . . with shame. Then she turns to face him. "No more!" she hisses into his eyes.

Other people come to stand next to them, reaching for the pumpkins . . . oohing and ahhing over the nice shapes.

He is alone. None of his tagging brothers. She looks over at his old truck in disbelief. He is red-nosed, watery-eyed from the cold, his black beard gone chestnut in the sun . . . wearing a mangled red felt hat that looks like something his papa may have scoffed up off the floor of a junk . . . and his usual pair of holey whitish jeans. She hollers, "NO MORE OF THIS SHIT!!" and grabs him in the crotch.

The people on both sides of them admiring the pumpkins and colored corn get deathly quiet.

Norman grins . . . his grin that makes him look like he has half a brain . . . his eyes on her hand as it withdraws.

She says, "You come over tonight and do the REAL THING, Mr. Letourneau . . . alone without an audience to protect you . . . Act like a grown man for a change . . . No more games! Maybe YOU got patience . . . but I give up, okay? I GIVE UP! Have it your way. Forget the condoms if that's what it's got to be. Jesus Christ! Forget it! Forget it! We're all going to be dead before long anyway . . . What does it all matter?

She flings her hand out at a passing cart, a two-year-old in the seat, pink-faced from screaming in the store. She shudders. Turns back toward the dark watery eyes. "Bring your goddam bare pecker right over tonight and let's us get started."

"Okay, okay," he says . . . not grinning . . . In fact he looks pale and scared. He sidles closer, gives her a squeeze, hides his face in her hair. He listens to the carts squeak past, to the ernk of the automatic doors . . . to voices.

FOUR

Gallows Humor

1

WHEN ERNIE TRAIN shows up in the spring at E. Blackstone Babbidge's trailer in Miracle City, he doesn't go right up and knock at
the door. He stands for a while smoking with one hand on the fender
of an old truck, watching his half-brother through the kitchen window and smiling his famous smile. Ernie Train. THE Ernie Train
. . . hair blackest of blacks and combed with force off his forehead.
Bare-looking blue eyes, tall bare white teeth, clean close shave . . .
so much bareness . . . the honest, wholesome look he is famous for.

There's only a soft light in the Babbidge kitchen. But outdoors
there's a big mercury lamp fixed high on a pine above the doorway
. . . It almost blinds him. Ernie chuckles to himself, mashes his
cigarette on the heel of his cowboy boot. Then he cups his mouth.
"BAD NEWS TRAVELS LIKE A WILDFIRE! AIN'T YOU
HEARD YOUR GODDAM BROTHER IS IN TOWN? THE
GOOD-LOOKIN' ONE!"

Faces appear in the windows and doors of the trailers and camps
up and down the weedy, washed-out road.

Blackstone appears on the steps which have wrought-iron rails.
His dark hair is in a turmoil, his salvage shirt looks full of bullet
holes . . . but it's really battery acid.

Ernie Train gives him a funny little wave.

Blackstone steps down. Some of his children appear in the doorway behind him . . . eyes wide. They have never seen a shirt like
Ernie's before . . . not in real life. It looks like maybe satin. In the

queer glare of their father's big mercury light, there's no guessing at the shirt's true color.

One of the older girls whispers, "Miss Lily-Ann . . . come see this man that looks like Ernie Train across the eyes . . . REALLY. Hurry!"

Ernie Train says, "Hell, Gene . . . what's all this top security?" He squints into the mighty light. "What you keep in this here fort?"

Blackstone murmurs, "My family."

More people step up to their doors and windows along the road.

Ernie laughs his high "Heeeeeee-hah!," the laugh he is famous for, then says, "Guess what I'm driving these days, Gene . . . A little six . . . a Maverick . . . an OLD Maverick . . . can you believe!!! She's my ship! Heeeeee-hah! Probably wondering where my ship is, aye?"

Blackstone keeps his icy stare on Ernie's bright shirt. "Where?"

"Well." Ernie sighs. "She *almost* made it. She didn't coast to a stop till I was fifteen feet from the pumps . . . of your store down there. Nobody around so I just left'r." His accent, like Blackstone's, is Aroostook, eddying with *r*'s.

Blackstone says, "Well, let's go down. I got a can."

Ernie says, "Thanks, Gene!"

They stroll toward the back of the truck talking cars. Blackstone wonders, "What's she got for rust? Fender walls probably gone, aye?"

The back of Ernie's shirt is embroidered with a rattlesnake getting ready to strike. And Ernie is wearing something expensive that is either rolled on or combed into the hair, the kind of scent that rides like an uneasy memory on the night.

2

When it's time for the first hymn, Ernie Train is the first one up off the pew. He leaps.

Ernie sings louder than anybody. This is his third Sunday . . . and he has smiled through almost every minute of it. "Very nice man," they all say.

His shirt this morning is a quivery glittery lavender material with a giant musical note on the chest pocket. The whole right side of the face of the child standing next to him has a lavender glow.

Ernie knows all the words to ALL hymns by heart. He never holds a hymnal, just hooks his thumbs in the belt loops of his tight, tight jeans. He stretches out the words to certain hymns to make them fancy. But as far as anybody at the Egypt Fundamentalist Baptist Church can tell, Ernie Train has never accepted Jesus Christ as his "personal Savior."

Today's first hymn ends and Ernie collapses onto the pew grinning madly. Blackstone sits beside him looking grim as usual. Ernie winks at certain women. There's a drop of sweat on the back of his neck.

Pastor Paul leans on the pulpit. There's a yellow rose in the lapel of his pale-gray summer suit. He says, "Friends, Marty Williams is at the Osteopathic this morning on the intensive care list. I was with him last night and let me tell you right now, he needs our prayers."

Even as Pastor Paul speaks, the women from Mushy Meadows and the widow of Walt Perkins squeeze their eyes shut.

The hard heel of a child thonks a pew.

Ernie Train glances around and points at the guilty child, then mimes a giggle with his hand over his mouth.

At the piano Miss Nancy is turning pages. She has on her new beige summer sandals. When she glances Ernie's way, he blows her a kiss.

Pastor Paul mentions other sick people. Then he reminds everybody about the fellowship supper. And then he welcomes visitors from Fryeburg. Ernie waves at the visitors . . . smiles his big bare white-teeth smile.

On the other side of Blackstone, his wife, Lillian, sits with a sweet and drowsy smile. She has a new perm, short and tight, the kind of tight curls she used to point out looked "old" on other women.

Pastor Paul opens his Bible.

When Ernie moves a certain way, shafts of light burst from his glittery shirt. The shirt he wore last Sunday was a plaid of pinks with white piping. The shirt the Sunday before was a BIG YELLOW.

Pastor Paul tells about the puppy he found when he was a little fellow in Ohio. He weaves excerpts from the Scriptures into the story and anecdotes about people who thought all you had to do was accept Christ as your personal Savior and that would be it . . . home free. Unh-unh, says Pastor Paul. There's more.

Another drop of sweat appears on Ernie's neck.

Pastor Paul says, "We must seek out the Lord's Word! It is not going to follow us like a lost puppy. WE are the lost puppies, friends. God is the Master!"

Blackstone has shaved well . . . around the mustache his face is stark. Even a little sore-looking. He watches Pastor Paul studiously. Even when nobody else is paying attention. Pastor Paul's eyes and Blackstone's eyes are locked together. Pastor Paul says into Blackstone's eyes, "It is not up to us to ever wonder or question, but to KNOW. If we know what the Almighty commands, there will be no doubts. Because His Word is perfect."

"Amen!!" somebody in the back cries out.

Pastor Paul's eyes close and open slowly. "His Truth is complete! Every question you could ever ever EVER think to ask is answered in the Scriptures. God is one step ahead of us all the time, you know. He knew our questions BEFORE He made the first man and woman. Imagine that! He knew their questions before they had LIPS!!!" Pastor Paul sighs. "God is incredible, isn't He?"

Lillian gives one of her husband's hands a squeeze.

Pastor Paul whispers, "Friends, there are no mysteries." He shakes his head, chuckles softly. He holds up his Bible. "We can be life's experts. We can know everything." Everyone is looking up at the Bible. He waves it harder. "But . . . but . . . my friends . . . BUT!! . . . we can only know everything by opening this book . . . by SEEKING. We must study the Scriptures daily. Daily. Not once a year, once a month, once a week . . . but EVERY DAY. We must study the Scriptures every night after supper . . . OR . . . before supper . . . OR . . . get up early and do it. Sounds like work, huh? Wellll . . . what does living an endless death sound like? What does the job we could have with Satan sound like? PLAY???" He waits for a few gasps. He says, "We must study the Scriptures with DILIGENCE . . . till we are EXHAUSTED." He pretends he is going to give the Bible a toss into the many upturned faces. Blackstone's hands lying on his lap suddenly jerk.

3

After the service, the widow of Walt Perkins watches Blackstone rise from his pew, his icy-eyed children gathering around him . . . and Ernie down on his knees groping for a baby's shoe under the pew. She waits till Blackstone is mixed into the crowd before she finds Lillian chatting with some other Miracle City women . . . She takes Lillian's hands into hers. All the Miracle City women smile sadly at the widow . . . this widow who has pimples like a young girl and tall awkward girlishness and hands that SQUEEZE.

The widow says into Lillian's eyes, "My dear Miss Lily-Ann . . . I have bad news. You must listen for all you're worth to what I've got to tell you, dear . . ."

The eyes of all the women widen on the widow's long pimply girlish face.

She whispers, "I have seen the aura of death around your husband's head."

Lillian's hands try to worm free . . . a small try. The widow grips harder.

The women turn to look at Blackstone but he's nowhere in sight.

The widow says, "I saw it six times around my beloved Walt's head but I didn't pay any attention. I knew it was a sign from God but I didn't know what to make of it. It was a sign to me . . . that my husband was planning the taking of his own life . . . a sign to me to warn Walt of the Lord's Judgment on those who throw away His most precious gift. But I chose to ignore the sign, Miss Lily-Ann. I must live with that. But now . . . there it is . . . your precious husband . . . the aura was there through this whole service. I couldn't let you leave without warning you . . . So now it's in your hands."

Lillian pulls hard . . . pulls free. She moves away in a polite way, smiling all the while . . . her hands tingly from the widow's squeeze. She pushes through the little group that is shaking hands at the door with Pastor Paul. "Excuse me! Excuse me!" she says.

Her new church shoes clack down the high granite steps. Out in the sunny dooryard, she catches up with Blackstone and hooks her arm through his, drops her head on his shoulder. Under her cheek, his shoulder is like a rock.

4

The moon rises before dark, a moon you can see through, like Klee-nex.

As the last brush strokes go on the ell of the Shaws' old Cape, everybody is smiling . . . everybody except E. Blackstone Babbidge, who sits on the Shaws' well cover with a squashed Coke can by his foot. But he doesn't look angry. He is just a man sitting absolutely stock still.

Lillian and Miss Barb are still up on ladders slapping on brick-red paint.

"Oh! My aching back!" gasps Miss Carole, who is lugging empty paint cans to the barn. "I thank the good Lord it's only every ten years you have to paint!"

"What if you get sick of the color before ten years?" Mr. Ken teases.

"I'm already sick of the color!" she calls back from the barn.

Everyone watches Lillian's and Miss Barb's big brushes closing in on the last unpainted square . . . getting smaller and smaller.

"Almost done!" somebody shouts.

"Countdown!" somebody else shouts. "Five! . . ."

Then, "Four!"

On the hot top by the barn the thunking basketball stops and boys with number shirts and T-shirts cut short over their stomachs scream along with the others. "THREE!!"

"TWO!"

"ONE!"

Then cheers and applause. Lillian waves the brush. Her yard-sale tank top is spotted brick-red. She tosses the brush into the air and Jeff Greely catches it by the bristles.

More cheers.

Blackstone doesn't move. He is watching a boy with a number 44 on his shirt lean into the white Chevelle parked halfway into the barn. Then suddenly the music blares.

Mr. Ray bows to Miss Lisa and points to the Shaws' broad treeless lawn.

She shakes her head.

He points to the see-through moon.

People lugging empty paint cans and ladders to the barn laugh at this.

Finally Mr. Ray and Miss Lisa dance. They do an old-fashioned square step although the music from the Chevelle is for much more frenzied dancing.

There's children running in and out of the barn, throwing paper cups, throwing potato salad, jumping off the garden wall . . . mostly kids from Mushy Meadows or the big bully white-haired kids of Mr. Brian and Miss Connie. Among them stride the young Babbidges, their shoulders squared.

Lights come on in the house, women inside fixing more coffee . . . opening more bags of chips . . . kids running through the big rooms screaming, "Kidnap! Kidnap!"

"Be careful now!" Miss Carole's voice calls.

Out on the warm lawn, pairs of paint-spotted people dance.

Blackstone whomps a mosquito on his forearm.

Junie has just showed up from work . . . from the mill . . . her hair tied up in a piece of white rag. She is instantly surrounded by friends. She and Wendy Ginn dance with the boys with numbers on their shirts, 44 and 18. Wendy Ginn has long white hair and earrings that look like bunches of dimes. Somebody turns the Chevelle's radio up louder. The young people shake their shoulders, shake their hair. The white rag in Junie's hair flashes and signals in the deepening twilight. From the doorway of the big house, Miss Barb sighs, "Some people aren't acting very Christian tonight."

Small kids gather into a screeching mob and circle the big house and barn, crackle through the sumac beyond the garden. "When you kidnap, you are supposed to give up!" screams one of the Babbidge children. Blackstone's head turns.

"More potato salad if anybody is interested!" Miss Jean calls from the picnic table by the garden. As the pack of children comes screaming from the sumac, they knock a fistful of plastic forks from Miss Jean's hand. "Lord! Lord!" she giggles.

"That's enough, you guys!" warns Miss Sue. "How about a little bit of civilized behavior?"

Lillian says, "And you kids watch out for Miss Carole's garden now. She's got some real pretty flowers!"

The night smells hot. Hot paint. Hot, fresh-cut grass. And hot stillness.

As the kids come sweeping around the house again and again, there are more of them each time . . . some making the wails of police cars.

Blackstone seizes Jason Robert by the front of his striped muscle shirt and murmurs, "Simmer down."

"Yessir," says Jason Robert, always squinting like he doesn't understand. He has a big splat of brick-red paint between his eyes. When his father releases him, he vanishes.

In the barn, a light comes on. Mr. Bob shows three men his boy's new three-wheeler.

Mosquitoes whine around Blackstone's head as he squats back onto the cement well cover. He swipes at them with his denim cap.

While state and local news is on the radio, the older kids vanish. When the music comes back, there's only Mr. Ken and Miss Terry dancing.

The mob of little kids bursts out from between parked cars, Christopher Babbidge in the lead. Some of them are waving branches they've ripped from sumac.

"Those kids are going to get poison!" gasps Miss Carole.

"That kind isn't poison. That kind is okay," somebody assures her.

"Still . . . one of them will get a poked eye if they aren't careful." Lillian sighs.

When the big kids reappear, Wendy Ginn asks her parents if she can go with the others to get pizza in Dana's Chevelle. The parents say NO.

Lillian finds a place on the grass to stretch out and Miss Penny gives her her moist newborn, grim-faced Josh, to hold . . . newly adopted by the Stevenses, who are visiting from Fryeburg. Lillian sighs. "Eensie weensie little man."

The big kids decide not to go for pizza, but they disappear for a long while behind the parked cars.

The little kids get wilder and wilder, climbing over somebody's new Subaru. Miss Carole shoos them off. Jason Robert has rejoined the mob. He climbs up onto the garden wall with his arms out for balance and several white-haired children and a couple from the Mushy Meadows gang try to beat him off with their sumac limbs.

It is dark now, the moon solid, vast, and spotted.

Somebody turns the music up even more. The dancers sway to a slow one. There are shoes and sneakers scattered . . . paper plates . . . Coke cans. One of the boys takes his number shirt off and slings it into the grass.

"Do you want to dance?" an unfamiliar voice asks Blackstone. He raises his eyes. It's Junie, her left cheek sucked in, her eyes on the middle of his ragged black T-shirt. Her voice is willowy, a voice he's never *ever* heard her use. He doesn't answer her.

He just stands up with suddenness.

He lays his denim workcap on the well cover. He puts his right hand on her back, steers her toward the dancers, and whispers into her hair, "You are stoned and drunk . . . You got no business that way."

She faces him with an aimless little grin. "How do you know so much?" she says mockingly.

She puts her arms around him.

The kids go howling past, one shrieking, "Don't let him get away! He's got the sacred scrolls!!"

Junie mashes her face hard into Blackstone's chest. He tries to get her to dance the waltz, but she won't move her feet, just muckles onto him harder, like for dear life.

Lillian watches with her head cocked.

The music switches to a fast one.

Blackstone pulls one of Junie's arms down, but she just puts it back. "People are looking at you, June!" he says.

The kids go screaming past again . . . one dragging another by the foot. Some are police. One tickles Junie with a sumac branch as he passes. Junie giggles.

These days she is as tall as he is, maybe taller. When she raises her head quick, they are eye to eye. She squints at the hundreds of hairs of his mustache, the mass of it, dark and unwelcoming, his mouth buried there.

"For crissakes, what do you want?" he snarls.

She pushes against his dungarees.

She feels the fright jerk through his waist.

The fast music stops. The weatherman says a seasonable warm front is expected.

The boy with the 44 on his chest appears, gives Junie's blouse a hard pull. "Hey, Funny Junie! What's going on here? Leave Mr. B. alone." The boy gives her blouse another hard pull. She shuts her eyes tight, drops her arms.

The boy takes her by the arm and leads her toward the cars where the other older kids are all tittering. "What a riot, Junie! What a show!"

Blackstone reappears on the well cover . . . stock still. There's no expression on his face . . . nothing like rage yet . . . just an aura . . . like a warning from God.

5

The old trailer is so small there's no place to get away whenever Blackstone gives one of his kids a strapping. Everybody just stands there feeling HUGE. Or they go and get on their mattresses face up or face down, but motionless, listening to the belt crack and the terrible cries.

The oldest daughter, Eugenia, warms milk in a little red-rimmed pan, smiling her sad smile.

When they all got home from the house-painting party, there was Ernie Train and young Mark at the little supper table, where they have a lot of their great bullshit sessions . . . The table lately has become their territory.

When the strapping in the little back room began, Mark and Ernie stopped talking mid-word.

Now Ernie, who is buffing a pair of dark expensive-looking tooled leather boots, keeps his head down so nobody can see his face.

Mark's eyes are on his coffee cup. You'd think there was a story on that cup the way his eyes are fixed there . . . But all it says is GEMINI and shows twin women wearing something like togas.

When it is over, Lillian says . . . almost cheerfully, "Mosquitoes are thick tonight. I wish we could get that screen door fixed."

Eugenia pours the warm milk into a little plastic cup and says firmly, "I hope you kids realize that you acted like a buncha savages at the Shaws' tonight."

Blackstone comes out from the wee back room. He's still buckling his belt and his eyes sweep over the many faces of the kids he's spared.

Junie, stretched out on her mattress, covers her eyes.

Lillian pulls open drawers, finds the gummy tin of Bag Balm.

When she reaches the little room with the bunk beds, she can smell Blackstone's rage . . . just as she had smelled it on the ride home with the Greens, Mr. Ken talking a blue streak about the new fans in the church kitchen . . . Blackstone stone-faced, reeking.

She sees the sheets and blankets in a ball in the corner which means Jason Robert has put up a fight.

"Come out," she says softly.

He is under the bunks . . . only one bare foot, one bare leg shows.

"Jason, I need to look at your legs," she says. She picks the lid off the Bag Balm, sticks her finger in to see how runny the heat has made it.

Jason Robert snivels softly but doesn't move. "I *hate* him," he whispers. "Don't you?"

She squats down with her back against the wall. She closes her eyes.

Jason sobs, "Next time he hits me, I'm going to KILL him."

"Oh, Jason! Don't talk like that!"

Jason snickers. "Yep . . . I'm going to bash his head."

Lillian says, "Don't blame your father. He was so unhappy at the party. He's VERY shy."

"Then he'll be GLAD to die," says Jason Robert. "When I kill him, he'll say 'Thank you!!' "

6

It's been one year now since they've moved from Luke's to Miracle City . . . Seems like 101 years. Night after night, Junie is wakened by the sound of Blackstone grinding his teeth in his sleep. She can look right onto the mattress next to hers and see his dark hair on the pillow. The sheet that covers him and Lillian looks pink by the glow of the security lamp outside. Junie knows Lillian is awake listening, too. They are both light sleepers.

Junie drifts off now and then but is wakened again and again by the grinding teeth.

Tonight it seems he is going to snap them off at the roots. They actually CRACKLE.

Junie cries out, "Mama!"

"What?"

"Make him stop."

Lillian gives him a little poke.

The crackling stops.

7

At Sunday dinner, Ernie Train doesn't sit at the table but by the door, his long creamy fingers brushing the strings of his smooth-going guitar. He sings "If You Could See Me Now" softly to himself. He seldom eats meals, just snacks. Crackers, coffee, Mountain Dew, ice cream, and raw baloney. "I'm on a diet," he always tells them.

Everybody is looking at him, waiting for him to stop singing so Blackstone can say grace. Finally he comes to. "Oops!" He giggles and gives them one of his big bare white smiles, his bare shaved face blushing.

Blackstone says the grace with his icy eyes wide open.

"Daddy!" scolds Jennifer Ann. "Close your eyes."

"How do you know his eyes are open if your eyes are closed like they ought to be?" Stacy wonders.

"Everybody eat," Blackstone commands.

Mark loads his plate with nothing but whipped potatoes, then shakes ketchup on it. Since he's been working in the woods for Sargent, he has raised a soft-looking beard . . . and a more enormous appetite.

Blackstone rolls up the sleeves of his wrinkled church shirt and the moon tattoo emerges.

Mark says, "Uncle Ernie, play something from the old days . . . when you and Dad was young fellers."

Ernie smiles broadly, strums a little.

Blackstone loads his plate with deer meat and potatoes. Lillian pushes the oleo tub toward him. Ernie watches Lillian's hand on the tub.

Ernie hums "Good-Hearted Woman, Good-Timin' Man."

Mark leans back on two legs of his chair and claps his hands right in the middle of the song. "Very good! Very good!" he says. "But that ain't what I meant. What I meant was those songs from the sixties. Those hippie songs. Drug songs. Protest songs. Hate-the-system songs. You know. The ones with the real weird words . . . like . . . like 'White Rabbit.' You know 'White Rabbit'?"

Ernie smiles, strums a little bit of "Torn Between Two Lovers."

Junie says, "Mark, could you gimme the ketchup, please? . . . If there's any left."

Mark has the ketchup down on the floor by his foot. The table is too small for anything but plates. "That's the seventies," he sort of sings out as Ernie persists with "Torn Between Two Lovers," his voice soft and husky, nothing like the wild heee-hah singing he's famous for on his records and TV appearances.

Jennifer Ann whispers, "Is the man ever going home?"

Lillian says, "Shh! That's not nice."

Ernie leans toward the table, his pale pink shirt quivering liquidly up and down his narrow back. "Honey, you don't have to call me 'the man' for the rest of your life. You can call me 'Uncle.' I'm your Uncle Ernie. Gawd. Gene, don't you ever talk to these kids about me? Don't you pass on some of those good old Aroostook stories . . . your old heller days?"

Blackstone's mouth is full of deer meat. He shrugs.

Mark says deeply, "Dad don't talk about *yesterday*."

Blackstone's and Mark's eyes meet.

Jennifer Ann whispers something to Michelle. The two of them giggle.

Blackstone points at them both with his fork. "In about ten seconds one of you is going to get a scorched ass."

Lillian gasps, "Blackstone! I've never heard you use that word before!"

There's a long silence, just the clinks of forks against plates and the sounds of gentle eating.

Mark says, "Cripes, Ernie . . . Don't you know any of those old protest songs from the good ol' days?"

When Mark says "good ol' days," Blackstone breaks out into one of his huge scary grins. All his little teeth show.

Lillian says, "How about some good Christian songs, Ernie. You do them beautifully. Everybody agrees."

Ernie has stopped strumming. No humming either. He's just looking at Lillian with his big strenuous smile.

Lillian gives Mark a raw look. "Well, your father fought in that war. Maybe he doesn't want to relive that terrible terrible TERRIBLE time. It was a terrible time for him, nothing anybody at this table, praise God, will ever know. I just think those songs will . . . well, you know . . . they were AGAINST the war, against what your father was doing . . . It's kind of . . . of . . . AWKWARD."

Blackstone snarls, "It don't bother me a bit! Sing away, Ernest. Give it hell!"

Lillian looks down at her plate. "I just don't want to see you get upset." She sighs. "You know how . . . upset you can get."

Blackstone swallows a whole mouthful of unchewed deer meat. "Jesus Christ! I ain't no goddam baby."

"Daddy! Watch your words!" Eugenia scolds.

"Daddy said swears," Jennifer Ann says solemnly.

At that very instant a car slows up in front of the trailer, almost stops . . . then drives away. They all know the sound of it . . . another one of Ernie's fans who has found out he is staying here. They come driving by for a peek. Sometimes they knock on the door. Sometimes it's the phone. But mostly they just want a peek. Maxine Letourneau next door can hardly take her eyes off him. Ernie screams "HEY MAXINE!" when he sees her out there and she gives him a grave nod. Nobody can believe the real Ernie Train is here in Miracle City.

Ernie says softly, "I don't want to cause no trouble here, Gene . . ." He reaches out to prop his guitar in the corner.

Blackstone bellers, "Go ahead, man! Play us a couple of them good ol' acid tunes . . . and protest 'em songs. There's plenty of those I recall. Play away!" He wipes his mustache with a paper napkin, then rolls the napkin between his palms till it's like a nut.

Ernie obeys.

8

Both the living room and kitchen floors have mattresses night and day. There's only one big soft chair. Blackstone is in it with his arms folded across his chest watching a bowling tournament on the TV.

There is a tremendous pounding up and down the little hall of the trailer, in and out of the bathroom and small back room of bunk beds. It's Junie in her bedroom slippers that look like polar bear feet, chasing the kids, making them shriek. The slippers have rubber claws. They're a present from one of her boyfriends at the mill . . . a guy named Greg.

The kids run all over the mattresses, hide behind the room divider, hide behind Lillian . . . shrieking, "Bear! Bear! Killer bear!"

Junie snarls.

Mark comes in from the yard, from the old engineless, rear-endless Ford van which is his TERRITORY . . . his private place. His space. He has his mattress there, his music. It's real cozy. He says, "Potatoes and fake gravy AGAIN! I'm gonna gag."

Lillian says, "Praise God for His gifts."

Mark grunts. "I'm a Gemini. I like variety."

The TV makes dull clattery sleepy bowling noises. Blackstone's eyes are fixed there like there's nothing going on in the room. All around his chair the children surge, screaming, "Bear! Look, Daddy! Bear! KILL it!"

Lillian sighs, "June Marie, are you planning to come to supper in your bathrobe? Or are you going to get dressed like a decent human being?"

Junie snarls, seizes Jason Robert by the wrist. Jason screams at the top of his voice.

Out in the dooryard, there's the slam of a car door and the "Heee-hah!" of Ernie just getting home from one of his quickie trips to town.

Anastasia gasps. "Stacy! Where's that spare roll of toilet paper? Andrew's got a booger."

Jennifer Ann lands squarely in her father's lap. She is red and gasping, hides her face in his neck. She whispers, "Daddy! The bear is really Miss June, isn't it?"

He doesn't look at Junie, who is flinging Jason Robert onto a

133

mattress, wearing her bear slippers on her hands now. Jason Robert gags on his laughter as she tickles him under the arms with her paws.

"Look, Daddy! See Miss June's hands!" Jennifer Ann insists.

But Blackstone doesn't look at Junie. He just rocks his breathless Jennifer back and forth . . . "Simmer down, baby," he says deeply . . . and slides his eyes back onto the bowling tournament.

9

The truck is yellow, not the type of yellow trucks come in. It's more of a TONKA yellow or decorate-your-own-milkcan yellow. It's a yellow with brush strokes. The driver is Severin, Armand Letourneau's son, half-Passamaquoddy . . . just half. But for his clothes and the white, freshly lit Marlboro in his battered-up hand, he could pass for one of those olden-days Indians in a tawny photograph . . . built tall and powerfully bony, bare-faced, thick-lidded eyes . . . a face of dignity, distance, and defeat . . . an old boy . . . perhaps eighteen.

"Holy shit!" howls Mark Babbidge. "That's my old man walkin' up ahead. Pull over."

Severin rams the floorshift down into second and the old truck screams.

Mark moves over on the seat for his father.

After Blackstone is aboard, the truck turns onto Farrington Road and barrels down through the tunnel of trees. Mark rides with a hand on each knee. His neck which is naturally thick, naturally muscular, is more thick all of a sudden, thick with anxiety . . . thick with readiness. He looks *ready* for anything. He says, "We're going up to Severin's old man's house to bury a dog . . . Dad . . . Imagine that." He grins at his father, the split-toothed grin that ancient Greeks would be aroused by.

Blackstone's pale eyes are fixed to the cold haze thickening between the mountains below.

Mark says to Severin, "Dad knows how to bury dogs. He's had PRACTICE. Right, Dad?"

Blackstone says, "Simmer down, Mark."

Mark's right knee jerks. He says to Severin, "My old man is the one that had all those dogs he didn't take care of . . . let 'em stay

134

out in the weather. Remember? Your ol' Uncle Lucien took care of that. They ain't kiddin' when they say that ol' boy's got a heart of gold. If it weren't for types like him, think of all the sufferin' that would be allowed to go on in this ol' world. Know what I mean, Sev?"

"Yep," says Severin, giving his Marlboro a vicious suck.

Across the open field Horne Hill rises brutishly out of the haze. The barren top of it is pink with morning, although it's still gravely blue where the old truck clangs along up the grade.

"Severin's dad's got a heart of gold, too . . . Can't even bury his own old dog . . . Imagine that, Dad. I mean . . . Severin's dad thinks of his dog like . . . like a KID or something!"

Severin says, "Well, Papa has emphysema. That's why I'm doing it for him."

Mark narrows his eyes. "I thought you said he was broke up over it."

"He is," says Severin. "Wicked broke up . . . okay?"

"You said he . . . CRIED," says Mark.

"Yep . . . he cried," says Severin.

Mark's eyes slide over onto his father's blackened hands. "Well, the only thing *my* dad felt was pissed off at Big Lucien. And I said, 'Gee, Dad, why don't you go right down there an' give ol' Gross Monsieur Pluto a knock right on the side of the head? You gonna just let him do this to you?' But the old man . . . he don't have nuthin' to say to that 'cause he knows Big Lucien . . . man of gold . . . he has him by the balls. Without that junkyard job, Dad might as well go up in the woods and hang himself . . . Right, Dad?"

Blackstone is stock still.

Mark chuckles. "And NOW since Dad and Luke had their tiff . . . Big Lucien owns the very ROOF over Dad's head. The plot thickens . . . Right, Dad?"

Severin pitches what's left of his cigarette out into the roadside weeds. He says, "Why you walking, Gene? . . . Your truck conked out somewhere?"

"Yep," says Blackstone.

"Need any help?" Severin asks.

"No," says Blackstone. "I'm all right."

"You in a rush to get home? This dog business shouldn't take long

. . . But if you gotta get back, I'm obligin' . . . Dog can wait . . . He ain't complaining." He keeps his eyes straight out on the road.

"I appreciate it . . . but I'm fine," says Blackstone.

The sun strikes Armand and Patty Letourneau's old white farmhouse at the exact moment they round the corner. The yellow truck clangs and clatters into the yard, stops under the huge shade trees. The men get out. Severin pulls a bright new rolled bandanna from his dash. He ties it around his hair which is silky hair, peaceful hair, pleasurable hair . . . long . . . clean . . . black. You can tell it's his pride.

He pulls a shovel from the back of the truck.

Mark says, "Shit, Dad, don't this remind you of the big day we buried them dogs?"

Blackstone leans over the bright yellow hood of the truck, the visor of his cap so low there's no eyes, just nose and the mass of his mustache.

Mark says, "But thirteen dead dogs ain't much of a massacre, is it, Dad? You've probably seen PILES of human people in Nam. Death probably don't bother you one little bit . . . Right, Dad? Death and sufferin' . . . you can get immune to a thing like that, right?"

Blackstone says softly, almost lovingly, "Simmer down, Mark."

Severin walks toward his father's house with the shovel.

Mark leans over the yellow hood alongside his father, so they both face the view of the great heartachingly beautiful bald mountain . . . both faces bright yellow. There's a little squeak in Mark's big neck.

Blackstone murmurs, "What the hell's the matter with you?"

Mark grins. "It's gotta be SOMEWHERES that happens to some guys, right? . . . That you get immune . . . Right?"

10

When Lillian comes to pick Junie up from her shift, she has balled-up blue Kleenexes all over the Malibu's dash and a red, red face. They sit there a while with their windows down listening to the rapid thrum of the looms in the mill and the thrash of the river and the click click click of the left turn signal which hasn't shut itself off.

With her tightly curled older-lady hairdo and scratchy polyester clothes, Lillian is no longer Junie's twin.

She says, "I guess you are beginning to figure out just how stubborn and bull-headed your stepfather is . . . what I've had to put up with these past two years . . . haven't you?"

"I guess," says Junie softly, sucking in her left cheek. She lays her head back . . . closes her eyes, the looms still beating in her head.

"I mean . . . like that old truck has been on the side of the road a WEEK now . . . and he's like . . . STILL AT IT. He might as well give up on it. Everybody says it. No need beating a dead horse, for gosh sakes."

Junie sighs.

Lillian studies the group of women talking by the loading platform. She says, "He's crazy, isn't he, Junie?"

"Sometimes," says Junie.

"He hasn't slept more than ten minutes all this week . . . He just keeps at it and at it and at it and AT IT . . . thinking he's going to figure out the big mystery, you know. Well, there's no mystery. The truck is junk! Ernie suggests one of us give him a push with the Maverick or Malibu. But no . . . He just don't want to do what makes sense! I say he oughta just get Lucien to junk it out . . . get fifty bucks for us . . . so we can get some groceries and stuff. We can't support a family including HIS BROTHER on your check forever. And Mark's boss is all done with that Effingham lot. So Mark says he's starting back to school in September . . . And I'm not going to be the one to discourage *that* miracle . . . And if Lucien would just come up with some money . . . pay Blackstone even HALF of what he owes him . . . Jesus, Jesus, Jesus!!!" She presses her fists to her eyes. Then she looks at Junie with a smile, eyes wide. "I don't know what I'd do without you, sweetie. You are my best friend."

Junie narrows her eyes. "I thought Big Lucien was RICH. How come he can't pay guys right? Luke used to say Big Lucien was sitting on a fat pile."

Lillian giggles, reaches to wedge some of Junie's dark raggedy hair behind her ear . . . hair that's a little heavy with the lanolin of the mill. "Your real father . . . dear man . . . has . . . well . . . let's say it costs a *lot* to have a heart of gold."

"Are we leaving Blackstone, Mama?"

Lillian sighs. "I pray to the good Lord to give me the strength to break with Blackstone. I get up every morning and say to myself, LET'S GO . . . But . . ."

"He's got some kinda power over you, huh?" Junie says.

"Junie . . . there ain't nobody perfect. When you add up all the good 'n' bad of people, Blackstone is the best the Lord God makes. My husband has his good points."

"What's those?" Junie asks.

Lillian giggles. "Now, June Marie . . . look at what you've done! You've got me laughing. Thank you! Thank you! Thank you!" She gives Junie a big squeeze.

11

On the black ride home, Blackstone's old off-green International comes into view. Lillian squares the Malibu headlights on it . . . stops.

Blackstone is pawing through a metal box of tools on the ground. Lillian gets out, stands with her hands on her hips, says almost cheerfully, "My goodness, Mr. B.! What if it's not to be fixed? How about gettin' Lucien to let you use the ramp truck to haul it back to our dooryard . . . at least get it home where nobody will bother it. And you'll have better light at home . . . and FOOD, you know."

He doesn't answer. He keeps pointing the weak flashlight into the toolbox like the Malibu headlights don't exist.

Lillian says, "My goodness! My goodness!"

He finds what he's looking for, then strides back to the open hood, points his flashlight there.

She follows close behind him and looks in at the hoses and belts that never make sense to her . . . watches his hand work the wrench.

"Want me to hold the flashlight?" she asks.

He looks at her, his pale eyes shrunken with exhaustion. He puts the flashlight in her hand . . . easy . . . almost giftlike.

The next night there's a blowing black cold rain. When Lillian shows up at the mill, she wears a plastic rain cap, the accordion kind . . . the kind she used to say she'd never be caught dead in. As they head back up the dark highway toward Miracle City, Junie dozes . . . the rapid thrum of the looms always on the edges of her dreams.

When the Malibu comes to a stop in front of Blackstone's truck, Junie doesn't wake up.

Blackstone isn't working on the truck, just leaning over on both forearms, staring into the ragged-running engine, his salvage shirt black with rain.

Lillian steps out. "Any luck?" she asks . . . The engine, to her, sounds pretty good.

His voice seems to come from the thrashing howling woods. "No."

She steps up close to him and says, "I brought you a little supper. *Please* eat it. Sit in the Malibu with me out of the rain."

His mustache seems to tremble, but it's really the wind. Everything trembles, everything flutters.

Lillian shivers. "I've been praying, Blackstone . . . that the Lord will guide you in getting this truck on the road again."

Blackstone has nothing to say to this. He just listens to the engine, his arms folded on the fender. He says, "It's going to turn out to be some small thing . . . something really stupid, you know. It ain't any of the things that make sense . . ." He tells her about the carburetor, the old one, the one he just put in, and everything he tried in between. He says, "She's got about as much power as a baby fart."

Lillian smiles.

He shifts his forearms, sighs.

"Where's your flashlight?" she wonders.

"Wore out," he says.

"Want me to stay and keep my headlights on ya?" she asks.

"No . . . Go home and get your girl to bed . . . and yourself . . . Just get the hell out of here." He leans closer to the ragged skipping roar.

Lillian sighs. "I'm going to get down right now on my knees and pray for you . . . I can't stand it anymore, Blackstone!" She starts to squat down . . .

He muckles onto her narrow shoulders, yanks her to her feet, and says, "Don't let me see you do that, Lily-Ann . . . Keep some respect."

13

When Junie gets out of work the next night, Ernie's Maverick, loaded with guitars and piles of bright shirts, is parked over by the river below the mill. She hasn't laid eyes on Ernie for days and days . . . except at night when he sleeps in his car by Mark's van or with his pillow and sleeping bag on the floor between the table and the sink. He is not the "home type," Lillian likes to say. He is nothing like his half-brother.

Junie sees Ernie's arm wave.

She crosses the lot, swinging her corduroy bag.

He has a woman with him, dark looks, gypsy earrings, a cheek full of snappy gum.

"What you doing way over here?" Junie asks Ernie.

He smiles his big smile, taps the ash of his cigarette on the side of the car. "Don't want to be recognized."

Junie looks back at the clutch of women having a smoke around Jeannie Cooper's Bobcat, all of them laughing loud. She says, "Oh, yuh . . . I forgot about that."

"You want to drive, Junie?"

"Sure!"

He gets out, hiding his head with drama, lunges long-leggedly to the other door.

The woman doesn't say anything when Junie flops into the driver's seat and slings her corduroy bag into the back.

As Ernie gets himself situated, Junie studies his T-shirt . . . A plain white T-shirt . . . not his usual way of dressing. And on his lanky upper arm, a tattoo of a dragonfly. His hair is a mess. And on his long, long neck there's about eight hickies . . . in rows.

He chuckles. "Nothing difficult about this old girl. She drives like your average automatic . . . Just turn the key and ram'r into drive."

"Okay," says Junie. She turns the key once and the little car hums to life. It is bouncy and needs alignment but has such a dreamy little purr to it as it heads out over the bridge back to Egypt.

"How you like wool, June?" Ernie says. He rides with his arm stretched out the window, fingers wide like he's trying to catch something from the air.

"It's a job," says Junie.

Ernie nudges the woman. "This here little girl is my brother's stepdaughter . . . named June." He adds, "June, this is Mary . . . from Old Orchard."

Junie says, "How do you do."

The woman says, "You got bears up this way?"

Junie giggles. "Naw . . . they hide."

Ernie opens and closes his hand on the warm night, his big smile plastered all over his face . . . his leg jiggling. "Hey . . . June . . . Want to go to Portland with us!!! We can turn this ship around right now! Don't you ever get restless?" He nudges the woman. "All she does is work and gives her pay to my brother for the bills. They got a trillion hospital bills . . . BABY BILLS, I call it. This little gal don't EVER have any fun for herself. It really pisses me off." He whispers into the woman's hair, "CHURCH people."

Junie says, "Someday I'm going to get a Two-Eighty Z."

Ernie says, "Oh yuh?"

"Yup!" she says, grinning.

"That ain't practical," he says. "In fact, that ain't CHRISTIAN. Christian girls drive . . . station wagons, don't they?" He nudges the woman. The woman moves her gum to the other cheek.

Junie feels frantically for the turn signal. Ernie reaches across and flicks it for her, then sinks back to his seat. The Maverick purrs onto the Graves Falls Road and they start up the grade. When Blackstone's old truck slides into view, Ernie sits up board-straight.

"Want me to stop?" Junie asks.

"Jesus, NO!" he cries. "We just stopped when we came by to get you and he was too pissy for my tastes."

"He's worried, I guess." Junie sighs.

"Give him the horn!" Ernie shouts. "Scare the shit out of him." He stretches over and squeezes the horn as they pass. "Heeeeeeeee-hah! You son of a bitch!" He hoots into the night.

14

The two-ton truck which says LETOURNEAU'S USED AUTO PARTS, EGYPT, MAINE on the doors is waiting for Junie in the parking lot of the thrumming mill. It's Blackstone with his head back against the cab, the visor of his workcap very low . . . like he might be sleeping.

Junie doesn't have the door closed yet when he's pushing the shift into gear. He says, "Your mother says you sleep all right riding along."

"What?" The truck smells like brake fluid . . . and black bananas. Junie glances around quick, can't see any bananas.

"If you are tired, just go ahead and sleep. I've got to pick up an automobile."

"Oh," says Junie. "Where's *your* truck?"

"Right where you might suppose," he says deeply. He doesn't look at her. He NEVER looks at her.

They get onto the road going west into New Hampshire. The old truck rides rough.

Junie watches the moon, a moon in its last quarter fixed firmly in the thick, unbearably black murk of an August sky. Then her eyes slide over to the breadth of Blackstone's upper arms with the sleeves of his salvage shirt rolled tight.

They ride along saying nothing, headlights coming up behind them fast, passing, leaving them in the blackness. The truck rolls past variety stores with gas pumps, all closed. The road is endlessly black with a faded double yellow stripe.

When they reach the place where the car is, Junie whispers, "Won't the people be in bed?"

"Not these people," he says.

He backs up under the trees and Junie squints at the big side mirror. The cars and trucks and motorcycles look smoky-pink from the taillights of the ramp truck. Dogs snarl. But she can't see any dogs. The light from the curtainless windows of the house is a gray bare light. She sees silhouettes of people moving around.

"Hippies," says Blackstone, then he looks at her and grins.

"Oh," says Junie.

He bends the visor of his cap straight up, screels the door open, and disappears, leaving the motor running.

Junie's tongue moves first into one cheek, then the other. She looks over the wrenches and sets of keys on the dash . . . used matches . . . and rags. She can hear him flinging chains around on the ramp.

She opens the door, drops down off the high seat. The air smells of strangers and of deep woods. Junie breathes deep of it, looks up at the house . . . then turns, looks into Blackstone's face.

His eyes are wide on her. He just stands there between the two bumpers with his hands hanging.

She giggles nervously.

He is stock still.

She says, "Want to dance again?"

The dogs have stopped barking but are growling, one or two of them only a few feet away.

Junie jerks her hips from side to side . . . like dancing.

He says, "This is a warning . . . Don't mess around with me . . . unless you mean real business."

She feels her way along the side of the truck. It is warm and vibrates against her palms.

She comes to within a foot of his face . . . eye to eye . . . jerking her hips like a little snappy dance, then she squeals and bounds away . . . ducks behind a windowless station wagon loaded with white industrial pails. The growling of the dogs moves along the other side.

Blackstone appears, his hand on the station wagon hood.

She ducks behind the next car, stumbles over a stack of bent lawnchairs . . . giggling. An endless minute passes.

Arms lock around her from behind. "Holy shit!!" she shrieks.

"Giggle again," he says.

She twists around, goes at his buttons, starting with the one at his throat.

He says, "You ain't got no business being like this . . ."

She starts at her own buttons and zipper, her eyes bright with the hippies' gray glare. There's what sounds like a refrigerator door slamming up at the hippies' house. The dogs are straining in their collars

143

. . . gasping, coughing. She slings her cutoff jeans at Blackstone's feet.

Then she hears the clink of his belt, closes her eyes. "I'll do anything you want," she says. "ANYTHING."

She hears the buckle hit against the station wagon door he's leaning against. She sneaks a peek at him through squinty eyes. In the house of hippies, somebody shouts, "Is that the thing that's got the ten-year guarantee?"

Junie kisses Blackstone, the kind of kiss she can feel in the walls of her mouth, then she shoves him away, goes careening away, feeling frenzied in her nakedness, hiding, scooching in the darkness beyond the next car.

When he finds her, he straddles her from behind.

"What are you doing!" she gasps. It is not how she pictured it: he is nothing like the young boys at the mill. Her elbow strikes the station wagon's hubcap . . . He is big and hot-feeling and wet . . . reeking. His passion is hardly distinguishable from his familiar and constant rage.

15

On the way back to the main road, nobody speaks. There's just the creak of the car on the ramp.

The moon is higher. It looks like a kind and crinkly face.

Then up on the main road, after about a mile of silence, Junie says in a livid voice, "I hate your ways, you old thing. You make love like an old wild goat." She squeezes her eyes tight.

After a few more miles, a warm watery-smelling breeze picks up and makes the rags on the dashboard flutter, makes Junie's raggedy hair squirm. With her eyes closed, the rocking of the truck, slow and easy from side to side, brings her close to sleep. She smells the homes of strangers on the breeze . . . a terrible, otherworldly smell. And she can smell Blackstone.

She opens her eyes, looks at Blackstone's old whitish jeans shredded and stained by his work. She slides down on the seat, cradles her head in his lap. This is the way they ride for the rest of the way. He doesn't question it.

16

It is an evening of early dark . . . fall coming on . . . silver and blue.

When the ramp truck comes rumbling down the weedy rutty road of Miracle City, everyone can see, plain as day, Blackstone's old off-green International winched up on back.

Eugenia and Anastasia rush out cheering, "It's home! It's home!"

The younger kids run ahead. Lillian hangs back in the doorway to hoist up Eugenia's thick-wristed, thick-necked, humorless son, Andrew. She squares him heavily on her hip.

The ramp truck has pulled up so suddenly into the dooryard it has gone into the clothesline, a towel of yellow roses plastered over its windshield.

Anastasia and Eugenia giggle madly, diving through the hanging sheets toward the side of the truck. Then all giggling and silliness stops.

The driver has only half a face.

The littler kids stare open-mouthed.

Lillian commands, "You kids, isn't Jonathan and Vikki in their yards? . . . Go over around and look. I'll call you when I need you for something! Go on!"

They don't seem to hear. They are stock still.

The shirt that is the usual salvage shirt says RICHARD over the pocket.

Eugenia and Anastasia have their horror written all over their faces.

The fellow's voice doesn't match his face. What would match would be a great ruined shriek. But his voice is young and quavery and a little bit teasing. "Gene around?" he asks.

Eugenia and Anastasia are lost for words.

"Yes," answers Lillian. "But he's asleep . . . for the first time in two weeks."

Richard has one very steady greenish eye. "Well," he says, smiling. "Here's his baby."

"Big Lucien's orders. Right?" says Lillian.

"Right," he says.

As the truck door swings open, all the kids jerk back . . . *way*

145

back. He ducks under the hanging laundry and under hemlock limbs toward the back of the truck.

As he unloads the International, the kids watch hard. The side of Richard's face that shows is the side that looks like taffy. The International sinks slowly into the tall weeds . . . The soft pale look of those weeds around its fenders is almost loving, like hands.

Lillian says, "Thank you for doing this. It's really nice of you . . . being so late and all. You must be missing your supper. My husband would *never* ask Lucien for the use of this truck for himself. He's . . . independent, you know."

The half-faced Richard kneels in the weeds, works the chain free of the bumper, says, "Don't thank me, Ma'am. It was boss's orders. I'd be home with my VCR if it weren't for a bossy boss." He grins his half-grin.

"He's got a blasted face," Jason Robert whispers.

Anastasia murmurs, "I wish Daddy was up." She turns suddenly and moves toward the trailer's wrought-iron rail steps, running her hands through her hair. Then she stands at the door staring at Blackstone, who is on the mattress nearest to the refrigerator. He lies on top of the blankets, fully dressed, spread-eagle, one forearm across his face to protect his eyes from the light.

17

Ernie's many shirts hanging out to dry are a spectacle, especially after a week of dark rain and gloom. The shirts zigzag all over the cramped dooryard. There's even a sort of emergency line tied from the trailer door to the broken bedsprings against the metal shed . . . Shirts, shirts . . . all of them the most ridiculous colors.

Parked among the shirts, within three feet of the wrought-iron-rail steps, is Lillian's Malibu. Its hood is up. Blackstone is bent into the motor, tools everywhere in the sun-dappled muddy yard.

A voice calls, "Daddy! Dinner is ready!"

Blackstone moves away from the car, takes the steps, kicks his boots against the doorjamb. Hunks of hard mud drop out of the treads.

Perched on the tall stool by the door is Ernie, all legs. "Hey, Stone Man!" He giggles. "Long time no see!"

Beside Ernie is a woman with her jacket on although the trailer is hot. Her jacket is short and chestnut-color, a shade darker than her dense, unmanageable, beautiful chestnut hair. Her skirt is ablaze with stylish stripy color, spills over both sides of her chair . . . over her tall tall leather western boots.

Blackstone kicks the door shut.

Lillian turns from the counter where she's peeling apples, sees him leaning against the refrigerator. The smell of broken motors drifts out of him. And the smell of his rage. He bends the visor of his workcap straight up and picks open his jackknife. His forehead is the only snow-white part of him.

"Any hope for the Malibu?" Ernie asks.

Blackstone shakes his head.

Lillian holds an apple to the light. It is dented, spongy, purplish. She cuts out a small good part and adds it to her pie.

Blackstone's voice trembles. "I have my next three weeks' pay tied up in these rigs and I haven't even earned it yet." He carves off part of his left thumbnail. "And no pay at all till the boss is done crushing. Ernie's car is out of gas. Till payday we're going to hoof it, folks."

Eugenia announces, "Food! It's ready! Jennifer! Benjamin! Chris! Jason! You better be done washing them hands! You've already had a century to do it!"

She buckles big baby Andrew into the highchair. Andrew looks like his father, they say . . . Guy Williams, who went back to Boston where his friends are . . . and entertainment . . . Too DEAD in Egypt, he was heard many times to say. But mostly the baby has his mother's looks . . . the usual Babbidge baby look, power in both hands and a chill in the eyes.

Ernie says, "Thanks a trillion, Eugenia, for doing those shirts for me." He tips an imaginary cowboy hat . . . his big smile plastered all over his face.

"It was nothing, Uncle Ernie. We love having you."

Lillian says, "Church was good, Blackstone. Everybody asked about you. Walt's wife especially. She has it in her head you're going to kill yourself like Walt did."

"That so?" says Blackstone. He bites his right thumbnail and spits a chunk on the floor.

Lillian sighs deeply. "When are you getting your hair cut, Blackstone? You are starting to look like a wild man."

Blackstone watches Lillian's hands cutting up the apples. Lillian's belted dress is a print of big peaches . . . the dress the pastor's wife used to wear a lot.

She says, "You could have it cut Monday night. Steve's is open till nine on Mondays."

"It's just hair," says Blackstone. "You afraid of hair?"

Ernie laughs, "Heee-hah!" and slaps his leg.

"No," Lillian says and smiles.

Junie comes from the little back room of bunk beds, bounding over the mattresses and sleeping bags. Blackstone studies her polar bear slippers. Junie says, "You want help with the apples, Mama?"

Lillian presses the paring knife into Junie's hand. "Yes, sweetie. Thanks." She gives Junie's back a little quickie rub.

Blackstone spits out another fingernail.

Lillian runs water into a pitcher, lines up several packs of Kool-Aid on the front of the sink. All of the smiling Kool-Aid faces are purple. She says to her husband, "I wanted to have our picture taken down at the mall before cold weather . . . You know, a family portrait we can all be proud of . . . You know, a CHRISTIAN-looking family. I'd like the big one for us and maybe one big one for your mother for Christmas . . . and little ones to send to the rest of your people up home. All your sisters keep nice albums, you know." She turns and faces him with a smiling purple packet in her right hand. "They are having a special at the mall next week. Mr. Bob and Miss Carole are going down Saturday and we can ride with them, they said. No excuses, Blackstone. They even said they'd loan us the money for the pictures till Lucien gets your pay to you . . . or we can take it out of Junie's on Thursday. Gosh . . . that gives you a whole week to get your hair taken care of . . . You must have enough money to get your hair cut."

Blackstone's mustache flickers. Then his many little teeth make a smile. "Women . . . I got forty-seven cents . . . and every penny we get into this house from now on is going into my truck. The truck is our only hope now. Your Malibu . . . she's hist'ry."

The table fills up with kids.

Mark pulls up a chair next to Junie and gives her arm a squeeze. "MUSCLE!" he says, doing the Popeye voice Luke is an expert at.

"Mama!" Junie whines. "He's really *squeezing*."

Eugenia says, "Mark! You animal! Shape up!"

Mark grins his big split-toothed grin, pitches a pea at Eugenia.

Lillian takes some little pouches of fast meat from the kettle of boiling water.

Blackstone pockets his knife. Fussily he arranges his workcap on a pile of papers next to the refrigerator. His hair is flattened to his head in the shape of his cap's brim. He sits down with a sigh.

Lillian works her way around the table, emptying the fast meat pouches into plates.

Blackstone starts to give the blessing before Lillian has gotten to every plate. "PRAISE GOD FOR THESE BLESSINGS AND FOR THIS FAMILY'S HEALTH AND WELL-BEING . . ."

All during the blessing the smaller children study the chestnut-haired woman who Ernie has his arm around.

"AMEN," says Blackstone.

Lillian finishes giving out the fast meat and sits, tucking her dress of big peaches around her legs. She says, "So . . . you sing, too, Miss Gail . . . That's wonderful."

"Yes," says the woman softly. "I've been working the bars on the lake this summer . . . and a little bit at Old Orchard, Portsmouth, Lewiston, Portland, Bangor . . . all the local stuff. My group is called the Brownfield Posse. Have you heard of us?"

"No, I haven't," says Lillian. "Do you make records?"

The woman sighs. "We've done demos. But . . . it's a hard business to crack."

"Uncle Ernie is famous," says Anastasia.

"Yes, I know it." The woman laughs. "He has a wonderful voice. A wonderful talent."

Stacy squints up at Ernie. He leans toward her and sings a line of "Pussyfootin'" in a comical off-key voice.

Mark spits a piece of fast meat out onto his plate.

Lillian's eyes widen on Mark's plate.

Blackstone has nothing but the fast meat on his plate. He just rubs his head, slow and hard, his thick dirty hair squirming through his fingers.

"Uncle Ernie . . . you are rich, aren't you?" Stacy asks.

Ernie frowns exaggeratedly. "Naw. A common misconception."

"What's *that* mean?" Jason Robert squints.

"Means I'm broke," Ernie says with a big smile.

Eugenia says, "Well, you certainly *are* famous. There was a carload of people here this morning taking pictures of your shirts." She giggles. "Ain't that a riot? The shirts out there hanging. They took pictures from all angles. We was in here laughing our heads off, wasn't we, Miss Lily-Ann?"

Lillian smiles, nods.

"Ain't you hot with your jacket on?" Jennifer asks the woman.

The woman is reaching for the margarine which is down by Anastasia's foot. "A little maybe," she says, smiling.

"Don't be rude!" scolds Eugenia.

Jennifer says, "I'm not being rude. I'm being *nice.*"

The woman smiles. "Yes, she's being nice. I just might take my jacket off in a minute." She looks around at the faces. "You all look so much like Ernie. There's a real family resemblance. But, heavens, Ernie! You and your brother are only half-brothers, aren't you?"

"That's right," says Ernie. "But we were raised real brothers by Grammie and Granpuh Blackstone. Our real mother is, you know . . . a problem person. But Grammie and Granpuh were SAINTS. I'll take you up to meet Grammie sometime. She's still alive. You'll LOVE Aroostook."

"It's THE county!" Anastasia giggles. "That's what Daddy always calls it."

Mark spits out another piece of the fast meat. "Jesus! What was that!" he croaks. "The gums of somebody's false teeth?"

The little kids shriek with laughter.

"False teeth!" Michelle howls.

The woman watches Blackstone butter a piece of bread. Then he folds it, dips it into the gravy of the fast meat.

Eugenia says, "Mark! You're not supposed to criticize food at the table."

Ernie leans to one side, picks out his tooled leather wallet. He says, "Get a load of this. Jeepers, I think I still have it. I've showed it to healthy women in all fifty-four states." He flaps through the photo section. "Ayup . . . here it is . . . hee hee. Get a load of *this*." He flattens a yellowed photo against the woman's hand. She looks at it and reddens. "Oh, Ernie!" She passes it back quick.

Ernie leans over the small table and flattens it into Junie's hand. "Pass it around, June," he says. "Bet you can't tell who it is."

Mark says, "Junie, let's have a look-see."

Junie pulls her hand away from Mark.

Mark jabs her calf with his workboot.

"Ow!" she cries. "Quit it, Mark!"

"Come on, Junie Loony, let's give that ol' picture a glimpse. It's nudity, ain't it?"

"Yessss," says the woman.

"What *is* it?" Lillian asks gravely.

"Rated X!" Ernie says deeply. "Don't anybody under eighteen look."

The woman's eyes flash to Blackstone and away.

Blackstone is looking at the woman, wiping his big mustache with a Happy Birthday napkin of red, yellow, and blue balloons . . . the last napkin in the household. Then his icy eyes slide over to the photo in Junie's hands.

Mark grabs for the photo but Junie flattens it against her leg.

Lillian is half out of her seat.

Mark puts his head on Junie's shoulder, trying to see the picture as she slowly turns it over.

Mark howls, "Holy fuckin' mother of Christ! It's the old man without a stitch! And who's those other naked people? . . . Hippies, ain't they, Junie? HIPPIES!!! By Jesus, Dad, *I* never known you had a heada hair like that . . . and a goddam full Christly beard to your belly button!" Mark's voice trembles. He seems about to burst into sobs. "In the old days EVERYBODY was hippies, huh Dad? Everybody . . . even your average REDNECK . . . even . . . even your Vietnam VET!"

Ernie says, "That's what I call my B.C. picture of Gene . . . BEFORE CHRIST. Get my meaning?"

Mark laughs an odd breathy laugh. "Poor Junie . . . can't take her eyes off the pecker. She's in a state of shock. Ain't never seen a stud that big before, have ya, Junie? Ain't never seen a stud that hairy. I don't expect you'll ever get that picture back, Ernie. She's gonna get it photocopied for sure and sell them to everybody at the mill . . . if I know her like I *think* I do." He makes another grab for the picture.

"Quit it!" Junie snarls.

Lillian comes at Junie from the other side. "Gimme the picture, Junie."

Junie squashes the picture harder against her leg, her eyes glassy with tears. "Ain't nuthin', Mama."

Lillian lunges for the picture.

"Cripes, I'm sorry." Ernie laughs nervously. "I didn't mean for all this."

Junie scrambles around under the table amongst the legs and feet and serving dishes. One small cold-looking potato comes bouncing out of the struggle and stops at the door.

When Blackstone moves, everybody freezes. He lurches to his feet. He takes a few steps to the nearest mattress and collapses . . . spread-eagle . . . then draws his tattooed forearm across his face . . . as if to hide his face from the light.

18

Blackstone works the timing light, his mind lost in the whirring clacking motion of the motor. It is 3:20 in the morning in Miracle City, moths flapping like mad against the mercury lamp above, the oniony smells of Miracle City suppers long gone. He stops to squash a mosquito on the side of his neck, sees Ernie . . . the big smile he is famous for plastered all over his face.

"Hey, Stone Man!" Ernie hoots. He puts his free hand out to lean against the truck fender, a warm-looking can of beer in the other.

Blackstone says, "What's up?"

Ernie closes his eyes, rocks to and fro. His ridiculous and resplendent silk shirt, black with enormous red roses, is unbuttoned. His jeans are cut off above the knees . . . a real hatchet job. He wears no belt. The jeans look about ready to drop.

"Wife and the girls say you got a couple calls here yesterday from some guy trying to track you down," Blackstone tells him. "Not a fan."

"Uh-oh." Ernie sighs. "Did he say he was my promoter? Did he say his name was Conroy?"

"I wouldn't know," Blackstone murmurs.

Ernie's grin is gone. He speaks in a dark raspy voice, "Old Ernie says to tell those kind of people to kiss my ass."

Blackstone lays the timing light down easy.

Ernie says, "You win."

Blackstone backs away from the truck. "Look," he says. "Get away from that engine, wouldya?"

"Heeeee-hah!" Ernie laughs. He sways.

Blackstone says, "What are you on, man?"

"A little little little LITTLE bit of everything." Ernie pretend-measures an inch with the fingers of his free hand.

Blackstone says, "Where's your Maverick?"

Ernie giggles.

Blackstone sighs. "When you get like this, man, you scare the hell out of me."

Ernie winces exaggeratedly. "Shhhhhhh! Don't say that, Gene. I'm going to be all right."

"Using yourself up on coke an' shit ain't the way."

Ernie resumes his big smile, gives a little hop. "Don't rail me, brother. You're beginning to sound like Granpuh just before he busted my goddam wrist! Yep . . . I see it before me . . . spittin' image of Granpuh . . . goddam repulsive bone-breakin' bastard. I say, man . . . leave me be! No sermons on this nice PINK night." He squints up into the mercury lamp fixed high on a pine. "Heeeeee-hah!"

Blackstone wrenches a red bandanna from his pocket, wipes his forehead and mustache. He sees that Ernie is barefoot, the right big toe bleeding blackly.

Ernie stops rocking, says softly, "Why you rail me? . . . You ain't clean."

Blackstone's eyes widen.

Ernie giggles. "Ain't NOBODY snort more coke, gulp more V.O., and gobble up more acid than you used ta . . . BEFORE

153

CHRIST." He giggles again. In the camps and trailers along the weedy puddly road, there's the thumps and whispers of stirring neighbors. Blackstone just keeps his usual grave silence. Ernie says, "Okay, okay, okay, Gene, you win. I say YOU WIN! I'm ready to accept the Lord. What do I do? Get on my knees . . . right?" He sways way to the left.

Blackstone grabs him by the arm. "Watch out for that fan, Ernest!"

Ernie looks at the hand on his arm. He whispers, "You was always such a hot shit. Rock of the earth . . . Rock of the fuckin' EARTH." He giggles. "I mean Grammie woulda had your shits bronzed if she had money. But Jesus. I ain't seen nobody more crazier'n you . . . Mister Man. I mean, I wasn't goin' to be the one to tell Grammie right out. Uh-uh. Not me. I mean . . . I never saw no meaner goddam ornery crazy guy than you. Ya gotta respect a thing like that, I say to myself. I mean . . . Gene, you used to be the friggin' ultimate." He looks up and down the road, from window to window, door to door . . . covers his lips with his free hand, says huskily through his fingers, "What I seen is . . ." He glances at the open doorway of Blackstone's glossy dark-green trailer with the bicycles against the step. "I mean . . . I seen you really tear ass and I ain't seen nuthin' like it since! Jesus . . . and I've seen A LOT! Jesus . . . my goddam brother. Damn it, Gene . . . I want to be with the heroes. I'll stay right here with you, Gene. Right here in this town . . . I'll get me a little place. Cute like this. Close by . . . gosh . . . why not. I say, fuck the world . . . fuck bucks . . . fuck fuck. Ain't no place like home and home is where your goddam brother is."

He looks up through the pink light to the stars. He rubs his face like he wants to rip it off.

Blackstone reaches inside the truck to switch off the motor.

The silence is sudden.

Ernie keeps talking . . . and sobbing. He stops to turn the beer can up for one last big swallow, then sinks to his knees in the weeds. He sighs. "You win. You win. I'll accept Christ. Help me, Gene. Help me do it." He folds his hands like a child at prayer.

Blackstone squats down in front of him. "Listen, man . . . it's your decision," he says deeply. "You give your heart and soul to the Lord. It ain't nothing to do with me."

A couple of camps down, somebody flashes their porch light.

"But . . . ," says Ernie, getting a grip on Blackstone's forearms.

"Will you guys shut the Christ up!!!" somebody hollers nearby.

Ernie tries to whisper, but it comes out half-whisper, half-howl, still gripping Blackstone's forearms . . . "But . . . be honest now, Gene. Don't give me no shit. Man to man, you know. Look me in the eye. Tell me like it is . . . There ain't NOBODY up in the sky, is there, Gene? No Big Guy in the Sky. No big Dad. It's just . . . sky. Right? Right? Are ya hearin' me? It's EMPTY . . . right?"

"I'm calling the deputy now!" a voice wails a few doors down. "Roger's dialing the phone now! He's dialed the first three numbers!"

Ernie squeezes more tightly on Blackstone's forearms . . . a squeeze meant to hurt. He says, "I mean . . . I mean . . . heeee-hah! . . . Look me right in the eye, Gene, and tell me I'm fulla shit . . . that . . . that you . . . well . . . I mean . . . ask ANYBODY . . ." He flings one hand toward the Babbidge trailer. "Ask 'em. Ask 'em all about it! Pin 'em down! Ask 'em who . . . Ask 'em . . . say . . . say this . . . say, you know it's true . . . that . . . fuck, Gene . . . listen, YOU know it's true and I know it's true that . . . around here there ain't no goddam God but YOU."

19

The tiny Coldspot Café isn't really big enough. The doorman starts turning people away. In the parking lot and along the lake, there's legs running through headlights, horns blowing, firecrackers, screams, and guffaws. Inside the Coldspot, the doorman's eyes glitter on the crowd.

Gail O'Wril and Ernie Train test the mike. It squeals so Ernie fools with it a little. The crowd gets terribly quiet. Ernie says close into the mike that he and Gail are going to start doing shows together in the area . . . that he loves this area . . . and wants to settle here. He says he wants to give up the big road shows for a while and lead a wholesome life here in this wholesome beautiful town of Egypt.

The cheers and hand clapping and whistling and foot stomping and catcalls go off like a bomb.

Ernie and Gail wait it out, smiling, nodding.

Then Ernie and Gail bring their mouths close to the shared mike like they are about to kiss it. In the barroom light there is something disquieting about Ernie's bare bare face, perfect black against the perfect creamy white, like a wooden man. In the doorway behind the doorman, a dozen faces stare.

On and on two voices run together, singing "My Last Hope," the song Ernie is most famous for . . . always sung solo and a bit mocking. But now with Gail the song seems thicker, sweeter, more generous . . . almost holy. When Ernie smiles his famous smile, it seems for once a true smile.

20

Blackstone folds his forearms on the table. Instead of closing his eyes, he looks hard into the eyes of his children and his wife. He says deeply, "LORD, HEAR US PRAISE YOUR NAME TONIGHT. EVEN THOUGH WE ARE PRETTY MUCH OUT OF FOOD AND WHAT WE HAVE ON THE TABLE SOME OF US TONIGHT HAVE SAID IT ISN'T MUCH OF A MEAL . . . WE ARE GLAD TO GET IT . . . THAT PROBABLY OVER IN RUSSIA THERE'S PEOPLE LIKE US BEING TORTURED . . . THAT EVEN WORSE THAN TORTURES, THEY CAN'T SPEAK YOUR BLESSED NAME . . . YOUR NAME THAT FEELS LIKE FOOD IN MY MOUTH. DEAR JESUS. SWEET JESUS. JESUS. JESUS. JESUS. JESUS. JESUS. JESUS. JESUS . . ." He covers his face with his hands so that the name spoken over and over and over is almost not recognizable.

21

When Lillian sees the doorless maroon GMC yard rig with the battered oxygen and acetylene tanks chained to the cab and the deputy's jeep and the brown sheriff's cruiser pull up under the trees out front, she tries to lock the door . . . but the old thing won't catch.

Eugenia tightens the sash of her robe, her face looking like a prizefighter's when she is so suddenly awakened. "Who is it?" she asks.

Lillian doesn't move away from the door. She has her head cocked, waiting for the door to make a noise. "Nobody I want to see."

Eugenia stands by the window, watches the jeep door jerk open. "S'pose there's trouble over there to Eve's . . . big drug bust or something?" she suggests huskily.

Lillian says, "My heart is going a hundred miles per hour, for gosh sakes." She grips a fistful of her blouse.

Eugenia says, "They're coming here . . . It's Big Lucien with them . . . Wonder what *he* wants?"

Lillian puts her foot against the door.

"Dear Jesus," Eugenia whimpers. "It's something bad, isn't it, Miss Lily-Ann?"

Lillian looks at her sneaker up against the door . . . a gray and rubber rag of a sneaker . . . not anything to keep out three men. There's a soft knock. Lillian says, "What do you want, Lucien?"

"Lillian . . . diss sheriff wants to talk wit you if he can . . . for a few minutes."

Eugenia breathes, "Dear Jesus."

Lillian shouts through the door, "What's he want to talk to me about?"

"Lillian . . . not good to talk wit a door in de middle . . . Very unplessant . . . Open up."

Lillian says, "Where's my husband?"

Lucien rattles the doorknob. "Lillian, dearie," he says coaxingly.

"WHERE IS MY HUSBAND!!" she shrieks.

Eugenia hugs herself, whispers to God.

Lucien says, "He iss gone to Sanford for a car . . . No reaching him . . . not now. But . . . can't wait for dat. De sheriff he wants you to hear him. He iss a *nice* person . . . a nice guy. I know him a long time . . . Please hear him. It iss about dat feller Ernie . . . He stay here wit you? . . . Some relation? . . . Aye? . . . A relative?"

"YESSSS," Lillian sobs.

"I don't know how to make dese words right . . . but de man found hung in woods . . . lit-tle bit ago. De sheriff he talk to you all you need to know, Lillian. Somebody has to go make some identification uff de man's body. He wants to talk to you about dat."

Eugenia wails.

Lillian says, "I don't want any sheriff in here."

"He iss juss going to talk wit you . . . He . . . he wants to make you feel better . . . need a lit-tle talk. He can tell you where Gene has to go to identify dat way. Also wants to talk to you a lit-tle bit about Ernie . . . about Ernie in general."

"No, please!" Lillian sobs. "Talk to Blackstone! I don't want any cops in my house. Please! Please! Please! Please!"

"Mrs. Babbidge," another voice calls gently.

"STAY OUT!!!" she screams.

22

Lillian stands by the gas stove heating a pan of milk . . . the last milk in the house. All night the family has been listening to Blackstone bawl. His grief frightens them. Some have kept their heads buried with pillows or teddies. Lillian knows he'll refuse the milk . . . say, no . . . give it to the babies. But then she'll insist. She'll say, but if you drink it, you'll do us all a favor . . . you'll do all of Miracle City a favor! You're keeping the whole wide world awake. She has never seen her husband cry before this. How childlike his shuddering shoulders, his kneading of the blankets! And all that sniffling and snuffling of the nose! And most disquieting of all is . . . yes, he wants the milk, thank you . . . sits up to the edge of the mattress to drink it . . . his face grotesque, full of bloat . . . he raises the cup . . .

23

Blackstone straddles a kitchen chair backwards, his head bent forward as if in prayer. Eugenia works the scissors with vigor, stabbing and chopping as if the black tufty hair was a monster fighting back.

Lillian comes from the bathroom in yesterday's cotton shorts and striped blouse. She stands by the room divider a long while studying

158

the hair on the linoleum. She says, "Well, look who finally brought Samson to his knees!"

Eugenia smiles.

Lillian starts a little pan of water and yawns, turns and looks into Blackstone's eyes. Then she turns back and studies the calendar, puts a few marks on it with a stubby pencil.

Eugenia takes her father's head into both hands, gives it a little rocking. "Little grayer than the last time I cut it, Daddy."

Lillian says, "Forty-five and half-alive." Then she giggles.

Eugenia says, "Miss Lily-Ann! You're a poet and don't know it!"

"Yep," says Lillian.

Eugenia leans forward and blows hard at each shoulder, then blows at the nape of his neck. She says, "I wouldn't wear that T-shirt today, Daddy. You'll itch all the way and have to stop somewheres."

"Right," he says.

As he stands, Lillian looks him up and down. She moves around the tiny trailer kitchen gracefully like on ice skates. "Well, now," she says. "If you get rid of that barbaric mustache, you'd look like a gentleman we could all admire."

He grins his rare wide grin. "I will when you shave yourself bald and cut off your tits."

"DADDY!" shrieks Eugenia.

Lillian turns the flame off under the gurgling pan. "I don't know how your people are going to be able to STAND you for three whole days," she says.

Blackstone says, "Ain't none of my people to mind a bit. They're each an' every one on the road to hell."

Eugenia sighs. "I wish I was going to Aroostook. I want to meet Grammie."

Blackstone lifts a chamois shirt from a rack behind the door, just ironed, blood red.

The hearse makes no sound. They just see the reflections of sun flutter over the walls.

"It's here," says Lillian.

Eugenia rolls her father's dress clothes up, works them tightly into an IGA bag.

Lillian says, "Blackstone, please hug me goodbye."

He hugs her hard. He buries his face in her neck.

159

She giggles. "None of THAT! We don't want it to get around about how passionate you are!"

Eugenia goes to the door and looks out at the hearse. It is silver-gray. The casket through the smoky glass looks black and vast and terrible.

Blackstone goes out, gets into the front seat with his bag of dress-up clothes. He puts the window down and rests his elbow there. The red of his shirt sleeve is the only color.

The women watch his face in silence. They can tell by the look in his eyes that the driver has just said something friendly. But Blackstone doesn't say much of anything back . . . He is not a friendly man.

FIVE

The Crusher

1

THE SKY is the bluest blue, a cartoon blue.

The crusher is red and vast and it howls. It is swallowing a 1976 Pinto. It's the same crusher and crusher crew Big Lucien always hires when he needs a fast buck.

The man who works the levers hardly moves . . . just his hair which the icy wind gives a funny flutter to. He is a small-built man. His hand on the lever is bare, gray-knuckled by the cold, his nose red, his knitted cap blue . . . too ordinary a man to be standing so close and so cavalier to a monster.

A fork loader brings the crusher a gored and rusty Rambler. The crusher eats the Rambler. The Rambler doesn't fight back. It just shivers as it enters the jaws. The windshield pops. The crusher howls lustily.

The crusher man working the levers slow and easy has a faraway look in his eye.

2

Gussie Crocker Letourneau is small . . . pint-sized, they call it . . . too small a young woman for her big "HAW! HAW!" of a laugh. And her hat is way too big . . . a wide-brimmed brown felt mountain hat. When she wears it, not a sprig of her pinkish Crocker hair shows. She is named August after her mother. The mother August is tall.

Gussie sits on the edge of the bed with a plate of canned stew watching the news. It's a big bed. It's the kind of bed that's so big they make special sheets for it.

Gussie is just home from work so she doesn't have her big winter boots off yet. And she hasn't eaten enough stew yet to smooth out her cranky expression. Josh and Bubba take up the rest of the bed. They are long-limbed babies . . . almost majestic . . . nothing like Gussie. In the darkness of the kitchenette a few feet away stands the babies' father, Severin Letourneau. All that shows of him is the white of his long johns and the glitter of his eyes. He is probably getting himself a second or third bowl of stew. He is always eating. He is just like a boy.

When the landlord unlocks the door and steps in, Severin doesn't move at all . . . not even to lay his spoon down.

The landlord always looks as surprised as they do when he barges in on them like this . . . like somebody has given him a big push into the room.

Lowering her spoon into her bowl, Gussie says, "You sure are quiet, Mr. Howe."

In the dark kitchenette, Severin keeps his silence. But he shifts a little. The light from the bedroom ceiling strikes his profile . . . gives him away. He is tall . . . long-tall. And he is sinewy and slope-shouldered . . . sort of like an animal made to wriggle out and away through cracks and crannies. He is trying to disappear now . . . but he can't. There is something about him that always catches the eye . . . his Indianness, his mother Patty's thick-lidded dark eyes . . . the red of his bandanna . . . the black and disquieting yield of his long, long hair. Even his long johns. How white! He is always showy without trying . . . twice as showy as his father, Armand Letourneau.

The landlord is staring hard at the long johns.

Gussie says, "Excuse the mess. I just got home."

The landlord's eyes glide contemptuously across the wall of Rocky and Rambo posters . . . and the poster of Smurfs. He studies the heap of toys and clothes in the corner near the heat register. "It's time we have a little talk, August," he says. He always brings the smell of something like vinyl into the room. Josh, the older, more majestic baby, works his way to the edge of the bed, sniffing the air. Josh has nothing on but a pajama top of jet planes on a yellow sky.

"Excuse me if I just interrupted your changing your baby's pants," says the landlord.

"I wasn't changing no pants," says Gussie.

There is a sound like maybe Severin is putting his spoon and bowl in the sink.

"Do I smell pizza?" the landlord says. He is smiling faintly.

"No," says Gussie. "It's stew." She gets off the bed.

"Oh," says the landlord. "Maybe you had pizza yesterday . . . or the day before."

Josh plops off the bed and runs at the landlord, his wee genitals wagging. He holds a set of keys out to the landlord, but the landlord ignores him. He says, "We have to make arrangements on this rent . . . tonight."

There are keys everywhere in the room. Sets of keys. Keys in huge clumps. Keys in cans. Keys on the wooden chair by the bed. Keys on the bed. Keys by the landlord's foot.

Gussie snarls, "I don't smell no pizza." She wrinkles her nose. "We haven't had pizza for the wickedest long time."

The landlord sighs deeply. "Dear, I don't care about your pizza. You can have all the pizza you want. We are talking about *rent* now." He smiles. His head is bald and pink with some hair on the sides. His face is pink and shaved . . . shaved to a blankness. His smile lasts only about two seconds.

Gussie says, "We haven't got any rent money this week, Mr. Howe. We was overdue for insurance for the truck . . . And last week was the sticker, you know how that goes . . . Front tires was fifty bucks apiece. And Severin doesn't get his pay regular, you know . . . We been hurtin'. They . . . "

"Your problems, dear, have nothing to do with me. I'm only here to make arrangements for you people to pay me what you owe me . . . tonight. Either that or I want you people and your . . . STUFF . . . out of here by Tuesday. I'm sorry."

Gussie looks at the landlord's feet which are surrounded by keys. She says almost cheerfully, "What if we promise to give you both our checks Friday? Severin's uncle should be done crushing by Friday . . . He's going to pay everybody off that day, you know. We'll be RICH. We'll come right over from work and sign every penny we got right over to you . . . like we did that other time. You were happy about that before. Remember?"

The landlord says, "That's not good enough this time. I'm sorry. Your January payment will be due January first. So we need to get caught up here now for November and December. Understand what I'm saying?"

Gussie steps a little to the left, then a little backwards. Everywhere she steps there's bunches of keys crunching. She says, "It's not like we're not trying, you know. We are trying, you know."

The landlord looks at her with a cool and level gaze.

Gussie still has her bowl of stew in her hands . . . a big bowl of stew for so small a woman. She rocks it menacingly and snarls, "Where you think we're supposed to come by that kinda money? . . . Rob a friggin' bank!!?"

The landlord throws his hands up like he expects her stew to wind up in his face. He chuckles. "It's none of my business where you get the money, August. I just need to see it in my hand right now . . . before I walk out of here in about two minutes . . . or I'll have to ask you to move. That's all there is to it. We don't need to go into your private life . . . your problems. Okay? Just get the money out right now and I'll make out the receipt. Please hurry." He shakes his sleeve back, checks his watch.

There is a scratching sound and the smell of a cigarette.

The landlord smiles. "Now the cigarette company doesn't let your husband have cigarettes for nothing, does it?"

Gussie swipes off her big hat, whaps the corner of the bed with it a couple times. She shrieks. It is hard to tell what it is she's shrieking but it sounds like swear words . . . the Bible kind.

The landlord is still smiling . . . faintly. And he says calmly, "Dear . . . dear . . ."

Gussie's words get clearer after a while. She's saying, "Get out, goddammit . . . Get the hell out! Goddammit . . . get out! Get out!"

The landlord says, "Okay, okay. I want you to listen to me now. I've listened to you. Okay? Okay?" He waits with patience while Gussie gets control of herself. Then he sighs deeply, glances at his watch again and continues. "Now . . . you think you are the only one to have troubles. I have listened to all your excuses. But, dear, I have bills, too. It's not my fault you people can't manage your money right . . . or don't have the initiative to get better jobs or training or however that goes." His lip curls. "That's not my business. None of my concern. I'm not in the welfare game. This is how I make my living. It's my *work*. So . . . I'm afraid I have to ask you people to find another place. I'm giving you till Tuesday or I'll have to . . ." He sighs. ". . . get a court order and have the sheriff help you move."

"Where?!" Gussie howls.

"Where?!" Josh howls. His set of keys goes sailing past the landlord's head, then smacks the wall and drops to the floor with the rest.

3

Three men watch Severin Letourneau shovel out the Firebird. Here in the yard he is just eyes, just frozen breath and a pair of bare hands . . . just the dingly-dangly dancing straps of his aviator cap, what Gussie calls his "Snoopy cap." He's not exactly a spectacle. But it is hard to keep your eyes off him . . . How such a tall, slouchy, narrow-shouldered boy can throw so much snow around so fast. And as the red-orange Firebird emerges, he shovels even faster.

One of the men asks, "How's the motor, by the way? Is this the one they tell me is seized up?"

Severin shrugs, panting hard, sticks the shovel in the high wall of snow. "I don't know anything about that motor . . . You have to talk with the guy at the desk." He cracks open a fresh box of Marlboros as he strides toward his yard buggy, a three-color Toyota truck with tanks for the torches chained to the cab. He returns with a jack and four-way wrench in his hands, a cigarette in one corner of his mouth.

The three customers talk about the Firebird and other Firebirds they have known as Severin works the jack and the Firebird rises. When the wind slams the dry top snow down the long aisles of cars, the three men pull their heads into their collars and turn their backs.

Severin reaches for the wrench. He has a peculiar way of working the wrench, all shoulders and elbows . . . his kind of showy way of doing it. When the second lug lets go, he loses his balance. His face slams into the fender. His cigarette drops into a snowy footprint. The men laugh. "Atta go!" one praises. Severin cups his hand to his mouth. His hand fills with blood.

One of the men says, "Jesus! You all right?"

"I'm all right," says Severin.

The three men chuckle. One says, "That looked pretty funny how you did that . . . Weeeooop, SPLAT! Just like that. Weeeooop, SPLAT!" They all laugh nervously.

One says a little bit softly, "They say from the neck up you bleed the worst. I heard that once."

Severin spits into the snow. He says, "I mighta swallowed my tooth."

"Awww!" one man says. "If you swallow it, the tooth fairy doesn't come."

The men laugh, slap their thighs.

Severin gags. There's a silence with the men now as they watch him on all fours gagging.

In the near distance the crusher is roaring steadily on and on and on and on.

Severin looks up with a lewd and bloody grin, the tooth held high in his fingers.

"Well, there, by Gawd! You get the fairy after all, dontcha?" One of the men chuckles.

Severin paws around in the snow for his cigarette. He stands up, leans against the Firebird, strikes a kitchen match over a patch of rust in a showy, showy way.

4

After the customers leave with their four Firebird wheels, Severin takes his yard buggy over to the blue Baptist bus in the very heart of the yard. He sits in the open doorway of the bus to smoke and bleed in private. The big wind whips the leaves and pine spills around the inside of the bus. A Dixie cup bounces around in there. Severin turns his broken tooth in his fingers. His fingers are so cold, he can't really feel the tooth. He drops it twice. Finally he thrusts his hands deep in the pockets of his army jacket. The blood keeps moving warmly down his chin. He thinks about August . . . not his wife August . . . but her mother, the tall one. Maybe he'll drive over there after work, see if she's home from work just yet. She will mix up some salty water for him to slosh around in his mouth. Or maybe just give him a rag to suck. You never know with her. She might not do anything. She might just reach out and touch him.

5

The first time he laid eyes on August Crocker was around the time his mother and father were having a little trouble . . . came close to divorce. Patty had a restraining order fixed up by her lawyer to keep Armand out. All the doors in the old place were locked but Armand thought of the bulkhead and was down there in the cellar banging and grumbling his way toward the cellar stairs. Severin called "Papa! Papa!" and he started to open up the cellar door. His mother said in her low, always-soft voice, "Don't be dumb, Severin. If he gets in here, he'll squeeze our necks." She said this just as Severin was already swinging the door open and there was Armand at the bottom of the stairs looking up at them from under the gray cellar light, his eyes bleary and twinkly with tears, a cigarette on his bottom lip . . . He was what Mon Oncle Lucien called a "no-handed smoker."

Severin had never seen Armand squeeze necks before. It was not in his hands he got mad. It was in his mouth. And the madder he was, the less came out of his mouth you could recognize . . . It wasn't even French exactly . . . just a bunch of yowling and pacing and menacing-looking grins . . . a lot of showiness. Armand wouldn't squeeze the neck of a fly. He was just a lot of bluff. He was scared of thunderstorms. He wasn't happy around firecrackers or big-caliber guns, even balloons. Severin never saw his father break any-thing in a rage. And yet he never saw him cry before either till that night at the foot of the cellar stairs, so it was a time of new things.

"Shut the door," Patty said softly and deeply.

When Armand heard this, he made a lunge. He was big-bellied

even then and hulking with winter clothes, big boots. The whole house shook.

Patty slammed the door, sat down with her back against it, her feet against the hall wall.

"Patty!" Armand bellered through the door. That was the last word they could understand. After that it wasn't words. Any other man would have bashed the door down. But Armand didn't even rattle the knob.

That's when the Crockers moved into the old Harlan Cobb place up the road from them . . . great gray fields, gray barn . . . a yellow monster of a house . . . a million windows . . . a million doors.

"If I had kids with pointed heads like those Crockers, I wouldn't let them out in public without hats on," Patty was telling everybody at the Coldspot, where she worked. At the Coldspot, which has the only decent pizza for miles, the only decent BLT, and the only tap beer, word about the Crocker heads could go a long way.

While Patty and Severin were out by the mailbox one day digging dandelions for supper, three or four Crockers went whizzing past on old bikes. Patty rested her digger on her knee and stared after the Crockers a long, long time like they were a great spectacle.

This was the same year Severin had trouble with his eyes, something which the doctor predicted he'd outgrow. But for a while Patty and Severin looked alike with their black-frame glasses, straight black hair with bangs, and gentle, gentle ways. He was absolutely his mother's son. And yet when his parents sometimes called to him to come sleep with them on a Sunday morning . . . there in the big front bedroom with the fox hunt wallpaper . . . and Armand's old curled-tail dog sprawled on the floor on Armand's side of the bed . . . Severin would push closest to Armand, his ear hard to the ribs, listening to the boom, boom, boom. And there in the dawn, his eyes wide open, knowing he was too old, way too old, almost ten, Severin would secretly suck his thumb.

One day when Patty and Severin were at the IGA, they saw the Crockers up at close range . . . about five almost-teenage Crockers mobbed around the magazine rack. "Terrible terrible thing," Patty moaned in what could have been within earshot.

168

In the parking lot, while she was unlocking her tangerine-color Super Beetle, she moaned it again.

Then out came the mother August with her cart. Against the white sleeveless blouse her pregnancy was like a goose's egg, outlandish, hard, almost luminous. Crockers of all sizes shuffled behind her. They mostly had white T-shirts stretched out at the necks like they put them on by climbing through the tops. They all had pink or brownish-pink hair . . . no hair styles, just tufts . . . even the girls . . . no barrettes, no bows. You could not tell the girls from the boys by their hair.

Patty was having a little trouble with the window crank. It had bad threads. But she worked at it so she could overhear what the Crockers had to say to each other. She said softly and deeply into Severin's ear, "Don't stare at them, dummy."

So the both of them with their look-alike black glasses and their look-alike bangs kept their heads aimed straight ahead, with just the eyes rolling over to the left every couple of seconds.

The father, Robby, had been waiting in the van which said on the side of it: ROB CROCKER, FINISHED CARPENTRY. Telephone number underneath.

"He looks like an Indian to me," Patty whispered. "I know one when I see one."

Severin's eyes rolled to the left . . . terrified . . . terrified by Robby Crocker's Indianness, terrified by all those pink tufty heads bobbing about . . . and terrified as always of something which he could never put his finger on.

Armand used to let Severin drive the Super Beetle up and down the dirt part of the road. Patty always looked a little alarmed as Severin reached for the keys on the wall, but she never argued with Armand. NEVER. Unless it was the one big thing she couldn't stand . . . his hanging around over at Big Lucien's on poker nights and going with Big Lucien to the bars. Even then she wouldn't argue. Her voice was too soft to be raised. With her Indian looks and delicate ways, half of Egypt figured she was Japanese. What Patty would do to Armand if he did the unspeakable . . . poker at Lucien's . . . was to stuff everything from all the bureau drawers which was his into IGA bags and line them up by the kitchen door.

Armand would just step over the bags, chuckle, then head straight for the bedroom where she was waiting with her back toward him. He'd make murderous-sounding love to her and Severin would be in the next room scared out of his wits.

So although Patty didn't agree that Severin should drive the VW, she said nothing to Armand . . . just waited till he had left for work, then she would look Severin in the eye and say softly, "You will probably crash and be paralyzed to your neck."

Usually when Severin drove the Super Beetle, he'd go as far as the Barstows' driveway and turn there. He'd always listen to the radio as he rode along. He was tall for his age so he could reach the pedals just fine . . . and could see over the wheel . . . In fact, to anybody watching the orange bug sputter past, it probably looked like Patty herself driving . . . the hair, the glasses, the gentle hands.

From the Barstows' driveway, Severin could see the great yellow house in the distance. It filled him with terror.

When school let out for the summer, Severin made fifteen or more trips a day in the Super Beetle. Patty said he was wearing the car out. She told Armand one morning as Armand was just heading out the door to work. He just chuckled and said, "Iss dat all women do, diss worry worry worry?"

After his truck was gone from the dooryard, she turned to Severin and said, "I heard of a boy over in Shapleigh who got cancer in his legs from not getting enough exercise. He should have listened to his mother and walked more."

Severin grinned. "You're just saying that. Worry worry worry."

"Well." She sighed. "Laugh if you want, but that sore spot on your leg could be anything."

Severin laughed. "I haven't got any spots on my leg. Gawd."

That day it turned off quite hot by noon. The window cranks in the Super Beetle were broken off and after the usual fifteen trips to Barstow's, Severin began to sweat hard. He decided it was time to drive all the way up as far as the big yellow Crocker house and turn right in their driveway. He was going to maybe even play a joke on them or something . . . like maybe put a rock in their mailbox or something squishy if there was anything like that lying around nearby.

Well, there it was . . . up close . . . the great yellow house surrounded by the black wet-looking stumps of maple trees cut long ago. And everywhere . . . in the tall grass, in the windows, behind the latticework of the piazza . . . Crocker faces. He decided this was a bad time to put surprises in their mailbox. So he twisted the shift into reverse and stepped on the gas . . .

Fate had it that the accelerator cable under the pedal popped off at that moment. The pedal just went flat. Severin gazed at the pedal with sweaty eyes. He reached down and gave the pedal a grave feel. It was flat, all right. The sun thrummed on the glass, the metal. And with the windows stuck in the up position, Severin began to broil. Gosh, the engine went fine. But what could make a pedal flat like that, he wondered.

Crockers scuttled out from under the piazza and stood there squinting at him. They wore wrinkly summer shorts and T-shirts with stretched-out necks. They looked cool and calm and refreshed. All of them had pink hair and pointy heads . . . heads far more pointy than he remembered them from the IGA. Severin was horrified. He took his foot off the clutch. The car bucked and stalled. He turned up the radio. He poked some channel buttons. The heat inside the Super Beetle was good enough to steam wieners.

Soon two Crockers about Severin's age came from down the road on old Columbias. They whizzed right over to the tangerine-color car parked in their driveway . . . probably figured it was some guests. They looked at Severin through the steamy glass. Severin averted his eyes. More Crockers came from the tall grass nearby and looked in at him from the west side of the Super Beetle. Next came five or six rotund white geese, their wee blue eyes snapping with rage and wonder. They were geese the size of small men.

Behind Severin's glasses were pockets of heat 100 degrees apiece.

He poked at the radio buttons some more and found a station where there was a kid his age winning a Black Sabbath album by being first caller. He put the kid's voice up full blast. The Crockers' eyes and the eyes of the geese widened on his face.

After a while more Crockers came. It seemed like hundreds. Their pointy heads looked creepy in the sun. All the Crockers were talking to each other. The little ones squeaked, but the older ones sounded more like ordinary human voices. The heat became a solid thing inside the Super Beetle . . . like a hand pressed over Severin's nose and mouth.

Then he saw the mother August come out of the house. The screen door gave a bang behind her like a gunshot. She was wearing a print sleeveless blouse, her belly riding along in front, her long shapely arms going to and fro as she strode down the long driveway. There was a baby wearing training pants on her trail. It walked like rocks hurt its bare feet. It had the most pointy head of all. He or she. Who knows?

As the mother August looked through the window at Severin, he saw that she had one eye that was out of control . . . a bobbing sort of eye. A few drops of sweat dripped down Severin's top lip.

The mother beckoned him with her large snowy hand.

He could feel his heart beating in his liver, in his intestines and urinary tract. In his mouth. He decided to open the door.

His dripping beating body got a fast rude switch to chill.

"What's wrong, son?" August's voice came in with the cool air.

"My car. It's broke," he said. "I was turning around in your driveway . . . that's all . . . just turning around. The pedal . . . it's flat."

He stepped outdoors and pulled off his jersey and wiped his long narrow body with it, tugged off his glasses, mopped his eyes. He felt the Crocker eyes on him, on this new stripped-down view of him. He started to jiggle around . . . having to take a leak . . . It felt like the school globe in his bladder. And his stomach growled. And he was dying of thirst.

August sent the almost-big kids for tools in the shed that hooked the house to the barn. She went down on her elbows on the sandy car floor and studied the pedals. Her great long tawny ponytail spread to cover her back and even part of her dungarees. When the tools arrived, it took her only a minute or two to fix the pedal and explain what went wrong. She stooped and wiped the black from her hands onto her dungarees. Every move she made was wide and easy like a ballet. At this point Severin's jiggling was almost tap dancing. She looked at him a long moment, her one good green-gray eye moving all over him. She said in her strange way of talking, a voice of some other land, "Son, lookit over yonder there's a tree. You're welcome to it."

He headed for the tree. If she had said, "Piss on that VW wheel," he'd have done it.

He looked back once and saw that she was turned away to give him some privacy . . . but the kid Crockers just kept staring at him.

Then one morning in late summer as Severin was munching on a bowl of Special K, his mother, Patty, was trying to run water on a kettle of dishes but was getting only a trickle. She padded in her waitress sneakers over to the back door and looked out through the screen to the near distances. She said in her sweet slight voice, "You know that cement thing out there? The thing you jump off of?"

Severin put his spoon down, blinked.

"What we are going to do, you and me, is open it and see what's in it," she explained. She pushed out through the screen door and Severin galloped long-leggedly after her.

The sky out there was gray, the sun a bright white fuzzy spot over the birches.

"Severin . . . you take one end," Patty said deeply.

They grunted and struggled. It was like opening a tomb. The black foreverness of the well appeared. The cover scraped and eeked as they worked it off. Then it finally thunked to the grass. Patty and Severin both leaned over and aimed their identical black-frame glasses downward.

"Can't see a thing," said Patty, deeply, sweetly.

"Me neither," said Severin.

Patty shivered, rolled her eyes. They both listened a minute to the soundlessness of the well.

"We need a flashlight, I guess," said Patty, looking distracted. "And . . . I guess . . . a ladder. Do you know where Papa keeps his ladder?"

"Ladder?" Severin began to feel his heart beating in his bottom lip.

"Yes," she said softly, deeply. "To get down and see."

"But it's probably too far, Mama. Papa's ladder will fall down in there and get lost!"

"Severin, it's not deeper than the extension ladder. It'll be about the same. You'll see."

"What about snakes?" he said, his lip curling.

She gnawed her lip a little bit, smiled. "Naw . . . there's no poisonous snakes in Maine . . . They just eat little bugs."

He followed his mother into the barn to look for the ladder. He followed her into the kitchen for the flashlight. "You are wicked brave to go down there," he whispered. " 'Cause some snakes squeeze."

Patty giggled. "Don't be silly. This isn't Africa."

When they were back at the well again, a woodpecker was at work overhead in the birches . . . thot, thot, thot, thot, thot . . . Severin looked at the row of cloth buttons down the front of Patty's pink waitress uniform and a wing of her shiny hair swinging across her face as she leaned over the well for another peek. "Okay, Severin . . . Come on. Let's get this thing down," she said.

They started the ladder down . . . down . . . down. The price tag still attached by a wire to a rung went flapping by . . . gone.

When the ladder hit bottom, the end stuck out about two feet.

"See," said Patty's sweet delighted voice. "Didn't I tell you?" She wiggled the ladder some. "Gosh," she said. "It's narrow down there. You'd better go down. You are thinner. I'd probably get my fat rear stuck down there." She giggled.

Severin said, "I think we should call a company to come." He hooked his thumbs in his belt like Armand often did.

"No," said Patty. "We can't do that."

Severin was starting to suck in quick doses of air. Severin was a good boy . . . nearly always obeyed . . . even though Armand and Patty never threatened him with a belt or spatula. Sometimes Armand mentioned *le loup-garou*, who was out there looking to eat kids who got into their father's cigarettes . . . And then there was elves of *Père Noël* who watched you at ALL TIMES. But usually the things he had to do for Patty and Armand which he didn't want to do involved school or disgusting food like beets and cottage cheese. But this. THIS. He imagined for a moment FIFTY elves with belts and spatulas. But none of that was punishment enough. He said softly, "No."

"Be brave now," his mother said. "It's nothing." Her hand touched his hair. She gave him a little push. She even guided him onto the ladder. The woodpecker . . . thot, thot, thot, thot . . . a sort of drum roll.

"Hurry up now. Let's find out what we have for water down there." Her voice was her sweet pretty everyday voice, ordinary, and close to his ear. She pressed the flashlight into his fingers.

Down, down, down into the darkness. The crusty walls framed his mother's face. He couldn't see her eyes because of reflections on her glasses. Down, down, down. Her face grew small as an aspirin up there. There was a sound below. A little watery echo.

"Okay," his mother's voice said. "You are probably down far enough. Put on your light now."

He didn't put the light on. He just held it tight, turning it in his fingers.

"Severin, you okay?"

He didn't answer her.

For twenty minutes she called, but he wouldn't answer her.

In a while there were the voices of men . . . men from the salvage yard. His papa was unnaturally quiet . . . not much to say. His papa's face appeared at the top. "Severin!" he said sharply . . . No answer.

Armand started down the ladder. The ladder jiggled and thrashed under the great weight of him. In no time Armand came out of the well with Severin in his arms . . . the rippling red-eyed dragon damp and stinking with triumph against Severin's cheek.

Severin sprang from those arms, ran into the woods, his mother, father, everybody pounding after him to catch up. "Severin! Severin!" they called. He lost them all among the creamy birches and a deep ravine with high stone walls. In time he came back out on the Harlan Cobb Road. And there was the yellow house on the distant hill . . . all windows, all doors . . . gables and ells.

He roamed the Crocker fields for a while. The sky was getting windy and silver. Cool. He stole rhubarb from the Crockers' garden for supper. He ate it, squatting in the grass. Then for a nice rest, he lay spread-eagle in their Queen Anne's lace. The perfume was all around his head like a crown.

He took off his glasses and rubbed his eyes. It felt great to have his eyes bare. Everything looked much greener.

The Crockers' back door kept slamming. The squeaks of little Crockers playing didn't seem far away at all. He could almost make out actual words.

He sat up to look. He saw the mother August was out there, too
. . . walking with a pail. She wore her white sleeveless blouse . . .
loose, flapping. The belly was gone. She got herself waist deep in
loud geese. They drove their heads into the pail. Then she put her
hand, her big right hand, on one gander's head. He yanked his head
away. She did it again. He would not hold steady. And yet there was
always an instant when the hand looked like a funny little cap, the
gander's blue and silly small eyes turned up toward the woman's
face. But all this looked fairly fuzzy to Severin . . . his glasses left
on the ground by his foot. He was standing straight up in the field,
knowing August would see him. And she did. Her good eye fixed
on him suddenly. Fixed steady.

6

At noon Severin Letourneau eats his sandwich while standing over
the heat register, the straps of his Snoopy cap dancing madly. The
front of his army jacket is soaked with blood.

His father's breathing is for a few moments the only human noise
in the room, although it sounds like the peeps of mice.

All the men sprawled out in the plastic chairs along the wall watch
the arrival of Wayne Hutchins. He is whistling something Christmasy. He walks with a sort of hop like a jay, heads straight for the
coffee maker by the file cabinet. "Good morning! Good morning!
Lovely day!" he says breathlessly.

Something cracks against the side of the building. It's the icy wind
getting meaner by the minute. Severin can feel his heart beating
along the broken root of his tooth.

Armand snorts, "Diss not morning, Hutchins . . . unless you are
on California time perhaps."

Wayne chuckles, carries his cup of coffee toward the vacant chair
between Carl the road commissioner and old Clarence Farrington
. . . two of the regular office hang-outs. There are eight lighted cigarettes and a cigar all going at once, the great gray mixed-up smoke
drooping around chair legs and boots. Wayne steps high over a silvery Sherman-tank-type object. It's the Moontrekker, what Big Lucien has just found in the trunk of a wrecked Ford Tempo.

Wayne looks back. "What the hell was that?"

There's the united chuckle of many men.

Wayne gasps, "Holy shit! Is it bigger than a breadbox or what??!!" He squats down and gives the Moontrekker an all-over feel. It bursts to life in his hands, twinkling and buzzing. Its bulldozer track churns. He lets it back onto the floor and it buzzes around merrily . . . then returns to his feet.

Wayne wonders, "That thing operated remote control or something?" He studies the hands of each man. Some of them hide their hands. Some hold their hands open. Some just keep stuffing their sandwiches into their mouths, gulping Cokes, looking bored.

Wayne sits down with his coffee, rubs one eye hard with his palm . . . turns to the road commissioner and sighs. "This ain't a normal place."

Crowe Bovey comes in from the back way, plunks a cold gummy fuel pump on the counter, glares at Hutchins . . . then paws through a pile of coats for his flat-looking sandwich. Severin watches Crowe hard all the while Crowe's back is to him . . . Crowe Bovey . . . Big Lucien's best yard man, they say. Big Lucien's slave, they say.

Big Lucien is behind the counter this morning, deep in his broken spring rocker. All anybody coming through the door would see of him is one of his green rubber boots.

One of the Moontrekker's little lights pops to life, then fades. Wayne is out of his seat, jabs the Moontrekker with his foot. The Moontrekker purrs. Wayne says, "It's you, Big Mr. Pluto, ain't it? It's you operatin' this dandy rig." Wayne peeks around the corner to get a better view of the boss.

Dave the desk man tells Crowe about the set of hubcaps Jimmy Fogg just called for.

Wayne Hutchins paws his denim vest for a smoke. He speaks to the Moontrekker. "If you are God, give me a sign."

A little hatch on one side of the Moontrekker buzzes open and a wee American flag appears, seeming to be waved by a tiny hand. Wee red, white, and blue search lights point in every direction. A tinny version of "Yankee Doodle" plays.

The men howl with laughter, Armand Letourneau sliding right down in his seat . . . "Haw! Haw! Haw! Haw!"

177

Crowe Bovey has vanished. There is just his mashed sandwich on the counter next to the gummy fuel pump and the phone.

The Moontrekker lurches forward and bumbles over old Clarence Farrington's left foot.

Armand laughs so hard he gets caught in one of his phlegmy coughs . . . spits into his handkerchief.

Now the Moontrekker is playing "The Star-Spangled Banner" and is headed for Gene Babbidge's foot.

Old Clarence Farrington says, "I heard the commies got bigger ones, you know."

"No way!" howls Dave the desk man. "You can't buy batt'ries in Russia."

When the tune ends, the little flag vanishes, the hatch flaps shut, the twinkling and buzzing stops. There is just the sound of the mean wind outside. Shy chubby Bobby Ward peels the Saran Wrap off his third jelly sandwich.

7

Severin watches the landlord's bright, bright house through its fortress of blue spruce trees . . . his right hand on the shift knob, ready for a fast getaway. A fresh Marlboro flutters on his swollen bottom lip. Both his babies are in the truck with him. They are crying.

When Gussie climbs back up on the high seat, she is gasping, her big-brimmed felt hat cockeyed. She slams the door three times before it latches.

"Anybody see you?" Severin asks, giving the shift a hard shove forward. The babies wail harder to drown out his voice. He kicks the clutch in, twists the key, and the engine comes to life raggedly.

Gussie snarls, "The man is going to be pissed when he sees we could only come up with one check." She takes Bubba onto her right thigh, Josh on her left. "Ride the horses! Ride 'em hard!" she tells them. Her big winter boots stomp the floor. The babies bounce. But they keep crying their wretched sleepy cries. "Ride the horses! Ride 'em hard! Ride the horses! Ride 'em hard!"

The truck crunches along down the white winding road.

"You always do that," Severin says softly. "You promise the guy more than we can handle."

Gussie stops jiggling the babies, looks at Severin through slitted eyes. She says, "Josh! Bubba! If you two don't shut up in about three seconds, I'll make the monster man smile at you again."

Both Bubba and Josh flash horrified glances toward their father . . . at his face lit ghoulishly green by the dash lights . . . the black busted tooth hole, the lip, the cigarette.

Severin says deeply, "Don't do that again, Gussie."

"Monse man," says Josh gravely.

Severin glares at his wife and says, "See what you got started?"

8

Gussie Crocker had invited Severin Letourneau to her sixteenth birthday party. Severin was sixteen, too, but told everybody he was eighteen. He had stopped needing eyeglasses by then but wore aviator sunglasses everywhere . . . even indoors . . . even in school . . . even on *cloudy days*. He seemed distant and manly to girls. He wore a red bandanna around his long slippery-looking black hair . . . bragged he was half-Indian to some . . . told others he was 100 percent . . . bragged he could fix cars . . . told Gussie he had been in prison for a while . . . "It was a rough place."

When he showed up at the party, it was the first time he had seen the inside of the Crocker house. The kitchen smelled bad. Like rotten fruit, he thought . . . before he realized it was the big weird pink cake on the drainboard . . . Gussie's birthday cake. But no Gussie. She was late, they said. "Have a seat."

Not far from him the mother August sat on a chrome-leg chair with perfect posture. She said, "I know it's time when I cain't reach my toes."

The mother August's belly was so great and straining it was shocking to look at. Severin tried not to look.

Robby mumbled, "Lemme see."

He squatted down to her bare feet, took the toenail clippers from her hand. He wore gray workpants, gray workshirt. There was the shape of a tape measure in one of his rear pockets. When the little fan on the floor swept Robby's way, his hair fluttered and flapped like a snow-white fighting cock. His palms looked stiff. But so did the foot. Coming together, the foot and hand made a little scratchy noise.

Crocker boys, nearly as old as Severin, came ramming and stomping into the kitchen through the way of the shed . . . grim, green-eyed, caught by the rain. They made a sopping pile of wet sweatshirts and socks on the floor. "Where's Gussie?" "Where's Gussie?" "Where's Gussie?" each one asked.

A Crocker dumping Comet into the pantry sink squeaked, "Ain't here!"

August kept her toes cocked, her eyes on Robby.

Severin tried not to look at the toes.

Robby mumbled something now and then. Severin could not make out a word of it. The toenails, looking waxy as suet, fell away in chunks under the clippers.

Two Crockers in diapers and plastic pants watched their father's hands work the clippers, their green eyes big with alarm. They didn't seem to trust his hands on her foot.

"Can't we have a party anyways . . . NOW?" wondered a small Crocker wearing a lobster claw potholder glove. As the fan swept around, pink hair on each and every Crocker child raised up like a flame, then died.

One of them with his chin in his hands, his eyes on the ghastly pink cake said, "You can't have a party for somebody without her being at the party, even if it takes FOREVER, even if she dies somewheres and we're all waitin' . . . You just gotta keep on waitin'."

Severin was deathly still in the old vinyl chair in the corner of the kitchen . . . his eyes barely moving behind his aviator sunglasses. Even as a Crocker toddler came up to him and put its hand on his knee, Severin Letourneau had nothing to say. Another one climbed up on the arm of the chair and touched Severin's aviator sunglasses. Then the buttons of his shirt. His rolled red bandanna. His face. The child had a hypnotic touch. Its face full of welcome. It put its arms around Severin's neck and hugged him hard. When it kissed Severin on the mouth, it had funny breath.

The mother's toenails dropped to the linoleum like hens pecking

. . . tat . . . tat . . . tat. The long toe of the right foot was erect and obedient in Robby's dark hand.

A jeep pulled up into the dooryard. Severin knows bad brake drums when he hears them. He turned his head and saw it was the deputy, Erroll Anderson . . . and Gussie.

The Crocker geese surrounded the jeep. The deputy looked out into a satiny ghostly row of blue eyes. The big rain smashed into those eyes, but the eyes didn't blink.

"Uh-oh," said a small Crocker in the kitchen.

"They're gonna tear the man's leg off if he gets out," said another.

"It's matin' season, you know," said another into Severin's eyes.

While some geese hissed, others hammered the jeep's fenders with their bills. The bodies of the old ganders were rotund, the younger ganders' narrow like darts.

"They go wicked bananas in matin' season," squeaked a very, very small Crocker.

Another Crocker reached up to feel the big pink cake.

The deputy honked his horn three times.

"Looks like Gussie's been caught stealing stuff again," one of the older Crockers said solemnly.

Robby wasn't doing any more clipping, just squinting at his wife's steamy left foot with a heartbroken expression.

The mother August wore a tired little smile.

Behind Severin's aviator sunglasses, his eyes ate Robby up. Patty was right about Robby. Gussie had said it was true. Robby was Passamaquoddy. There it was, plain as day, in the man's eyes and the mouth which was at all times braced into a beaten, ruler-straight line. Severin's eyes jerked back onto August's bare foot.

"Maybe it ain't stealin' little stuff this time . . . Maybe she's robbed some BANKS!" gasped a medium-sized Crocker.

Robby stood up then, mumbled something nobody could make heads nor tails of, then went out into the rain to deal with the situation.

A teenage Crocker sighed. "Gussie is a bad seed."

The mother August smiled at Severin as she got to her feet. She said, "Soon we'll have our cake." She went for spoons and forks in the drawer.

Severin watched her sorting the bent and greenish silverware. He imagined her with Robby in bed . . . the bed Gussie said had sheets hung around it for privacy. He could picture himself as Robby, his whole body orchid-color with passion, the veins in full bloom.

"It's a bad situation," said a Crocker close to Severin's ear.

"No, it's not," said another. "She'll get over it. Everybody says."

"It's something in Gussie that makes her do it," said another. "Something mental."

"No way," said another.

"It's something wrong," said another.

"No, it's not," said another dreamily. "It's nature."

After the party, the ordeal of the pink cake, the Kool Aid in plastic glasses, the presents, Severin asked Gussie to go for a ride with him in his truck . . . then pulled the truck up into the weeds about twenty feet from the Crocker mailbox, said something silly and breathless and dishonest, and with the inexhaustible and effortless fluids of a sixteen-year-old boy, made Josh.

9

It's as if the landlord knows about the new bolt lock. He doesn't push his key into the old lock, doesn't even jiggle the knob. It's as if he can see plain as day Severin standing there . . . alone . . . just home from work, his Snoopy cap in his hand. The landlord just goes ahead and speaks like he's looking into Severin's eyes. "Severin, we need to talk."

Severin's bashed and blackened hands clench.

"Severin," the voice says calmly, firmly . . . *commandingly.* "Open the door, please."

Severin steps closer to the door. The floor creaks under him. His heavy army jacket whispers.

"Severin. This is the last time I'm going to ask you. Either pay up the rent you owe or be out of here by the weekend. I gave you and your wife a chance but you broke your promise."

Severin inhales.

The landlord's voice is fatherly. "Severin . . . just open the door and let's talk about it . . . man to man. I don't really want the sheriff in on this."

Silence.

"Severin," says the landlord.

Severin steps closer, lays his forehead against the door.

10

The great yellow house on the hill is starting to look Christmasy from the road. Lights of all colors twinkle madly from the big bay window in the front room. Crockers bang doors, hurry from room to room, putting up paper elves, an elf to every window. There is fighting over the Scotch tape.

When the mother August comes in from her newest job, Robby's van is parked close to the door. Inside she finds that her girls have not remembered the dishes or the laundry. They are in the Christmas spirit for sure.

Robby's big La-Z-Boy chair by the kitchen window is empty though that's where she usually finds him when he gets home early. There is rock music upstairs . . . two different radios, two different stations.

Robby is not in the bathroom either.

Nor is he messing around in the shed.

When she strides into the purply-dark cold front hall where the washing machine is, she sees boxes of Christmas decorations strewed all over . . . a Styrofoam reindeer with wiggly eyes by her foot. She stuffs a load of dark colors into the washer, shakes in some soap.

He is sitting at the foot of the open stairway watching her. He says, "August."

She turns . . . discerns his face in the darkness between the bannister dowels . . . deep, deep old-man eyes . . . frightened eyes.

She unbuttons her long workcoat, pulls the black knit cap from her head. "It sure is getting Christmasy around here, isn't it, Robert?"

He mutters something, sounds like, "Little bastards."

With her good eye fixed on the mad twinkling light showing under the front room door, she sighs. "Christmas is their favorite, you know."

He says, "Come take a look at my hands."

She steps around the bannister.

He says, "It's something with my hands . . . I don't know what."
His hands lie in his lap.

11

Red and gasping from shoveling, Severin stands with his bare right
hand on the glossy fender of the Cutlass. "LEFT!!!" he bellers.

The yard wrecker roars and pops. Its iron tail arches toward the
Cutlass. Severin can see the face of his father in the side mirrors
. . . Armand's eyes scrinched against the unspeakable brightness of
sun and snow.

"LEFT! LEFT!" Severin screams.

Armand throws his whole body into the gears. The boom lurches,
the iron hook sweeping past Severin's face.

"HO!" Severin screams, cigarette bouncing on his scabbed-over
bottom lip.

The wrecker oozes back a bit more.

Severin squats, hooks on to the Cutlass bumper. "OKAY!!" he
calls and steps back. The car's back end ernks up and up. He studies
the safety chain, then chuckles deeply, leaves it to hang. He yanks
the shovel from the snowbank and flings it clattering into the wrecker bed.

Armand shuts the engine down, but he doesn't get out.

Severin waits for his father to make a move. Armand's decline is
not measurable in years but in seasons. This winter he is less of a
man than last fall. Last fall he was less of a man than in the summer.

Eventually he steps down out of the wrecker. He rubs his bare
hands together. "A big fat goof God made in making hell a hot place
. . . aye?" He grips the Cutlass fender to catch about six breaths . . .

Severin looks away.

"He would get to torture sinners lot worst have he make it nine
below and a . . ." He gasps. ". . . and a big wind."

Three aisles away the crusher howls. The fork loader is feeding it
a nice-looking Plymouth Satellite which shudders as it passes into
the jaws. Tomorrow the crusher will finish up for sure, they say.
Everybody will finally get paid. There is a festive feeling in the icy
air . . .

Severin says, "Three-eighths?"

Armand blows on his bare hands, nods, then ambles back to the wrecker for the torch. "Got anutter t'ing coming if dey t'ink I'm going to mess wit dat Bronco tranny today . . ." He gasps.

Severin looks away.

"I must have ten hands, dey t'ink. Why doan dey get Cunthead Hutchins to do it . . . And I do not mean do it wit Armand Letourneau's tools when Armand have hiss back turned around." He leans on the bed of the wrecker, studying the ground, and gasps.

The icy wind twirls the straps of Severin's Snoopy cap.

Armand says, "Dave, he know yesterday I was only one stripping . . . Gene out wit de ramp . . . Crowe on de tranny job . . . But who he say get Cheney's doors! Not Hutchins, who iss wit hiss feet up . . . but Armand, who iss about t'ree vehicles ahead off de fork loader . . ." He pants as he talks . . . but talks . . . talks . . . and talks. "Gross Monsieur Pluto only keep . . . Hutchins because he . . . feel sorry for de wife . . . de lit-tle girls . . ." He talks, he pants, then at last humps down under the rear of the Cutlass, reaches up to give the tailpipe a squeeze.

Severin paws through the heap of wrenches on the back of the wrecker. There are moments when wrenches all look the same. He glances over at his father's bent-over back, the torch coming to life with a trillion rebounding stars.

When the wind rises again, snow stings Severin's face like bits of glass. He hurries with the wrench for the shelter of the Cutlass. It's kind of cozy under the Cutlass.

Armand says, "Still got de hots, you . . . for dat El Camino off Mitchell's?"

Severin says, "Maybe. Why?"

A spark settles on Armand's sleeve. Sparks by the dozens. For a moment he is glittering madly. He says, "Go giff de man a call at dinnertime. I t'ink he iss ready to come down anutter hundred." The tailpipe drops. He gasps, grins. "It iss not official . . . but you offer it, he will bite I bet."

The walkie-talkie clipped to Armand's belt sputters, "Armand! Hello! Hello!" Armand ignores it. He leans toward the driveshaft, squinting.

"I'd give my left ball for that El Camino," says Severin. He holds the wrench out to Armand but Armand keeps squinting at the drive-shaft.

"ARMAND, YOU PECKERHEAD! YOU DEAF OR WHAT!??" the walkie-talkie sputters.

Severin's hand with the wrench in it drops to his side. He sighs. "Gussie hates El Caminos. She says she wouldn't be caught dead in one. She says they look silly. She says to ride in one you need to have golf clubs and white shoes and . . . Pepto-Bismol-pink pants."

Armand says, "Wrench."

Severin pushes the wrench into his father's hand and snarls, "Women can be a royal pain."

Armand works the wrench slowly, powerfully . . . swinging his great beer belly from side to side . . . his breath leaving him in round frozen white volleys.

Severin says, "Like this morning she was all over me about Corn Chex. She says . . ." He imitates her creaky Crocker voice. " 'How many Corn Chex do you eat per second? Two thousand per second? Or three thousand per second?' She's trying to be funny, in case you didn't know. She's pretty weird. An' she says I got a worm. A WORM. I say, 'Baby, you are a looking for a slap on the ass.' She shut her trap then. She knows I'm pretty pissy in the morning . . . Last thing I need is a buncha shit. But women will push you as far as they can, don't they?"

Armand says, "Yep."

In the distance there's the snap and crackle of the crusher's wicked work.

The Cutlass driveshaft thonks to the ground between Armand's boots. "Where's your marker, Severin?" he gasps.

Severin drives both hands into his army jacket pockets, feeling for the marker. He swipes the driveshaft off the ground, prints CUT 79 in big cautious letters, his bare hands aching with the cold.

The walkie-talkie hisses, "WHAT'S GOING ON DOWN THERE YOU GUYS? TAKING A SNOOZE?!!"

Armand ignores the walkie-talkie . . . just stands there huffing and puffing . . . watching Severin load parts onto the wrecker in a showy way.

12

Gussie sounds like twenty Gussies bounding up the apartment stairs. She has Josh under one arm, Bubba under the other, a Lavinski's shopping bag dangling from her teeth. She gives the door a kick. "Open up!" she snarls.

Severin unbolts the door, his left cheek full of Saltines.

"Feeding your worm?" she snorts as she barges past him, drops the bag to the floor, gives it a kick toward him, and commands, "Get a load of that Christmas present!" She shuts the door with her back.

Severin looks down at the bag, munching. "It isn't Christmas quite yet," he says.

"Bullshit on that waiting routine!" she snarls. She lowers the babies. They stand there nearly paralyzed in their oversized snowsuits. "Open it up! Open it up!" Gussie clamors.

Severin reaches into the bag.

The babies watch his hands produce a gray suede jacket which stinks of brand-newness.

Gussie says, "Put it on! Put it on!"

Severin drives his right arm into the sleeve.

"Beautiful! Beautiful!" Gussie swoons.

Tags flutter at Severin's left wrist.

Gussie shrieks, "Zip it up!"

His hands have trouble with the zipper. His mouth ajar shows the black space of his wrecked tooth . . . his monster look. He gives the zipper several frustrated tugs. He murmurs, "Zipper's stuck."

Gussie watches his hands, horrified.

Then up goes the zipper.

Gussie applauds.

The babies applaud stiffly.

13

Severin slouches on the edge of the bed . . . the bed which is big but not big enough. His children as they sleep sound like pots of water coming to full boil. From the window sill he picks a stretchy ponytail holder. He ties his hair back. He studies the street with its twinkling undulating Christmas lights outlining the shapes of the sagging mill houses. He paws the cluttered sill for his Marlboros, then lights one up. He turns, sees the back of Gussie's head . . . her crazy unreasonable pinkish hair. She isn't asleep. She's looking at something, he can tell.

"What are you looking at?"

"Your new jacket," she replies.

He coughs out some smoke. He narrows his eyes on the pale ghosty shape that is his new jacket on a plastic hanger in the doorway to the kitchenette.

She says huskily, "It's the first thing you've ever had for yourself that's nice since we've been married. It makes you look nice."

"I'd rather have that El Camino," he says.

She snorts. "That ol' thing! You need to get you some canteloupe-colored pants first."

Smoke settles peacefully over the bed.

Gussie sighs. "You don't like your jacket, do you? Be honest."

"I like it," he insists. "But I can't do nothing with it on. I can't check the oil in the truck. I can't even *lean* against the truck. While I got that jacket on I can't eat nothing or pat a big dog. What if I spill lighter fluid on it? Or beer? What if I bleed?"

They both look through the darkness at the jacket, nobody saying a thing for a while. Then Gussie says softly and creakily, "You will feel nice walking through crowds wearing that jacket. You will feel like King Shit."

There is the sound of Severin's lips on the cigarette and the sounds of Josh's and Bubba's flustered, frenzied sleep . . . then another sound . . . a thunk.

Severin reaches across the babies and seizes Gussie's elbow. "Don't talk!" he whispers.

"Maybe it's not him," she whispers back.

"Sh!"

They stare at the door for a while, then Gussie sings out, "Time's up!"

Severin locks his cigarette in his teeth and paws through the stuff on the floor beside the bed.

"What are you looking for?" Gussie sighs.

"My shirt."

"Here we go again!" she says. She sits up, clutching the covers. "The door is locked, Severin! Mr. Howe won't ever get in here again unless he uses a cannon. I don't know why you gotta act so tense."

Severin struggles into his shirt, his St. Christopher's medal flickering from the Christmasy light of the street.

He says, "Maybe Mr. Howe is planning a blitz. He's got a buncha cops out there. He's probably mad about that jacket."

Gussie shrieks, "I got that jacket on layaway! Paid over a long period of time! I haven't done nuthin' wrong!"

Severin pulls on his damp wool pants, fastens the belt. "Suppose Mr. Howe heard you got that jacket and he didn't happen to hear the layaway part. Suppose one of his friends saw you getting out of Nancy's car with that big bag?"

"I don't give a shit!" she snorts.

He collapses onto the bed on top of the covers, pinching his cigarette between his two fingers. He says bitterly, "Next time that peckerhead comes here, I'm going to pick him up and tie him into twenty knots. You watch. I've had it up to here!" He thumps his forehead. "Papa says it's against the law for him to bust in like he likes to do . . . that I got the right to lay him out. One step into this apartment again without us opening the door for him and he's gonna see my fist on the end of his nose!"

Gussie sighs, lays her strong thick hard right arm over her babies, and shuts her eyes.

14

There isn't much light, just a paper-shade wall lamp over the sink. The fixture in the ceiling is just an empty socket tonight.

Robby Crocker sits squarely in his La-Z-Boy, his eyes on the three men.

Crowe Bovey speaks. "Mrs. Crocker . . . you got a better light than that?" He gives his knuckles a couple of warning cracks.

The Crocker kitchen is nearly as cold as outdoors, even with the woodstove stoked. Some of the Crocker kids have their jackets on. Some have blankets around them. August says, "We are a little bit short on bulbs."

Ernest Bean says softly, "Let's take a look at that ring, Rob."

Robby's hands remain in a blueish bloated heap in his lap.

August says, "I don't think he's had that ring off since we were married."

A red-nosed child squints up at gorilla-sized Ernest Bean, who has a dark day's growth of beard, a plaid wool jacket with a Ruger patch on the sleeve, and there under his arm . . . a hacksaw. The child says squeakily, "Are you from the bank?"

"Bank? Me?" Ernest Bean laughs big deep belly laughs over this.

August says, "It's a thing with Robby . . . that ol' ring. He just doesn't take it off ever."

Robby mumbles something nobody can make heads nor tails of.

Severin, who is the third man, is wearing his army jacket and Snoopy cap. He is just a pair of hands, a pair of eyes.

A couple of wee Crockers begin to fuss.

"Get 'em outa here," Crowe Bovey says into August's eyes.

She opens her hand over the child's head.

Severin's eyes widen on that hand, that head, the head that isn't really pointy at all, maybe just a little bit narrow. When did the Crocker heads stop looking pointy to him? It was not a sudden thing . . . In fact, he hadn't noticed it happening.

August says, "Kids . . . go and be with the Christmas tree. The grown-ups have something private." She shepherds them out, her dark workcoat thwomps the door frame as she passes.

Ernest Bean says, "Rob . . . what's this with giving your ol' lady shit about taking that ring off? Huh? Huh?"

Robby's mouth tightens.

Crowe Bovey is smiling one of his haughty, faraway half-smiles.

Ernest says, "Think we can handle it, Rob?"

Robby's right thigh jerks . . . looks like he's getting ready to give Crowe Bovey a kick in the crotch. Crowe steps back and says, "You going to let us have a look at your hands or what?"

August returns.

Severin studies her briefly, then lowers his eyes.

She says, "You all need any soap?"

Ernest waves the hacksaw. "Naw . . . I guess not. I think it's going to boil down to this. How long's his hands been like this?"

She says, "Sudden like."

Ernest says, "A doctor ought to see this . . . don't you think?"

August just stands there in her big coat with her back to the hall door, her sluggish bad eye and her good eye moving over everybody at once.

Crowe says, "Well, it don't matter. That ring's coming off in about twenty seconds. It's cutting off his blood . . . We want to keep fartin' around or what?" He looks at Robby and Robby's right thigh tightens again. Crowe snorts, "You're going to be an asshole about this, aintcha?"

Robby is a small man, a small old man. His hair has been combed by a daughter, wet and parted in the middle. He doesn't look like much of a match for three fit and ready younger men.

And yet he fights . . .

He fights them for nearly two hours, scrambling about the kitchen, knocking down a canister, a box of salt . . . tearing at their jackets, ramming, grunting, kicking like hell . . . gets Crowe Bovey a good one in the crotch before it's over with, brings him down a peg, brings him to his hands and knees . . . takes that look off his face.

15

The crusher can't seem to get enough. Maybe two more days, Big Lucien tells the boys. The more weight, the more money. The old women send down fruit muffins. The sun is warm and the old collie lies in the open office door. The sky is storybook blue. There is Christmas in the air. The crusher eats a couple of Mavericks, a Bobcat, a Toyota, a Satellite, a Vega, a Bronco, and a good-looking Dodge Ram. All around the crusher is the mad, mad sparkle of crushed mirrors and glass . . . footprints, ruts, and goo. The fork loader gores a Pontiac . . . backs up . . . rams it . . . gores it again.

Severin slumps in the sunny doorway of the blue Baptist bus, smoking, watching the crusher crew work. He is about to toss down his cigarette and go back to work when he sees the bald-headed, bald-faced figure striding past, the beige trench coat aflutter, arms swinging. Severin doesn't move. The landlord just keeps on striding confidently along, glancing to his left and right . . . but he never sees Severin.

Severin lunges into the bus.

For an hour or so nobody knows where he is.

16

While Severin gets the laundry from the back of the truck, Gussie hurtles ahead with Bubba under one arm, Josh under the other.

Severin looks up at the windows of the yellow house, not one window lacking a paper elf or reindeer. Eaves drip. Two vast, spotted chimneys rise up into the fog.

As he staggers into the steamy furor of the Crocker kitchen, all five trash bags of laundry swung over his shoulder, a short cigarette on his lip, Gussie announces, "HERE HE IZZZZZ! IT'S SEVERINNNNN LETOURNEAU IN HIS NEWWWWW JACKET!!!" She throws out her hand. "TA-DAAAAAAAAAAAAAH!!!"

17

Severin sees the mother August has made a green pie. It sets there on the workbench in the grim half-light all ready to go. It is not a pie with a crust, but some sort of billowy chiffon thing. Everything the woman cooks takes on a kind of dreadful power.

They put the youngest babies on a blanket by the woodstove . . . Tami-Jane, who has a croupy cough, and Bubba, who has something sticky in his dark hair.

"You think they'll wrastle?" wonders one of the Crocker boys who has just come huffing in with an armload of popple sticks.

"I bet Tami will beat!" squeaks a small Crocker.

"Let's put 'em together . . . get 'em started," suggests another.

Gussie, counting forks by the sink, says, "Leave 'em be!" She and some of her sisters pass the forks around. Gussie goes to the window where her father is sitting, staring out. He is wearing his gray carpenter's clothes, but also a dressy button-up Sunday sweater. His hands are in his lap . . . less swollen since the doctor . . . heartbroken-looking hands. "Daddy, you want some pie?" Gussie asks. He puts his right hand out.

Gussie cuts into the pie with a big dark meat knife. Everybody watches the slice of green ease onto Robby's plate.

The mother August warns Gussie to cut the pieces small. She says it is "rich."

Gussie and her sisters get out some more plates. All the teenage girl Crockers have their pinkish hair cut "new wave" these days . . . not a lot different from Crocker hair's natural tendencies . . . just a lot more wet. Gussie tells one of her sisters about the landlord trouble she and Severin are having. She explains that Severin has been such a "gentleman" about it. "Till one day last week, ol' Mr. Big Shit comes hounding after Severin at the yard. Well, Severin says that was the last straw. No more Mr. Nice Guy. He grabbed Mr. Howe and threw him against a bus."

One of the new-wave Crockers puts a plate in Severin's hands. It's a big plate with rings like a bull's eye.

Gussie says, "Severin, tell about the look Mr. Howe had on his face when you threw him against the bus."

Severin shrugs.

"Go on, Severin. Tell them! Tell them!" Gussie clamors.

Severin shrugs again, says softly, "He looked pretty funny."

Gussie says, "Nawwww . . . dummy! Tell 'em what you told me . . . about the exact way he looked. It was funny the way you said it. Something like . . . ah . . . something about . . . his eyes popping . . . Tell that part!"

Severin murmurs, "Yeah, he looked funny in the eyes."

"And he apologized to you, right!?!"

Severin says, "Yep."

The mother August appears at his side, flops a piece of the green pie on his bull's eye plate . . . dead center.

18

The apartment over Allen's Oil looks empty. There's a big, big mattress against the telephone pole out front. Its blue-flowered sheet billows and booms in the wind. On the sidewalk is the soggy heap of a household, a green-apple cookie jar and a Rambo poster near-buried in the deepening snow. Mr. Howe has solved his problem.

19

That night they park the truck on a back road and leave the motor running for heat.

Toward morning, almost light, Severin wakes, hearing his heart beating outside his body, beating in the air. He is aroused, every bit of him readied for sex. The dream, he realizes with horror, was about Crowe Bovey. He and Crowe Bovey together. Not frantic fucking, Gussie style, not Gussie's noise, not Gussie's near-wrastling . . . nothing at all like that. It was just a kind of cloudy embrace. Sex with Crowe Bovey or any man is nothing Severin can imagine wanting to do. Awake now, he's shocked. Feels crawly. The arousal subsides fast. There's just the burbles of his sleeping children and Gussie's silence. And the sickening smell of exhaust. He grips the steering wheel, sits up straighter . . . looks over at Gussie's wide-open eyes. With the windshield buried in snow, they are in a blueish gloom . . . like a dream. Serene. Otherworldly. Gussie is staring straight into his face, her expression one of exhaustion, desperation, and fright . . . not the usual Gussie. For one long moment, Severin feels indomitable. He feels damn good.

20

Crowe Bovey is shoveling out a BMW when Severin's little yard buggy comes roaring up the aisle and stops.

Severin cuts off the engine, steps out. He can hear Dave the desk man's voice crackling over the walkie-talkie on Crowe Bovey's belt. "Headquarters to Wasteland! . . . Headquarters to Wasteland! . . . I've just sent a man down to see if you got your fingers up your ass, Bovey. Gotta have that wirin' harness *now*. Johnson's here looking eager." The voice chuckles to itself. "When Severin gets there, just give it to him to bring up . . . and that radiator if it's ready. He should be right along. Over and out."

Severin leans against a junked Datsun, says nothing to Crowe. He just gnaws on his left thumbnail. Today there's no wind. No crusher. Just cold silence like the North Pole. It's so cold today it breaks a record set in 1943, according to the old women up at the house. On weather, Tante Marie Louise and bald Mrs. Bean are the world's experts.

Severin sneaks a real quickie glance at Crowe's face. The glasses are gone . . . got gouged and bent in the scuffle up at the Crockers'. Without glasses the eyes look darker, squinty and rapt. Mean.

When Crowe throws the shovel, Severin nearly jumps out of his skin. The shovel smacks the door of the flawless wine-color BMW, leaves a dent. He pushes past Severin and thrashes through his tools on the back of the yard wrecker.

Severin snickers nervously before speaking. "They say it's thirty below and no wind chill . . . just plain old thirty below. Man, am I ever ready for a trip to Florida . . . lay on the beach . . ."

Crowe pushes past again, flings the BMW hood up, lays his tools on the engine. In the near distance, a yard buggy sputters . . . a couple of voices hoot back and forth. Wherever there is life, there's a doughy, snow-white veil of frozen exhaust and breath.

Crowe snatches up his hacksaw and goes to work.

Severin says, "Need any help?"

As Crowe rips through the hoses with the saw, there's the sound of liquid letting go. Thin, sweet-looking pink and green colors spread around his boot.

Severin says, "Me an' the ol' lady are moving down back tonight. Oncle Lucien found us a trailer in pretty decent shape. You are welcome to stop by any time. Ol' lady loves company. She gets a few beers into her and she'll make us enough spaghetti to feed a platoon. You like spaghetti?"

Crowe eyes Severin. "Yep," he says, then squats to unbolt the bottom of the radiator.

Severin starts up a frisky rocking from foot to foot, hands buried in the pockets of his army jacket.

The walkie-talkie on Crowe's belt squawks, "Jesus, Bovey, where's that wirin' harness! You guys down there jerkin' each other off or what?" The voice chuckles to itself.

Crowe tears the walkie-talkie from his belt and whales it into the

BMW's flawless fender. He turns to Severin, his eyes widening and narrowing on Severin's face. "Go up to the office with this message. Tell them this message, would ya? This is the message. Suck off. That's the message. You go on up there and give 'em that message, okay?"

Severin goes.

When he returns with words from the office, the yard wrecker is still there . . . but Crowe is gone.

Severin hunts around, sees fresh footprints leading up to an Eldorado . . . the door open. He looks in, sees a screwdriver and pliers on the seat.

"Hey! You hiding?!!!" Severin calls out, but his voice shrinks into the frigid unearthly stillness.

He climbs up onto the snow between cars, sinks to his hips. He works his way around a van, hollering, "Bovey! Where the hell are you!"

When he comes floundering back to the Eldorado, Crowe is standing there, his hands in his pockets, his strange eyes dead straight into Severin's eyes.

Severin gasps, "Man oh man . . . you freaked me!"

Crowe hunkers forward slightly. Then he turns away, moves toward the yard wrecker, still hunkering.

Severin calls, "You okay?"

When Crowe reaches the wrecker, he keeps his hands deep in his pockets . . . just stands there squinting at the doorless cab.

Severin calls again, "You okay?"

Crowe chuckles. "I think my hands are gone."

Severin says, "Jesus, that's bad. Better go up to the office and get 'em warm! Want me to drive you up?"

Crowe bellers, "I got WORK to do! This ain't junior high."

"Okay. Okay," says Severin. He goes to his little yard buggy and waits, playing with the clutch, the exhaust in a roiling white wall behind. Crowe keeps standing there by the yard wrecker, his hands in his pockets, his eyes squinty.

After a few minutes, Severin drives away . . . off to look for the coil for a Malibu he was supposed to have had ready an hour ago.

21

Six snowy geese stagger toward the open door of the shed . . . spring fever in their eyes. Inside the shed small Crockers squeak delightedly over a box of old wallpaper they've found . . . white roses on a gold scroll. A big gander snatches the box away, beats it with his wings. The other geese cheer him on.

The bank people arrive in a silver car that whirs. A man steps out on one side of the car, a woman steps out on the other. They don't slam the doors. They just touch them and they close.

The small Crockers come to the shed door and look out. "Uh-oh," one says forlornly.

When the bank people ask the small Crockers, "Are your parents inside?" some nod while some shake their heads.

The big gander has lost interest in the shredded wallpaper box . . . slings it to one side, heads for the intruders.

The other geese cheer him on.

"Look out," says one small Crocker.

The bank people are knocking at the wrong door, the door to the inner shed. "Maybe it's that other door," the woman says.

They start for the other door, the man shaking his sleeve back to check his watch. There are many doors to the big yellow house, but most of them have no steps. The man asks the small Crockers, "Are the geese mean?"

Some nod, some shake their heads.

The big gander has his neck out, headed straight for the man's pant leg. The man tries to get out of the way in a dignified manner. Another gander is snatching at the woman's dress hem. The man and woman quickly get back in their car. The geese drum with their beaks on the silvery surface.

The woman calls from the car window, "Kids! Please tell your parents that there's somebody here to see them. It's very important. Very very important. Please let them know we're here, okay?"

In the silvery surface of the car are the silvery invincible geese which, no matter how hard the Crocker geese poke at them, just don't back off at all.

SIX

Blackstone's Baby

1

TANTE JOSEPHINE'S knitting needles clash against a heap of showy fuchsia in her lap. She watches as old Tante Flavie opens the door for the young woman in the white fur coat. It's that "Greenlaw girl" come to see Dinah, but Dinah's not back from Portland yet. This is the first time the "Greenlaw girl" has set foot in Big Lucien's house. She and Dinah have been close all winter . . . ever since Dinah came from Western Mass. to start college.

Junie sucks in her left cheek and glances around the kitchen at all the faces of the old women . . . and then at Crowe Bovey, who is asleep at the table with his face in his arms. He wears a black and red wool shirt over his salvage shirt, both collars twisted.

"Please," says Tante Josephine. "Pardon you the sleeping man."

Junie sits at the table across from him. A cumbersome purring black and white cat instantly fills her lap.

Old Flavie shakes Crowe's shoulder. "Hey, dummy person! Dere's a pretty girl in diss room and you are sleeping t'rough de whole t'ing!"

The other women all titter over this . . . those who still have their minds.

"He work hard," says Flavie. "He work himself to death."

"T'row over him water dat iss cold," giggles Tante Marie Louise.

They offer Junie tea.

She says no.

They offer her Lorna Doones.

She says, "No . . . no thank you." She tells them she can only stay another minute. She rubs the cat's ears and listens to the old women talk about a tree that is dying in the dooryard. None of them agrees on why the tree is dying and it turns into a small fight. Part of the fight is in English, part in French.

In the next room beyond a little hallway of built-in china closets is the TV with the evening news . . . more old women, more cats . . . and a lot of high bare wallpapered walls. On the biggest, barest-looking wall is a little plaster Jesus dying on the cross.

Now and then Junie's wild, wild penny-color eyes spring onto Crowe Bovey, his hands, his hair.

The old women say, "Take off dat big coat! Stay awhile! Iss not very late. After all, it iss Saturday. Big visit night."

Junie says thank you but she can only stay another minute.

They ask her if she's sure she doesn't want some Lorna Doones. How about some leftover fruit salad? A piece of very nice cheese? How about a sandwich?

2

It's Tuesday morning. A cold, ugly, gray wind. A lot of red noses and runny eyes. Not much for business. Dave the desk man is flipping through some wrinkled *Hustlers* . . . yawning.

E, Blackstone Babbidge has just come in with a car on the ramp . . . the car a 1988 Buick, the "nose" completely gone. His stepdaughter, June Marie Greenlaw, had gone with him as she often does since she quit the mill. She is nothing like his own daughters, who stay pretty much to home . . . go to church, cook. Not this one. You hear about this one. Wrecked all three of her cars. Into drink. Into drugs. Go. Go. Go. Go. Gene's got no control over her. She's like a wild dog.

But it's caught up with her. Limping around after Gene, thin-faced . . . jumpy. No energy. "Dying, probably," says old Clarence Farrington, one of the many office wise men. "Burned-out, it's called. A pity. Drugs will do it. But you can't tell 'em nuthin'." This is what Clarence has to say when Gene's not around. Right now Clarence is telling the road commissioner all he knows about greyhound racing.

Junie stands over the heat register in her big coat, her wild, wild penny-color eyes on Gene.

Dave the desk man yawns again. When the phone rings, it's only the vet's office . . . something about a sick cat. Dave stands with the phone cradled in his shoulder, saying "Yep, yep" and rolling his eyes. Gross Monsieur Pluto is always having Dave make appointments for cats. Cat bills must be a fortune, they all say. Sometimes the man's heart of gold gets the better of him, they all say.

Gene is crouched on a stack of snow treads working a Rubik's Cube he found in the wrecked Buick. Out through the spotty glass door they can all see the Buick still winched on, "nose" down. The windshield has a spider-web break . . . blond hair and blood. "A twelve-year-old boy," the cops at the scene told Gene and Junie. It is plain to see Gene is having a bad time trying to figure out the Rubik's Cube.

The salvage office is not a bright officy place. Gene's stepdaughter's big white furry coat is the only bright thing.

Hutchins comes barreling in through the back room rolling a tire. He has his green LETOURNEAU'S USED AUTO PARTS workshirt on inside out. His denim vest with Sherpa lining is aged to practically a flat, blackish rag.

Four cigarettes are going now . . . one cigar . . . two smoldering pipes.

Old Clarence Farrington is now telling the road commissioner about how they found Rick Berry dead in his car over Shapleigh last night. "Suicide," he says, shaking his head.

Wayne stands the tire against the counter, turns to Junie, and says, "Let me make you coffee, honey. Two Cremoras, right?"

"I want Cremora in mine!" Dave the desk man sings out.

"I want mine black," says the deputy.

"Two sugars," says Richard, who has only half a face.

Wayne snorts, "Fuck you, you guys. I only wait on pretty ladies."

Crowe Bovey comes in through the back way, lowers a labeled alternator to the small pile of parts on the floor by the counter.

Junie says to Wayne, "I've stopped drinking coffee. But thanks, Wayne. You're sweet."

"Sweet as a snake," says Dave.

Junie's eyes slide back to her stepfather. In his hands the Rubik's Cube makes frustrated snapping sounds.

Old Clarence Farrington gives more details on the suicide.

Crowe Bovey warms his hands over the heat register. His eyes widen and narrow on Junie's white coat. It's been a year now he has gone without glasses. He knows the parts business by feel, they all say.

Wayne Hutchins steps over Buzzy Atkinson's outstretched legs, gives the sleeve of Junie's coat a sharp tug. "Get that old hot thing off, would ya?" he says. "We're all gonna wilt just looking at ya!"

Gene raises his icy eyes, studies Wayne a moment.

Junie says, "I'm only going to be here another minute."

The NAPA auto parts calendar on the wall behind her flaps madly in the blowing heat.

Old Clarence Farrington says the suicide wasn't much of a shock to him. He can tell the suicide type when he sees them. "Rick had a way about him."

"Sure it weren't the old ale that killed him?" Dave suggests. "The man drank himself foolish. Maybe his liver killed him."

"Naw . . . Ruger Blackhawk," says Clarence.

"Kids 'n' bills. Kids 'n' bills," says the deputy.

3

It is another Saturday night. Tante Flavie tells Junie that Dinah has gone to something that has to do with her college, but "come in anyway. Have a seat." They offer her tea and toast. She says no thank you. Cats surge around her dress boots, smell the hem of her coat. She tells old bald Mrs. Bean that her name is June Greenlaw . . . but the old women already know her name. There isn't much the old women don't know that goes on in Miracle City. They know all the details about how wild she is. And they suspect she's another one of Big Lucien's past babies turning up.

They ask her if she was born in June.

She says no, that her mother just liked June as a name.

They ask her if the classy-looking coat is real fur.

She says, "It's petroleum," with a quirky little smile.

They say the coat looks hot. "Take it off!"

She says she won't be staying long, only a minute.

Tante Josephine's knitting needles clash.

Crowe Bovey is not asleep at the table tonight. He has a habit of disappearing sometimes . . . lots of hidey-holes in the big old house.

Junie smiles into the eyes of the old woman they call Grace.

"BRAT!!" she shrieks at Junie.

Old Flavie says, "Not pay de old lady attention . . . She iss not right in her head."

All the while Flavie talks, she's busy. She crams folded towels into a drawer. She searches her loaded apron pockets for a comb. She combs Memère Poulin's hair. She shoos cats off the gas stove. She heaves a chunk of stringy wood into the Hearthmate . . . leaves the little door open to make a nice crackly light. She circulates. Her apron pockets clash. A collie dog sprawled under the big home-made supper table groans. It is a groan filled with peace and gratitude.

Suddenly the Moontrekker appears, all its wee lights flashing and soaring. There is a sinister whir.

"Ma Gawd!" gasps Charlotte, the newest old woman.

The Moontrekker turns slightly as if to consider her as she speaks.

The eyes of all the cats widen. All purring stops.

The Moontrekker bumps along down the steeply slanted floor toward the circle of rocking chairs.

Tante Josephine smiles pleasantly, her knitting needles keeping their rhythm even as the breadbox-sized Moontrekker makes a bee-line for her foot.

"Look out!" gasps old bald Mrs. Bean.

Memère Poulin's GI Joe doll slides off her lap . . . lands on the floor with a plop.

The Moontrekker veers away from Mrs. Bean's foot as she's about to give it a kick.

"They make such terrible toys these days, don't they?" sighs Mrs. Bean.

A tante cries, "LOOK OUT!"

The Moontrekker bams into a cat broadside. The cat leaps straight up, then vanishes under the table.

The Moontrekker circles the rocking chairs and woodstove again and again . . . whirring, scintillating.

"I told him not to give dat toy on dem kids. Dey abuse!" Tante Marie Louise sighs.

The Moontrekker charges Tante Marie Louise's feet . . . the feet dressed only in cloth bedroom slippers. Its bulldozer track bears down, up and over those feet. Tante Marie Louise giggles like a young girl. "What a funny feeling dat iss!"

Mrs. Bean sighs. "When I was a young girl, we was lucky to have a piece of rope to jump with."

Old Grace cocks her head, then throws up her hands and shrieks, "They are coming to cut off my head, Phil! Ma Gawd . . . Where's Debbie? Debbie! Deb-BEE!"

The Moontrekker sashays up to Junie's dress boots . . . classy boots . . . like her classy coat and her classy shaggy root perm. The wee lights wink and gleam. Then it rises up and over her boots . . . lovingly. Then it whirs away down the little hallway to the front room.

Old Tante Josephine looks into Junie's eyes and says evenly, "Our Gross Monsieur Pluto plays tricks on de old women . . . drive us . . . how you say? . . . coo-coo. De man more junk into diss house he brings . . . and he play wit it hiss own self. Dat not kids behind dat tonight."

Junie's eyes widen on the little hallway . . . says softly, "Oh."

As she is leaving a few minutes later, she leans her shoulder against a corner of the old house to retch.

4

On Junie's third visit to the Letourneau house it is early afternoon. She asks breathlessly, "Where's your bathroom?"

The Letourneau bathroom has what they call "the temporary door" . . . a Peanuts comforter nailed up for privacy. There's a black stain where the knob would be if it were a real door. There's cold milky-looking water in the clawfoot tub. Everywhere are sneakers and wet towels. The toilet is rounded up, brimming with something butterscotch-color and lustrous.

Junie gets down on her knees and has ten minutes of dry heaves.

When she reaches for toilet paper to wipe her mouth, she sees feet under the hanging Peanuts comforter. Small feet. Some in sneakers. One in snowmobile boots. One in striped punk socks.

"There's somebody in here," says Junie quickly. "I'll be just another minute!"

"Somebody in there," one of them whispers.

"What are you doing?" one asks.

"Sick," says Junie.

"You better hurry," says the punk socks.

Another pair of feet appear. Then the comforter shudders. "Don't push!" snarls one of the pairs of feet.

Junie gasps, "Please! I need a couple more minutes."

The comforter pulls a little to the left. One brown eye appears. "She's on the floor," says the eye.

More feet arrive.

"There's a lady in there," the eye tells the new feet. The quilt drops back into place.

Junie sees that a pair of American-flag-print sneakers are hopping around, like the wearer might have to pee in a desperate way.

Junie's mouth fills with wetness and the dry heaves resume. Then she unwinds more toilet paper to wipe her mouth. The toilet rumbles. The contents drop an inch.

"You are not supposed to flush it!" the snowmobile boots scream. "It's broke!"

"I didn't," Junie gasps. "I didn't touch it."

"It will flood soon," says the punk socks softly.

The Peanuts comforter flaps open and the bathroom fills up with kids, some Big Lucien's grandkids . . . some non-Letourneau Miracle City kids who hang out. Most young Letourneaus have dark dreamy eyes and roses of color on their cheeks like shame. One small Letourneau gazes at the toilet and declares, "Looks like lava, don't it?"

Junie gets to her feet. "It wasn't just me! Most of it was already in there when I came in."

One of the Miracle City kids says, "What if I do THIS!" and she mashes the flush handle with all her might.

"NO!" wails a Letourneau.

Everybody backs away.

"Junie," says Dinah's voice from beyond the Peanuts comforter. "You okay?"

Junie's eyes flash to the gum boots under the comforter.

"Dinah!" a tiny Letourneau sings out, draws open the comforter in one wide sweep.

Dinah steps in, sits on the loaded clawfoot tub. She could be Junie's twin, same thick shaggy perm, same round penny-color eyes. Another of Big Lucien's many babies. But her accent is Western Mass.

Something orange bursts out from under the tub. It's Clint, one of Big Lucien's most favorite cats. Clint throws his weight against the Peanuts comforter.

The kids shriek and make a big pile on top of Clint, all shouting "Get him! Get him!"

One child gets a hold of Clint's front legs. Another pries open Clint's mouth. Clint's orange-striped tail flicks like fire. A mouse leaps from his mouth, vanishes under the clawfoot tub.

Dinah says, "Jesus God . . . Ain't this bathroom busy?" She stands up and waves her arms. "Everybody out . . . NOW! You are being rude to company. OUT! OUT!"

As the bathroom empties of Letourneaus and non-Letourneaus, Junie's dry heaves resume. Dinah sighs, "Most morning sickness is in the morning. Maybe it's God speaking." She chuckles. "You know . . ." She chuckles again. "Like you get it worse as punishment when you been messing with your mother's man." This she whispers in a secret, secret way.

5

It's Saturday night at the Maine Mall. Junie has to throw up. They hurry out the back way at Sears and she does it by the fluorescent-lit loading dock. Dinah holds the bags, watches for people coming so she can kind of stand in front of Junie, who is down there on her hands and knees on the pavement. She says, "Doesn't the clinic have *any* kind of pills for that?"

"Naw . . . They weren't good for babies, I guess," says Junie.

205

Dinah's bottom lip thickens. "Neither is it good for the baby if you die."

Junie giggles. "I'm not that bad, I guess." She stands up with a groan, wiping her mouth with a Kleenex. "I guess I stink now."

They're sisters . . . anybody can tell. Same walk. Same way they gesture with the hands. Same voice, even. And both are dressed kind of classy tonight. One coat is furry and white. The other a handsome belted gray wool. They both have loads of make-up. Pantyhose. And what Tante Flavie calls "senseless shoes."

Whenever they're together, Dinah treats Junie like a queen, takes her arm when they go up or down stairs, keeps asking if she's thirsty. And Dinah's college boyfriend treats Junie special, too . . . looks long into her eyes with his soft gray calm ones and says, "How are you feeling today, June? You look lovely, if that's an indication." And all the old women's eyes are on fire with her. They say, in-your-condition-this and in-your-condition-that. Old Flavie asks, "Where does your boyfriend live?" Junie says Europe. Old Flavie makes her a baby book with shoestring binding.

The dark windy parking lot at the mall makes the two big coats flap and flop against the two sisters' legs. Dinah gasps, "I feel guilty now dragging you here. It's a long trip home."

Junie paws through her purse for another Kleenex, giggles. "It don't matter where I am."

They go clonking around and around the vast and windy parking lot, hunting for Dinah's little car. "All little cars look the same," says Junie.

"Oh, no they don't. I know my little darling when I see it!" says Dinah.

When they find it, Dinah unlocks Junie's side first, waits for her to get in, shuts the door softly for her.

While the engine warms, they go through their bags with the dome light on . . . a few things for the baby, a few things for themselves . . . like matching blue chicken potholders for the houses they will have someday.

Severin Letourneau says, "Wait. It's locked."

There's the clatter of a padlock, then the door of the old tool shed creaks open. The three visitors duck low to keep from banging their heads on the door frame. They eye the low ceiling warily. Buzzy Atkinson and Raymie Bean squat. Severin stands. Crowe Bovey claims the chair . . . the only chair.

Raymie Bean says, "What the hell's going on here?" His breath smokes from the cold.

Severin looks old tonight, his eyes very Indian, his mouth a tight line . . . his hair dirty and wild. "Not a hell of a lot," he says deeply. He drops his cigarette butt between the gray boards of the floor.

There's a rose-color, rose-smelling candle for light.

There's a big mattress with three shapes under the covers. Crowe Bovey's eyes widen and narrow on the shapes.

Buzzy Atkinson picks some plastic dinosaurs from one pocket, a fireman Weeble from the other . . . arranges them around the rose candle. He does all this without taking his orange work gloves off.

Crowe says, "You know those things make fumes?" He points at the Coleman stove opened up on a pine board by the door.

Severin says, "Yes."

Crowe cracks his knuckles impressively, sounds like he's breaking the bones of his fingers one at a time. "No way you can get that set up outside?"

"Maybe," says Severin. "Guess we oughta."

Raymie Bean says, "I'm in the dark about this. What happened to the trailer Mr. Pluto got you, for crissakes? I mean . . . couple weeks ago you were a trailer person. Now you're a . . . an *elf*."

Severin says solemnly, "Ain't grandfathered."

Crowe says, "Is that anything to do with sex?"

"Code man says it's the new thing they passed . . . last election. It reads: You can't do this, you can't do that. Enough rules to choke a horse. It's the new way, Mon Oncle says. Everything has to look nice. Can't look dumpy, he says. Dumpy ain't allowed . . . unless it was something dumpy before the new rules. If it's dumpy and new, they give Mon Oncle stiff fines. All the towns are going this new way nowadays." He draws a match up the wall before he even has a Marlboro shaken from the pack.

"Buncha bullshit," says Buzzy.

Raymie Bean scowls. "You mean this lean-to–chicken shed, or whatever it is . . . is grandfathered . . . the nice trailer, it wasn't?"

Severin chokes on some smoke. "Funny, isn't it?"

Crowe has started a beard about two weeks ago, something else he can yank on and wrench at. It already seems shorter on one side. He snorts, "What some of these do-dee-doo-dah yuppies in this town need is a few rounds from a good Winchester between the eyes." He gives his beard a tug.

"Who is this code feller, anyways?" Buzzy wonders. He spanks his gloves together. They make a cloud of dust.

Severin shrugs. "I don't know. He's just always coming into the office, looking for Mon Oncle. You seen him, aintcha? He drives one of those Caravan things."

"Yuppie bus," Crowe snorts.

"Yeah, I think I know who you mean now," says Buzzy.

Severin sighs. "There's always been a lot of complaints, you know . . . People not liking the looks of Mon Oncle's business. Put up a fence here. Put up a fence there. Can't have too many unregistered vehicles showing from the road. Used to be that other code guy a while back. He was more the phone type. This one is the in-person type. But I never heard him say his name. He probably said. But there's always so much going on up at the office, you know. I only half-listen 'less it's directed at me." Severin chuckles. "Names don't matter anyway. It's the position."

Crowe bends down, picks up a blond beech leaf from the floor, tears it into smithereens. "Know thine enemy," he says.

Severin says, "Mon Oncle will figure out something. He always does."

The men are silent a while, watching the rose candle flicker in the icy draft . . . watching their frozen breath swirl. The shadows of the dinosaurs and one fireman Weeble sway on the gray board walls. The only decoration the walls have is a little pink plastic Jesus dying on the cross which the tantes forced Severin to tack up. They said no home was complete without one.

7

Parked in the darkness outside the Babbidge trailer, Dinah says, "What's the matter?"

"I forgot his black tape . . . this kind of tape they use for fixing wires. He wanted me to look for some."

"Him?" Dinah sneers. She gets quiet a long moment, her fingers drumming on the stickshift knob, her eyes slitty with contempt. "What HE really needs is an eggbeater up the ass . . . damn old letch."

Junie looks up at the fuzzy light of the small kitchen window. They always leave a light on for her . . . even when everybody's trying to sleep . . . all those human forms on their mattresses, their arms thrown over their eyes to keep the light out. For her. Now that she's pregnant they, like everybody else, treat her like a queen. She murmurs, "He is not a bad person."

"Move out of there," says Dinah. "Come stay up to Papa's with me. Papa would want that. You know how Papa is . . . Heart of gold. He'd want what's best. Come on. I'm gone to classes most days. You could have my room to go to during the day . . . to rest. Really rest. Anybody else as sick as you would be in bed. Do it for the baby. Okay?"

"I can't."

"You've got to get away from him."

"I can't."

"You gotta leave home some*day*. You can't stay glued to that tribe forever. It's not NORMAL. If you really love him, you won't keep hanging around being another mouth to feed . . . *Two* mouths to feed pretty soon. And what about your mother? She's going to catch you at it after a while. She's going to SUSPECT something, if she already doesn't. If you really loved her, you'd quit messing with him and get the hell out. FAR out. Like after I graduate, I'm going back to Mass. You could come down there. You'd love Pittsfield . . . Lots of guys. More jobs. You can meet Mom."

"I want to think about it," says Junie.

"Okay," says Dinah. She gets out to open Junie's door. Then she takes Junie's elbow and together they walk around Blackstone's old pale-green International and the toys. Dinah tells her to watch out for that rusty Thermos bottle lying on its side at the foot of the steps. You'd think Junie really was a queen. Junie giggles, teetering in her classy high-heeled shoes . . . stepping high. She is starting to really *feel* like a queen.

8

The code man steps around a puddle to get to his Caravan, lays his clipboard on the seat.

The old ramp truck is coming fast . . . clanging and bouncing and squeaking and throwing slush. The code man sees through the windshield the scarred, ravaged face of Richard Collins. The truck isn't slowing up at all. The code man shouts "Hey!" and leaps to the left against the salvage office door. The old truck moans like an animal, slides broadside on the ice, coming flush with the code man's face, cornering him. The yellow-gold lettering on the truck door which spells out LETOURNEAU'S USED AUTO PARTS, EGYPT, MAINE looks like a scream.

The driver drops to the ground, almost on all fours.

The code man looks level into Richard's one eye and says, "What can I do for you?"

The code man knows what Richard's noisy breathing means. It means he wants to slam the code man down and kick his face in.

"Why don't you leave my family alone?" Richard says. The voice is a young boy's voice on the verge of tears . . . although there's nothing like tears in the clear wide-open green eye.

"I'm sorry, but it's something I can only discuss with Mr. Lucien Letourneau, who owns the property on which these infractions are being made. I seem to be having a problem locating the gentleman. If you will, please urge him to contact me as soon as possible."

Richard's blackened hands flex and unflex.

The code man sighs. "Please move your truck, sir, so I can get my vehicle out of here."

The only thing that moves on Richard is the breeze in his hair.

The code man sighs again. "Mr. Collins, I wouldn't suppose you are trying to interfere with the duties of a code-enforcement officer . . . are you?"

There's no real answer from Richard. He just backs away and bounds back up onto the high seat of the truck, bangs the door shut. The engine makes a monstrous roar.

9

It's near midnight in the big dark slanty-floored Letourneau kitchen. All the old women have gone to their beds. Junie Greenlaw hasn't gone home yet. Every time she makes a move to leave, Dinah says, "Cripes! You can stay another few minutes, can't you? It's Saturday night!"

"Good place to be on a wintry Saturday night . . . sitting around the opened door of a woodstove, a half-bottle of Zeller Schwarze Katz left, and good company," Dinah's boyfriend, Michael Mattson, says, baring his palms to the fire, his quiet eyes on Junie.

Junie's coat is off. It lies like a dead white beast over the back of a chair.

"Tell Michael his fortune!" Dinah insists.

In the near dark the two sisters are hard to tell apart . . . but for the eagerness of one, the weariness of the other. And with the weary one there is the old white sealer pail by her foot in case she doesn't make it to the bathroom to vomit.

Crowe Bovey is at the table asleep with his face in his arms. He's a quiet, quiet sleeper, never stirs . . . unlike his agitated daytime self.

Junie says, "I don't really know how to give fortunes. It was just one of my schemes when I was a kid."

Dinah giggles. "Do that one on Michael that you told me about . . . You know . . . that one that . . ." She leans toward Junie, whispers in her ear. They both giggle.

"Okay," says Junie. Junie fixes her chair so it's facing Michael's chair, sits as squarely as she can . . . closes her eyes, breathes loudly.

Michael grins. "Looks real."

Junie touches her eyelids lightly.

Cats watch from various high places, from various cozy chairs. When Junie opens her eyes she has a dazed and mystical expression.

Dinah practically loses her mouthful of wine in her lap. "What a riot!" she says.

Junie speaks in a mystical voice. "I see . . . I see women coming. Women coming from everywhere. In Camaros, in Trans Ams, in Two-Eighty Z's, in Volvos . . . all those fancy kinds of cars driven by women with piles of money. Sexy women . . . like you see on TV . . . Sissy Spacek, Cher, Brooke Shields . . . all of them looking for Michael Mattson. Coming for miles. Even some coming from overseas . . . even Russia. They get a special pass to get out. All headed this way . . ."

Dinah is laughing herself silly . . . causing a few cats to put their heads up and look around.

Junie continues. ". . . Stopping in Boston to get directions. 'Where's diss place dey call Egypt, Maine?' the ones from Europe say. 'Damned if I know,' says a guy in Boston. 'Some place in the boonies, I guess.' They all ask directions. A few rich Boston women join the crowd headed north. 'Where in the hell is Egypt, Maine?' they all ask. It's that town where Michael Mattson lives . . . That very nice blond fellow who is majoring in art therapy who wears that crazy purple sweater a lot . . . wears a watch. Oh! *That* Egypt, Maine! Now they all know the way. They are all headed up this way in a big swarm of spinning mag wheels, the dust 'n' dirt flying out from their tires . . . a big cloud of dust on the turnpike . . . very dangerous-looking . . . attracts a lot of attention . . . All the news guys join the crowd headed this way . . . All those women showing up at once to give Michael Mattson a big kiss and whatever else you want, even all their mon —" Junie stops cold. She has happened to glance toward the shadowy table and seen Crowe Bovey's face . . . wide awake, watching her hard.

Michael Mattson says, "Quick, June! Tell me what happens! Don't leave me hanging now!" He chuckles, downs the last of the wine.

Junie looks confused.

Dinah turns in her chair, points at Crowe. "Hey! Go back to sleep!" She tosses her balled-up paper napkin at him, misses.

Crowe gets to his feet, stretches, says hoarsely, "Time all little kid-dies were in bed, isn't it?"

Michael Mattson scowls.

Dinah says, "You mean it's time all old dinosaurs like yourself crawled off into their caves. That's what you meant to say, isn't it?"

He sneers, still stretching. "Go to hell," he says. He ambles stiffly across the sloped floor, runs himself a glass of water, drinks it at the sink. Junie squints at the back of his LETOURNEAU'S USED AUTO PARTS shirt for a whole minute like there's several para-graphs written there.

10

Just after midnight, Dinah's little car whines to a stop outside the Babbidge trailer. Dinah sucks in her left cheek. "Well, here we are . . . Back again!"

Junie says softly, "I been thinking."

Dinah looks at her sister's face.

"I been thinking about moving up with you at the house . . . till I get squared aw —"

Dinah throws her arms around her, whispers into her hair, "It's where you belong, you know . . . With your real sister and your real tantes and your real papa . . . Your *real* blood!"

11

Crowe Bovey sits cross-legged in the dark, oiling a rifle with a rag. Nobody could call this a room. It's not even a closet. It's just a pitch-dark, cold, mousy-smelling space full of guns. The guns are old. 1920s. 1930s. 1940s. Whole series of guns with tight, almost silky action.

Crowe Bovey kills. He kills a *lot*. There are stories about Crowe Bovey's killing. Legends. The old men call him the Grim Reaper. The old women call him a nut.

His favorite targets are crows, jays, squirrels, and skunks . . .

things he can kill in masses. He just loves to pile them up, they say. It doesn't have to be a thing you can cook.

Now and then Big Lucien and Crowe go out into the barn for a little private talk. "Leave de yellow grosbeaks alone, Crowe. Dey are not even edible," Lucien says very, very, very softly.

Crowe Bovey keeps his truck's gun rack full of guns in case there's a woodchuck standing pretty in somebody's field when he is a mile or more away from Big Lucien's domain.

Without his glasses, how can he see to shoot? everybody wonders. He's a man who knows his target by sense of smell, some insist.

But in the dark dark space under the attic stairs, with footsteps creaking overhead, these are not the guns Crowe kills with. These are his quiet guns. Rifles he has bought and traded with quiet shrewdness over the years . . . rifles standing in sturdy rows . . . unmarred. His babies. His fortune. They are worth thousands.

12

When Junie comes into the trailer after midnight, her stepfather is at the tiny table with one sleeve of his salvage shirt rolled up, a tin of Bag Balm open between his outstretched forearm and a ketchupy pile of plates. She need not look at the pink angular burn of the cutting torch on his arm. She knows the look of such a burn by the look in his eyes.

She steps over a pair of boots, a toy shovel . . . making her way to the table. She can smell something bad. She need not look at the refrigerator. She knows what a refrigerator on the blink with all its food spoiled looks like by looking into Blackstone's eyes. She says, "Ain't you got a cold rag for that burn? Let me fix one."

The formidable mustache barely moves. "Go get your mother off the bathroom floor," he says.

She steps over the mattresses, all the children and grown children and children of the grown children curled against each other in half-sleep.

She pushes open the flimsy bathroom door.

She in her bulky white coat and her mother in her soft raggedy nightie fill the whole tiny bathroom to its limit.

Lillian's face is bloated as from fists . . . but it's really from crying . . . This is how hard Lillian cries lately.

Junie says, "Mama, get up and come out. He says he wants you."

Lillian bawls, her mouth a big square. "I try!" She throws herself against the pipes of the sink. She wails, "Oh, sweetie . . . Oh, I'm terrible, aren't I? You think I'm terrible, don't you?"

Junie squats so they are face to face. The smell of the toilet and the damp mildewed linoleum sets Junie's nausea off in waves. She says softly, "Oh, Mama . . . get up."

Lillian buries her face in Junie's big coat and sobs. "Out there in the world it's so crazy, you know. I always kind of . . . go to pieces. I'm not USED to it. You gotta be USED to it . . . you know . . . you gotta be quick or something. Well, you weren't used to it, were you? . . . And you did okay at the mill, didn't you? And you weren't used to it. What's wrong with me?!!! I can't get USED to it. I'm a freak!"

"Mama, let's get out in the kitchen. I can't stand it in here."

Lillian wrings her hands. Her eyes are shrunken in the red bloat of her face. "June, you remember me at all my jobs, don't you?" Before we lived over at Freddie's . . . and before that when we stayed down to Sanford that summer. Remember?"

Junie says, "Yup."

Lillian says, "I just couldn't STAND those jobs . . . I mean . . . nobody is supposed to LIKE work. Work is SUPPOSED to be awful, but . . . I just couldn't STAND it."

Junie nods gravely.

"It's just so crazy . . . What makes all those other people keep getting up each day and GOING? Gosh, the worst part is the *going*. When I wasn't at work I dreaded it so bad . . . Looking forward to the next day with . . . you know . . . so much dread. What's the matter with me!!! I'm a freak, aren't I?"

Junie says, "I don't know, Mama."

"I mean . . . it was like I already lived my life and I could see my life . . . you know . . . GONE." She half-giggles, half-sobs. "You know . . . now . . . being at home, being Daddy Blackstone's wife . . . It's . . . gosh . . . great. It's being . . . I don't know . . . you know . . . I open my eyes each day and I get up and start doing my things . . . You know, straightening up, getting the kids ready for the bus . . . all that stuff. Everybody says, 'Ain't you bored, Miss Lily-Ann?' . . . You know . . . them at church . . . they say, 'You must get cabin fever.' I say a big no . . . 'NO, I don't. I keep busy. I got the kids. I got Blackstone.' " She drags her nose and mouth across the sleeve of her nightie. "But . . . I'm not making any money here. I mean . . . we don't have anything . . . It's all on HIS back. I ain't worth shit!" She screams . . . the blood-curdling kind. "He hates me! Don't he? He hates me! He hates me!" She screams, "He HATES MEEEEEE!"

Junie can feel the wine and cheese she ate at the Letourneaus rising in slow billows.

Lillian raves.

Junie says, "Mama . . . let's go . . ."

"He NEEDS me to work! To HELP. But Lord God, I can't! I can't! I can't! I can't! . . ."

Junie embraces the toilet and retches.

13

All that shows of Severin Letourneau under the two-tone Monte Carlo is the legs of his stained and pilly wool pants and his old boots.

A mufflerless part-Pinto yard buggy comes screaming up the aisle and stops short. It's Glenn, one of Big Lucien's many part-timers . . . so blond and fair a man, he's almost silver . . . except for the hands . . . black, bashed hands . . . and his smudgy eyes which he has a habit of rubbing. He revs the Pinto, makes the engine crackle and pop . . . studies Severin's legs and feet for a moment. "Dave thinks you got something against your walkie-talkie," he says to the legs.

"That's right."

Glenn gives the yard buggy the gas, makes it buck and hump . . . then says, "You ain't seen Hutchins, have you?"

"No," says the legs.

Glenn rubs his eyes. "Dave sent him down a couple of hours ago . . . figured he was with you."

No response. Just the sound of the wrench working.

Glenn says, "Well . . ." He yawns, rubs his eyes. "If you see him, tell him they want him up to the office."

From under the Monte Carlo comes a grunt. "And if *you* see him, ask him where my three-eighths drive extension is and my ball peen hammer . . . which means he's probably been using the extension as a punch, and if he has, I'll hammer it up his ass. You can give him that message for me. That's the message."

"All rightie! All rightie!" Glenn sings out and veers away down the next long aisle of snowbound junks.

14

Dinah studies for her sociology quiz in the front room. Noise doesn't bother her. Now and then she looks up at the TV to catch a clamorous bright commercial . . . or to dig around in the cushions of her chair for her pen. Her shaggy dark hair is knotted up in the silky purplish scarf she borrowed from Junie.

Junie is on the couch with five cats and Crowe Bovey. Crowe's at the farthest end of the couch, asleep sitting up . . . head back, mouth open. By the light of the lamp, his uneven beard shows up black and brown, orange and gray. There is so much about Crowe Bovey and the tense patchy tortoise-shell cat in his lap that is alike.

Junie hunkers with a blanket around her, her knees up . . . a blue plastic industrial pail on the rug next to her. Now and then she lifts the newspaper that covers the pail and vomits or near-vomits.

People hurry through the front room on their way to other parts of the house. There's always a small army of old women or kids between Junie and the most exciting parts of each show she watches. They are making taffy in the kitchen tonight. The thoughts of taffy make Junie grab for her pail.

Dinah giggles.

"Got jokes in that book?" Junie asks, wiping her mouth on the striped towel she keeps beside her at all times.

"No. I was just thinking about something."

"What?"

"Can't tell," Dinah says, winking one of her round penny-color eyes. This means she's getting ready to tell Junie another secret about men.

Junie's bottom lip thickens sulkily. "I've told you all *my* secrets, haven't I?"

Dinah lowers her book and fixes a hand to one side of her mouth to block her whisper from leaking out to the noisy kitchen. "I'll tell you after we're in bed. It's too gritty and lewd and JUICY for . . . you know . . . tender ears." She flicks her eyes toward the kitchen.

"Okay," says Junie, settling deeply into the ruptured old couch.

An ad for turkey stuffing comes on.

Junie grabs for the pail . . . chokes and gags.

A couple of cats panic and lunge away.

"Jesus," says Dinah. "Are you going to make it or what?"

When Junie is done, she positions the newspaper over the pail in a dainty way. Then she puts her head back a while, looking at the ceiling with tears in her eyes.

Dinah lowers her book now and then to check on Junie. After lowering the book for the fifth time and seeing Junie still staring with tears at the ceiling, she says, "They should have pills for that, June. It's not right. With all the great inventions they have, for crying out loud! . . . Like Astroturf and heated toilet seats. It just makes me mad."

Junie just keeps staring up.

After more time . . . a cat sharpening its claws on the wallpaper . . . Tante Josephine helping Memère Poulin to the bathroom and back . . . three long columns of sociology in eensie print and three photo captions . . . a cat knocking a vase off the trunk . . . another column of sociology, part in italics . . . Dinah glances up.

Junie has pushed all the cats away and lies with her head in Crowe Bovey's lap.

Dinah raises the book fast, pretends to be lost in the eensie print of her book.

When she looks back again, Crowe is awake, his hand stiffly, hesitatingly descending on Junie's hair.

15

Everybody is watching Severin. Severin's the one who just found Wayne Hutchins's body in the Road Runner, they say.

"Seems like everybody's doing themselves in these days," says Clarence Farrington, rubbing his knees.

"Naw . . . Ain't no more than there's ever been," says Dave the desk man. "It's just you hear about it more . . . with TV and newspapers and so forth."

Dave is wearing a salvage shirt that says WILLY over the pocket. All Dave's salvage shirts say WILLY instead of DAVE. Willy, the old desk man, was built a lot like Dave . . . thick in the middle, pacy and pompous. The shirts don't say DAVE because Big Lucien says he has to start being more conservative . . . No more new shirts.

There's John, the new guy. His shirts say ARMAND.

A sheriff comes in through the spotty glass door, asks how to get down back. Everybody studies his holster, the handle of his gun, his belt buckle, his cop shoes . . . his big-brimmed hat . . . everybody except Severin, who is over by the heat register quietly smoking, looking straight at the back of Dave's shirt which reads LETOURNEAU'S USED AUTO PARTS in yellow-gold . . . because that was the first thing he saw when he stepped up to the window of the Road Runner, the back of Wayne's shirt.

16

At noontime, it starts to rain. A cold rain . . . close to snow.

The office is hot and crammed with customers staring at the floor and the walls . . . and at their own feet.

One needs a taillight lens to an '87 Taurus, one needs a timing chain to a '72 Dodge, another needs a tranny. Where's Crowe?

"Down back screwing Mrs. Connie Mains in that old Buick without a nose," says John, the new man.

Dave says, "Somebody go stop him. We need that tranny now."

All the office wise men chuckle.

Clarence Farrington says around his pipe stem, "Isn't that Connie Mains one of them he's had down back before?"

"High class cunt," says the road commissioner.

"Watch your mouth," says Dave, glancing at the customers.

Severin and shy Bobby Ward offer to go down back and stop Crowe. They leave in a hurry out the back way. But they don't go anywhere near the Buick without a "nose." They just go climb up into the blue Baptist bus and have a smoke. They watch the rain out through the smashed windows. There are hundreds of cigarette butts and dozens of balled-up and flat cigarette packs on the floor. Severin and Bobby don't have much to say. Just Bobby squinting over the many roofs of cars at the Road Runner, murmuring, "Cops're all gone. Got their fill, I guess." A long pause, then he says with a nervous chuckle, "Wonder what got into ol' Wayne anyways."

They smoke hard and fast, one after another.

Severin keeps gazing out into the rain although the rain is getting too thick to see through. His eyes are blurry and wild.

Bobby throws his wobbed-up Camel pack on the floor.

Severin keeps his face turned away so Bobby can't see his eyes.

Now there's a wind and all the cigarette packs and old leaves skid around in a frisky happy kind of way.

Bobby Ward lights up another, then sucks at it hungrily like it's his first, then says gravely, "Ain't this place the goddamnedest hell hole you ever worked at?"

17

Junie can hear Big Lucien out in the kitchen talking softly into the phone. When he is talking *that* soft, he's mad, they say. He's been on the phone for hours trying to find places to put the families that the code man says have to leave Miracle City. Big Lucien has friends everywhere, friends who owe him favors, they say. It won't be long. He'll have the problem solved.

18

Between Junie and the TV are the sleeping bags and mattresses of the one family Big Lucien hasn't found a new home for yet. The husband is Glenn, one of Big Lucien's many part-timers. The wife is named Sonya and she spends all day with her next youngest baby on her hip in front of the TV. Sonya's hair has a vast dark patch, not much left of her old bleach job. She never sits down. She just rocks from foot to foot in front of the TV, the baby's long floppy ragdoll legs all asway. Sonya wears shorts and no shoes even though it's winter. She never needs to go outdoors. She just goes from foot to foot there between Junie and the TV. And she smokes. And she smells funny. Junie can't keep anything down with Sonya nearby.

The baby on Sonya's hip is named Kenny. There's something wrong with his legs. Junie asks Sonya about the legs, but Sonya just shrugs . . . gives one of the white, white legs a pinch and says huskily, "Can't feel nuthin'."

In the night Junie tells Dinah the latest about Blackstone's baby . . . how that baby is moving a lot now . . . how she can't help but think that the baby is *many* people . . . all the Babbidges of the past and all the Letourneaus going all the way back to France . . . and the Greenlaws and the Blackstones . . . "Blackstone was my stepfather's mother's maiden name" . . . and then Harris and Welch and Pollard and Karnes. All those people! All that blood!

Dinah says life is like an hourglass . . . shaped like that. All those people squeezing down into one pair of people and those two people together are responsible for millions more.

Junie smiles.

The next day Junie stays up in Dinah's and her little room, a cold room with worn blue linoleum and a high white metal bed. She listens to the rings of the wall phone down in the kitchen, the slam of doors, the chirps of kids and old Grace screaming, "If they cut off my head I'll shoot 'em! . . . If they cut off my head I'll shoot 'em!" over and over and over and over.

Junie lies there on the high bed all morning . . . the baby in a quiet mood, too . . . even as she leans over the edge to vomit. She imagines the baby's face. The eyes. Icy eyes.

Her great silent solid belly begins to frighten her.

At noon, Tante Flavie gives the door a couple of whacks. "Coming in!" she shouts. And she comes in.

19

There is a special on the TV. All the old women are granted the best soft chairs of course, the couch, the La-Z-Boy, and various other chairs that are comfy. Sonya rocks from foot to foot, still in her shorts. She's had her Kools pack in her free hand for some time, but still doesn't have one lit yet. She's been too busy smacking her kids. Smacks them in the mouth. She's not a screamer. A kid never knows quite when its mouth is going to get smacked.

Right this moment Sonya is crossing the rug with barefoot stealth and catches another one by surprise . . . SMACK!

"Waaaaaah-aaaaah!"

Junie has a soft seat, too. The old women wouldn't have it any other way. She is feeling better tonight, they say. Tante Marie Louise thinks there's even a little color to the poor girl's face.

The old women keep asking Junie if the TV special is bothering her. It's all about a baby who couldn't live but a few days. Junie says, "Oh, it's okay." and she smiles . . . looks back at the TV. The first part of the program shows the parents as they were, a re-enactment, before the birth. They are either using a real pregnant actress or stuffing her with a pillow. Junie studies the woman's maternity blouse . . . an almost ethereal pink check.

Somebody comes from the kitchen where the men are playing cards. Junie knows it is Crowe. She has memorized the sound of his boots coming and going. His joints crackle as he squats next to the arm of her chair. It seems when he's not cracking his knuckles, the rest of his body does it by itself.

One of the old ladies asks him how the poker game is going. His answer is a sound with his lips like spitting out a hair.

Junie doesn't say anything to him. She and Crowe never ever talk. Not even the night he fondled her hair. That night when Dinah had said she was going up to bed, Junie had got up quick and took hold of her pail. When she looked back at Crowe on the couch, he was squinting at the palms of his hands.

The voice of the mother on TV speaks as it shows her making orange juice. The voice talks about what the baby means to her and "Gary," her husband. The music is scary . . . like a horror movie . . . like a thing hiding in the shadows. The program has all the old women in a big grip. Big Lucien's most current woman, Carleen . . . who is not pregnant yet, they all marvel . . . leans against the doorway to the downstairs bedroom sawing at her long nails with an emery board. She works as a bank teller, has a lot of different sweaters and skirts . . . and neat boyish honey-color hair . . . with just a touch of gray.

There's big laughs in the kitchen, something tickling the poker players. It doesn't take much to set them off.

Carleen says, "I can't stand these true story deals where you know ahead people are going to die . . . It just gives you no hope."

Sonya's children are quiet on their mattress, their eyes fixed dreamily on the show. They are towheads like their father, Glenn. Towheaded, slumpy-shouldered, somnolent. They rarely play.

One of them has been feeling Junie's left ankle for the last twenty minutes . . . named David . . . He is always doing things like that . . . Seems like he never knows it's happening . . . Seems his hands just can't get enough of cats and socks and old wool sweaters . . . and dolls. As the baby is born on the TV, David wears such a sweet and uneasy smile.

One of the other kids sighs dreamily. "Look at the baby. Ain't he cute!"

"Iss not a he . . . iss a she," says one of the tantes.

The camera shows the baby's face a long while.

Old bald Mrs. Bean says, "Gawd! This is awful. That's not the real baby of course, but . . ."

"Oh, yes it is!" says Mrs. Leighton, one of the new old women. "They said they got these pictures of the actual baby."

Tears fill old bald Mrs. Bean's eyes.

After a string of commercials, they start surgery on the baby. The father's voice talks as the doctors start opening up the chest.

Crowe stands up suddenly, his dark eyes sweeping the room . . . sneering . . . like everything and everybody are a stupid joke. He says loudly, "Don't the public just eat up other people's troubles. Goddam sicko TV shit!" He stalks out . . . goes back to the poker game in the kitchen . . . back to the laughing and hooting of the men.

Junie feels a small wave of nausea. She has her pail nearby just in case.

In the kitchen the wall phone rings once, then stops.

When the baby dies, all the old women and young women weep.

20

There's a northeaster the next day . . . a mean one.

Big Lucien is out ramming around the dooryard with the junkyard plow . . . lights whirling on all the walls. The little kids run to the windows. But the big kids, home from school, are bored.

Lillian and Jennifer Ann come for a little visit. They bring some of Eugenia's warm prune cookies. Fat and steamy-looking, Jennifer Ann looks *older*, even though it's been only a week since Junie moved out. Lillian lays her black suede coat on a chair. The child David gives it a quickie feel. Everybody has some prune cookies. Junie has as many as she can get her hands on. "You are getting an appetite, sweetie?" Lillian asks.

"Yep," says Junie.

Lillian smiles, sits beside her . . . close.

David has lost interest in Lillian's jacket . . . but two kittens find it now . . . get cozy on it to wash each other's necks.

Between the couch and *Days of Our Lives* Sonya stands with her usual shorts and bare feet . . . baby and cigarette.

Lillian's older-lady-type beige pants are wet to the knees from her snowy walk . . . pants Junie has never seen before . . . And Lillian carries the smell of that other household . . . queer and far away . . . no part of this household.

Junie lays her head on Lillian's shoulder.

Jennifer Ann is sitting on the edge of a wooden chair in a way that makes Junie know she is sore from one of Blackstone's merciless strappings.

As it turns out, Lillian and Sonya are old friends. There is a little conversation . . . Sonya turning away from the TV now and then to look Lillian's way. But mostly Sonya just keeps her back to the couch, rocking from foot to foot . . . the long loose legs of the baby jerking this way and that. They talk about Martha and Franny and Noreen . . . people they both know. And Kim. And Roach.

Big Lucien makes the snow thunder against the house.

Lillian wants Roach and Kim's new address.

Sonya says there's no name for that road, but she can draw her out a little map.

Junie still has prune cookies in her teeth, works her tongue around. Blackstone's baby is stock still . . . must be listening to the TV, the plow, the ringing phone, the voices. Rapt.

Sonya uses the couch's wooden arm for a desk. Junie has to move her elbow some. What Sonya does is rip off a corner of *Your Weekly Shopping Guide* for the map. Junie's eyes widen on the words "make a left here" and "look for a bridge after the dam." The handwriting is the prettiest Junie has ever seen, prettiest in the world, probably. Great long tails and sweeping curlicues as effortless as human hairs. And even as Sonya does this astounding thing, she keeps the baby with the bad legs secure on her hip.

"Isn't that the old town road?" Lillian asks.

"No," says Sonya. "It's offa that."

The baby with the bad legs is named Kenny. He raises a set of keys to his mouth and gives them a noisy suck. He is looking right into Junie's eyes. His eyes are almost silver.

Lillian giggles. "Won't Roach and Kim be surprised when they see me! Gosh. It's been a dog's age."

21

There is a tap-tap-tap on the door to the trailer that's not grandfathered . . . the infraction-of-the-code trailer . . . the trailer where Severin and Gussie and Bubba and Josh are living again . . . in secret . . . heavy drapes, no lights.

Severin lifts a corner of one of the drapes.

It's Richard Collins and Crowe Bovey. Richard carries a dark rifle, his ruined half-face grave and expressionless.

Severin opens the door.

Crowe says huskily, "Are you busy?"

Severin says, "Just waiting around for the old lady to get home and cook." He grins his gap-toothed monster grin. Behind him is only the insipid yellowy light of a lamp with a towel over it.

Richard marches straight to the flimsy made-to-look-like-wood eating table and places the rifle there with a flourish. He says, "What do you think of that dandy item?"

Severin stands with his hands deep in the pockets of his wool pants, his eyes on the gun.

Richard says, "Check her out . . . Tell me what you think."

Severin reaches for the rifle, hefts it. With an eye to the scope, he points it around the room . . . stops with it aimed at the gaudy deer rug on the wall. When he brings it down both Crowe and Richard are looking at him hard. Severin's eyes drop to the worn gray bolt. He runs his thumb over it. "Jesus," he breathes. "Ain't loaded, is it?"

Crowe sneers.

Richard says, "Maybe . . . maybe not." He takes the rifle, jerks the bolt back. "You're not familiar with guns, are ya?"

Severin shrugs.

Richard pushes the gun back into Severin's hands.

Crowe's eyes widen and narrow on the gun. "How many weeks' pay was that one, Richard?"

"Traded," says Richard.

Crowe says, "Louie's?"

"Nope, place over to Mechanic Falls. He deals a lot of black-powder shit, but I ain't into that."

"He didn't have —" Crowe stops short as a car pulls up outside. All three study the door. The car drives away. A key turns in the lock. Gussie comes ramming in with a Narragansett sticking out of the pocket of her workjacket. She looks hard and long at the two shadowy visitors, then turns to pull the door shut.

Severin asks, "Where you been?"

She looks at the rifle under his arm. "Over to Bean's camp on Ace Pond!" she hoots. "Christ! Weren't we celebratin'! Can you believe that?!!"

Severin says, "Keep your voice down, wouldya?"

"We wasn't celebratin' Valentine's either!" she snorts. "But we *was*

226

celebratin' that a bunch of us are gettin' the shaft! Man oh man . . . Ain't many bosses gonna celebrate with you the fact that they are about to lay you off!" She pushes her big felt hat to the back of her head. "Steve's a decent dude. I tell him that all the time." She squints around the shadowy trailer, at the usual spattering of Lego bricks and busted cheap-made superheroes. "I say, 'Steve, you are a decent goddam boss!' He likes that." She laughs mightily, "Haw! Haw! Haw! Haw!"

Severin says, "Watch it, Gussie! You're being too loud."

"I'm not being loud. YOU are being loud!" she snarls.

Severin says, "Keep it up and the whole world's gonna know there's somebody living here."

She reaches for a fistful of Severin's shirt. "Give me the truck keys! I gotta go get the creatures."

"You're not driving," he says. He lays the rifle on the table with both hands . . . daintily . . . like he expects it to go off.

Gussie flattens herself against Severin's back, giving his pants pockets a frisking.

Severin says, "Lay off that shit, Gussie. I'll go over and pick them up in a few minutes. Just go in and lay on the bed a while, okay?"

"Gimme them keys!" she screams. She feels the chest pocket of his salvage shirt.

He draws back. "Go lay down a while, Gussie. You're not safe driving those kids."

She steps squarely in front of him and grabs the front of his shirt. "GIVE ME THE GODDAM KEYS . . . NOW."

He reaches down under his wool pants to a pocket of his dungarees. His hand reappears with a key. She snatches it and leaves like a storm, giving the door a reverberating slam.

The guests have nothing to say. Two big clown spots come out on Severin's cheeks.

They can hear the truck start up in the distance where it's kept hidden in the trees at all times.

"She's gonna get it tonight!" Severin blurts out. "I've had it with her shit. Now and then she gets like this. Nothing a good slap across the head won't fix."

Richard snorts, his ruined nose flaring.

The truck clamors past the trailer and is gone.

Richard reaches into his pocket, arranges a half-dozen .308 cartridges one by one on the table. He sighs. "Ain't they pretty."

Crowe cracks his knuckles luxuriously.

Richard says, "In the old days, somebody tried to take your home, you'd put one of these inside their head." He holds one of the shells toward the light. "But nowadays . . ." He sighs, his clear green eye fixed to Severin. "Nowadays when they come to make you go, you take a shell like this one here . . ." He rolls it between his fingers. ". . . and you put it in your own head."

22

The code man has found the little camp filled with Crockers in the woods behind Miracle City, one of the waferboard camps Big Lucien had taken the liberty to have built after the new codes. Code man doesn't leave a stone unturned, they say. "What a beagle!!"

23

Big Lucien is not at supper tonight . . . one of his headaches coming on. When you pass the room where he lies, there is silence . . . which is worse than his screams. The screams will come in time, though.

Sonya is not at the table tonight either.

The women talk about the Crockers . . . about what you get when you marry an old man. "You get the burden," they say.

Crowe Bovey turns to Junie and says, "Can you reach the applesauce?"

Junie fetches the applesauce.

The women talk about the house the Crockers lost . . . about how you never see the people from out of state who bought it . . . Well . . . you don't see them *close up*.

"Phantom people!" says Mrs. Bean with a giggle.

"Peckerheads," Crowe Bovey sneers.

"No! No! You! Say you a good Contrition for dat rotten word!" Tante Josephine scolds.

"Peckerheads," Crowe says into her eyes.

Sonya's kids look at Crowe's mouth.

Creamsicle, one of Big Lucien's latest cats, wants to go out. He shows this by staring at the doorknob.

"Dere iss no room in diss house for Crockers," says Tante Lucienne.

"Dere iss no room for even one more person," says Tante Flavie.

"Papa will figure out something," says Dinah . . . her face still showing the scarlet brand where Sonya gave her a hell of a slap just before supper. There's so much bickering among the women these days, but only Sonya goes so far as to slap you.

The phone rings. Tante Flavie answers it with "Hello! Hello! Hello! Whatcha want!" It is somebody looking for Big Mr. Pluto. It's Bob. "No! No! No! He iss on de bed. Goodbye."

Creamsicle is still staring at the doorknob. Other cats circulate. Some clean up around the chair legs of Sonya's kids.

"Sit in your chair right," Sonya's husband, Glenn, tells one of the kids. "Squirm, squirm, squirm. You got ants, right?"

After a while the tantes get up from the table, some to sit by the Hearthmate, others to pick up plates.

There is talk about the weather . . . six storms in ten days . . . another storm on the way.

More women get up, pick up plates.

Junie keeps eating. She's never been so hungry. She cuts another piece of raisin pie . . . piles it onto her bread 'n' butter . . . eats it all.

Crowe Bovey and Glenn eat without a word . . . both looking sleepy . . . the sleeves of their thermal shirts showing at their wrists . . . ragged and rotted by their work.

Flavie rams a chunk of ash into the Hearthmate with her foot. "Somebody else do somet'ing around here PLEASE!" she commands. "Somebody get de door for dat cat!!!" With her eyes turbid and black behind her glasses, she is glaring at Junie.

"Goddam cats," says Crowe into Junie's eyes. "Ain't good for nuthin'."

24

It is 4:05 A.M. according to the apple clock over the refrigerator. The morning after another big poker game.

Junie pads into the kitchen in her polar bear slippers and robe . . . down the long cold slanty floor which sometimes speaks like a human voice. It says, "Yup, yup, yup, yup, yup."

The glaring overhead light has been left on. The kitchen is a mess. There are pans everywhere with pink greasy water in them, playing cards on the floor. V.O. bottles. Jim Beam bottles. Squashed beer cans. Paper bags. In one of the bags a tiger cat is curled. Crowe Bovey is at the table . . . wide awake . . . alone. He wears an unfamiliar plaid shirt buttoned to the throat. He watches Junie coming toward him.

She says, "You guys know how to party, dontcha?"

He glances around the room . . . then, with a flourish, dislocates all the fingers of his left hand . . . Pop! Pop! Pop! Pop! Then punches them back into place.

She picks a beer can off the drainboard, gives it a shake . . . It sloshes. "I'm starved," she says, glances around. There's a squashed hot dog on the floor, too disgusting for even the cats to take an interest in. Junie just stands there looking out into the bluish moony night through the window over the sink.

Crowe says, "Get me a glass of water, would you . . . while you're right there."

She gets a tumbler, runs water into it twice . . . fills it to brimming. She turns. He's leaning out of his chair with his hand out. The glass is so full, it splatters the floor, runs down his wrist into the cuff of the plaid shirt. A couple of kittens run over to sniff the wet floor.

Crowe drinks the whole glass of water without stopping . . . his eyes on Junie. Then he wipes his beard on his sleeve and studies the glass with his squinty dark half-blind eyes. "More," he says.

She runs the water hard into the glass twice, fills it on the third. Again he has his hand out waiting. Again it is brimming and rushes down his wrist.

He finishes the second glass . . . burps. He says, "Know where the aspirin are, don't you?"

She gets him an aspirin. Runs more water.

As he washes the aspirin down, she waits.

He holds the glass out to her, licks his mustache, and gives his knuckles a revolting series of pops and snaps, his eyes squinty on the empty chair across the table from him. "Come sit down," he says.

She sits across from him, one hand in her lap, the other on the table.

He burps again. Says, "Aaaaah."

She says, "You gotta work in the morning, don't you?"

"That's right," he says, sneering. Burps again. "I'm a . . ." He lowers his voice. ". . . a slave." He grins . . . not a nice grin.

"That's only in four hours," she says.

"Golly," he says mockingly.

She feels the baby move. Since the sonogram, Noah is his name. She and Dinah thought it up. She wanted it to be from the Bible. Dinah had said, "You can't get any more Bibly than Noah!"

Sonya says kids at school will make fun of him. "Better call him Michael or Justin or Josh . . . a name everyone else uses." But nobody ever listens to Sonya.

Crowe reaches across the table and gets a grip on Junie's hands with both of his hands. He is pulling her hand toward him slowly . . . squeezing.

25

The screams begin. There is always one of the women stationed by his bed in case he gets one of his big seizures. Each woman has to put in only an hour. They rotate. The room is kept dark, they explain. A box of tongue depressors on the dresser. You just got to sit there and wait.

"Know what to do in case of a seizure, Junie?" old Flavie asks.

"No, what?" says Junie.

Dinah hugs herself, says close to Junie's ear, "Jesus, Junie . . . you are brave. I wouldn't go in that room with him like that. I wouldn't TOUCH that room with a ten-foot pole . . . not with a TWENTY-foot pole."

26

Crowe takes Junie to Kool Kone. His truck is black and newish. He calls it Prince like the old collie. It rides smooth. He drives with his head cocked, his eyes squinty. He drives slow like an old man. He always takes a few guns in the gunrack . . . a couple of handsome expensive-looking high-powered rifles and a beat-up taped-up shotgun. He keeps a handgun under a wool shirt on the seat. "I carry a permit," he tells her. He talks about guns all the while they lap their ice creams. She hardly understands any of it. She just listens to his voice. She is glad to get away from the house, all the kids and cats . . . away from Big Lucien's blood-curdling screams . . . away from old Flavie telling her she doesn't make banana bread right.

27

After three seizures, Big Lucien is back to his old self. The first thing he does as his old self is bring another family to stay awhile . . . Friends from Bangor, he calls them. And their big bouncy crazy grinning black dog. There are mattresses in the back hall now . . . a cot in the kitchen. And the dog. He's everywhere. Prince *hates* the grinning dog. Flavie says she thinks Prince has stopped eating.

28

Crowe and Junie start to skip suppers. When Crowe gets off from the yard, he doesn't even wash up. He just warms up the truck and says, "Let's go."

The days are getting long and muddy. They sit in the Kool Kone parking lot with the windows down lapping their ice creams. People are walking around in their shirt sleeves. Crowe's eyes follow them in that dazed half-blind look he gets. It doesn't matter to him that he can't see, he tells Junie. He knows everybody in Egypt by the makes and models of their cars.

As Junie gets nearer her "last month," her face gets a little plump.

Her color is like a rose to each cheek. "The ice creams are doing it," she tells Dinah.

"Love is doing it." Dinah giggles.

29

He invites her to his secret space under the stairs. He says, "Don't knock any of those guns over, please."

But she can't see any guns. She can't see anything. It's just black and cold. She hits her head on the stairway. She says, "Don't you keep a flashlight?"

He says, "I've been through a few."

She tries to get comfy on the quilts. They are loaded with sand . . . and probably spiders.

Crowe gets comfy beside her.

Crowe talks. He talks about salvaging, about how he grew up Methodist, about going to the top of Mount Washington with his aunt, about bears. He tells all he knows about bears. He tells her a ghost story. He talks about guns. He talks *mostly* about guns. He talks and he talks and he talks in his old-fashioned old-mannish hesitating way till her head rings with his voice.

Finally he is thumping around in the darkness, pulling his pants off . . . hurling them into a pile somewhere. He says, "This don't hurt babies, you know." His lovemaking is only a few hard jabs and then it's over. Goes back to talking. He lies with his arm over her and his voice close to her ear makes her hair flicker. He talks all night. He talks till his wind-up clock goes off at 6:30, then he paws around for where he left his pants.

At supper that night, he's quiet. Not a word to say. Just "Pass the bread" and "Peas, please" . . . Keeps his head down.

At bedtime, Junie starts toward the stairs to go up to Dinah's and her room.

"Where you going?" he says, squinting, trying to distinguish her from the shadow of the door.

Back again in the black cold space under the stairs, he starts in talking.

She asks him, did he find a flashlight anywhere?

He says no, but he will. One will come along. He tells her about the transmission he took out this afternoon. He covers every step there is to taking out a transmission . . . and names each tool. He tells her about the rear end he took out and all the steps to that. He tells her about coon hunting with Benny Leonard and his boy. Tells her all he knows about radar. He tells her about his dead wife Kathy's fear of snakes. "Eeeeeeeek-eeeek!" he mocks Kathy's fear. He tells her about a big squash he once grew. And his snowmobiles. There were eight. He tells about the black over-the-hill balloons Kathy got him on his thirtieth birthday. He says Kathy had a sicko sense of humor. He tells her some more about bears. She falls off to sleep during one of his long involved facts about bears.

The next day she finds a flashlight under the sink but the batteries are dead.

That night he says some batteries will come along. They are always showing up in cars. Then he remembers the story of his Uncle Walt's motorboat.

Junie loves his voice. She loves the way he says "tudstools" and "booshes" and "ruds." She hates the cold, mousy-smelling dark and she can't get comfy on the quilts. But she loves his mouth close to her ear. She is happy. She roams around the Letourneau house all day, flushed and fat with Crowe Bovey's voice.

30

It has turned off cold again . . . typical spring. They sit in the empty Kool Kone parking lot with the motor running. Not many people in the ice cream mood today. Crowe is dark under the eyes and he's quiet. When he's done with his ice cream, he just rests his head back and plays with the wheel. Every one of the knuckles on his right hand is torn wide open. It's nothing he has to explain. It might as well be the hand of E. Blackstone Babbidge. Only difference is Crowe won't let his heal. He keeps picking and picking at the scabs.

The radio is on low . . . country-rock.

Junie has a banana boat. She could eat THREE banana boats. But the clinic doctors say, "Watch out for your weight, dear."

When the code man's Caravan wagon pulls in, Crowe stiffens and starts to twist and pull on his lengthening mustache.

Junie says, "What's the matter?"

Crowe grunts, sitting up straighter, squaring his shoulders . . . looks ready for a big fight.

The code man has his family with him . . . a couple of small heads . . . and the wife.

The code man gets out.

"I oughta take my Weatherby and blast his fucking brains out . . . is what I oughta do," says Crowe.

"Who is it?" Junie asks.

"The goddam devil is who," says Crowe.

The code man passes in front of Crowe's truck, eyes on the big sign that tells the ice cream flavors. The code man wears his leisure clothes today . . . a yellow golf shirt, camel-color sweater, and gentlemanly pants. He stands in front of the flavors sign a while, studying it.

Junie looks at the code man's family in the Caravan. She wants to lap the boat-shaped dish out but not in front of Crowe. He has told her before it looks childish.

"What's so bad about him?" she asks.

Crowe is rigid.

The code man talks through the little order window. He smiles and gestures.

Crowe is almost crouched on his seat. His foot moves onto the gas, gives it a small push. The pistons race some.

Junie looks at the foot, his cracked gray workboot with rawhide laces. She says, "Wanna go?"

His dark eyes have a washed-out greenness to them on this cold bright day. There is something new about him every day . . . something changing . . . reversing itself. He says huskily, "Asshole yuppie mother-fucker," and crouches a little more.

The code man's order is ready . . . four little white ice creams in a cardboard carrier. There's an exchange of money.

New blood suddenly beads up on Crowe's knuckles.

"Come on, Crowe. Let's go visit Severin and Gussie. Let's just go." Junie touches his arm.

The code man with the four little ice creams in the cardboard thing comes striding toward Crowe's truck. As he passes in front of the grille, Crowe stomps the gas, makes the engine scream. The code man jerks around, looks up into Crowe's eyes. But only for a moment. The code man's face relaxes at once. He continues to stride along in a natural way.

Crowe blows the horn . . . really hammers it with his bleeding hand, splattering blood everywhere. The code man ignores this.

Junie says, "Crowe, let's go . . . Come on."

He says, "Not till I go over there and kick his face in."

Junie says, "Why don't we just go?"

He says, "They have a way about 'em, those kind of people. Those type. Fuckin' cold bastards. Makes you wanna fill their fuckin' faces with lead."

Junie gives her banana boat dish one quickie little lap. The baby doesn't move. He is listening to Crowe's voice and his mother's voice, to his mother's speeding blood and the worry of her heart.

31

The baby is overdue, but he's dropped, the clinic doctors tell her . . . which means it won't be long. They say he's going to be a big baby. But she knows this. She even knows how the baby will look. He will look like all of Blackstone's kids. She takes a lot of walks in the salvage yard now that the mud is gone. She loves the feel of the space, the sun, and the drone of bees. There are daisies and devil's paintbrushes between some of the cars. She picks them for old Flavie, who she's just had an argument with. There are also other things between the cars . . . a pink playing card, a rag, a split-open Johnny Cash tape cassette, the ribbon of it tangled in the weeds. She stuffs things into her sweater pockets. How terrific it would be to find money that robbers had left in a car . . . a big bag of bills. She paws through the cars. She checks the gloveboxes and under the seats. She comes home with her pockets bulging . . . a catnip mouse, a Matchbox car, a dollar's worth of change, a candle, a spoon, aviator sunglasses, a rolled-up *National Enquirer*, clothespins, .22 shells, a wax banana, a book on horoscopes, a coffee cup that says MOM . . .

32

They get married. Elope. No flowers. No rice. No cake. None of that. Right in front of the justice of the peace and the witness, who is the justice of the peace's mother, Crowe makes a crack about Junie being "big as a house." Then he brings it up again when he can't get his arms around her for the kiss after the marriage words. There are colored glass squares in the window by the fireplace. There's an ethereal, almost heavenly patch of purple on the left shoulder of Crowe's dress-up sweater, a yellow one on his neck. He tries for the kiss again. He looks tense and crazy with love for her.

Then he keeps picking at his dress-up sweater. He won't leave it alone.

All the way out to the truck, he grips her wrist . . . leaves it marked red.

He drives slowly as always, squinting at the road. They plan to drive around a little and look at the way people have their yards fixed. They can't go far. No money. "No money for a motel," Crowe says, his voice shaky. More than anything, they want a motel.

On Route 25, he pulls the truck to the shoulder . . . shuts the engine off. He says, "No motel."

She says, "It's okay, Crowe. Someday things will be nice."

He has nothing to say to that . . . just picks something invisible from his button-up dress-up sweater. Then he squints at her belly. "Open up your shirt," he says.

It's a cream-color maternity top, a gift from Eve, who often visits. Across the bodice are embroidered violets, pink roses, black-eyed Susans, daisies . . . and one smiling snail.

She giggles. "Not here, Crowe!"

He says, "Yeah, here."

She says, "A car might come by."

"Hell with them," he says. He has trouble with the tiny cream-color buttons . . . so weathered and ruined are his hands.

"Come on, Crowe! Don't be dumb!" she almost sobs.

"I just want to look, for crissakes," he says.

He fumbles from button to button.

She whispers, "I look disgusting . . . like a watermelon."

He says, "I just want to look. I've never SEEN you before, for crissakes."

The belly emerges.

Her voice shakes, "Please, Crowe . . . that's not the way I really look." She tries to yank her blouse back together, but he spreads it open again . . . tries to feel the shape of the baby.

The baby starts to writhe and unbraid under his hands.

"PLEASE don't look anymore!" Junie laments, trying to hide her belly button that's as big as a grape.

"I got a right now," he sneers.

"A right! What right?" She gives his hands a shove. "Ain't your baby anyway, Mr. Big Shot!"

He spreads his fingers wider, harder. He has no wedding ring. He has insisted that in his line of work you could get your finger ripped out if you wear a ring. His hands are just plain hands . . . softly, darkly haired . . .

There's a sudden jab. It's Noah. He jabs again right against the palm of Crowe's right hand.

Crowe squints at the spot. "Well," he says, his lip curling. "It's finders keepers, losers weepers, you know."

33

Crowe and Junie have moved into the camp in the trees that the Crockers were just booted out of not long ago . . . It breaks the code . . . breaks the LAW.

From the little plastic window, Junie can see a kind of murky view of the mountain, its menacing rock face. Then down on the path she sees Dinah coming . . . dressed in shoes not made for such a steep walk . . . urban shoes, Dinah calls them . . . stupid shoes, old Flavie calls them.

Every night is the same. Junie gets the tea water on. Her dishes are put away. Her kitchen looks nice. Crowe is always asleep at the table with his face in his arms. One sleeve of his salvage shirt will sometimes look like a tiger got a hold of it. Dinah likes to study him a long moment and say, "Is that all that man ever does?"

Noah is two weeks overdue now. Cramped for space. Charged and ready. Every night is the same . . . the belly getting bigger and bigger and bigger . . .

Dinah flounces into one of the deep flowered chairs, kicking her shoes off into a pile . . . The tea pot whistles . . . and the two sisters use their secret, secret voices to talk about men.

The little kitchen smells like onions and meat.

The tea has a dot of milk.

It is just exactly like Junie pictured life should be.

34

On Monday morning the code man finds the camp in the woods occupied. He has had it "up to here" with Mr. Letourneau. You can trust Big Lucien Letourneau about as far as you can throw him, he tells the people back at Town Hall with a sigh.

35

Back at the crowded Letourneau house again, Crowe says not to worry.

That night after supper while Junie watches TV with the others in the front room, Crowe combs his hair, combs his beard, puts on his plaid shirt and his brown dress-up button-up sweater, and loads the truck with guns . . . guns in suede carriers . . . guns in boxes . . . guns wrapped in blankets . . . and he drives off.

When he gets back after midnight, Junie is asleep on the quilts in the empty black space under the stairs. She can smell another household on him . . . strangers and their ways. She knows in his pocket is the money for a house of their own . . . like life should be. She is wild with joy. She lies there listening, waiting for him to pull off his boots and lie down . . . to push his face between her shoulder blades like he often does. But he just keeps squatting there in the darkness.

She says, "Crowe? Crowe? What's wrong?"

He sobs.

She can't imagine for all the world what his sobs mean. She has no understanding of this.

36

On Thursday the code man discovers Gussie Letourneau making red Jell-O in the outlawed trailer. All she had to say to him was a soft "oh" and her eyes blurred with tears. But as he was leaving, Josh got him square in the back with a rock.

37

On Friday, when June Bovey visits the hospital clinic, the doctors admit her and induce labor.

38

That night a breeze picks up . . . smells sweet of summer . . . smells sweet of the hills. There is a human-shaped form hanging from the hemlock in the open space by the lilacs. It's the code man's effigy.

In the moon-blue light a dozen men circulate, talking loud, charged. One is dousing the hanging shape with gasoline. Another man is all ready with the match, eager to give it a toss. The breeze picks up again, makes the hanging shape sway. The shape resembles a naked man . . . vaguely pink.

Old women are screaming from the upstairs bedroom windows.

Somebody assures them they don't have to worry . . . It's not the real code man.

The first three tossed matches miss, taken by the breeze. The men take bets over whose match will do it. Who's got the balls to hit the mark? " 'Fraid?" one taunts another.

Now some are throwing matches at each other.

Somebody assures the old women they can go to bed now and not worry. This is just a bunch of bullshitting, they say.

Sounds like a cannon when a match finally makes the mark.

The men cheer and toast each other with their beers.

Sonny Ballard waves his arms and swoons . . . "Oh, dear . . . Oh, dear . . . Put out the fire! . . . Put out the fire! This poor code officer will never make it to work tomorrow!"

Norman Letourneau makes a noise like a fire truck, runs up to the burning man . . . drunkenly close . . . madly close . . . unzips himself and pisses into the crackling brilliance.

The others whoop and howl.

"Crazy bastard," they all say.

"No, it's not a real man," somebody insists. A couple of old women have come down onto the piazza in their nightclothes.

"It's just an old union suit stuffed with rags," Glenn tells them.

The old women aren't convinced. Tante Flavie is on her way inside to call the STATE POLICE.

Little Lucien runs after her, seizes her wrists.

The shape burns up to nothing fast . . . drops to the ground . . . small as a sock . . . somebody pokes it with a stick.

Glenn says, "See . . . It ain't nuthin'."

A couple more men come loping to the piazza, stinking of soot and drink and hysteria. They lean in close. Grinning.

The women look them up and down. Tante Marie Louise crosses herself and mutters something soft and unforgiving.

Old bald Mrs. Bean looks back out to the smoking, glowing last little piece of the code man and says croakily, "Even to pretend isn't very nice."

SEVEN

The Man of Gold

IT IS a warm mint-color evening which smells of wet streets and wet brakes.

Across the tailgate of the Chevy Luv there is printed with a bold unshaky paintbrush: GOD BLESS AMERICA, GOD BLESS PRESIDENT REAGAN. The bumper and fenders are plastered with faded REAGAN–BUSH '84 stickers and one new sticker: MORE NUKES, LESS KOOKS. Behind the wheel is Maxine Letourneau. She is smoking hard and slow and deep, her round arms and square hands making the steering wheel look eensie.

At the street where you turn to the Cumberland County jailhouse, the Chevy Luv's brake lights burst to life. One light is red, the other a tulip of shattered plastic with a clear white star of light. Big Lucien has been messing with the Portland whores again . . . and drinking . . . drinking hard . . . which makes him brawl, makes him lewd. It happens now and then. Maxine gives her Tiparillo another desperate suck, trying to keep her cool . . . For it is she who has got stuck the last three times having to pick him up. The other women say to leave him, make him walk.

There's a plastic child-safety seat. But the child has only one knee in it. He looks like a middle-aged man with his red-and-white-striped hockey shirt and shaky thick girth . . . Firstborn of Norman and the hippie woman . . . Spoiled rotten, they all say. He rides along with his head and shoulders out the window, his dark curls fluttering in the wind. When he sees people on the sidewalk, he bellers, "Look out!" And then he laughs his deep manlike laugh.

"Sit down, Matt, before you fall out," Maxine commands.

There's no empty parking spots, just hydrants and Police Parking

Only signs . . . and people looking startled as Matt screams, "Look out!!!"

The Chevy Luv chugs around the block again and again.

Matt sees a man locking up a small silver car. "Look out!!" he howls.

"You want the cops to come out and give you a frisking?" Maxine snarls, flicking a Tiparillo ash into the wind.

The Chevy Luv chugs around the block again. "Do you see Pepère?" wonders Maxine.

"No," says Matt.

"Keep your eyes peeled . . . 'cause I can't take my eyes off the goddam road." She sighs.

The Chevy Luv starts down a side street. It turns out to be a dead end. As Maxine backs the truck up, Matt roars, "LOOK OUT, GRAMMIE!!!!" Then he laughs heinously.

"Quit the shit!" Maxine snarls.

"Shit quit shit quit!" Matt booms, then laughs till he gets tears.

"Sit down, you big galoot! I can't see around you!" Maxine commands.

Matt ignores this . . . Still riding with one knee in the child seat . . . looks sort of like George Washington crossing the Delaware . . . his eyes narrowing on the dilemma of humankind, the smallness, the silliness, the lack of forethought. Then he raises one chubby hand to protect his eyes from the city's brightness . . . and a sudden warm look comes to his face . . . warm with indulgence and forgiveness. Then he snickers. "This is Poo-poo land."

The Chevy Luv starts down a tree-lined, car-lined street of shops. "Where in the hell are we?" Maxine growls, pitches her Tiparillo butt out.

"One-way street!" somebody shouts from an awninged doorway.

"Look out!!!" Matt calls back.

"Jesus Christ," Maxine breathes.

"Poo-poo land," says Matt.

"Portland," Maxine corrects him. "Keep your eyes peeled for your Pepère. Maybe the jail people decided to keep him for good this time . . . the old fool."

The little truck works its way back to the jail building. There's a man waiting there. An ordinary man. A man you'd never ever notice on a city street. He has thinning hair. Work clothes. He has narrow cringing shoulders like he's ducking a thrown shoe. Weak-looking shoulders. A small man. What some would call a "shrimp." Over the pocket of his dark-green workshirt there is embroidered in yellow-gold: BIG LUCIEN. He steps toward the curb. The Chevy Luv squeals to a stop. The door opens. Without a word, the child bounds into his arms.